D1109826

# Cold Truth

*Also by Mariah Stewart*
*in Large Print:*

Dead End
Dead Certain
Dead Even
Dead Wrong

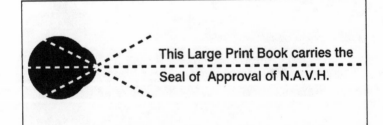

For Chery Griffin, the very best and truest of friends, who laughs and occasionally cries with me; who never fails to offer support, encouragement, and — dare I say it with a straight face? — her wisdom; and who, as Victoria Alexander, is a most excellent partner in whine

As the Founder/CEO of NAVH, the only national health agency solely devoted to those who, although not totally blind, have an eye disease which could lead to serious visual impairment, I am pleased to recognize Thorndike Press* as one of the leading publishers in the large print field.

Founded in 1954 in San Francisco to prepare large print textbooks for partially seeing children, NAVH became the pioneer and standard setting agency in the preparation of large type.

Today, those publishers who meet our standards carry the prestigious "Seal of Approval" indicating high quality large print. We are delighted that Thorndike Press is one of the publishers whose titles meet these standards. We are also pleased to recognize the significant contribution Thorndike Press is making in this important and growing field.

Lorraine H. Marchi, L.H.D.
Founder/CEO
NAVH

* Thorndike Press encompasses the following imprints: Thorndike, Wheeler, Walker and Large Print Press.

I believe that in the end
the truth will conquer.

— John Wycliffe

# Prologue

Under the hot lights of the television studio, Regan Landry shifted uncomfortably in her chair even as she reminded herself that her appearance today on *This Morning, USA*, the daily show that followed the network morning news program, was business, and therefore need not be pleasurable.

This would be her final televised spot on the tour promoting *In His Shoes*, the last book she'd co-authored with her father, Josh Landry, before his death eight months earlier. She didn't have to be comfortable; she merely had to be good, good enough to do justice to her father and their work.

In the past, it had been Josh who'd done the book tours, the television appearances, the magazine and radio interviews. Regan had always watched from the wings as he captivated every audience with his wit and easy charm, mesmerizing them with the gritty details of his research into the minds of some of society's most loathsome killers. Josh's own murder had changed all that.

While Regan was not as comfortable in

the spotlight as her father had been, she felt she owed it to him — and to his many fans — to keep the schedule that their publisher had arranged before Josh died. For years, her father had returned for book signings at many of the same bookstores across the country, some of whose patrons had never missed a visit. Some readers had become so familiar, he'd known them by name. Regan believed he looked forward to the signings as much as his faithful fans looked forward to seeing him and hearing him talk about the research he'd done to prepare for each new book.

Regan had been tempted, but she couldn't bring herself to back out of the tour, and in retrospect was glad she had not. She'd come to look upon the past few weeks as a sort of pilgrimage, following in her father's footsteps, accepting the sympathy of his longtime readers, many of whom had pressed letters or cards into her hands. Their thoughtful words of condolence and remembrance had given her great comfort; at each bookstore, there had been moments when she'd truly felt her father's presence. The book tour which she had dreaded and had hoped to avoid had become a journey that, in the end, had brought her the first peace she'd known since the day Josh had died.

"Are you all set there?" Heather Cannon, the perky morning hostess — dubbed "America's kid sister" by the media — took a seat in the chair opposite the one in which Regan sat, and smoothed her skirt with one hand and her hair with the other.

"Fine, yes. Thanks." Regan nodded somewhat stiffly.

As a regular morning viewer, Regan had watched hundreds of celebrities — movie and television stars, athletes, musicians — sit in this very seat. It suddenly occurred to her that perhaps some of those same people might be sitting at home watching her.

It was a thought she wished she had not had.

She pressed sweating palms against her thighs and tried to force calming breaths into her lungs. So far, it hadn't worked.

"Can we get you some water?" the hostess asked. "Are you sure you're all right?"

"Yes. I'm fine."

"Everyone gets a little stage fright here." Heather flashed her most reassuring smile. "Once the cameras begin to roll, and we start to chat, you'll be fine."

"I am fine," Regan insisted.

"Not too late for a little water," Heather offered again.

"Thanks, but no."

"Okay, if you're sure." Heather nodded to someone behind Regan. "We're a go whenever you are. Regan, watch the red light on the monitor . . ."

For a moment, Regan couldn't remember where the monitor was, but she followed the lead of her hostess.

*Sorry, Dad. I'd hoped to have made a better showing.*

"For over twenty years, Josh Landry was the gold standard when it came to writing true crime bestsellers," Heather began. "He made a highly respected career out of investigating old, unsolved murders with the intent of cracking them, and then told the story in one of his many books, the last few with the assistance of his daughter, Regan. Tragically, Josh Landry was murdered last year at his farm outside of Princeton, New Jersey, by a man named Archer Lowell, who had targeted Landry as part of a bizarre murder-triangle that had, for several months, stumped even the FBI. Regan Landry is here with me today to talk about the last book that she and her father wrote together."

Heather reached across the spare distance and touched Regan lightly on the arm. "Regan, how hard has it been to carry on in your father's footsteps?"

"No one could fill my dad's shoes, but I couldn't not go on this tour. He was very, very proud of this book, and I felt obligated to go on with the schedule. Dad always looked forward to seeing his readers, and I felt I owed it to them — and to him — to take this last trip."

"Do you think it will be the last trip?" Heather leaned closer. "You're not thinking about continuing your father's work?"

Regan hesitated for a long moment.

"I hadn't planned on it. My intention was to finish out this tour for him, then move on to something else with my life. But before I left last month, I'd started cleaning out my dad's house with an eye toward getting it ready to put on the market. In the course of going through his files, I came across some notes that he'd made regarding different cases he'd looked into over the years — books he'd planned on writing in the future — and I have to admit, some of those cases are stories just begging to be told."

"Ah, so there might yet be more Landry true crime?"

"Possibly. I have to give it a bit more thought, but my dad left some pretty interesting notes and interviews, even some correspondence from people who may or may not have been involved in violent crimes."

"Correspondence? From killers?"

"Some, claiming to be. It's pretty scary reading, actually."

"Your father didn't turn these letters over to the police?"

"In some cases, apparently, he did, and only kept photocopies for his file. In others, I can't really tell, because I don't know if the files contain all his notes. Sometimes he'd remove material if he was working on something and forget to put it back in the file, or just as often, he'd stuff papers into an otherwise empty file, so I never know where I will find things. His housekeeping was notoriously poor — notes pop up in the darnedest places. I'm still trying to sort things out and organize the files. To answer your question, I can't tell what's been handed over to law enforcement because I don't know what the files originally contained. And others, well, it's hard to know which letters were from real criminals."

"Because some of the letters might be

from people who just got a charge out of writing to him and saying they had committed certain acts, to get his attention?"

"To be sure, there was some of that. He'd mentioned several times that he'd get letters from one state or another, describing killings or whatever, but when he'd contact the local police, he'd be told there were no bodies buried where the letter said there'd be, that sort of thing."

"So it was hard for him to know who was on the level?"

"Yes. But he did amass a wealth of information on many cases that he'd shared with police and with the FBI over the years."

"Any notorious cases, ones we'd recognize?"

"Oh, sure. He had several boxes of material on the Hillcrest Rapist, the Bayside Strangler, and the Six-Year Killer, to name just a few."

"The Six-Year Killer who was active in Massachusetts, so named because he seemed to surface and kill every six years," Heather interjected.

"Right."

"Have you read through your father's notes on that case?"

"Some of them. I haven't had time to read through all of it."

"Any insights?"

"Not yet. I've been skimming through merely to see what there is. And again, I haven't had time to organize things in a way that would make any sense or would give me any feelings about the case — or any of the cases — one way or another."

"Which case do you think you'd be most likely to pick up first? Assuming, of course, that you decide to go ahead and write a book on your own."

"I can't really say." Regan shrugged. "There are boxes of files I haven't even opened yet. Who knows what I might find in one of them?"

"Well, I feel certain that one of those files will be calling your name, and maybe by this time next year we'll be looking at a new Landry true crime bestseller. I know I will be first in line for my copy."

Heather turned to the camera. "We'll be right back with Regan Landry to talk about *In His Shoes* . . ."

Heather turned back to reassure Regan. "You did just fine. You're a natural."

"Thank you. You're making this a lot easier than I thought it would be." Regan smiled for the first time that morning. "And if that bottle of water is still available, I think I'd like it now."

He sat back in the chair and rewound the tape, then pushed *Play.*

"There are boxes of files I haven't even opened yet," the pretty blonde was saying. "Who knows what I might find in one of them?"

Who indeed?

Well, *he* knew what she would find in at least one of those boxes. Or many boxes, depending on how disorganized the man really had been when it came to record keeping.

And assuming, of course, that Josh Landry had kept the letters *he* had written so long ago. Letters meant to taunt, letters meant to tease and intrigue, and, yes, to frustrate.

He smiled, recalling how Josh Landry had ignored the first few, perhaps thinking them the work of someone who was merely seeking attention. Of course, that had been before his body of work — he loved that expression — had been discovered, so to speak.

He'd certainly given old Josh something to think about, once upon a time. By the time Landry had figured out he was on the level, it had been too late. Way too late. And by then, of course, he'd moved on, bored with the game and in need of fresh surroundings and new challenges.

Over the years, it had been grand, watching the police here and there trip over themselves, looking for clues, frantically searching for suspects. Their confusion had merely reinforced his belief in the stupidity of the law enforcement community in general. He'd yet to meet his match.

He rewound the tape to the beginning, and watched it again.

Pretty thing, that Landry girl. Smart, too.

Was she smarter than her father had been?

He pondered the thought, stopped the tape, and rewound it and played it again. Watching her had made him think of other pretty things. Pretty things and pretty places, from long ago and far away.

He walked to the expanse of windows that looked out on the desert that lay beyond, and thought back to the town where he'd grown up, where it had all begun. His first mischief. His first willing venture into the dark places where his mind had led.

He turned back from the vista and paced the length of the cavernous living room, scents and sounds and images from the past now alive in his mind. Long stretches of wetlands lush with tall reeds and grasses that whispered softly and beckoned in the breeze. Long arms of beach over which gulls soared and screamed. Summer afternoons spent in a small boat, catching crabs in a net under a rickety two-lane wooden bridge. If he closed his eyes, he could see it. Hear it. Smell it.

Once he had been a child of the sea. What, he asked himself, was he doing here, surrounded by hot sand and blazing sun? Perhaps it was time to think about going home.

Besides, he'd pretty much come to the end of his run here. Sooner or later, the police would start putting two and two and two together and they would get six, sure enough. Within the past two weeks, several bodies had surfaced. Might not the sheriff's department start to catch on to the fact that those naked bodies that had turned up recently in the desert were not the run-of-the-mill border killings they'd been dealing with over the years, but something of a different nature? It was far from unusual to find the body of a young girl along the border — the count had been growing steadily for years — but his victims had all met their end in the same precise manner. Surely soon someone would notice and would begin to question the possibility of such coincidence.

He alone knew there were many, many more bodies, here and elsewhere, and that there were no coincidences.

All things considered, maybe it *was* time to go home. Return to the scene of the crime. Literally.

He sat on the plush leather ottoman and rewound the tape, suddenly feeling old. How much longer could he safely keep on, he wondered.

Over the years, he'd been lucky, but how much longer before his luck would run out?

He'd had one close call, about three weeks ago, the memory of which, even now, made him dizzy. He'd just dumped his latest kill in the foothills in the state park outside of town, and was walking back to his car, her clothes in a plastic trash bag slung over his shoulder, when he ran smack into a park guard.

"What's in the bag?" the guard had asked.

"Oh. Just some trash I picked up at a campsite about a half mile up the trail there," he'd replied, even as he'd patted his jacket for the small revolver he always carried there and wondered if he'd need it now.

20

"Don't it just kill you, the way people will leave their shit around?" The guard had shaken his head in disgust. "You wouldn't believe some of the stuff we've found up there."

"Oh, I bet I would." He relaxed and shifted the bag from one hand to the other.

"Well, thanks for being a good citizen and pitching in here. We appreciate the help, you know, not enough staff to keep track of everything."

"Hey, my pleasure."

"Want me to take that?" The guard reached for the bag.

"No need. There's a Dumpster in the parking lot at my apartment building. I'll drop it in on my way past."

"Well, hey, thanks again."

"Glad to help." He'd nodded and strolled on off to his car, glancing back casually, but the guard had already disappeared. He'd opened the rear door and casually tossed the bag inside.

He'd slid into the driver's seat of his Mercedes SUV and stole an anxious glance in the rearview mirror to reassure himself that he had not been observed. It was then he'd realized that his hands were shaking and he was sweating. But he hadn't been caught, and since the body he'd left deep in the hills hadn't been discovered for another ten days, the guard had remembered only vaguely that someone had been around the park that night. The well-meaning public servant couldn't remember anything about the stranger except that he'd been kind enough to dispose of some trash left behind by a careless camper.

Still, it had been an unpleasant experience, one necessitating finding a new dumping ground and a new vehicle, just in case the guard had noticed. Both had been easy enough — there were endless places in the desert to hide a body and it had taken him less than a morning to trade in the black Mercedes for a silver one — but things hadn't been the same.

He hit *Play* and watched the tape again.

He was overcome with nostalgia every time that Landry girl and Heather what's-her-name talked about the Bayside Strangler. Nostalgia and — dare he say it? — a perverse sort of pride. And it sure did bring on the memories.

He rested his head against the back of the chair and closed his eyes. It was there again, that smell of the bay, the salt air, the scent of marine life rotting in the hot sun on the beach across the road from the house where he'd grown up. He inhaled sharply, as if hoping to catch and hold those scents, those memories.

He shook off the bit of sudden home-sickness, reminding himself that *that* was a part of his past, no more. He'd done what he'd done and moved on. There was nothing there for him now. Well, there was some family, but he cared about as much for them as they cared for him. Over the years, their contact had been cursory at best.

But then there was that little bit of unfinished business.

Now, that *did* rankle, just a wee bit. A sloppy bit of work on the part of an amateur *that* had been, and he admittedly had been an amateur in those days. Of course, he hadn't planned on making a career of it. Back then, who could have foreseen the path his life would take?

Even so, only an amateur would have left so much to chance. Only an amateur would have taken such risks. Only an amateur would have panicked the way he'd done, instead of going back another time to do what he'd gone there to do.

And God knows, only an amateur would have left one of them alive.

# One

The early-morning fog had yet to be burned off by a sun still snoozing behind low-lying clouds, but the gulls were already circling over the bay and the shorebirds had begun to forage along the waterline. Although almost summer, the air still bore a bit of a chill, and the remnants of a cool spring night hung in the damp air. Waves rolled gently onto the beach, tiny swells outlined with white foam that left damp impressions on the pale yellow sand. Overhead, a gull screamed at the intruder who crested the top of the dune.

"Oh, shut up." The woman barely glanced at the ornery bird that swooped over her head and continued to rain gull curses down upon her.

Detective Cassandra Burke stood with her hands on her hips, and through the fog sought the outline of the Barnegat Lighthouse across the bay. She'd just ended her fourth night of surveillance of a motel where suspected drug sales were being conducted, and she was both exhausted from lack of sleep and stiff from inactivity. She toed off her shoes and left them in the sand, then set off for the marina a mile down the beach. She'd walk the kinks out, then run back. Two miles wasn't really long enough, but it was the best she could do this morning. Maybe she'd feel better. Maybe not. But she had a meeting at eight, and needed to sandwich in a little exercise, then a little breakfast, before she headed to the police station.

The sand on the bay beach was coarser than that on the ocean side, and allowed a more solid footing. She walked briskly, sidestepping the spiny helmets of the dead and dying horseshoe crabs that had washed up onshore overnight and had been unable to crawl back before the tide went out. When she reached the inlet, she paused long enough to watch a few large power boats — charters, mostly — as they set out to sea with their passengers, sport fishermen who had paid for the privilege of casting their lines into the Atlantic with hopes of snagging a few feisty blues before the sun set later that day.

She waved to the captain of the *Normandy Maid* as it passed, a half-dozen or so eager fishermen on deck, their baseball caps shielding their faces from the sun that would soon enough grace them with its presence, their arms and noses slick with SPF 35. It wasn't much of a living, running a charter, but for those who'd never done much else, it was a way of life, a life she knew well. Her father had captained his own boat, the *Jenny B*, named after her mother. He'd never made much money, but he loved to go to work every day. In the off-season, he ran the only boat storage facility in Bowers Inlet, but his life was out on the water. Few days passed that didn't find Cass here, at the point where the bay eased into the ocean, watching the boats head out, and remembering. As a very little child, she'd watched from her mother's arms as her father's boat chugged by.

"Wave to Daddy, Cassie," her mother would say. "See him there, on the deck? Wave to Daddy, honey . . ."

And Cass would wave wildly. Most days, her father would salute as he passed, touching just his right index finger to the brim of his hat.

A few years later, Cass stood on the rocks nearest the water, holding tightly to her little sister's hand.

"Wave to Daddy, Trish," she'd say. "Wave to Daddy . . ."

The alarm on her watch buzzed, bringing her back to the present. She turned away from the inlet and started back down the beach, running so fast her muscles barely had time to burn before she reached the spot where she'd left her shoes. If she was going to grab something to eat before her meeting, she'd have to leave now.

She wanted real food. Through the wee hours of the night, she'd had enough coffee to keep her wired for several days, while Jeff Spencer, the only other detective on the town's small police force, had packed away enough cream donuts to make her sick just to watch. Eggs and sausage and toast should do it, she was thinking as she slipped into her shoes. And orange juice. Her stomach rumbling, she headed back to her car. If she drove fast enough, she might even have time for a short stack of pancakes.

"Detective Burke?"

"Yes?" Cassie paused midway across the lobby of the new police station.

"The lady at the desk there . . ."

"Sergeant Carter." Emphasis on *sergeant.*

"Right. Sergeant Carter. She said you were working on my son's case . . ."

"Your son is . . . ?"

"Derrick Mills." He spoke the name softly.

"Yes. Derrick. Yes, I'm working on that case." Cassie swallowed back a sigh. Derrick Mills was one of five kids arrested for selling drugs at the regional high school three weeks ago. She wasn't blind to the father's pain and embarrassment and wished she could ease it somehow, even as she knew she could not.

"I was wondering what we had to do, you know, to get the charges dropped. He's a good kid, Detective. Top athlete, good student. He's got a scholarship to play baseball in college next year."

"I'm sorry, Mr. Mills. I really am. But Derrick should have thought about that scholarship before he offered to sell cocaine to Officer Connors."

"Detective Burke —"

"Please, Mr. Mills. Save your breath. I've made my report and my recommendations, and they stand. There's nothing I can do. Now, if you want to talk to the county DA's office, you go right ahead and make that call. But right now, I'm late for a meeting. So if you'll excuse me . . ."

"You know, I expected more from Bob Burke's girl." His voice had dropped to a low growl.

"Don't even go there." She shook her head and walked past him.

Cass made an effort to not glance back at the angry father while she fought down her own anger. It wasn't the first time someone had invoked her father's name, as if somehow having known him entitled them to special favors from her. It certainly wouldn't be the last. It just flat-out pissed her off every time.

The meeting had been changed from the large conference room to a small room adjacent to the chief's office.

"Denver must have whittled down the guest list," Cass said as she took a seat across the table from Jeff Spencer.

"So far, it's you and me, Burke." Jeff rattled a bag in her direction. "Hey, there's one last strawberry cream here. I believe it's got your name on it."

"Jesus, how can you eat that crap all the time?" Grimacing, she turned her head away from the bag with the donut rolling around in it.

"I don't understand that sugar phobia of yours." Spencer shook his head.

"I don't understand why you're not so wired from all that sugar that you're buzzing around the room like a popped balloon."

"Ah, you're both here. Good. Good." Chief of Police Craig Denver stuck his head through the door that led from his office. "Let me grab my coffee . . ."

Denver disappeared momentarily, then was back in a flash with his oversized mug and a manila file. He took a seat at the head of the table and busied himself with a napkin and a coaster and his glasses, as if postponing whatever it was he had brought them here to discuss.

"I hate this part of the job," he sighed. "You both know that the administrative details of this job drive me crazy. Paperwork, reports, statistics . . . waste of my time. But you don't get to pick and choose, not in this job, not in any."

Cass bit back a grin. She'd heard this same spiel right about this time last year. And the year before, and the year before. She suspected that the intro was for Spencer's sake. He'd only been with the department for a few months.

"Let me guess. The insurance company asked for an updated training manual again," she deadpanned.

Denver nodded.

"Updated and expanded."

"And you want one of us to volunteer to sit down with Phyl and proofread the

30

pages before she sends them in." Cass toyed with a fingernail.

"That about sums it up." Denver smiled.

"It's Spencer's turn." Cass twirled her pen. "I did all the proofing last year. And the year before."

"Then you have the experience, don't you?" Spencer's eyes narrowed. His wife had already issued an ultimatum about him spending too many of his off-duty hours on department business and he'd sworn he'd make an effort to spend more time with her and their new baby, and less time working.

"Fair is fair, Spencer, and I —"

Phyllis Lannick, the chief's secretary, poked her head in the doorway.

"Sorry to interrupt, Chief, but Officer Helms is on the phone and he says it's an emergency. He sounds rattled." She pointed to the phone on the small table behind him. "Line two."

Denver raised an eyebrow as he reached for the phone.

"Emergency, Helms? Hey, hey. Slow down. Take a deep breath and start over . . ."

The chief went silent then, listening. The color drained from his face.

"I have Burke and Spencer right here.

31

They're on their way. Goes without saying that no one touches anything until the scene has been processed. Keep everyone out of the area until I can get the county CSI out there." He hung up and turned to his two detectives.

Before either could ask, he said, "The manual will have to wait. They just found a body out near Wilson's Creek."

"A body?" Cassie asked as if she'd not heard correctly. "Where along the creek?"

"Right outside of town, near Marsh Road. Just look for the cars. Apparently all three of our patrol cars and a couple of emergency vehicles are already there, parked along the roadside before the bridge. You won't be able to miss them. Try to keep everyone in line until the county people arrive. I'll meet you there." He shoved his chair out from the table, muttering, "Just what we need, a homicide right as the season opens."

"Homicide?" Cass paused on her way to the door and turned.

"That's Helms's take on it. See if he's right . . ."

The body lay on its side on a rock worn smooth by the fast-moving stream known locally as Wilson's Creek. The woman had

32

been young — late twenties, early thirties, Cass was thinking. She knelt carefully to visually inspect the victim, whose unseeing eyes were open and whose silent mouth still held its last scream. Bare arms, lightly sunburned to right above the elbow, were flung over her head, one hand trailing in the water. Her very long dark hair spilled over her face and into the creek, where the swift current wrapped some strands around her fingers. One leg was curled over the other, almost demurely.

"You didn't touch her, did you?" a voice from behind asked tentatively.

"No. Of course I didn't touch her." Cass looked up to find the county's lead crime scene investigator, Tasha Welsh, surveying the scene.

"Good. Hope you all watched where you walked." Tasha's eyes scanned the entire scene, the two detectives, the body, the uniformed officers milling about the black-and-white cruisers parked up a slight rise on the side of the road.

"Actually, we came in along the stream." Cass motioned behind her, indicating the direction.

"That explains your wet jeans." Tasha approached the body slowly, then turned and looked at Cass, who held a camera in her right hand. "Start from here, this angle, and work your way around that way . . ."

Tasha pointed to Spencer and said, "Either smile for the camera or move."

Spencer moved.

"Blood on the inside of her thighs," Cass noted as she snapped another shot.

"She's probably been raped. And grass stains on the backs of her heels, Burke." Tasha pointed to the victim.

"Which means she most likely was dragged for at least part of the way," Cass said as she aimed the lens again. "Should be easy enough to find a drag trail if he came in from the road. Go take a look, Spencer, while I finish up here."

"You want to start on the road up there?" Spencer pointed to the area where the shoulder was widest.

"I want to start all along this area. Go tell Helms and the others to space themselves out and begin looking for depressions in the weeds. Remind them to tread lightly, though. We don't want to lose any evidence by stomping on it."

"They should know that," Spencer said over his shoulder.

"Yeah, they should. Remind them anyway. If there's anything here, I'd like to find it before it's obliterated by someone else's footprints or by the rain they're calling for this afternoon."

Cass continued to photograph the body for another ten minutes before turning her attention to the growth of cattails off to the right of the body. They stood as tall as cornstalks and as thick as blades of grass. Anyone coming through there would have left an obvious trail. She stood quietly and surveyed the terrain. Up there, off the shoulder of the road, was a stand of bamboo that could have provided some cover. She'd start there.

There were tire marks from a dozen cars — possibly even from the cruisers — on the soft sandy shoulder, but she stepped carefully around them anyway. The bamboo ran for about twelve feet along the roadside, then dropped off into marshland where only rushes grew. They had yet to reach their full height, and to Cass's mind, the logical place to walk if one was carrying or dragging a body would be right there at the point where the bamboo and the marsh met.

Predictably, about ten feet in from the road at the point where the bamboo ended, the grasses were slightly tamped down into a narrow path, which continued for another twenty-five feet into the marsh and ended in a larger, more haphazard depression. Cass looked over her shoulder, up to the point where the path actually began, and could almost envision the scene as it had happened.

*He carried her from the car through the bamboo,* Cass thought, *then she must have become heavy, and he let her down back there, right where the weeds begin to bend. He dragged her down this far; the dragging of her body made the path, such as it is. Then he dropped her here.*

Why had he dropped her here?

She stood for several long moments, listening to the light breeze set the rushes in motion. The body was fresh, the young woman hadn't been there for long. Late last night, Cass surmised. She squatted down near the depression and studied it, looking for something that would help her to see what had happened here. It took her almost ten minutes, but she found it: two sections of reeds, bunched and broken, spaced almost two feet apart, at either side of the top of the depression.

Cass could see the woman now, face-down in the marsh, her arms outstretched, hands grabbing on to the only things she could reach . . .

36

She stood and walked back up the path to the road, snapping shots of everything she felt relevant, then she caught Spencer's eye.

"Got something, Burke?" Spencer called, and she responded by waving him over to where she stood.

"I think I found the path the killer took into the marsh," she said when Spencer joined her.

"This is his way in, and out, I suspect," she told him. "And down here — please watch where you walk — look here . . ."

She led him down the path and to the depression in the reeds.

"I think she may have been unconscious when he took her out of the car and began to carry her down here. Then, when he got about here, she either became too heavy or woke up and began to fight, and he dumped her on the ground over there."

"What makes you think she was still alive?" Spencer asked, and Cass pointed to the bunched and broken reeds.

"I think she grabbed on to the reeds and tried to crawl away. I think this is where she was attacked. I think he hurt her here."

Cass knelt on one knee to obtain close-up shots of the broken stalks.

Spencer stepped off the path and looked around.

"He could have taken her down this way," he pointed toward the left, "right to the stream. He might have waded through it, just like we did, to avoid leaving footprints."

"Let's check it out."

They picked their way through the marsh to the bank of the stream. From there they followed the current back to where the body lay.

"Find anything?" Tasha asked without looking up from her task, scraping under the victim's fingernails into small plastic bags, one for each finger.

"We found evidence that she may have been alive when she was brought down here." Cass stepped from the water onto a nearby rock and described the scene they had discovered in the marsh.

"I agree, she died here." Tasha turned to drop the bags into a container. "Fixed lividity here on the right hip and along the thigh and upper arm. Just the way we found her. Rigor's set in, we got the flies but no maggots yet, so we know right off the bat that we're within twelve hours. Body temp right now is 85.1 degrees Fahrenheit, so, since we know that the body loses about one and a half degrees every hour after death, that means . . ."

"She's been dead about nine hours." Cass looked at her watch. It was just a few minutes after nine. "Which takes us to around midnight last night."

"That's my best estimate, though it could have been a little less. It was cool last night, could have lowered her body temp a little faster." Tasha stood up and motioned for the county medical examiner. "Dr. Storm, she's all yours."

"Thanks." The ME, a stocky woman in her early sixties, stepped forward, her expression solemn.

Tasha stripped off her gloves and dropped them into her open bag, telling Cass, "I should have something for you by tomorrow. At least by then I'll know if he left any DNA. I'm hoping there are some skin cells under her nails, if nothing else. Then we'll see what Dr. Storm has for us. In any event, I'll be in touch as soon as I know something."

Cass nodded. "I'd appreciate it."

"By the way, cause of death appears to be manual strangulation," the tech told Cass. "Looks like she was sexually assaulted, but we'll have to wait for the ME's findings to know for sure. We'll also want to know which came first, the assault or the strangulation."

Tasha closed the black bag into which she'd tucked the samples she'd painstakingly collected. "I'll head on back to the lab now, and try to sort this all out."

She smiled at Cass, then added, "Then you get to figure out what it all means."

"With luck."

"Anyone know who she is?" Tasha hoisted the bag over her shoulder.

"Not that I'm aware. Helms found her clothes in the marsh, they've been bagged for the lab. Jeans, T-shirt, bra, panties, one brown leather sandal, canvas purse," Cass told her.

"Guess you weren't lucky enough to find a wallet with ID in the purse?"

"No wallet."

"Well, I guess that's your job, right?" Tasha started toward the county van, which was parked up near the road. "To figure out who she was and why this happened to her?"

"We'll do our best." Cass fell in step alongside Tasha.

"When was the last time you guys in Bowers had a homicide?"

"Aside from the hit-and-run we had last month, this is it. We've had a few domestics over the years, but for the most part, this has been a pretty quiet town. I guess if you had to depend on us to keep you busy, you'd be pretty bored," Cass said when they reached the van.

"Please, we have plenty to do without your homicides." Tasha opened the back of the van and set the bag in. "We cover the entire county. There's always something going on somewhere. And there's no shortage of rapes, assaults, burglaries, you name it. Plus, things will start to pick up now, especially when the kids start coming for senior week."

Tasha grimaced. "I hate senior week. Then, of course, straight through till Labor Day the entire county is hopping. All these little shore towns with their rentals — families and college kids — and then there's the day-trippers. Over the past few years, we've had a bunch of homicides. I hope this is the only one you'll have to deal with."

Tasha opened the driver's-side door and hopped in.

"I'll get back to you as soon as I can," she told Cass.

"Thanks. I appreciate it. I'll make a set of photos for you and send them over." Cass stepped back and watched the van pull onto the highway, then scanned the small crowd that gathered around the officer who had found the body, and who was now retelling the story for the newly arrived chief of police.

Denver stood quietly, occasionally nodding, until the officer concluded his verbal report. Then, without so much as a comment, the chief followed the path to the body, and stood over it, wordlessly watching the ME's ministrations. Finally he turned and looked up to the crowd at the edge of the roadway. When he met Cass's eyes, he held them for a very long minute before turning away abruptly and walking back to his car.

Cass watched Denver's Crown Vic pull away from the side of the road before motioning to Spencer, who was in deep conversation with one of the EMTs.

"I'm going to go back to the station and check for missing persons," she called to him.

"I think I'll stick around here for a while longer, grab a ride back with Helms," Spencer replied.

"Okay. I'll see you there."

Cass walked back down toward the stream, pausing about ten feet from where the body lay sadly exposed. The limbs, where rigor mortis was beginning to set in, were covered with eager flies seeking an opening. The medical examiner was still conducting her inspection of the body, and Cass found she could not bear to watch this latest invasion of the unnamed woman. She crossed the stream and followed the trail along the other side to the two-lane road where she'd left her car. She got in and turned on the ignition, her movements becoming more and more robotic with each passing moment. She turned the car around and drove, not to the station, but to a lonely stretch of road.

Six miles down, she took a right on a narrow lane that led toward the bay. Minutes later she reached a run-down house that sat off the side of the road, the sole structure for another quarter mile in either direction. In the overgrown yard sat the shell of an old Boston Whaler, its hull dry-rotted. Cass parked the car behind the boat and walked around to the back of the house, where three rickety steps led to an even more unstable back porch, which once upon a time had been painted white.

Time and neglect had stripped the wood and weathered it gray. The screen on the back door had long since eroded, and the windows no longer closed tightly. Cass sat on the top step and looked off into the tall cattails that grew from the marsh straight on up to the back of the dilapidated garage. Off to the left was a pond, and from where she sat, she could see a small blue heron wading through the water, head down, cautiously stalking its prey.

She balled her hands and covered her eyes, but all she could see was the body of that dark-haired young woman sprawled out upon the rock.

Oblivious to the sweat that covered her face and dampened her light blue T-shirt down to her waist, she sat immobile and tried to control the emotions that churned within her. Of course, she'd seen dead bodies before, but she'd never reacted like this.

Well, hadn't her therapist warned her that this might happen someday? That if she persisted in a career in law enforcement, sooner or later she might have to deal with something that might take her back to a place she'd rather not go?

The ringing of her cell phone jarred her, and she answered it on the second ring.

"Burke."

"Are you on your way in?" Spencer asked, his voice tense.

"Yes."

"Good. I'll meet you there. I just heard from Denver." He paused. "Apparently we have a situation."

"I'll be there in ten minutes." She hung up and slid the phone back into her jacket pocket.

She sat for another few moments and watched the heron grab something from the water, throw its head back, and swallow its meal in one quick motion. The wind hissed through the cattails, the hushed sound soothing her as few things could. She remembered countless nights when she lay awake in the room under the eaves, right up there on the second floor, listening to that very same sound as she fell asleep. It had comforted her then and it comforted her now.

A moment later she was walking toward her car, her hands steady, her pulse almost normal, wondering what, on this day marked by murder, constituted a "situation."

Craig Denver sat in the chair the town council had surprised him with as a gift for his twenty-fifth year on the job and simply stared out the window next to his desk. For years, he'd wondered what he'd do if this day ever came, and now it was here, and he was still wondering.

He spread the piece of paper that had arrived earlier that day in a plain white envelope that bore no address. Phyl had found it on the floor of the lobby, near the front door, when she was on her way into the building after having picked up lunch for herself and the chief. She would have tossed it, except for the fact that it was sealed. Her curiosity piqued, she'd opened it, and having glanced at the message once, took it immediately to the chief's office.

The paper itself was undistinguished, everyday computer stock, the kind that could be purchased at any one of a number of chain office-supply stores. It was the message that had caught Phyl's attention, a message comprised of glued letters cut from newspapers and magazines, much as a child might do for a homework assignment.

Hey, Denver! Have you found her yet?

She'd carried it down the hall, holding it between two fingers to avoid getting her prints on it, walked into the chief's office without knocking — something she rarely did — and dropped it on his desk. He had unfolded it, then stared at it for the longest time.

46

Finally, he asked quietly, "Where did this come from?"

"I found it on the floor in the lobby."

"You didn't see anyone . . . ?"

"No one. I'd just picked up lunch from Stillman's, I wasn't gone ten minutes. I didn't see anyone on my way out, or on my way back in."

"Okay." He'd nodded slowly. "Thank you."

Most of the force was still out at Wilson's Creek, so he dusted the envelope and the white sheet of paper for prints. There were none except for the smudged partials that he suspected would prove to be Phyl's. He'd reached for the phone, and called in Spencer and Burke.

Denver sat back in his chair and sighed deeply, wanting nothing more than to start this day over and have it turn out differently.

Coincidence, or copycat?

Either way, it wasn't good.

Either way, shit was going to be stirred up, sure enough, and he wasn't the only one who was going to have to deal with it.

He rubbed his eyes wearily and waited for his detectives to arrive.

# Two

Cass flew into the parking lot and swung into her reserved spot. Once inside the building, she waved absently to the desk sergeant as she walked briskly through the lobby.

"Spencer here yet?" she asked over her shoulder.

"He went back about a minute ago," the sergeant replied.

Cass followed the hall to the chief's office, knocking on the door although it stood partially open.

Denver motioned her in without looking. He sat at his desk, a thick file in front of him.

"We've had an odd development."

He slid a piece of white paper across the desk, and both detectives leaned forward to get a closer look. "This was found in the lobby today."

Hey, Denver! Have you found her yet?

"That would refer to the victim we found out in the marsh?" Spencer asked.

"Yes."

The chief tapped his pipe on the edge of the desk. The bowl was empty of tobacco, as it had been every day for the past four years since he'd successfully given up smoking. He still, however, had a need to handle it in times of extreme stress. Like now.

"So he's taunting us?" Spencer again.

"In a way. He's deliberately trying to remind us of one of our old cases."

"How old is old?" Spencer asked. "Two years? Five?"

"Twenty-six."

"Twenty-*six?*" Spencer looked from the chief to Cass, then back again. "Twenty-six *years?*"

Denver nodded as he slipped on a pair of thin plastic gloves and opened the file. He took out another white envelope and removed a sheet of white lined notebook paper, which he unfolded and held up for both detectives to see. The message had been composed with letters cut from newspapers and magazines.

Hey, Wainwright! I left something for you on the beach!

And then a second sheet from a second envelope.

"George Wainwright was the chief of police here in Bowers Inlet for almost thirty-five years," Denver explained, his voice softening.

"Well, the notes sure look the same. Did you ever find out who sent those?" Spencer pointed to the letters that lay, one next to the other, across the center of the desk.

"We know who sent them. We just don't know his name."

"I don't understand . . ."

"The Bayside Strangler mailed those letters to Chief Wainwright," Denver said.

"The Bayside Strangler?" Spencer leaned forward in his seat. "Hey, I heard about him. Geez, he must have killed, what, nine, ten women . . . ?"

"Thirteen," the chief told him. "He killed thirteen women, back in the summer of '79."

"All in Bowers Inlet?" Spencer asked.

"No. Just the two here," Denver replied. "But over the course of that one summer, he hit several of the other small bay towns as well — hence 'the Bayside Strangler.' Killion Point, Tilden, Hasboro, Dewey — he hit all of 'em at least once. Then the killings just stopped."

"Just like that? Like, he just left the building?"

"In a manner of speaking, yes," Denver said dryly.

"And there was never a suspect?" Spencer frowned.

"Nothing. No idea who he was or why he started, why he stopped." Denver shook his head. "No one had ever seen this guy. We had no description, no evidence to help us narrow down the field. And think about how huge that field was. Besides the permanent residents of all these little towns, you have the summer people. The ones who come back every year and own or rent the same house, the ones who used to live here but come back in the summer because their family still owns property here. You have the rentals — Christ, they change every week or two. And then you have the summer help, the kids who come for ten weeks to work at the shore, then leave and go back to wherever they came from. Day-fishers, day-trippers."

"So he just moved away . . ."

Cass spoke up for the first time. "Most serial killers only stop because they die or go to prison. Moving away doesn't usually stop them from killing."

"I guess if there'd been a serial killer

someplace else with the same MO you'd have heard about it."

"Maybe, maybe not. If he'd gone on another spree like he did here, it would have made the papers, but we may not have seen those papers out here," Denver said.

"Twenty-some years ago, there wasn't any way to track something like that," Cassie noted. "No national data banks, no central records."

The chief nodded. "You're right. Chances are, he just moved on. Now, the young woman found in the marsh . . . do we know who she is?"

"Not yet. There was no ID, no wallet," Cass said.

Denver stared at her.

"Chief?" She waved her hand in front of his face.

"No ID at all?" he asked.

"None. Why?"

"Just coincidentally, the Bayside Strangler always took his victims' wallets," he replied. "Of course, not knowing if this woman had a wallet on her at the time, we don't want to jump to conclusions."

"That's a pretty odd coincidence," Spencer pointed out.

"She might not have carried ID. I can't tell you how many times my own daughter has gone out and left her purse or her wallet right there on the kitchen counter."

"Still —" Spencer began, but Denver cut him off.

"We're not going to connect the dots just yet, Detective. Understand?" Denver shrugged. "As tempting as it is. It's more likely that someone is trying to throw us off."

"Yes, but —"

"Let's focus on our victim, shall we? Start checking the missing persons reports, statewide. I wouldn't be at all surprised to find, in the end, that we've got a guy who's killed his wife or girlfriend and has enough knowledge of the Bayside Strangler to try to muddy the waters. It was no secret that the Strangler had sent Wainwright taunting notes. Anyone could have remembered that. And the fact that the victims' IDs were stolen, well, maybe this guy figures if he takes the wallet, he sends the letter, everyone will assume there's a copycat Strangler out there and take the heat off him. Let's not automatically buy in to that, all right? I wanted you to be aware of what we dealt with before, but let's not assume. Let's start by finding out who our victim is.

"Put your focus on her," Denver repeated, "so that we can find her killer."

"But we can compare the evidence, right?" Spencer asked as he stood. "The old to whatever new forensics comes up with?"

"Back then, fingerprints were the best you could hope for, and unfortunately, this guy didn't leave any. None that we found, anyway. Thank God, investigative techniques have come a long way since then, but we don't have anything to compare."

Spencer scratched behind his right ear. "All those crime scenes and no evidence? Hard to believe."

"Today, a good CSI can get prints off a victim's skin. Scrapings from under the nails. Fibers and hair. They can test trace found at the scene. Dirt found on carpets, all sorts of things. Back then, the techniques were not quite as sophisticated. DNA was just a glimmer in the eyes of a few scientists twenty-six years ago." Denver seemed distracted for a moment, then said, "I was a rookie here in 1979. I worked that case. I have to admit, seeing that body this morning took me right back. It's uncanny . . ."

"Then, you remember those cases firsthand," Spencer said.

"Like it was yesterday. The first victim

here in Bowers Inlet was a thirty-four-year-old woman named Alicia Coors. She disappeared from her home and was found the next morning on one of the dunes down past Thirty-sixth Street. And that was just the beginning. Every few days, there'd be another, somewhere in the area. All women about the same age — late-twenties to mid-thirties. All were sexually assaulted and found dumped in one of the marshes. Cause of death in each case, manual strangulation. All left posed in the same manner."

"How were they left?" Spencer asked.

"Pretty much the way that woman was left this morning."

"Why would he do that?" Spencer scratched behind his ear.

"That's a question a profiler might be able to answer. Unfortunately, back then, there were no profilers." The chief shrugged. "I don't know what motivated him then, and I don't know what's motivating someone now. And I don't want to jump to conclusions. So let's just follow the evidence and hope it leads to the truth."

He stood up, a clear indication that the meeting had concluded.

"Spencer, I want you checking missing persons immediately."

"On my way." Spencer got up and headed out the door.

"Anything in particular for me?" Cass asked.

"Yes. I'd like a word with you." He pointed to the door and said, "Close it."

Cass did as she was told, then turned to face the chief.

"Are you going to be all right with this?" he asked.

"I'm fine."

"Seriously, Cass, if it's going to be a problem for you . . ."

"It's not going to be a problem." Cass was beginning to bristle.

Denver sighed. "I'm asking because I'm concerned about what you might have felt, looking at that body today . . ."

"She wasn't my first dead body, Chief," Cass told him softly. "She won't be my last."

"I'm aware there have been others. But this one . . . I just wasn't sure if this might not be . . . troubling for you."

"Of course it troubles me, but not in the way you might think." She smiled at him with true affection, grateful for his kindness, understanding where he was going with this. "I appreciate that you . . . remember. And that you care enough to ask.

56

But I'm fine. I have to be. This is my job."

He nodded. "I'm going to have to take your word for it. Give the county CSI team a call and see if they have anything yet."

She started for the door, then turned and said softly, "You know, Chief, I didn't see her that day. I never saw her body."

"I'm sorry I brought it up, Cass. I really am. It's just that . . ." He shook his head, not certain that he could put into words what he wanted to say.

"It's okay. Thanks, Chief." She walked through the door and closed it behind her.

Denver rose and walked to the window and watched a pair of catbirds as they diligently built their nest in the tangle of rosebushes not ten feet away.

*"I didn't see her that day. I never saw her body . . ."*

Denver wished he could say the same. When he'd seen the young woman's body this morning, he'd had one of the first true déjà vu moments of his entire life.

And even now, in his mind's eye, he could still see the body of Jenny Burke, lying on her back on the floor of her bedroom, her hair spilled around her like a dark halo, her eyes open but unseeing. For just a moment, back there in the marsh this morning, it had been Jenny's face he'd seen. It had been the hair, he told himself. It was just all that long dark hair, and the way the arms had been positioned.

Of course, that was where the similarities between the two situations ended. The crimes — and the crime scenes — had been totally different. And Jenny had not been sexually assaulted.

And, he reminded himself, Jenny's killer had been found hiding in the garage, covered with Bob Burke's blood. He'd been arrested, tried, convicted. The Strangler, on the other hand, had never been identified.

It had just been the hair, Denver told himself again, that had reminded him of Jenny. All that long dark hair, spread out over the rock, had, just for a split second, brought back that day. For just a moment, he'd been a rookie again, standing in the doorway looking at the first dead body he'd ever seen. That it had been the body of a woman he'd known had marked his baptism with that much more fire.

He'd hated to bring it up to Cass, but he'd needed to put it on the table. Had he overreacted? Maybe so.

Oh, hell, of course he had. He had forgotten that Cass had never made it to her mother's bedroom before the killer had turned on her. She wouldn't have known the way the body had lain, the way the hair had fanned out.

*"I didn't see her that day. I never saw her body . . ."*

He shivered, remembering that nightmarish day.

They'd talked about it, when she'd come in for her interview. She had her reasons for becoming a cop, and he respected her for it. But she had to know up front he'd been there that day, and if she had a problem with that . . . if working for him would be a daily reminder of things she couldn't deal with, she needed to face up to it before she started.

"No," she'd said. "I knew who you were before I applied for the job. You knew my parents before . . . *before.* I know what you did that day. I want to work for you."

"I won't give you special treatment because your folks were old friends," he'd told her, "or for any other reasons."

"I wouldn't expect you to."

"Well, you scored highest in your class in all areas. You're the best marksman in your group. I'd be a fool not to hire you, wouldn't I?"

"It could be construed as discrimination, sir," she had said, a tiny smile turning up one side of her mouth.

"Yes, well, we wouldn't want to discriminate against you, would we? Don't want the FOP on my back."

"Thank you, Chief Denver," she'd said before she left his office that day. "I'll be a good cop."

And she had been. When the detective position had opened up three years earlier, she'd been the first to apply. He'd had no doubts that she'd qualify, and he'd been secretly pleased when she'd beaten out all the other candidates for the job. Only the fact that she couldn't be everywhere, day or night, had prompted him to ask the town for a second detective earlier in the year.

In his heart, the chief knew that he'd been bound to her by the events of that day twenty-six years earlier, and he made an effort to never let it show.

Was she aware of it? He wondered sometimes.

True to his word, he'd never shown favoritism in any way, and in fairness to her, she'd never asked for any. She did her job well, was well liked in the community, and had been commended on a number of occasions. Today was the first time in her ten years on the force that he'd ever even brought up the subject of their shared past. He hoped it would be the last time he would feel compelled to do so.

He picked up the stack of photos of the still-unnamed victim and studied them, one by one.

*Coincidence, or copycat?*

*We'll know soon enough,* he thought as he tossed the photos back onto the desk. *If someone's following in the footsteps of the original Strangler, he'll strike again in the next week.*

*And then, God help us, all hell will break out.*

*Again.*

# Three

Cass stepped over the heap of mail that lay like poorly dealt cards on the floor inside her front door. She snapped on the nearest lamp — an ugly old porcelain thing that had belonged to her grandmother — and picked up the litter, which she proceeded to sort. Junk, junk, junk, bill, bill, junk, magazine, junk. She took the entire pile into the kitchen and tossed the junk into the trash before setting the two bills and the magazine on the counter.

She turned on the overhead light and opened the refrigerator, took out a beer, twisted off the lid, and took a long, steady drink while she listened to the messages on her answering machine. Cass wasn't sure which aggravated her more, the hang-up, or the message from her cousin, Lucy, reminding her that she'd be coming into town next week but hadn't yet decided how long she was staying and hoped that Cass wouldn't have a problem with that.

Damn.

The last thing Cass wanted right now

was company, who would have to be, at the worst, entertained, and at best, tolerated, for an indefinite period of time. Even if that company was one of her closest living relatives and had been, once upon a time, her closest friend.

Her rumbling stomach reminded Cass that she hadn't eaten since breakfast, and suddenly that seemed like a very long time ago. She pulled one of the two chairs from the table and sat down, then pushed back the other and rested her feet on the seat and her head in her hands. Seeing the dead woman's body that morning had shaken her more than she'd let on. Being reminded that she'd have to share her home with Lucy for the next month was merely the icing on that day's cake.

Between now and Thursday, she'd have to find time to put fresh sheets on Lucy's bed. Stock the kitchen with real food. Have something to drink in the refrigerator besides a six-pack of beer and some iced tea from the local convenience store.

And she'd have to find time to vacuum. Dust. Clean the bathroom. All the chores she generally put off until she could avoid them no longer. She bit the inside of her lower lip, wondering when, in the midst of a homicide investigation, she'd find time to make the house hospitable.

The fact that Lucy's ownership in the beach house was equal to hers wasn't lost on Cass. Their grandparents had left everything to be equally divided between their only two grandchildren. That Cass had chosen to live in the house year-round had never been an issue between the two women. Lucy, who was married and had a lovely home in Hopewell, was content with her month at the Jersey Shore every year and couldn't care less that Cass had made the bungalow her permanent residence. God knew Cass was grateful that the other eleven months of the year she had the house to herself. And she should be grateful — she *was* grateful — that Lucy was coming alone this year and not bringing her husband and her two kids with her as she had every other year.

What was up with that, Cass wondered as she took another swig from the bottle, well aware that she was deliberately focusing on Lucy as a means to avoid thinking about the body they'd found in the marsh.

The phone rang, and Cass stood to glance at the caller ID before answering. She picked it up.

"Hello."

She listened for several moments without response, then said merely, "Thank you. See you in the morning."

The body now had a name and a story.

Linda Roman.

Cass leaned back against the counter and picked at the label on the beer bottle until only slim shreds remained intact, the peeled-away slivers tucked into the fist of one hand.

Linda Roman had been thirty-one years old, a year younger than Cass. She lived in Tilden, she worked in a branch of Cass's bank, and she had a husband of four years and an eighteen-month-old daughter.

*Too young to really remember her,* Cass thought. All that child would ever know of her mother she'd learn from others.

Cass sighed wearily. At least she'd been older when she'd lost her family. She had vivid memories of her mother and her father and her sister. If she tried really hard, she could almost recall the sound of their voices. Almost, but not quite. It had been a long, long time ago.

Twenty-six years this month.

And now another little girl would have a sad anniversary to mark, year after year. It occurred to Cass that what Linda Roman's daughter would most remember of her mother would be the date on which she died.

Cass emptied the bottle into the sink and tossed it into the bin, which she rarely, if ever, remembered to put out on recycling day. She opened the refrigerator and searched for something she could reheat in the microwave for dinner, but nothing appealed to her. She called in an order for takeout and took a quick shower in the bungalow's one small outdated bath.

It was long past time to renovate the bathroom — not to mention the kitchen — but every time Cass thought about it, and considered the options, she got a headache. Once last summer, at Lucy's insistence, she'd made it all the way to the local home-improvement store to check out what was available, but she'd returned home in less than forty minutes, her head spinning. All she'd wanted was a simple tub with a shower, a new toilet, a new sink. Some new tile. But she'd found all the selections overwhelming and left with less of an idea of what she wanted than she'd had when she'd set out.

*I like things simple,* she was thinking as she dried her hair and towel-dried her legs. *Simple, easy, basic.*

The only real improvements she'd made

since she'd moved in were to purchase a new microwave — a necessary fixture because it enabled her to reheat leftovers or takeout faster — and a new refrigerator, because the other one had given up the ghost three years ago. Other than those two items, she hadn't even bothered to change the color of the walls or the old carpets.

*But I will,* she assured herself. *As soon as I have time, I will.*

She recognized her procrastination for what it was. Just as she recognized that for the past hour, she'd thought of anything but the body in the marsh.

Linda Roman.

Cass dressed in sweatpants and an old rugby shirt left behind by an old boyfriend, and slipped into a pair of rubber flip-flops. She rarely wore anything else on her feet in the summer months when she wasn't working, though she'd be hard-pressed to explain why they appealed to her so much. They were not very practical, as foot-coverings went, and yet she'd bought them in almost every color she could find. Pink, yellow, red, blue, white, turquoise, and this year's new favorite, orange.

She walked the four blocks to the new Mexican take-out restaurant and picked up her order. She considered staying and eating there — the place was almost empty — but the owner of the restaurant was all too eager to discuss the crime with her.

"Hey, Detective. You in on that investigation? The body down by Wilson's Creek?" he asked.

"Yes."

"Well, were you there? Did you see it?"

"Yes, I was there."

"Must have been something, eh?"

"Yes."

"So, you guys got some clues? Suspects? I know they're saying on the TV that you got no leads, but sometimes they say stuff like that to throw off the killer, you know?"

"The investigation is just beginning." She had her wallet out, waiting for him to give her a total for her order so she could pay and escape, but he was holding on to the bag containing her food as if it were a hostage. He held her captive and was going to take advantage of the situation, so he'd have some inside dirt to dish with the breakfast crowd in the morning.

"I heard they just found out who she was. Linda Roman was her name, they said. Didn't ring a bell with me. Did you know her?"

"No. I didn't know her."

"Someone who was in earlier said they knew her from the bank. You bank there?"

"Yes. Now, if I could just —"

"Say, I'll bet my cousin Roxanne knows her." He snapped his fingers. "She works for that bank. Different branch, but I bet they all know one another. I think I'll give her a call and see if —"

"Dino, I hate to cut this short, but I need to get moving here."

"Oh, right, right. Sorry." He laughed self-consciously and rang up the total on the old-fashioned cash register. "It's just so weird to have something like this in Bowers Inlet, you know? When I heard about it this morning, I said, 'Hey, no way.' Then when some of the guys from the newspaper stopped in at lunch and told us what was going down, I said, 'No shit!' "

Cass handed over a ten-dollar bill and waved off the change, anxious to leave the small storefront and its owner's excited curiosity. She pushed open the screen door and headed back onto the quiet streets of Bowers Inlet. The sidewalks were deserted now at almost eight p.m., the other year-round residents no doubt all at home watching the special news reports pertaining to the murder. She wondered who among them might have known Linda

Roman; who, behind the shades of the houses Cass now passed, might be grieving over her death. As a cop, Cass knew she shouldn't let it get to her, but it did. God knew, it did.

She turned up the narrow walk in front of her small house, noting that once again this year the grass grew in stubborn tufts from the coarse sand in the front yard. This weekend she'd make it a point to pull it all up and rake out the sand so that it lay flat and weedless. Maybe she'd even put a pot of some kind of summery flower out there near the sidewalk. If she got around to it. Which she probably wouldn't.

Gramma Marshall used to keep pots of petunias out there at the end of the walk. Red petunias. The pots were still in some forgotten corner of the garage. Cass had never tossed them out, but neither had she ever filled them. Lucy, on the other hand, would look for them if Cass suggested it. Lucy couldn't sit still for more than five minutes, and had never been one to let things be.

She went up the worn wooden steps and through the screen door that opened onto the porch that ran across the front of the house, noted the screening that encased the entire porch had a rip here and there.

*Put it on the list of things to do,* she told herself as she unlocked the front door and headed for the kitchen. *Just put it on the list.*

Cass slid some of the burrito from the take-out container onto a plate, and took a bottle of water from the small pantry. She tucked the bottle under her arm and grabbed a fork from the drawer next to the sink and carried her dinner into the living room, where she sat on the same worn sofa she'd sat on as a child, and looked under the cushions for the TV's remote control. She caught the special report on the day's events on the local station, and stared at the screen as the anchor repeated all the details of Linda Roman's sad death.

Cass sat the bottle on the coffee table and rested her elbows on her knees. She'd been fighting off a bout of melancholy since early that morning, carrying it around inside her and trying to pretend it wasn't there. Everything she'd done all day — from the interviews she'd conducted, to the photos she'd viewed and the reports she'd written, to the beer she now swallowed — everything had been calculated to keep her from focusing on what had happened to Linda Roman in that marsh, because thinking too much could take her down roads she did not wish to travel. It was too late now, however. She'd made eye contact with the still photo of Linda and her family. She'd allowed herself to feel what Linda Roman's child would feel, and she knew she was lost.

"Son of a bitch," she whispered as videos of Linda Roman appeared on the television screen. Linda with her husband on their wedding day. Linda with her newborn daughter. Linda and her sister on the beach with their babies not two weeks ago. Watching was making Cass sick.

Literally.

She put the water down on the table and went into the bathroom, and threw up until there was nothing left in her stomach to be expelled. Only then did she return to the living room, where she turned off the television and the outside lights, picked up her plate of food, and carried it into the kitchen, where she dumped her food into the trash. She checked the lock on the back door, and went to bed. Once under the covers, Cass curled up in a ball and mourned for Linda Roman and for all the Linda Romans whose beautiful lives had been taken from them for no reason, other than that someone had *wanted* to, that someone could.

★ ★ ★

Sleep had been a long time coming, and had not lingered long enough for Cass to shake the fatigue that had been plaguing her. On top of everything else — or perhaps because of it — the dream had come back, and in its aftermath, Cass had dressed and fled the house, heading for the deserted beach. From half a block away she could hear the pounding of the surf, and it led her on through the night. She walked directly to the ocean and welcomed the cold spray as the waves threw themselves with abandon onto the shore, welcomed the sensation of the swirling tide tugging at her ankles in the dark.

She walked along the beach to the nearest jetty, where she sat in the company of her own ghosts until the sun came up. Then, knowing if she was to do her job she'd have to keep her own emotions in check, her memories at bay, she retraced her steps to the bungalow, her focus regained, her back straight with determination. She dressed for work, committed to bringing justice to Linda Roman, ready to begin the search for the man who had killed her.

# Four

Two days later, at 5:32 in the morning, Cass sat at her desk, rereading the report she'd come in early to complete. She made a few more changes on the computer screen before hitting the *Print* button. While the pages spit out, she stood for a much-needed stretch, her hands clasped behind her head. She'd been seated for well over ninety minutes, and found her knees and rear in want of a change of position.

The coffee in her cup was cold, and she needed the caffeine.

The remains of the pot in the lunchroom being the color of tar, she opted to make new. She rinsed out the carafe and filled it from the water cooler. Thanks to the chief's obsession with drinking water and with the impurities contained therein, he'd insisted on a cooler for the department. Cass figured if it was better to drink straight, it would make better coffee. She used it every chance she got.

The old coffeemaker chugged and hissed as if in agony. The groaning ceased, and

Cass started to pour a fresh cup, when she thought she heard a sound — a rustle? a shuffle? — from the hall. She peeked out the doorway and looked around, but there was no sign of anyone, no lights in any office other than her own.

*Must have been the coffeemaker,* she thought, and she returned to the job at hand. She finished pouring, then picked through the plastic container of sweeteners in search of a pink packet amidst the blue and white ones. She found one, poured it and some creamer into her cup, and headed back to her office through the blissfully quiet hall.

Cass really liked coming in early, when the night shift was still on the streets and the offices were, for the most part, empty. It was worth the loss of a few hours of sleep to have time to think without the background noises, the ringing phones, the chatter. Not that she'd had a full night's sleep since they'd found Linda Roman's body. Three or four hours a night had been all she'd managed.

So far this morning she'd written up her reports on three of the seven interviews she'd completed since Linda Roman had been identified earlier in the week and was ready to put them into both the department file and her personal murder book. She'd never done this before — kept a murder book — but over the winter, she'd met a detective from Los Angeles who mentioned having used this as a means of logging in all the data gathered during an investigation. The orderliness had appealed to her, so on her way home the previous night, she'd stopped at a nearby shopping center and picked up a three-ring binder. Since arriving at the station, she'd photocopied the evidence list and the statements from the officers who had found the body. Later she would print off another set of the photos she'd taken at the crime scene and add those to the book.

She grabbed her pile of reports from the printer as she passed it, then returned to her office and sat down to proofread before printing out a copy for the chief.

All the interviews had been pretty much the same. There'd been no deviations. Everyone Cass had spoken with had assured her that Linda Roman had been well liked and admired by everyone who knew her. She'd been described as intelligent, fun-loving, caring, a wonderful mother, sister, friend. No one knew of any enemies, anyone who might wish her harm, anyone she'd had words with or who had cause to be angry with her. She'd graduated from the regional high school, gone on to Rider College, graduated, come back home, and married her high school sweetheart. She and her husband were hard workers, active in their church, and all in all appeared to be the all-American boy and girl, all grown up.

It really pissed off Cass that someone had robbed them of their happily ever after.

A sound from the hall caused her to glance up. A solemn-faced Craig Denver stood in the doorway of her small office.

"You're early today," she said, knowing that the chief almost never arrived before eight. "Just in time, though, to take a look at these hot-off-the-press reports — which are pretty good, if I do say so myself. I'm printing out a set for you, and you can . . ."

Something in his expression caused her to stop in the middle of the sentence.

"What?" She tilted her head to one side.

"We have another one," he said, his words clipped and tense.

"Another . . ." She stared at him blankly.

He nodded. "Another body."

"Another body . . ." She pushed back from the desk. "Where?"

"She was left in the alley behind the

Daily Donuts on Twenty-eighth Street. Guys coming in this morning to empty the Dumpster found her lying near the fence."

"Okay," she said more to herself than to Denver. "I'm on my way. I'll call Jeff . . . I'll call Tasha . . ."

She opened her desk drawer and took out her digital camera and slipped it into her bag.

"I called Jeff, he'll meet you there. Wife wasn't happy to hear my voice, didn't want to wake him. Don't know how he's going to handle that, but he's going to have to address it, and soon. This wasn't the first time she gave me a problem when I called. In case you're wondering, though, I called you first. Didn't get an answer at your house or your cell, so I called him. In any case, we have two uniforms there already, they responded to the call. They'll keep everyone away from the scene until you arrive."

"Are you coming?" She stood and hoisted her bag over her shoulder, then reached over her desk to unplug her cell phone from the charger and slipped it into her pocket.

"I'll meet you there." He nodded, and she went past him.

He stood in her office for a long minute

before snapping off the light.

Craig Denver hated this. Hated the fact that someone was coming into his town and killing his people. Hated what it reminded him of, hated the memories it brought back, hated the way the whole thing made him feel inside. He walked ten steps down the hall to his own office, and stepped inside. He was halfway to the desk when he saw the flat white envelope that lay on the floor midway between the desk and the door. He stared at it, trying to will it away.

He knew what it was, and had a sinking feeling he knew what it would say.

Opening the top drawer of the filing cabinet, he reached in and pulled out a pair of thin rubber gloves, which he slipped on. Just a precaution, though. He knew there'd be no prints on the envelope, nor on the single sheet of paper he'd find inside.

He slid the paper out and held it up. It gave him no satisfaction to be right.

Hey, Denver! Remember me?

The body of the young woman had been left on the ground, uncannily positioned in much the same manner as Linda Roman had been. On her side, arms over her head, her long dark hair covering her face. It took all of Cass's willpower not to turn her over, just to make sure it *wasn't* Linda Roman.

*Snap out of it,* she demanded when she realized she was simply staring at the body. *Take a deep breath. Do your job.*

She put in a call to the station for some portable lights. Although the sun would soon be up, the cloud cover and mist would keep the scene too dark to gather much evidence.

She dug the camera out of her bag, set it for flash, and began taking pictures of the body, of the scene, the alley, the fence. She found herself growing angry with the person who had taken this young woman's life and left her lying naked on the cold black asphalt, with the morning drizzle running off her body.

And probably washing away evidence.

She was grateful to see Tasha walking toward her. The CSI lugged her black bag, which some joked weighed almost as much as Tasha herself, who barely hit the scales at one hundred pounds and was maybe five-two if she stood up really straight. With her dark blond hair cut short, she looked like a pixie. A tiny pixie who had nerves of steel and a stomach of cast iron.

Cass had never heard of Tasha backing away from anything, neither a crime scene nor an accident. It was said that even the most gruesome sights — those that made the big guys gag and cringe — barely made Tasha blink.

"Well, shit, would you look at this," Tasha said as she set down her evidence bag and opened it. "Two in one week?" She shook her head and looked up at Cass. "I'd say we have a problem here."

"I always admire the way you get right to the point, Tasha." Cass crouched down and took another few shots of the body.

"What's the point in pussyfooting around." Tasha pulled on her gloves. "You got two bodies in what . . . four days? Two victims who, at first glance, bear a strong resemblance to each other. Bodies positioned the same way — and look at that hair, the way it's covering her face. I'd bet you a month's salary that she's been manually strangled and raped, just like the other one, but you're too smart to take a bet like that, Burke."

Tasha bent down next to the body, and eased the hair from around the victim's neck.

"Oh, yeah. There they are." She studied the bruises, all the while murmuring to the dead girl, "Ah, honey, what did he do to you?"

Cass snapped a few more pictures.

"Burke, did you get her fingers?" Tasha asked, and Cass nodded. "One of them looks to be broken."

"I'm pretty much finished with the body from this angle. I'm waiting for some lights so I can begin to look around the alley. I'd hate to kick evidence aside and miss something important." Cass stood and straightened her back. "She's all yours."

"Well, don't go too far with that." Tasha pointed to the camera. "As soon as I'm done on this side, I'm going to want to turn her over. You can give me a hand. Let me see what's what under these fingernails . . ."

Cass stood back and waited for Tasha to finish her ministrations. A car pulled into the driveway, its lights illuminating the scene. Jeff Spencer got out of the driver's side and hurried up the walk.

"Where have you been?" Cass asked.

He shrugged, mumbling something unintelligible.

"Jeff, we have another homicide here," she pointed out the obvious, taking care not to raise her voice. "Second one this week. We need —"

"Yeah, yeah, I know what we need," he muttered under his breath as he walked past her, toward the body.

Cass stared at his back, then shook it off. *Must have had a bad night,* she thought, then turned to wave to the officers that pulled into the drive and started to unload the lights.

"Yay. Lights. Up here." She motioned them along. "Set them up right here . . ."

The lights brought new visibility to the scene, and the area was carefully searched for anything that the killer might have brought with him or left behind. Several cigarette butts near a hole in the fence went into a small plastic evidence bag, as did a drink container from a local fast-food restaurant and a dirty white sock. Any or none could have a connection to the killer. Only lab analysis would tell, and that not for a few more days, if ever.

"Huh . . ." Cass heard Tasha say softly.

"What?" She turned to see the CSI kneeling behind the body, a pair of tweezers in her right hand. She appeared to be inspecting something on the back of the dead woman's head. Whatever it was, it was invisible to Cass. "What did you find?"

"Some fiber" was the reply. Tasha crooked a finger at Cass. "Take a shot of this for me before I remove it."

Cass leaned forward to line up the shot as she was directed. Tasha slipped the thread into a bag, which she sealed and marked. She looked at Cass and said, "I found some similar trace tangled in the hair of our first victim."

"The same type of fiber? Blanket? Carpet?"

"Too long to be either. It's long and thin."

"Rope, maybe? Something he might have used to tie them up with, subdue them?" Cass's mind started to consider different possibilities.

"Nooo," Tasha said slowly. She held the bag up as if inspecting its contents. "I don't think it's rope, it's not that substantial. It looks thinner, more delicate. I can't wait to get back to the lab to check it out."

"Did you analyze the fiber you found on Linda Roman?"

"Not yet. I was concentrating on the trace from under her fingernails, trying to find skin cells, something that would give me DNA. The fiber is still in the evidence box, but I think it just moved to the top of the list."

"You'll let me know?"

"Do I get a set of those prints?" Tasha

nodded at the camera Cass held in her right hand.

"I'll run them off as soon as I get back to the office."

"Then you'll be the first to know what the little fibers are."

"Chief, there are reporters from four television stations and nine newspapers in the lobby," Phyllis announced through the intercom.

"Yes, I know," Denver replied. "I haven't decided what I want to tell them."

"May I come in there for a moment?" Her voice sounded shaky.

"Sure," he said, somewhat taken aback. Normally sure and confident, it wasn't like Phyl to be so hesitant.

The intercom clicked off and seconds later the door between the chief's office and his secretary opened. Phyl came into the room holding a can of Diet Pepsi in one hand and a chewed-up pencil in the other. She set the can on the chief's desk, and twirled the pencil between her index and middle fingers.

"What's on your mind, Phyl?"

"I just saw the pictures of this new one — this new murder victim — on Detective Burke's desk. The body from this morning.

I think I might know her. I think I might know who she is, Chief."

"You do?" He frowned. His detectives were still checking missing persons leads.

"She does manicures at the Red Rose Salon down at Fifth and Marshall."

"You have a name?"

"Lisa. I don't know her last name. But I'm pretty sure her first name is Lisa."

"Did you tell this to Detective Burke?"

"No. She was on the phone, and I was so startled, I just backed out of her office. It's taken me a few minutes to collect my thoughts. I could be wrong." Her eyes misted, and her hands, he realized, were shaking.

He pushed the button for Cass's extension. "Burke, I need you to come in here. Now."

Cass appeared in the doorway in less than a minute.

"Is something wrong?" She studied his face. "Please tell me there hasn't been another body . . ."

"No. But Phyl thinks she knows who our lady of the morning is."

"I think she's the manicurist at the Red Rose. Lisa something. I could be wrong, Detective. God, I hope I'm wrong. But I saw the pictures on your desk. I didn't mean to, I just came in to bring you a phone message that had been put in the chief's box by mistake. And the pictures were there, right on your desk . . ."

"I'm so sorry you had to see them, Phyl. They weren't pretty. And it must have been a shock, once you realized that you might recognize the woman."

"It was. It still is." To steady herself, give her hands something to do, Phyl took a sip of Diet Pepsi. "I can call down there, to the Red Rose, if you want. I'll see if she's there . . ."

"No, no. I'll do that." Cass glanced at the chief. "I'll do that right now, and I'll let you know as soon as I find out."

"Do it." Denver nodded. "Do it right away."

"I'm on it." Cass disappeared through the doorway.

"And then there are all those reporters. The sergeant on the front desk is getting a little rattled. Everyone wants to know what's going on," Phyl said as if to prod him.

"I'll come out and speak with them. Not much I can say, though."

He rubbed his chin and wished he had taken more time to shave this morning. He knew he'd be appearing on the six and eleven o'clock news all across the state, with a serious five o'clock shadow.

"Chief, Chief!"

"Chief Denver, is it true there's a serial killer in Bowers Inlet?"

"Chief Denver! Chief Denver . . . !"

The crowd of reporters pushed forward the minute Denver started down the hall toward the lobby. It was as if they had smelled him. They moved en masse, and he held up both hands to stop them in their tracks and quiet them.

"Okay, let's just settle down here," he said, feeling like a first-grade teacher. "Everyone take six big steps back, please. Spread out a little, give yourselves some space, for crying out loud."

The crowd did as they were told, then raised their hands and waited to be called on.

*Yep,* Denver thought. *Just like grade school.*

"Okay, let me first say that, yes, there have been two murders this week here in Bowers Inlet. Both victims were women in their thirties — the second victim hasn't been identified as yet, but appears to be of an age similar to Linda Roman, who as you all know was thirty-one."

"Were both women killed in the same manner?" someone called out.

"I'll need to see the medical examiner's report on the second victim before I can answer that," the chief replied.

"I've heard that both women were very similar in physical appearance — young, pretty, with long dark hair."

"I can confirm that, yes."

"Is the killer typing his victims, then?" a dark-haired woman in the back asked, a tinge of apprehension in her voice.

"I'd be looking for a red wig if I were you, Dana," someone called across the room to her, and there was a scatter of nervous laughter.

"We don't know about that," Denver said. "I wouldn't make any assumptions just yet. For all we know, the killer had some connection to both women."

"So you think the same person killed both women." It wasn't a question.

"The evidence is still being analyzed."

"Can we get details on the investigations?"

"I'll have a report available to you by six." Denver glanced up at the clock. That would give him almost two hours to decide what to release. "You can wait around for it, or you can leave your name and fax number, and we'll fax the report to you."

"Why can't you just tell us what you have?"

"I don't have a whole lot yet. I'm still waiting for the reports from the lab and the medical examiner's office. I was just about to sit down with my detectives and go over this with them, when you all showed up. I thought I'd deal with you first, let you know we're working on getting something together for you so that you can all meet your deadlines. I don't want to give you incomplete information, so if you'll excuse me, I'd like to return to that meeting."

Denver smiled perfunctorily and started back to his office.

"Chief Denver, how many victims do you need to have to consider this the work of a serial killer?"

The chief stopped in mid-stride and turned around slowly.

"I think it's a little early to start throwing around terms like that. I also think it's irresponsible, frankly, since you'll only serve to panic our residents, who are already upset enough."

"But how many, Chief?" The question was repeated softly this time. "I've heard two or three. Which is it?"

Denver turned heel and returned to his office, closed the door, and buzzed for his detectives to come in and bring their notes.

"We have a positive ID on this morning's vic."

Cass didn't wait until she was seated to begin her verbal report.

"Lisa Montour. Age thirty-one. And as per Phyl, she was in fact the manicurist at the Red Rose Salon in town. I called the salon and found that she hadn't come in yet today. Called her roommate, she said Lisa went out to meet up with some friends last night, but didn't come home. The roommate didn't realize *that,* however, until the salon called this morning."

"Can we get the names of the friends she was meeting?" Denver asked.

Cass held up a stenographer's notebook.

"The roommate gave them to me, along with phone numbers. She was supposed to go with Lisa last night, by the way, but got home from work really late and was just too tired to go out. I've already spoken with two of the four she was supposed to meet, but they both said Lisa didn't show up. They figured she got home from work and maybe just fell asleep."

"What time did she leave her apartment?" Denver sat back in his chair. "Walk me through what you've got."

"Her roommate — Carol Tufts, her name is — said Lisa left around nine-fifteen for Kelly's down on Twelfth Street. Should have taken her ten minutes at the most to get there."

"She was driving?"

"Walking. Her car had a flat, and she had no spare tire, so she decided to walk. Carol said she offered her the use of her car, but Lisa said she'd just as soon walk, since it was a nice night."

"When was the flat tire discovered, do we know?" Denver asked.

"Yesterday morning. According to Carol, the tire was flat when Lisa went down to leave for work in the morning. Found the tire flat, realized she didn't have a spare, so she had someone from the salon pick her up, and got a ride home yesterday afternoon." Cass looked up from her notes. "I'll bring the tire in for inspection."

Her cell phone vibrated against her hip, and she glanced at the number.

"It's the lab," she told the chief. "I think I want to take this."

Denver nodded, then turned his attention to Jeff Spencer, who'd been silent since he'd entered the room.

"So what do you have to add to Detective Burke's report, Spencer?"

Spencer shrugged. "Not much."

"Well, you were there at the scene this morning, weren't you?"

"Yes. But Burke had things pretty much in control when I arrived."

"What time did you get there?"

Spencer rubbed the back of his neck and shifted in his seat.

"I don't recall what time I arrived."

Denver stared at him. He didn't want to have this conversation. Especially he didn't want to have it *now.*

"You having a problem, Spencer?"

"Yes, sir. As a matter of fact, I am." Spencer's face was emotionless.

"Solve it. Take care of it. And do it fast." Denver stood, hoping to walk off his temper. "There's a killer in my town. He's just getting his game on. I don't have time to baby anyone through their personal problems. If you're not one hundred percent on this, Spencer, for God's sake, tell me now."

"Well, Chief, I hadn't planned on talking about this yet. What with these murders and all." Spencer's face flushed, the first reaction he'd shown since he sat down.

The chief motioned at him to go on.

"I'd really rather wait until . . ." Spencer's voice dropped and he shot a glance in Cass's direction. She was wrapping up her call.

"No semen found on either body, though both women had been sexually assaulted. The position of the bruises on each woman's neck is exactly the same, the thumbprints the same distance apart. Trace is still being examined, but Tasha found one interesting thing."

She leaned on the corner of Denver's desk, oblivious to the exchange between the chief and Spencer.

"Tasha found little bits of fibers in the hair of both victims. She's going to analyze them to see if they match." Cass looked up from her notes.

"Have this morning's vic's clothes been found?" Denver asked.

Cass nodded. "In the Dumpster. Neatly folded. Just like Linda Roman's were."

"Well, that tells us something about our man," the chief noted. "Speaking of which . . ."

Denver held up the envelope.

"Communiqué number two," he said dryly as he opened it and held it up.

*Remember me . . .*" Cass read aloud.

"I think it's clear he wants us to think

he's the Strangler. He wants us to believe that he's back. The question is, of course, is it really him? Or is it someone who thinks it would be fun to make us think it's him? And either way, what do we say to the press?" The chief returned to his chair and lowered himself into it. "I promised to have something for them by . . ."

He turned his left wrist to look at his watch.

"In about another hour and thirty-five minutes. What do I tell them?"

Neither detective spoke. The room was suddenly very, very quiet.

"If I tell them, they'll have a field day with the story. And it will egg him on. The killer. He'll like it, I think."

"And if you don't tell them, will we be putting more women at risk?" Cass asked. "Isn't it better if the public knows what's going on, so they can protect themselves better?"

"I think we can let them know that another woman has been killed by what appears to be the same person. That alone should let women know they need to take care; we can address the issues of safety with the public without adding to the hysteria by sensationalizing this more than it has to be." Denver tapped his fingers quietly on the arms of his chair. "And of course, the summer season recently opened."

"You get a call from the mayor, or something, like how this is going to be bad for business?" Spencer asked.

"This isn't Amity, Spencer, and I think I can safely say our killer isn't a great white shark." Denver stared at him coldly. "I only bring it up because our population will triple by the end of the month. Which will give him a greater selection of victims to choose from."

"Which means we have to do everything we can to find him, and stop him," Cass said, then shook her head. "Stupid statement. It's obvious we have to find him before he kills someone else."

"To that end, Burke, I want you to get with Tasha and go over everything she has. And I want you to get Lisa Montour's car down to the garage and have it gone over with a fine-tooth comb, especially that tire."

Cass tapped Spencer on the shoulder. "You coming?"

Before he could answer, Denver spoke up.

"No, he's not. And close the door on your way out, Burke."

Cass paused at the doorway and looked back over her shoulder. Spencer's neck had turned beet red and Denver's eyes were beginning to narrow as he focused on the detective who remained seated.

"Was there something else, Burke?" the chief asked.

"No, I just . . ."

"Close the door on your way out."

Cass did as she was told.

She returned to her office and dialed Tasha's number, wondering what was going on between Spencer and the chief. Whatever it was, it hadn't appeared that either one of them was happy about it. She couldn't remember the last time she'd seen Spencer that quiet, or the chief so tense. Her instincts told her it had more to do with Spencer's attitude than with the recent homicides.

Well, if anyone could adjust someone's attitude, it was Denver.

Forty minutes later, Cass had left voice mail for Tasha, called Carol Tufts and asked if she had the key to Lisa Montour's car, and arranged for Helms to meet her at Lisa Montour's apartment.

That done, Cass left the station, walking out the side door just as Jeff Spencer's wife pulled into the parking lot and stopped by the front of the building.

Within seconds, Jeff came down the sidewalk, a box in his arms. He balanced the box on one knee while he opened the rear door and slid the box across the seat before getting into the passenger side.

Puzzled, Cass stood on the steps and watched as the car left the lot on two wheels.

*Well, shit,* she thought. *That doesn't bode well.*

"You on your way to pick up that car, Detective?"

She turned at the sound of the chief's voice.

"Yes, I'm meeting Helms there. I spoke with our vic's roommate. She said the car keys are still on the hook inside the front door, where Lisa left them."

"Good. I'm on my way to the mayor's office to go over what little we know before the press conference he decided to call. Want to trade places?"

"No thanks."

Denver started to walk past her and she touched his arm.

"Chief, Detective Spencer just . . ." She pointed to the street.

"Ex-detective Spencer. He's no longer with the department."

"What?" Her jaw dropped.

"His choice. He's going back to Minnesota or Michigan . . ."

"Wisconsin." She supplied the name of Spencer's home state.

"Whatever," Denver grumbled. "His wife hates it here, she hates the beach, she misses her mother, she misses her sister, she hates that he's at work all the time, she hates that she has no friends here, the baby's always sick, he's never around to help her . . ."

He paused. "Did I miss anything?"

"If you did, it probably doesn't matter."

"I knew there was something going on there, his attitude has changed over the past month or two. So we had to have a chat. Told him that I need him to be on the case, one hundred percent, you know, we have a killer here, we need his full attention and if he can't give it to us, he needs to rethink his career choice." He paused again. "Apparently he had already done that. He'd applied for and was offered a job at a police department fifteen miles from his hometown."

"So he's leaving? He's just walking out?"

"Easier for some than for others, I guess. So, yes, to answer your question, he took accrued vacation, sick days, and personal time and is probably, as we speak, packing to leave, if his wife hasn't already done that. He starts his new job on the first of next month."

"Just like that?"

"Hardly just like that, he's had this planned for weeks. To give him the benefit of the doubt, he did say he'd planned on giving his notice early in the week, but we found the first body. Then the second."

"I thought he seemed a bit off," Cass said, recalling the way Spencer had held back and let her take the lead, not just that morning, but at the crime scene earlier in the week. "But I figured maybe he was just tired. You know, so much going on around here all of a sudden, and they have that new baby."

"Well, he's taking that new baby and leaving us holding the bag."

"Did you ask him to stay for a few more days?"

"What would be the point? Mentally, he's already out of here. Might as well let him go. He wouldn't be much use to us anyway, not in the state of mind he's in right now."

Cass thought back to that morning, when Jeff had been late getting to the crime scene, and had been pretty much ineffective even after he arrived.

"So, I guess it's you, me, and a couple of uniforms against our boy, Cass."

Denver walked down the steps and didn't turn back until he reached his car.

"Finish up with the car and with Tasha, then go on home and get some sleep. You never know what tomorrow will bring."

# Five

Her newly found enthusiasm for healthy living having been inspired a few weeks earlier by a visit from an old friend of her father's who happened to be a holistic physician, Regan Landry added a banana to the skim milk, yogurt, and assorted powders in the blender and hit the *Pulverize* button. The little appliance whirred noisily while she found a glass and searched for a straw. She hit *Stop* and a blessed silence followed. She poured her breakfast into the glass and sat down at the small round kitchen table and opened the newspaper. Bored after a few minutes of skimming the headlines, she searched under the paper for the remote control and turned on the television that sat on the counter across the room.

She changed the channel, searching for her favorite morning show, *This Morning, USA.* Once she found it, she turned up the volume and resumed her cursory scanning of the *New York Times.* An article about an upcoming auction of American antiques at Sotheby's caught her eye, and she'd just gotten to the sampling of early Pennsylvania furniture when something on the screen caught her attention. She reached for the remote and increased the volume.

". . . certainly of interest to anyone having plans to visit the New Jersey shore this summer," Heather Cannon was saying.

The screen split, half now occupied by a man in a police uniform who looked uncomfortable in front of the camera.

"I feel your pain," Regan muttered.

"Chief Denver, with the finding of a third body there in Bowers Inlet, the reports coming from the South Jersey area are telling us that the signs all point to the likelihood that this is the work of a serial killer. Can you confirm that?"

"You know, Heather, I hate that term, it stirs up so much . . ." The chief shifted in his chair.

"Will you confirm that there has in fact been a third victim?"

"Yes, there has been a third victim."

"And that all three victims have been young women in their early thirties . . ." Heather addressed the camera directly so that the man she was interviewing by remote would feel she was speaking directly to him.

"Yes, all three victims have been young women, all local women. The first two lived in Bowers Inlet. The young woman whose body we found last night lived in nearby Tilden, but she was left on one of our beaches."

"Now, the information that we have indicates that all the women were dark-haired and similarly built . . ." Heather paused and looked up from her notes. "Is there a significance to this similarity, do you think?"

"Right now we have no way of knowing. Yes, so far, there has been a resemblance between the victims, but whether or not we should read something into this, we just don't know."

"The most disturbing bit of information we've received is that you have correspondence from the killer . . ."

"Well, let's just hold up here." The chief was clearly agitated. "What we have are letters that were received after the bodies were found. I want to make that clear. They could have been sent by someone other than the killer, someone thinking to have a bit of fun with us. Right now, I don't know for a fact who is sending the letters."

"But they could be from the killer . . ."

"Of course they could be," he snapped.

"And the letters are sort of a taunt, aren't they?" Heather glanced down at her notes. " *'Hey, Denver, did you find her yet?'* I understand was the first note. And the second was, *'Hey, Denver! Remember me?'* Both notes were comprised of letters or words cut from newspapers or magazines?"

"That's right."

"And was a note found after this latest victim?"

"There was."

"May we ask what it said?"

"It said, *'Hey, Denver, have you figured it out yet?'* "

"Any ideas on what you're supposed to be figuring out?"

"A few."

"Any you're willing to share?"

"It would be premature." The chief of police of Bowers Inlet stared stonily into the camera.

"So what would you tell people who are planning to spend a week or more in your community this summer? I understand Bowers Inlet has many rental properties and enjoys a population boom in the summer."

"I'm telling the vacationers the same

105

thing I'm telling our year-round residents. Be aware of your surroundings. Don't go off alone. If you're going out at night, go in a group. But you know, those are things you should probably be doing anyway, no matter where you are. You need to watch out for yourself. Have a cell phone with you or a can of pepper spray. If you think someone is following you, report it."

"So, in other words, stick to the basic safety precautions . . ."

Regan tapped a finger on the tabletop, then rose and left the room as the interview concluded. She went down the hall to her father's office and turned on the overhead light. Something that had just been said had caused a little bell to go off in her head.

*Hey, Denver, did you find her yet?*

*Hey, Denver, remember me?*

Where had she seen it . . . ?

She pulled several files from a drawer and leafed through them. *Not this one . . . not this one.*

*Then maybe here . . . Nope.*

She returned the files to their places and opened the next drawer.

*Here. Here it is.*

Hey, Landry, remember me?

The note, on plain white paper, spelled out the message in letters of different sizes and colors — letters cut from magazines — giving a jumbled, schizophrenic appearance to the sheet of paper.

At the top of the page was a small circle with the number seven inside. Regan's father had written that, she was positive. That was the way he numbered pages when he was setting up the earliest drafts of his work. He might take notes from several files and integrate them for a single chapter or project. The fact that this note was numbered — and the message indicated that there had been previous contact — made Regan think there were more notes from the same author. She pulled several files from the next drawer, and in the fourth one she went through, she found a manila file holding one more message, along with several pages of notes written in her father's hand.

*Hey, Landry, did you miss me?* was numbered eleven.

Regan sat at her father's desk and began to read through the pages he had written. She paused to flip the file over to read the notation he'd made across the top.

*The Bayside Strangler.*

She read the rest of the file, then picked

up the phone and called information for the listing of the Bowers Inlet Police Department.

"I'd like to speak with Chief Denver," Regan told the person who answered the phone.

"He's not in. I can take a message."

"My name is Regan Landry. I'm a writer — I write true crime . . . I have some information he might be interested in, in connection with the current homicides there."

"You have information about the homicides?"

"I have information about some old cases . . . some notes that were written to my father . . ."

"I'm not following you."

"Look, please leave my name and number for Chief Denver and ask him to give me a call. It could be important." Regan hung up after reciting both the number at the farmhouse and her mobile number.

She went into the kitchen and made herself a pot of coffee, poured a cup, and took it back to the office. She sat and stared at the file she'd left open on her desk.

What did she really have here?

A couple of notes that someone had sent to her father some years ago. A few pages of preliminary investigation Josh had started. Was there more?

She sighed. Damn his lousy record keeping. If, in fact, he'd started numbering the notes as he received them, where were the others? Perhaps he'd handed them over to the police. To the FBI.

Maybe there was another file — or two, or eight, or a dozen. Knowing her father, there could be many more, or none. He could have passed them on. Or not. He could have lost them, thrown them out, or put them in a box and simply forgotten about them as another more interesting project presented itself.

She looked across the room to the long row of wooden file cabinets that she knew were stuffed with files and boxes of notes. In the basement, there were boxes of files she'd helped him move several years ago when he'd run out of room up here for his current works and asked her to empty several drawers and pack them up for storage.

Regan ran a hand through her hair and told herself to slow down. Just because the notes received by her father and the Bowers Inlet chief of police were similar — okay, they were exactly the same — but what did that mean?

*Hey, Denver, remember me?*

*Hey, Landry, remember me?*

Not exactly original thoughts. Someone from anyone's past might say the same thing. And anyone being coy or cautious might structure the notes in the same manner, cutting out letters and gluing them to the paper. What did that prove, anyway?

She opened the file and took out the two sheets of yellow legal paper. At the top of the first sheet, Josh had written, *Victims attributed to the Bayside Strangler, June 1979–August 1979.* There followed a list of thirteen names. After each name was a date, and the name of a town:

| | | |
|---|---|---|
| Alicia Coors | June '79 | Bowers Inlet |
| Carol Jo Hughes | June '79 | Bowers Inlet |
| Cindy Shelkirk | June '79 | Tilden |
| Terry List | July '79 | Dewey |
| Mary Pat Engles | July '79 | Tilden |
| Heather Snyder | July '79 | Hasboro |
| Jill Grabowski | July '79 | Killion Point |
| Mindy Taylor | July '79 | Hasboro |
| Cathy Cleary | August '79 | Tilden |
| Allison Shea | August '79 | Dewey |
| Trina Wilson | August '79 | Killion Point |
| Lorraine Otto | August '79 | Hasboro |
| Regina Daley | August '79 | Killion Point |

The second sheet had no header and consisted of two columns, one of dates, the other locations, but no names. The dates spanned several years, and the locations varied, state to state. The names of the Bayside Strangler's victims would be easy enough to trace. Perhaps Chief Denver could verify the names of the Bowers Inlet victims when he called back. *If* he called back.

Regan sat and stared at the yellow pages for a long time. She compared the two lists her father had printed up. Except for the inclusion of the names on the first list, they were identical in form.

If the first was in fact a list of the Bayside Strangler's victims — names, dates, and places — what was the significance of the second list?

She studied it, line to line. No matter how long she stared at it, the list made no sense:

| | |
|---|---|
| May '83 | Pittsburgh |
| February '86 | Charlotte |
| August '86 | Corona |
| March '87 | Memphis |
| January '88 | Turkey |
| November '90 | Panama |
| November '91 | Croatia |

| | |
|---|---|
| September '93 | Somalia |
| April '95 | Bosnia |
| February '98 | Pakistan |
| others???? | |

Since it was in the folder along with the Bayside Strangler notes, could she assume it had something to do with those killings? And if so, what?

She stole a look at the clock. It had been more than an hour since she'd called Chief Denver. She'd have to be patient, give him a little more time.

Regan slid the lists back into the folder, added the two notes that had been addressed to her father, and placed the file on one corner of the desk. She took one more look through the big file and, convinced there was nothing more to be learned from it, replaced it in the cabinet. She lifted out the file behind it and returned to the desk. Settling into the big chair her father had used for more than twenty years, she began to page through the contents, front to back. Once satisfied she'd uncovered nothing that could add to the information in the thin file that sat on the corner of the desk, she put that folder back and took out another. And another.

She'd gone through five file folders by

noon, another three by mid-afternoon, when she placed a second call to the Bowers Inlet Police Department. Denver was not available. She left another message.

Stopping only to eat a makeshift meal around seven that evening, she plowed through file drawer after file drawer. At eight-thirty, she stopped to make another pot of coffee, and it occurred to her however many files remained in the office, there were three times as many in the basement, and God only knew what Josh might have stashed in the attic.

So far she'd found nothing that referred to the list her father had handprinted with dates and places, nor had she found any other letters that may have been sent by the Bayside Strangler. Perhaps Josh had turned them over to someone in law enforcement after all.

But he would have kept copies, she reminded herself, if he'd planned on writing a book on the subject. He would have kept copies of all the correspondence, regardless. He'd done that before, she knew. Throughout the day she'd come across several such files. But where were the files that would relate back to the list? They had to be there. It was a matter of finding the right drawers. Or the right boxes.

As Regan studied the mysterious list for perhaps the tenth time, the thought occurred to her that she could have already bypassed something that might be a clue to the lists' meaning.

*How will I find it if I don't know what* IT *is?*

Somewhat disheartened by the thought, but nonetheless determined, Regan read on through the night. Her father had always relied upon his instincts in times like this, she reminded herself. Perhaps it was time to put her own instincts to the test.

He stood upon the wooden boardwalk at the top of the dune and inhaled deeply, filling his lungs with as much of the bay as he could draw in with one breath. This, more than anything, this scent, meant he was home.

With one hand at his forehead acting as shade, he scanned the horizon. Far into the bay, fishing boats headed to the Atlantic. The sun hung over the water like a red-hot ball. The narrow beach was littered with the remains of a dozen horseshoe crabs and hanks of seaweed. The scents all blended together, and if he closed his eyes, he'd be a kid again, searching the sand for treasure.

Across the bay, Old Barney stood watch. As a child, he'd played at the base of the Barnegat Lighthouse, had fished with his brother from the rocks. At least the light-house remained, whatever else might have changed.

And change had come to the bay communities, there was no denying that. Over the past week, he'd driven through all the small towns that dotted the shore, one by one, reliving treasured moments here and there. He'd been stunned by the amount of development that had come to the area since he'd been away, townhouses and condos and single family homes all the way back to the Pines, some built over what had once been marsh. Shopping centers out on the highway, flanked by fast-food restaurants and discount stores. It had made his head spin.

Well, a lot can happen in twenty-six years, he reminded himself. A lot can change.

*Now, me, I haven't changed at all.*

In his eyes, he was still the same guy who had left at the end of that summer, armed with new skills he'd developed over the course of three months. The need inside him, once awakened, had been a tough taskmaster, demanding ever more satisfaction. Over the course of the years, he had fed its desires hundreds of times.

As lately as last night.

He smiled, remembering. How could he have thought he'd come all this way and not feel that drive within him build to a scream?

Especially after having visited the scenes of his earliest escapades. He remembered — and relived — each one.

He had an uncanny memory for such things.

He walked the length of the beach, rehearsing what he'd say to his brother when he rang the doorbell of their old family home later this afternoon. Reminded himself to smile, to pretend to be happy to see his family again after all these years. Be gentle with his sister-in-law, who had — let's face facts here — never cared much for him. Admire the children. Beam at them, as if delighted by their very existence. He needed to get used to them, since he planned to be around for a while. It wouldn't do to be estranged from the only family he had left. Might it not appear odd somehow, if he and his brother lived in the same town and never socialized?

He sighed. It all sounded so dreary.

There were lots of ways for him to pass

the time, now that he was back. There were more places for him to visit, places he remembered well, when he was ready. He'd know when the time was right. Some things weren't meant to be rushed.

He raised the binoculars to his eyes and focused on an osprey that was circling overhead, and felt perfectly content.

He'd promised himself a place on the water, and having already put the house in Texas on the market, there was no time like the present to start looking for a new home. A permanent one.

Right here in Bowers Inlet.

# Six

Cass dropped her bag on the kitchen counter and plunked herself into a chair, grateful to be home after near round-the-clock duty for the past three days. With Spencer gone, she was once again the sole detective for the department, which would, under normal circumstances, keep her moving from sunrise to sunset. Throw a serial killer into the mix, and the hours of sleep each night diminish in proportion to the number of bodies found.

And just that morning, there'd been another body.

Cass had felt a twinge of guilt when she realized her first response had been relief to learn the body had been found in nearby Dewey. Once she'd finished walking the crime scene with Dewey's chief of police, at his request and with Denver's blessing, her boss had sent her home with instructions to get some sleep. But she'd run into Tasha on the way to her car. The county crime scene tech had all but begged Cass to photograph the scene for her since

Dewey didn't have anyone who could line up a decent shot. So Cass had stayed, and stayed, telling herself she could sleep later.

Well, right about now, she could sleep right here, standing in the kitchen. Or she could drag her tired bones into the living room and just pass out on the sofa. Yeah, that sounded even better . . .

She'd just stretched out and closed her eyes when a thought popped into her brain.

It was Thursday.

*Shit. Thursday.*

With a groan, she forced herself to sit, went into the bathroom, and splashed cold water on her face. Then it was a quick fly through the bedroom, where she changed into sweat shorts and an old T-shirt and pulled on her sneakers. Grabbing a headband from a drawer, she wrapped it around her wrist and picked up her gym bag. Back to the kitchen, where she took two bottles of spring water from the cupboard and tossed them into the bag she'd dropped by the back door. Already late, she hurried outside and hopped into her car.

Four minutes later, she parked and got out. It was dusk, and the lights on the poles surrounding the small playground had just turned on. From across the asphalt she could hear the distinct tap-tap-tap of a ball being dribbled. As Cass jogged across the court, that ball sped toward her, thrown by the lone player, a tall young girl whose white shorts were a sharp contrast to her long brown legs. Cass tossed her bag aside, then caught the ball with one hand. She started toward the basket, dribbling methodically, her eyes on her opponent. She took her shot, which was skillfully blocked. Back and forth they went for twenty minutes, until Cass, totally winded, called a time-out.

"I thought maybe you weren't coming this week," the girl said as Cass handed her a bottle of water. "I thought maybe you were too busy, you know, with that killer."

"It has been a tough week," Cass admitted as she opened her own bottle and took a long drink, "but Khaliyah, you know that I'll always be here. Some weeks later than others. It was close, though. I didn't get home until late."

Cass reached into her bag, searching the contents.

"I have something for you," she told the girl.

Cass handed over a cell phone.

"For me? This is for me? Really?"

"I'm thinking that with all that's going on, you should probably have one with you."

"You mean those women getting killed?"

"Yes."

"He's only killing white women, though, right? Older white women?"

"So far." Cass ignored the reference to age. All of the victims had been around Cass's age of thirty-two.

"Well, in case you need a reminder, I'm black," the girl whispered as if sharing a confidence. "And I'm not old. Those women who were killed were all in their thirties, right?"

"And they also all had long dark hair." Cass tipped her bottle in the direction of the girl's hair, which was tied back in a ponytail. "Long dark hair like yours. Black or white, young or old — and some other time, we'll talk about what is *old* and what is not — you never know what he's thinking, Khaliyah. Best to have it, if you need it."

"So, do I have, like, so many minutes a month . . ."

"No. So you can call me anytime, day or night. I already programmed my numbers in. Home, office, cell. So you can always reach me if you need me. Here, let me show you . . ."

"I know how to use it. All my friends have them." Khaliyah studied the phone for a minute, then touched a button.

Cass's phone rang. She reached into her bag for it.

"Hello?"

"Hello, Detective Burke. This is Khaliyah Graves. I want to thank you for the new phone."

"You are very welcome. Don't lose it."

"I won't. I promise. It's the best present I ever got." Khaliyah's eyes were shining. "Thank you, Cass."

"You're welcome." Cass disconnected the call. "Now, tell me, how'd school go this week?"

"Well, it's just summer school, and we only just started classes on Monday. At least I got the good Spanish teacher, but the trig teacher — so-so. We have our first test tomorrow. Jameer said this teacher gives the hardest tests."

"So you're still seeing Jameer?"

"Sort of. My aunt doesn't really want me to have a boyfriend, you know." She wrinkled her nose.

"Your aunt is a smart woman. As much as I like Jameer, I think you're too young to be too involved with any one guy. And remember, at the end of the summer, he'll be leaving for college."

"Did I tell you he's going to Georgetown to play basketball? Just like Allen Iverson?"

"Only about a hundred times." Cass smiled.

"Maybe I'll go to Georgetown, too," Khaliyah said wistfully. "Maybe I could get a scholarship. My friend Tonya has a cousin who got a full ride there for track. Maybe I could get one for basketball. That's what you did, right? At Cabrini?"

"Right. And I think your chances are great, if you keep the grades up and do as well on the court this season as you did last. We'll talk to your coach and your guidance counselor over the summer and see what they think. I'm sure they'll have some good ideas on where to apply and how to get the most financial aid." Cass took a long pull of water. "Did you get your Advanced Placement scores back yet?"

"Yes." Khaliyah smiled broadly. "All fours."

"Excellent. I'm proud of you."

"Thanks," Khaliyah said softly.

They sat in silence for a few minutes, sipping their water, watching the swallows swoop around the lights on the court.

"It's getting late, I should get you back

home so you can study for that test and maintain your perfect record."

"Fifteen more minutes?" Khaliyah got up and began to bounce the basketball.

"Ten." Cass stopped to set the alarm on her watch, then set about to steal the ball.

Twenty minutes later, Cass was dropping Khaliyah off in front of her aunt's house.

"Thanks again for the phone." Khaliyah's eyes were shining. "I can't wait to call Tonya. She's had her own phone since middle school."

Cass waved to Khaliyah's aunt as the girl hopped out of the car, calling, "Aunt Sharona, look at what Detective Burke gave me . . ."

Cass grinned to herself and drove away, thinking how little it took to make Khaliyah's brown eyes light with happiness.

It had not always been so.

Cass had met the girl after having been called to a grisly scene five years earlier. Khaliyah's mother had been stabbed to death by her boyfriend, when she'd discovered that he'd raped her only child. Only twelve at the time, Khaliyah had endured more, had seen more, than any child should, but there was something in her

124

spirit that had kept her strong enough to testify against the man who had attacked her and murdered her mother.

During the months leading up to the trial, Cass had spent a lot of time with Khaliyah, and the young girl had responded to the detective's kindness and truthfulness at every step of the investigation and throughout the trial. Along the way, Cass had become a mentor to Khaliyah, who lived with her mother's sister and her family. As much as Sharona loved her niece, the woman was already overworked with five children of her own and two jobs and had little time for the emotional needs of a damaged child. Cass had stepped in and become Khaliyah's advocate, her best friend, and the big sister she'd never had.

It had been Cass who had made certain that Khaliyah got all the counseling she needed in the months and years after her mother's death, Cass who had encouraged Khaliyah to ask to be tested for the top academic track when she reached high school, Cass who had paid for the summer school classes that had allowed her to catch up after having lagged behind in junior high. It had been Cass who had recognized Khaliyah's athletic promise and enrolled her in basketball camp, and Cass who had helped Khaliyah get the part-time waitressing job at the diner where all the local officers stopped for meals during the day, and who had sat down with Khaliyah's aunt and asked her to permit Khaliyah to take the PSATs this past year. Come the fall, it would be Cass who would work with the guidance counselors to look at the options for college, help her seek out the financial aid she would need, and take her on campus visits.

It was not lost on Cass that perhaps she was trying to replace one lost younger sister with another, but she'd shrugged off the thought. Khaliyah was smart and brave, brave enough to sit in open court and describe what had been done to her, what had been done to her mother. She had endured and survived, and was, in Cass's mind, deserving of whatever advantages Cass could help her attain. She'd have done the same for Trish, if she'd had the chance. Now she'd do for Khaliyah. She knew what it was like to lose your mother, to have that core of strength and confidence taken from you. She, too, had been placed with relatives, and though she'd never doubted her aunt and uncle loved her, she'd never quite been able to completely settle there. Whatever she now did for Khaliyah, it was to help her through the toughest times and make certain that she knew there was someone who would stand behind her. Cass never regretted a minute of time she spent with her.

It was almost nine-thirty when Cass arrived home and crept into the stone driveway next to her bungalow. This year, she was going to get these stones replaced if she did nothing else. Macadam, maybe. Something nice and smooth . . .

Exhausted, she started to open the car door, then realized the lights were on inside her house. Had they been turned on when she left?

A shadow moved across the kitchen window.

Taking her bag from the front seat, she felt around for her gun. Holding it down, her finger on the safety, she exited the car but left the door ajar so as not to slam it. She crept up the back steps, and peered through the window. The shadow moved through the front hall into the living room.

Cass eased the door open and slid inside, lowering her bag to the floor silently as she proceeded toward the front of the house. She rounded the corner, her gun level in front of her.

"Don't move," she told the figure who stood in the middle of the living room floor.

"Oh, for Christ's sake, Cassie, don't you get enough of that cop drama during the day?"

"Lucy." Cass exhaled loudly and lowered the gun. "Jesus, Lucy, I could have shot you."

"A simple 'Gee, it's nice to see you' would suffice."

Muttering under her breath, Cass went outside and closed the car door.

"I brought dinner with me. Or have you eaten already?" Lucy said as she came into the kitchen. "And how 'bout a hug?"

"No, actually, I haven't eaten." Cass embraced her cousin lightly.

"Good. Chicken parm and pasta. I stopped at that place right as you come into town?" Lucy hustled to the refrigerator and opened it. "Get two plates, Cass, I was waiting for you."

"Where are David and the twins?" Cass asked.

"The kids are both at sleepover camp this summer — they've gone before, but it never ceases to amaze me that they're old enough for real *sleepover* camp." Lucy shook her head. "I don't know where the years have gone, Cass, I swear it."

"And David?"

"You want a little wine with this, Cassie? I brought a bottle with me, it's right there on the counter, by your elbow."

Lucy fixed two plates and popped one into the microwave.

"Yay, a new microwave. The old one finally pooped out, eh? With any luck, the stove will follow suit and you'll have to get a new one of those, too. Have you seen the kind that has two ovens? A little oven on the top and a full-sized one on the bottom? It's super."

Cass popped the cork on the wine bottle as Lucy found two glasses.

"Well, we could probably spring for a few real wineglasses, but I suppose it tastes just as good in these fat little tumblers." Lucy smiled brightly and took a sip. "Yum. Cass, why don't you sit down — you look like you're about to pass out on your feet — and I'll just find us some knives and forks . . ."

"The second drawer next to the sink." Cass sank into a chair.

"Where they have been for the past, oh, thirty-five or so years." Lucy turned and opened the drawer. "No one can ever accuse you of rocking the boat, Cassandra Burke."

Cass stuck out her tongue at Lucy's back.

"I saw that. I saw it in the window glass." Lucy grinned and handed Cass the flatware just as the microwave beeped. In one motion, Lucy removed one plate, handed it to Cass, then slid the second plate into the microwave.

"I already moved my stuff into my room," Lucy told her. "I hope you don't mind."

"Why should I mind?" Cass shrugged. "The house is as much yours as it is mine."

"Only because Gramma's will left it that way. We both know it's your home, Cassie. I don't mind. I'm glad you decided to live here. It keeps the old place alive. I'm grateful for my little bit of time down here in the summer."

The microwave beeped and Lucy took the plate out and placed it on the table, across from Cass.

"I may want to stay a little longer this year, if that's okay." Lucy pulled out a chair and sat down. Her eyes were on her plate. "I mean, if it's not inconvenient for you . . ."

"My home is your home. Literally. Stay

as long as you like."

"Thanks. It might just be a few weeks. I'm not sure."

"Luce, what's going on?" Cass took another sip of wine. "Are you and David having problems?"

"Problems?" Lucy speared a piece of chicken and studied it. "If you call finding out your husband has been playing footsies with your next-door neighbor for the past six months and everyone on your block knew but you *having problems,* then, why, yes, David and I are having problems."

"Lucy, I'm so sorry." Cass set her fork down on the side of her plate. "I don't know what to say."

"Not much to say." Lucy's eyes filled with tears. "The bastard."

Lucy nibbled at her food, sniffing all the while. "I'm sorry, Cass." She shook her head. "I know you probably don't really want to know about it. I know you don't do *emotional,* and right now, I'm awfully emotional. And am likely to be weepy on and off for the next few months. I'll try to do most of my best crying when you're at work."

"Lucy . . ." Cass protested weakly.

"It's okay, honey." Lucy wiped at her eyes.

"Lucy, you can feel free to cry whenever you need to or want to. I'm so sorry you're going through this. I wish I could make it better for you." Cass met her cousin's eyes across the table. "I don't know what else to say."

"You could say, 'David is a total creep and bastard and he was never good enough for you.'"

"David *is* a total creep and a bastard, and I never did think he was good enough for you, Lucy."

Lucy nodded. "That was good, Cassie."

"I never understood what you saw in him. He's not worthy of your tears."

"You're getting better at this."

"Actually, I thought you were crazy to marry him in the first place."

"Nice, honey. Thank you."

"To tell the truth, he always reminded me a bit of Mr. Janner."

"Mr. Janner?"

"Sleazy guy who ran the movie theater when we were kids and who always seemed to have teenage boys hanging around him."

"Okay, perhaps we can ease up a little now. I get the point, and I appreciate it. We'll reserve the right to reopen the David-bashing at a future time. And I might need a shoulder to cry on now and then. Just a little."

Cass reached across the table and patted Lucy's hand. "You can cry on my shoulder anytime."

"I might take you up on that, you know, so you might want to think twice." Lucy began to tear up.

"What are you going to do?"

"You mean, am I going to divorce his sorry ass?"

Cass nodded.

"Yes." Lucy took a deep breath. "One of the reasons I wanted to stay here a little longer was to have some time to get my game plan down, you know? What I want and how we're going to tell the kids and all that. Oh, I know they're not babies, but still, it's going to be a big shock, and I need to find a way to tell them. I just need some space."

"You can have all the space you want, Luce. If you want to talk, we'll talk. If you want to be alone, that's okay, too. And you can stay until you feel like going back. Whenever that might be."

"You're still like a sister to me." Lucy's eyes filled with tears. Again.

"Hey, you know what they say about blood being thicker, and all that."

"I want you to know that I appreciate it. I'll try to stay out of your hair."

"Truthfully, with this sudden rash of murders, I'm almost never home. And when I am, for the most part I'm asleep."

"You just go about your business. I'll do my own little thing."

"Oh, shit." Cass frowned. "I meant to change the linens on your bed before you got here. And I was going to go food shopping."

"I can do the grocery thing tomorrow, not to worry. And you can just tell me where the sheets are. Oh. Wait. Let me guess." Lucy grinned. "Same place they've always been, right? Honestly, Cass, you walk into this house and it's 1950 all over again. Nothing has changed since Gramma died."

"I haven't really had a lot of time to spend decorating, Lucy. For the past few years, I've been the only detective in town. We finally hired another one, and his wife decides she hates it here and she wants to go back to Wisconsin. So he, being a good husband, packs it in and leaves us in the middle of a couple of nasty homicides. Long story short, I'm back to being the only detective in town." Cass blew out a long breath. "Which is a roundabout way of saying I just haven't had the time."

"I thought you looked tired. You have dark circles under your eyes. Hey, I have some really good eye cream that takes that dark puffiness away." Lucy pushed back from the table. "Come on, if you're finished eating, I'll get it for you."

"I'm finished eating — thank you very much for stopping to pick up dinner — but I'm exhausted, Lucy. I think I'll turn in."

"No, no, you need to try this cream first. Come on . . ."

Cass got up wearily and locked the back door. She swung her bag over her shoulder and followed Lucy out of the room.

"Leave the kitchen lights on, Cass," Lucy was saying as she went up the steps. "I'll come back down and clean up from dinner. I'll be awake for a while yet."

She reached the top of the steps and said, "I'll just grab that eye cream for you . . ."

Cass stood in the doorway of Lucy's room and watched her cousin open a satchel.

"What the hell do you have in there?" Cass laughed. "You clean off the department store cosmetic counters? What is all that stuff?"

"Oh, different products for different

things. Vitamin C day cream, it has an SPF of 25. Vitamin E night cream. Makeup. Shampoos. You know."

Cass, who used one all-purpose face cream — when she thought of it, which wasn't often — and who had used the same brand of shampoo since she was a teenager, shook her head and took the small jar Lucy held out for her.

"Here, come in the bathroom and I'll put it on for you."

"Lucy, I can handle putting creamy stuff under my eyes. I'm assuming that's where it goes."

"Don't be a smart-ass." Lucy turned on the light in the small bathroom, which was barely big enough for both women. "Give me that jar."

Cass rolled her eyes while Lucy dabbed the cool white cream onto her skin.

"See, you don't want to rub it in, you just want to smooth it on a little."

"Right. Thanks. I'm going to bed now."

"Cassie, you ever think we were maybe switched at birth?" Lucy grabbed her cousin by the arm and pointed to the mirror that hung above the sink. "You look so much like my mother, and I look so much like yours. You have the light hair, I have the dark."

"Well, our mothers were sisters, Luce. We do share lots of the same genes." Cass stared into the mirror. She and Lucy did share a strong resemblance. "But I never realized how much you look like my mom. And how much like Aunt Kimmie I look, now that you mention it. Of course, since we are four months apart, it would have been hard to switch us in the hospital, you know?"

"Seems like the resemblance grows stronger as we get older," Lucy noted. "Not such a bad thing, though, right? They were both knockouts."

"They sure were. Last time I saw your mother, she still looked fabulous. I can only dream of looking that good when I'm her age."

"She takes good care of herself, though I think she gets too much of that Arizona sun. You'll look great, too, when you're in your fifties if you take care of your skin. Oh — I have a wonderful little concealer you have to try. It will just wipe away those puffs and lines under your eyes. I'll just leave it in the bathroom for you to use in the morning."

"And they say rest is essential, right? Well, I'm all for getting some rest."

"Okay, then, I'm going to make up my

bed and you go right ahead and crawl into yours. I have a feeling you're going to give that under-eye cream a severe test."

"Are you sure I can't give you a hand?"

"Go to bed, Cassie. I'll see you tomorrow."

"Okay." Cass yawned. "Lucy, I'm glad you're here. And I'm sorry you're having problems."

"I'm glad I'm here, too. And as for my problems, well, a little retail therapy might help. Would you be upset if I did something about that sofa in the living room?"

"Whatever." Cass laughed and went to bed.

Downstairs, a small notebook in hand, Lucy began to plan the bungalow's makeover. If she couldn't be happy, she could at least be busy.

# Seven

FBI Special Agent Mitchell Peyton only wanted one thing on this Friday afternoon: an uninterrupted ten-minute block of time in which to finish his lunch.

He scowled as the fifth phone call in a row was put through to him. *Okay, I'll settle for five.* He counted to ten, put down the sandwich he'd been about to bite into, and tried to talk himself into not picking up the receiver.

He wished he could make himself not answer, just once.

"Peyton."

"Mitch, it's John Mancini. Got a minute?" As always, the boss wasted little time with small talk.

"Sure."

"Come on down, then."

Mitch hung up and rewrapped his sandwich — his favorite, roast beef and provolone with horseradish on a crusty whole-wheat roll — in the heavy white butcher's paper Andre's Deli used for some of its best work. He put Andre's latest masterpiece back into the bag it had been delivered in, then opened the bottom drawer of his desk. Not that anyone in his office would walk off with someone else's sandwich, of course.

Yeah, right.

"Bunch of sharks around here," Mitch muttered, and dropped the sandwich into the open drawer, then took a long drink from the bottle of water that sat open on his desk before setting out for the elevator.

"He's expecting you. Try not to let him go on for more than eight to ten minutes. He has a meeting with the director at noon," Eileen Gibson, longtime secretary to John Mancini, said without looking up from her computer when Mitch entered her office. "The coffee's fresh. I just made it."

"Thanks, Eileen." Biting back the urge to refer to her by the name the field agents called her behind her back — the Little General — Mitch paused long enough to pour a cup. He ignored what he knew coffee would do to his near-empty stomach.

He rapped his knuckles on the inner door, then let himself in.

"Be right with you. Have a seat." With

one hand, John motioned vaguely in the direction of the chairs that stood on the opposite side of the desk from where he sat, and with the other, he finished scribbling whatever note he'd been in the midst of making.

Mitch folded his long legs as he sat on the chair closest to the window and sipped at his coffee.

"Nice job you did, wrapping up the Kingsley case, Mitch."

"Thanks. I had a lot of help on that one."

"True. Everyone on that team is to be commended. And will be commended, officially. I'll be seeing to that in about forty minutes. But I do believe it was your investigative — and computer — skills that put the pieces together. Very impressive."

"Thanks, John."

"Actually, you did such a good job, and I'm so impressed, I'm going to ask you to look into something else for me." John Mancini leaned back in his chair. With his shirtsleeves rolled up and his glasses hanging from his shirt pocket, no one would suspect him to be the head of a special investigative unit that operated within the FBI. "You know who Joshua Landry was?"

141

"Sure. He's that true crime writer who was killed last year by one of the three murderers who had hooked up in Pennsylvania and switched hit lists. Sort of a *Strangers on a Train* meets Ted Bundy and friends, if I recall."

John nodded. "Close enough. The three met by accident in a holding room in the courthouse and had a little too much unsupervised time alone. They seemed to have made some type of deal to kill for one another — each would knock off three people who had at some point in time pissed off one of the others. None of them ever admitted to it, but it was pretty apparent that an agreement had been reached among them. Anyway, Landry crossed paths with one of them some years ago and had apparently made one hell of an impression. Enough so that he was gunned down in his barn one morning last fall. Shame, really. He was not only a good writer, but a smart investigator. He'd have made a hell of an agent, I always thought."

Mitch sat quietly, waiting to find out what all this had to do with him.

"One of the things that Landry did that set him apart from other writers in the genre was he'd look into open cases, usually older ones, cold ones. If he solved them, he'd write a book about it. More than once, he'd turned over information or evidence to us or to the local law enforcement agency, which helped lead to an arrest and conviction. He was a pretty sharp guy."

"Sounds like." Mitch was still wondering.

"I was there the day he was murdered. Spent some time with his daughter — did I mention he had a daughter?" John looked across the desk.

"No, but I know you're working up to it."

John laughed. "We've worked together too long, Mitch. I got a call from Regan Landry — that's the daughter — this morning. She's been going through her father's files for the past few weeks, organizing things and what all, thinking about selling his house. I'm not surprised. It's a beautiful spread he had, but Josh was killed there. Guess that spoiled any really good memories she might have had of the place. Anyway, she tells me she's going through some boxes and found some notes Josh made about the Bayside Strangler. Remember him?"

"I don't have to remember him. Every time I turn on the news, I hear about another murder that's being attributed to a copycat Strangler up there in some Jersey resort town. At least, last time I heard, they were still suspecting it was a copycat."

"Right. That's the official word. Well, it seems Regan has some correspondence from the real Strangler that was written to her father years ago, as well as some notes that Josh made that Regan isn't sure how to interpret. She thinks they may somehow relate to the old case. I'd like you to make a trip up there — Landry's farm is right outside of Princeton — and look over what she's got. If something Josh had in his files could help ID the original Strangler, who knows? Maybe it could lead to the killer who's trying to follow in his footsteps."

"If she has information about the Bayside Strangler, shouldn't she be contacting the department investigating these recent killings?"

"She's called the chief of police up there in Bowers Inlet several times, but he hasn't called her back. So I'm thinking he's in over his head, not calling back the writer because, hey, she's just a writer and what he needs isn't more publicity but a few leads."

"That's a big assumption, John."

John nodded. "Could be unfair, sure.

But I've seen the local chief on TV. Looks like he's really trying to get a handle on things, but my impression is, he's overwhelmed. He mentioned on the *Today Show* he has one detective. One detective, and all these bodies. Think about it."

Mitch did. He didn't envy the chief of police who had to try to track a serial killer with only a small department and one detective.

"So . . . ?"

"So I'm sending you to go through Josh Landry's paperwork and see if you can find anything there that might shed some light on the case."

"Wouldn't it make more sense to send an agent to the scene and give them another set of hands and eyes?"

"That's next on my agenda." John handed Mitch a business card. "Here's Regan Landry's phone number and address. Give her a call and let her know you'll be stopping by tomorrow. I already told her I'd send someone up, tell her you're it."

"Okay." Mitch took the card and stood. "I should know after a day or so if there's anything there."

"Good. I'll wait to hear from you," John said. "Oh, and on your way out, tell Eileen to track down Rick Cisco and get him on the line."

It was nearly ten p.m. by the time Mitch turned off the light in his office and gathered the file containing the information about Josh Landry he'd printed off the Internet. The hall stretched long and quiet before him as he started toward the elevator. Light spilled from the doorway of the office five doors down from his. He rapped his knuckles on the frame and peered inside.

"You almost done?" he asked.

Rick Cisco looked up from his desk, where a ream of paper spilled out from a fat file.

"Just about. You heading out?"

"Yeah. Thought I'd stop at Henry's for a beer on my way home. Want to join me?"

"I need about ten more minutes."

"Sure." Mitch dropped his briefcase on the floor and slid into the lone visitor's chair.

"I have a few more things I want to print out . . ." The agent's focus was on his computer screen. "I'm leaving for New Jersey first thing in the morning and I want to get a handle on this case."

146

"Let me guess. You pulled Bayside Strangler duty."

"Yeah. How'd you know?"

"Mancini intimated earlier he'd be sending someone to work with the police, right before he asked Eileen to track you down."

"Should be an interesting case." Rick stood and leaned over his desk to replenish the paper supply in the printer. "I spoke with the chief of police up there today. They really have a mess on their hands. Bodies piling up, no witnesses, no suspects. Very little trace evidence. This guy has been very, very careful, all the way around. He's left very little behind. No semen, no saliva, no blood."

"Fingerprints?"

"They're trying to lift them off the victims' skin — all the vics were manually strangled — but it's been tough going. They're sending the prints on to our lab, see if we can get something usable." Rick sat down and hit the *Print* command and watched the first few sheets of paper feed through before turning to Mitch. "Of course, if there are no prints on file that match, it won't much help us at this point."

"Well, I'm heading to New Jersey, too,

and coincidentally, my assignment is related to yours, though I'm sure it won't be as interesting. I'm going to be going through the papers of a writer who may have received some correspondence from the Bayside Strangler. The original one. The real one. Whatever we want to call him."

Mitch filled Rick in on the information he'd gotten from Regan Landry when he'd called her that afternoon.

"So what's she got in the files that the FBI needs to look at?" Rick asked.

"She says she has a lot of notes that her father had made and some letters from someone claiming to be the Strangler."

"Why would he have contacted a writer?"

Mitch shrugged. "Who knows? I guess that's one of the things I'll find out. Not as exciting as directly working a serial killer case, though."

"I don't know about that." Rick grinned. "Have you seen this Regan Landry?"

"No."

"Well, I have. She was on one of those morning news shows not too long ago."

"And . . . ?"

"Short and sweet, good-looking. Interesting face. Lots of long curly blond hair and nicely put together, if I recall. And smart. She came off as being really, really smart." Rick stood and packed the printed material into the file, which he tucked under his arm.

"Well, we'll see how smart she is when we start going over her father's notes." Mitch followed Rick to the door and snapped off the light. "I'm still thinking you got the best deal, though. I haven't had a good serial case in a long time."

"You had that guy in California last year," Rick reminded him as they headed for the elevator.

"Yeah, but that was an easy one. Something tells me this is going to be a lot more involved."

"What makes you say that?"

"You've got two possibilities here. One, he's the real Strangler. Two, he's a copycat. If this is the guy who has been around for — what is it, twenty-some years? — he's good, Rick. He's really, really good. Where's he been all this time? You know he's been up to something — they don't kill, then stop, then start up again unless something has intervened."

"Like maybe a prison term." Rick hit the *Down* button.

"Maybe. Could be you'll get a match

off those prints there."

"I've already requested that any prints we find be run through NCIC on a priority basis."

"And if he hasn't been in prison, where's he been?" Mitch asked. "And then we have to consider the possibility that this guy is not the real deal."

"The chief up there in Jersey — Denver's his name — seems to be weighing in heavily on the copycat scenario."

"Either way, you've got your work cut out for you," Mitch said as the elevator doors opened and they stepped inside the car. He hit the button for the lobby. "The original Strangler or someone following in his footsteps, he's going to be hard to bring down. He's killed how many now — three? four? — in a short period of time, and no one has a clue as to who he is or what he looks like."

"And it isn't going to get easier the more time that passes. According to Denver, every day more people come into town for the summer season."

"If you're the killer," Mitch noted, "that's good news. The more potential suspects the law has to weed through, the less heat on you."

"If you're the killer, it's great news. The

higher the population, the more potential victims get added to the pool. There's no telling how high the body count could go before we find him."

The two men stepped off the elevator and signed out at the main desk in the lobby.

"I'll meet you at Henry's," Mitch said as they walked out through the back door to the parking lot. His car was just ten spots off to the left, Rick's a little farther out in the lot.

Mitch unlocked his driver's-side door, thinking about the files that awaited him at the Landry farm and the possibility there'd be something that might aid in the search for a killer.

At the same time, Rick was electronically opening his own car, wondering just how high the count would go before the killer was stopped, and how long it would take before he was tracked down.

# Eight

"What are you all dressed up for?" Cass stopped just inside the front door as Lucy was coming down the steps.

"Cassie, it's Friday night." Lucy dropped her purse on a chair and leaned over to tighten a strap on her sandal. "Aren't these cute?"

Lucy raised her foot and wiggled it, showing off the pink flowers that ran across the toes. "I picked them up in that little shop out on Route Nine this morning."

"Yeah, they're real cute, but I don't understand why you're wearing them or why you're dressed up." Cass walked past her into the kitchen, where she lifted the lid on a pot. "Ummm. Chicken noodle soup. That's great, Luce, thank you. I am just dying."

"Well, let's hope you revive soon. The Clarks' clambake is tonight."

"What?" Cass frowned and spooned soup into a bowl.

"The Clarks. Cathy and Eddie Clark?

152

They were in my mom's class at Regional? They own the marina out near the lagoon?"

"So?"

"So they invited everyone who's come back for the dedication of the new high school to a big party, which is tonight. It should be a pretty lively group, since the all-class reunion of the old high school is next week. I know you got an invitation for it, everyone who ever went to Regional did."

"Lucy, I'm in the middle of a serial homicide investigation. Four women have died in the past week. I have been pulling double shifts for almost a week now. I'm exhausted. I need sleep. I have to be sharp tomorrow. The FBI offered to send us some help and he's coming in the morning for a briefing. One agent. Dead bodies piling up, no suspects, and they send us *one* agent." She made a face. "I guess I shouldn't complain, though. At least there will be someone else to help share the load. Not that I look forward to sharing my case with the Feds, but sometimes you just have to bite the bullet, you know? We need help. *I* need help. I could kill Spencer for walking out the way he did, but there it is. Anyway, I'd like to be coherent when I have to sit down and talk with this guy."

She rubbed her eyes with the palms of her hands.

"God, I hope he's not an asshole." Cass sighed deeply. "In any event, the last thing I feel like doing is partying."

Cass downed several spoonfuls of soup before looking up from the bowl, to find Lucy staring at her.

"What?" Cass asked. "Look, there's no reason you can't go. You don't have to stay home and baby-sit me. I'll be asleep before my head hits the pillow. I'll never even know you've gone. Besides, it's coming up on nine. Don't you think all those clams will have been baked by now?"

"I can't go by myself, Cass. I haven't seen any of these people in a hundred years. No one will talk to me."

"Why would you want to go to a party where no one will talk to you?"

"They would if you were with me. You still live here, you know everyone. People will talk to you."

"The question was, why do you want to go?"

"I just . . . I don't know, I want to feel connected to something, I guess." Lucy sat in the chair opposite from Cass, leaned her elbows on the tabletop, and rested her chin in her hands. "I feel so . . . so . . . ."

"Spit it out, Luce."

"I feel like I don't belong anywhere right now. I don't feel as if I even have a home anymore. My rat-bastard husband took that from me." Her eyes brimmed with tears and her bottom lip quivered. "Everyone in town must know what's been going on. I feel like I don't have anything left now. I feel like I've lost it all."

Lucy picked at her nail polish.

"Stop that," Cass told her. "You just paid for that manicure."

"Right." Lucy clasped her hands together. "Anyway, if I don't belong there, I have to belong somewhere. I was hoping it would be here. I was hoping, oh, I don't know, that maybe I'd see some of my old friends and reconnect with them. Maybe I could start to build a life for myself away from Hopewell. Maybe bring the kids here to live with me — not here, to this house, I'd get my own — but here in Bowers Inlet. Maybe I could even get a job."

"Not — gasp — a job!"

"Very funny. There are things I could do. I just haven't worked in a long time because . . . well, there were the kids, and then . . . well, I didn't have to. David always gave me a very generous allowance. I will say that for the man."

Lucy crossed her legs under the table and Cass could feel the slight breeze stirred up by her cousin's foot, which was bouncing with nerves and tension.

"You're right, though. You are tired, and I am a totally thoughtless, immature, self-centered bitch for not even taking that into consideration. I'm sorry. I was only thinking of myself."

Lucy forced a smile, then stood up and patted Cass on the back. "Finish your soup, then go ahead and turn in. I'll go up and change. I'm sorry I wasn't more con-siderate. I don't know what I was think-ing." She tried to lighten up. "Well, of course, I obviously wasn't thinking. I'm re-ally sorry."

Lucy began rinsing out glasses at the sink. Her shoulders were bunched and tight. Cass could tell even from looking at her back that Lucy was trying not to cry.

"I'm sorry, too. Sorry I didn't realize how hard this situation has been for you."

"I think you've had other, more impor-tant things on your mind."

"Well, look, Luce, how 'bout we go for an hour. Would you be content with just an hour? I honestly don't think I'd last much longer than that."

"It's okay. Really. You should go to bed."

"Oh, hell, Lucy." Cass finished the last bit of soup. "I can get changed in a flash."

"Are you sure? You don't have to . . ."

"I'm sure. The soup revived me. Besides," Cass pointed to Lucy's hot pink Capri pants, "we can't let those go to waste."

"Well, yay! I'll come home the minute you tell me you're ready to leave, I promise." Lucy's face lit up. "Now, you run upstairs and take a real quick shower while I straighten up the kitchen a bit."

"I'll be down in twenty minutes."

"I'll be up in fifteen to do your face."

There were a surprising number of people still standing around the bar in the tent that had been erected in the Clarks' backyard to celebrate the festivities surrounding the demolition of the old high school and the dedication of the new one. Beyond the tent, a wooden dock, weathered gray, separated the back of the property from the bay.

"Hey, Cass. Over here," someone called when Cass and Lucy entered the tent.

Cass nudged Lucy with her elbow. "There's Connie — remember her from basketball?"

157

"Sure." Lucy nodded, then waved. "Hi, Connie!"

"Is that Lucy Donovan? For heaven's sake, girl, come right on over here . . ."

Cass ordered a club soda and lime for herself and a beer for Lucy from the young bartender, and joined in the conversation with several old classmates.

"I can't believe you're a cop," someone in the group teased. "Aren't you the one who used to sneak beers from that refrigerator in your aunt's basement and go sit out on the jetty and toss 'em back?"

"That was Lucy," Cass denied with a straight face.

"Liar, liar, pants on fire." Lucy laughed. "I heard that."

Cass spent several long minutes admiring the photographs of old friends' children, a few more catching up with classmates who had moved away and returned for the weeklong festivities. She hadn't realized that so many people had gotten so involved with this old school–new school thing. To her, it was little more than one old building coming down, a newer one going up. But then again, she wasn't as sentimental as some.

The recent killings were the main topic of conversation, much as she'd suspected they might be, but as the evening wound down, the chatter became lighter, less intense, more personal. Signaling Lucy by pointing to her watch, Cass made it clear it was past time to go. True to her word, Lucy said her good-byes and looped an arm through Cass's.

"You are the best, you know that?" Lucy told her. "I had such a good time. It was fun to see everyone again, I don't know why I didn't keep in touch with those girls. Thanks, Cassie. I owe you."

"Drive me home and we'll call it even." Cass tossed the car keys and Lucy caught them with one hand.

"Poor Cassie, hunting serial killers by day, being dragged around town by her selfish, loony cousin by night." Lucy got behind the wheel of Cass's car and slid the key into the ignition. "God will reward you for your good deed."

"I hope it's with a good night's sleep."

Here and there throughout the tent or around the bar, classmates had gathered to catch up with one another's lives. Just inside the tent, a group of middle-aged men gathered at a round table. They'd spent most of the night talking about the old times, and doing a little catching up as well. Many of them had remained close enough to the shore towns to come back every summer with families of their own, often returning to the same houses in which they'd grown up. Some still lived in those towns. Others had left the Jersey coast to seek their fortunes elsewhere.

In groups of threes and fours, they struggled to be overheard above the music, which was loudest this close to the speakers.

"Howard, how's your sister doing these days?"

"Hey, Ebberle, that your Corvette parked out there? You trying to recapture your youth, or what?"

"Did you see Debbie Ellis? Can we say *face-lift?*"

"Check out the rock old Paulie's young wife is sporting. You know he never gave Patsy a rock that big . . ."

He was standing halfway between the table and the bar, listening to some idle chatter, when he saw her, and his heart stopped beating in his chest.

". . . so I said, listen, Hal, you can give me a better deal than that on this boat. You know she's been sitting in dry dock for — Hey, buddy, you all right?"

His companion tapped him on the back.

"You've gone white as a sheet, like you've seen a ghost."

The friend followed his gaze across the bar.

"You're looking at Bob Burke's girl there? Yeah, she's a cop here in Bowers Inlet now. And a damned fine one, too. I hear she's won all kinds of commendations. She's living in the old Marshall place on Brighton, old lady Marshall left the house to her and her cousin."

"She's beautiful. She looks so much like her mother." He somehow managed to get the words out.

"Oh, no, no. You're looking at the other girl. That's the cousin, Kimmie Donovan's daughter. You must remember Kimmie if you remember Jenny. The Marshall sisters? They were some ten years, maybe fifteen years or so ahead of us, I don't recall exactly. Kimmie married Pete Donovan . . . used to race cars on Sunday nights down on Lagoon Lane?"

He couldn't take his eyes off her.

"But you're right, man, it's unbelievable how much Kimmie's girl looks like Jenny. It's all that dark hair. Boy, she was a looker, that Jenny Marshall. Damned shame, wasn't it, about her and Bob . . . they had another daughter who was killed,

161

too. Bastard. Wiped out that whole family, or tried to. Cassie was lucky to get out of there alive, that's for sure. Damned shame. I hope that bastard Wayne Fulmer rots in hell for what he did to that family. I heard he died about ten years back, still in prison. Stomach cancer, I heard. I hope he suffered. I hope he suffered real bad. He got off easy, you ask me." The companion took a long swig of his beer.

"They should have turned him over to us, you know? We would have known what to do with that bastard, after what he did to Jenny and Bob and that little girl of theirs. Boy, that was a summer to remember, wasn't it? First that wacko Fulmer goes nuts and all but wipes out the Burkes, then all those women got themselves killed. Damned Bayside Strangler." He took another sip of his beer. "Hell of a thing for the town to be remembered for, isn't it? And now it's déjà vu all over again, like they say. I told my kid she goes no place without three or four other girls and a couple'a guys while we're down here. You never know what this bastard is thinking . . ."

He'd been murmuring agreement. *Yes, yes, of course, the man who'd been convicted of murdering the Burke family got*

162

*off easy. Yes, yes, dying of cancer was too good for him. He should rot in hell. Yes, it's crazy that someone's going around acting like the Strangler. Yes, you can't be too careful . . .*

He barely heard a word, hardly knew what he was saying.

He said his good nights, then hurried to the parking lot. The last he saw of her was the sweep of long hair as she got into the car.

He stood in the shadows and watched her drive away, his heart pounding and his knees shaking, wanting her.

The car turned right at the stop sign and disappeared into the night. But it was okay, he told himself.

She wouldn't be hard to find.

# Nine

Rick Cisco wasn't certain what he expected to find when he arrived at the Bowers Inlet Police Department, but it wasn't the welcome he'd been given. Fresh coffee, fresh Danish, and a warm handshake from Chief Denver had made him feel as if he'd stepped into the Twilight Zone. He wondered if there was something else going on in Bowers Inlet that he hadn't been told about. Like Pod People taking over the identities of the locals. He couldn't recall ever having been greeted as graciously by a local agency. Usually his entry into a case came by way of some pushing and shoving and was accompanied by grumbles and dirty looks. No one ever wanted the FBI involved in their cases.

He sat in the chair offered to him by the chief, and waited for the other shoe to drop.

A few minutes later, there was a knock on the door, and he turned to see a tall slender woman with chin-length cinnamon-colored hair and uneasy cops' eyes. She wore jeans and a white shirt with the sleeves rolled up, and he suspected she might be the other shoe.

Chief Denver made the introductions. "Detective Cassandra Burke, meet Special Agent Eric Cisco. Agent Cisco will be working with you on the recent homicides."

"Great." She flashed a smile.

"It's Rick," he told her, wondering if the smile was for his benefit or the chief's. He figured he'd find out soon enough.

"Cass," she replied, the smile still in place. "Hopefully, two heads will prove to be better than one."

"Chief Denver was just telling me that you've recovered very little evidence."

She nodded, all business now, the smile history. "This is one wily little bastard. He knows what he's doing, no question about that. We figure he watches his victims for a few days before he strikes; he always seems to know when his target will be most vulnerable. He seems to be choosing women who have a pattern of being out at night. He knows exactly where they will be, and at what time."

"He took one woman right out of her own driveway," Denver interjected. "She did shift work at a fast-food place and apparently was picked up just as she arrived home. A co-worker dropped her off in front of her house, but she never made it inside."

"You checked out the co-worker?"

"An eighteen-year-old girl who was home within ten minutes of dropping off the victim," Cass said.

"No one heard anything, saw anything?" Rick asked.

"No one's come forward if they have," Cass told him, "and as frightened as everyone is right now, I have to think if anyone had information, we'd know about it."

Rick turned to the chief. "I'm assuming you have extra men on the street at night."

"I have all my cars on the street, twenty-four/seven. But I only have so many officers, Agent Cisco," Denver explained. "We're all working around the clock on this case, but he just hasn't given us much to work with."

"Would you like to go over the files?" Cass asked.

"Yes, thanks. That's a good place to start."

"Detective, you'll show Agent Cisco where he can hang his hat while he's here?" Chief Denver pushed back his chair and stood.

"Sure." Cass stood as well. "If we're done here, we can start right now."

"Great." Rick took the hand the chief extended. "Thank you. I don't always get this pleasant a reception."

"Women are dying in my town, Agent Cisco. I want it stopped. I'll take whatever help I can get, wherever I can get it. I want this bastard brought in."

"I'll do my best." Rick nodded and followed Cass from the room.

She led him down the hall and into a small room that was crowded with two old wooden desks, one of which looked naked except for the phone, a yellow legal pad, and a lone pen. She paused next to the other desk, which was piled high with files and papers.

"You'll need a chair," she murmured, mostly to herself, then went back out the door.

Moments later she returned, rolling an old leather number on shaky wheels.

"Sorry," she told him, "but this was all I could find. If it wobbles too much, we can trade. It won't bother me."

"This will be fine." He rolled the chair behind the desk and sat in it.

"Where would you like to start?"

"With the first victim."

"Fine." Cass shuffled through several files. "Linda Roman was our first vic. Here are the basics."

She handed him a copy of the report she herself had filed. He skimmed it quickly.

"Early thirties . . . married . . . one child. No known enemies, no one stalking her . . ." He went on to the second page. "Found near a creek, apparently within hours of having been killed . . ."

"Here are the photos from the scene."

Rick laid the report to one side of the desk and picked up the top photo.

"She looks as if she's been posed," he noted. "This isn't a natural position, arms over the head just so. Legs bent at that angle."

Cass handed him another stack of pictures.

"Victim number two. Lisa Montour."

He studied it for a moment, then said, "Same age, same hair. Same pose."

He looked up at her.

"Number three?"

"Toni DeMarco." She slid one packet of crime-scene photos across the desk, then a second. "And this is Yvonne Hunt, number four."

"So close they could be superimposed on one another," he murmured. "He's reliving something. Re-creating a scene. The women even look alike. Same age, same body type. And all that dark hair. Notice how in each picture the hair is sort of fanned out . . ."

"We noticed, Agent Cisco." There was a touch of starch in her voice now, as if offended. He wondered if she'd been waiting to feel offended.

Well, he'd been waiting for that, that little bit of resentment, to come out eventually. He was going to nip it in the bud right now.

"I'm sure you did. And it's Rick. If we're going to be working together, let's keep it casual, okay?"

"Sure," she said dryly.

"Look, let's get something straight. I'm not here to take your case away from you, or to try to make you look bad, or to steal your thunder. I was assigned to come up here and lend a hand. And that's what I intend to do."

"You don't consider yourself the lead, now that you're here? You don't feel the need to be in charge?"

"No. Until I'm told otherwise, I'm considering us equal in this. Partners. But since you've been on this case since day one, I'm ready to follow your lead. Agreed?"

She studied him with brown eyes that were almost too big for her face.

"Agreed. Okay. I'll take you at your word." She sat in her chair, a wry smile tugging at one corner of her mouth. "Not that it makes any difference."

"It makes a difference, Cass. I know that the Bureau has the reputation of sometimes coming in and strong-arming the locals. I don't work that way. My unit doesn't work that way. I'll help as much as I can, I'll do whatever I can to work with you. We have resources that you don't have and we will use as many or all of them, whatever we need to get the job done. But I won't take over your case, and I won't try to screw you over to take the glory when we get this guy." Rick sat back and studied her face. "And we will get him, you and I."

"I hope you're right." She returned his stare for a long moment, then said, "Well, now that we've gotten all the obligatory territorial bullshit out of the way, let's get back to work."

"Getting back to our victims, then. Just give me a minute or two to read through the report from the medical examiner . . ." He scanned the information.

He turned the pages so quickly, she wondered if he actually read any of it.

"The autopsy reports reveal all the classic signs of asphyxiation. Petechia at the eyes, broken hyoid bone in the throat . . . and of course the telltale bruising around the neck." He laid the photos of the four victims side by side across the middle of the desk. "Any other injuries?"

"Lisa Montour had a broken index finger on her right hand. Other than vaginal bruising, signs of the rape, no other injuries." She rested her elbows on her desk. "And no, no semen, he must have used a condom each time. No bite marks, no saliva, no nothing. We're trying to see if prints can be lifted off the victims' skin, but we're still waiting on that."

"No other trace?"

"Some fibers on the clothing of each matched, some gray carpet fibers, probably from the trunk of the car he transported them in, but it's so generic it's of no help. We know it was from a GMC vehicle that was made between 1998 and 2003, but they haven't gotten it down any more exactly than that."

"Your lab person is good?"

"She's very good. We can meet with her on Monday, if you like."

"Great." He glanced at the lab report again. "What's this trace found in the hair of the first three victims?"

"The threads? We're not sure. That's something we'll ask Tasha about on Monday. She was trying to analyze it, but with the finding of another body, she had to put the fibers aside."

"I'll be interested in seeing what it is." He slipped the files she'd made for him into his briefcase. "I'd like to see the crime scenes if I could. I realize it's the weekend, if you have plans you can just direct me . . ."

"No. No plans. I don't mind. Besides, it's always good to walk a crime scene after the fact. Sometimes you see things you might have missed the first time around."

It was almost one in the afternoon when Cass pulled off the side of Bay Lane and parked her car. They'd already walked the marsh where Linda Roman's body was found, stood in the alley where Lisa Montour had been left, and visited the lonely stretch of beach where Toni De-Marco had been discovered.

"This is where the last victim was found," she told Rick as she got out of the car. "We've already photographed everything, so you don't have to watch where you walk."

Rick opened the passenger door and stepped out onto the soft sandy shoulder.

"You probably got some good prints along here, as soft as the sand is," he commented.

"Not as good as you might think. It's soft now because it rained yesterday morning and it's been cloudy ever since. The day we found her, it was hard-packed."

He followed her along the side of the road.

"This road doesn't appear to be heavily traveled. Is there more traffic along here during the week?"

"Not really. It leads to the remains of an old lighthouse. Hardly anyone comes this way anymore. You might get some people crabbing off the bulkhead, but not at night. The pier was taken down a few years ago — it was so badly deteriorated, it was an accident waiting to happen. There are no houses down here, it's too swampy to build on. There's no nice beach, the water comes right up to the marsh along here. So there's not much reason to be down here, especially at night." She stopped and pointed to the ground. "This is where we found her. You saw the photos, you know that she was posed right out in the open."

Rick stared at the place where Yvonne Hunt's body had been found.

"It would've taken a few minutes to have gotten the pose just so, wouldn't you think?" he asked. "He must have felt pretty confident that no one would be coming along while he was doing it."

"You're thinking that he must be local."

"Would an outsider know that this is a road to nowhere? Would a stranger to the area risk being seen by taking the time he'd need to lay her out the way he did?"

"I wondered, too. As a matter of fact, I mentioned it to the chief. But before you start thinking that this narrows the field, you should know a couple of things. First of all, during the season, our population increases greatly. Remember that we're a resort town. We get a lot of renters starting Memorial Day weekend. Renters and summer people who move down in June and stay right on through September. And keep in mind, a lot of folks have rented here for years. Add to all that the fact that there's a big high school reunion next week, and you have a lot of people who are well acquainted with the traffic patterns."

"What year reunion is it?" he asked.

"All years. They just built a new high school, and they're taking down the old one. So we have people coming down from the 1930s classes clear on through to last year's class."

"Swell," he muttered. "Not much chance of narrowing it down, is there?"

"We can maybe eliminate certain years. I mean, I doubt anyone past the age of, say, sixty-five or so would have been strong enough to overcome our last victim. She'd been taking karate lessons for about four months, so she had some basic skills in self-defense. Someone too much older would have had a tough time with her. I'd have expected to see more defensive wounds on her. As you know, there were none."

"Maybe we should bring in one of our profilers, get a little insight into this guy, get some ideas as to why he's doing what he's doing."

Cass shrugged. "Fine with me."

"I'll call and see what we can arrange. Maybe we can get someone here early in the week. Hopefully by then we'll know what that trace fiber is, the threads that were found in the vics' hair."

"You think that might be important to the profiler?"

"I think whatever it is, it's part of what he needs to do to make this thing work for him."

"His signature."

"Yes. I think whatever it is, it has to do with his signature."

"Did you want to look around a little more?" She gestured vaguely.

"What's back this way?" Rick tilted his head to the right.

"It's a bird sanctuary."

Rick parted the rushes that grew almost to the roadway and walked farther into the marsh. Cass leaned back against the car, waiting for him to return. Two days ago she'd walked the entire length of the fence that enclosed the bird sanctuary. She knew he'd find nothing of interest there.

"Any other way in?" he asked as he walked toward her.

"There's a dirt road about a half mile up toward the highway. It winds through the marsh, sort of a loop, then out again on the opposite side."

"What's the main attraction?"

"In the sanctuary?" She thought it over, then replied, "I guess the blinds are pretty popular during the migration times — we're just coming to the end of one of those. Heavy bird migrations mid- to late-April through mid-June, then again in the early fall. There's a big bird count on New Year's Day every year. And there's a cabin where you can buy bird books, bird calls, that sort of thing. You can ride through in your car, follow the loop around, or you can stop at the observation posts. There are several of those. Places where you can get out of your car and walk a sort of wooden boardwalk farther into the marsh."

"Sounds as if you're well acquainted."

"My mother was part of the group that petitioned the state to set up the sanctuary. It was her favorite place. She spent a lot of her spare time here, training guides, walking the wetlands to look for injured birds, tracking rare birds and photographing them. She even worked in the gift shop when they got shorthanded, though she much preferred being outside."

"She sounds like quite the nature girl."

"Yes, she was."

"Was?"

"She died when I was six."

"I'm sorry."

"So was I. Anything else you want to see?"

Rick looked around, his glance returning to the bird sanctuary.

"I think I'd like to drive that loop on the way back, if you can spare a few more minutes."

"Sure."

Cass got into the car and started it up,

waiting while Rick fastened his seat belt before making a U-turn in the middle of the road. She drove the half mile, then took a right on the rutted dirt road.

"It would be nice if the county or the state could get around to paving this one of these days," she said as she stopped in front of the long wooden gate that stretched across the roadway.

"Is it locked?" Rick asked.

"No, I'm sure it's just closed. Lots of people come out here. You can see by the tire marks there's been a lot of activity over the past few days since the rain."

Rick got out of the car and walked to the gate. He lifted it and moved it to one side. Cass pulled the car up and he got back in.

They drove in silence for a few minutes, the road winding slowly, dividing the preserved area in two, the salt flats on one side and the more solid ground of the marsh on the other.

"There's one of the blinds." She pointed to a wooden structure that sat surrounded by tall rushes and cattails. "That one looks out over the marsh, so if it's marsh birds you're interested in, you might spend some time there."

She pointed out several more blinds along the way.

"This one was named for my mother," she told him when she stopped at the top of the loop. "It looks out into the bay. One time during the migrations in the spring — when the birds fly from South America to the Arctic? — she brought me with her to watch the birds gobble up the horseshoe crab eggs on the beach down there. It's not as dramatic as it is on the Delaware Bay, but it was certainly something to see. At least for a six-year-old. All those birds swooping around, calling and scolding . . ."

She sat for a silent moment, then drove on, but not before he saw the sign on the side of the road. *Dedicated to the memory of Jenny Burke, whose tireless work helped turn a swamp into a sanctuary.*

"Seen enough?" she asked.

He nodded. "I think so."

She accelerated, heading for the exit, then paused to wave on an incoming car, then drove out through the gate.

The driver of the other car slowed to a stop as Cass passed, watching in his rearview mirror from behind dark glasses as she negotiated the bumpy dirt road.

She had no way of knowing he would sit and stare after her until her car had long since disappeared.

# Ten

"Hey, I thought you weren't going to work all day."

Lucy, who was sitting on the top step of the front porch, painting her toenails a deep red, called to Cass even before she had the car door closed behind her.

"I got tied up."

"I hope he was cute." Lucy raised one foot and wiggled her toes. "What do you think? Is it too dark? Would it look better if I were tanner?"

"It looks fine," Cass said without looking. The color of her cousin's toenails was the last thing on her mind.

"So, was he?"

"Was who what?"

"Was he cute?" Lucy grinned. "You were meeting with that FBI guy this morning, right?"

Cass paused on her way up the stairs.

"Actually, he was, I guess."

"You guess?" Lucy laughed out loud.

"Yeah, I guess he was okay."

"What did he look like? Tall, dark, and handsome?"

"That fits." Cass stepped around Lucy and went into the house.

"Hey, come back here!" Lucy got up awkwardly and followed Cass inside, walking on her heels to avoid smearing the polish. "You can do better than that. And what's his name? Was he nice?"

"Lucy, this wasn't a blind date. He's with the FBI. He's only here to help us out with these killings."

Lucy pulled two chairs out from under the kitchen table, sat in one, and propped her feet up on the other.

"But you must have had an impression of him. You spent all day in his company."

"Okay, my impression is that he's very smart, very professional. He wasn't what I expected at all." Cass rummaged in the refrigerator, which was filled to near-capacity, thanks to Lucy's trip to the local market. She brought out a block of cheddar cheese and set it on the counter while she looked for a knife.

"I bought a cheese slicer," Lucy told her. "It's in the drawer with the flatware."

"This?" Cass held up the slicer and Lucy nodded.

"There are crackers in the cupboard next to the cereal, but don't eat too much. I bought crabs for dinner." Lucy shook the bottle of nail polish, then opened it and began to paint the fingernails on her left hand to match her toes. "It was for myself because I didn't hear from the kids this morning. They're supposed to call on Saturdays, right? I figured they probably called home and talked to their dad and he probably didn't remind them to call me on my cell phone, so I went food shopping and stopped at the Crab Shack, thinking we could pig out later. Well, there I was, in line, waiting for our crabs to be cooked to order, and doesn't my cell phone ring?"

Lucy paused to beam.

"And there were my babies, both of them. They did call home, and they had forgotten my number, so David gave it to them and told them to charge the call to the house phone — I should thank him, I guess — so I got to talk to both of the boys. I almost cried, I was so happy to hear from them."

"How are they doing?"

"Having the time of their lives, and no injuries so far." She knocked on the wooden cabinet. "They want to stay for an extra session. You'd think two weeks of football, two weeks of lacrosse would be enough, but nooooo. They want two weeks of ice hockey as well."

"What did you tell them?"

"I told them to take it up with their father. I guess I'd rather have them at camp having fun than home dodging bullets between David and me." Lucy looked as if she was about to cry. "The longer they stay at camp, the longer I can put distance between me and David. The longer I have to think about what I want to do, where I want to go . . ."

She stared out the window for a time.

"Anyway, it was so good to hear their voices. I miss them every day. They've never been away from me for more than a long weekend."

"They're eleven this year?"

Lucy nodded.

"I guess that's old enough."

"Old enough for what?"

"Old enough to go a few weeks without seeing their momma."

"Oh, you." Lucy laughed. "I'll see them next weekend. I can't wait. I know it's not even been a week, but I miss them. Parents can go for visits after the second week, so I'll drive up on Saturday for a while. You're welcome to come with me if you like."

"We'll see. As much as I'd like to see Kyle and Kevin again, I hate to commit to anything. With the investigation and all."

"I understand." Lucy bit the inside of her lip. "I guess I need to find out when David is going to be there. So I can go at a different time."

"The boys won't think that's odd? That you don't go together?"

"I'll just tell them that I've come up from the beach, which would be the absolute truth." She waved a hand at Cass. "Now, go on. You were talking about how . . . what's his name? The FBI guy?"

"Rick Cisco."

"Cisco? Like the Cisco Kid?"

"I can't imagine anyone calling him that and living to tell about it," Cass mused, "but yes, like the Cisco Kid."

"So you were telling me how he wasn't what you'd expected."

"I've never worked directly with the FBI before, but from everything I've heard, they're a pain in the ass to deal with. Like, once they come into an investigation, they take over. They like to be in charge. Their way or the highway. And that once the case has been solved, they take the credit. If the case goes bad, they put the blame on the locals."

"You think that's the way this guy, Cisco, is going to do it?"

184

"Well, we'll see. He says we'll be working together, equally. He's not going to take over the case, he's not going to claim credit once we catch this guy, yada yada yada. The jury's still out on him." She paused to reflect. "And he was adamant that we would catch this guy."

"Well, that's a good thing, right? You want to work with someone who has that kind of confidence, right?"

Cass nodded.

"I want so badly to catch this bastard. And soon. It's been over a week." She shook her head. "Every day he's out there, some other poor woman is at risk."

"You think the Cisco Kid can make a difference?"

"He's another pair of experienced hands. That alone makes a difference." Cass cut off a paper-thin slice of cheese. "Want one?"

"No, thanks. Not right now." Lucy bent close to the table as she applied polish to a fingernail. "So what did you do with him today?"

"Gave him a copy of each of the victims' files. Took him to all four crime scenes." Cass went back to the fridge for a beer. "Last one. Want half?"

"Actually, I'd love half. Thanks."

Cass got two glasses out of the cupboard and split the beer equally between them. She set one on the table in front of Lucy, who was still absorbed in polishing her nails, and took a thoughtful sip from the other.

"He wanted to go through the bird sanctuary," she said.

"Why?"

"He just wanted to see what was there, behind the fence, since our last victim was found right outside there, on Bay Lane."

"I haven't been out there in . . ." Lucy tried to remember. "I don't even know how long it's been since I was there. Maybe not since I was a kid."

"I hadn't gone in years."

"Remember when your mom used to take us there?"

"Yes." Cass took another sip, then said softly, "They put a memorial up, near one of the blinds. A plaque with her name on it."

"That's really nice, Cass." Lucy put the brush into the polish bottle. "Hadn't you seen it before?"

Cass shook her head. "I sort of remember someone sending me a letter some years ago, that they were going to dedicate something, but I think I was still in college at the time and missed it completely."

"I'd like to see it. Can we go?"

"I'd be happy to take you tomorrow," Cass told her, "but right now, I'm so tired, I just want to sleep. I hope you don't mind."

"Nope. Not at all."

"No parties you can't miss tonight?"

"Actually, someone at the clambake did mention something about a party tonight, but since you were such a sport, going out with me last night when you were so beat, I wasn't even going to mention it."

"You could go alone, you know. You really don't need me to tag along."

"I'm just not ready to go places alone." Lucy held up one hand against the argument she knew would be forthcoming. "Don't say it. I know how old I am. I know all that. It's just that, after so many years of being married, I'm not used to going places alone, not social places, anyway. I know that must sound silly to you, but you've always been so independent, Cass, you've never needed to lean on anyone. If I ever had any real confidence in myself, I must have lost it somewhere along the way. I guess I need to work myself into my new life gradually." She tightened the lid on the polish and set it aside, then picked up her glass and drank from it. "Besides, I don't mind hanging out with you. I like your company."

"Thanks, Luce."

"Why don't you take a nap, and I'll run out and pick up a DVD or two, and we can do beer and popcorn and movies tonight?"

"Beer and pretzels?" Cass asked.

"Sure."

"That would be great. Thanks." Cass rose and started toward the steps. "And there's nothing I want more right now than a nap. I can barely keep my eyes open."

"Do it. I'll go now. Can you think of anything else you might want?"

"Right now I can't think, period. But thanks." Cass was almost to the top step. "Nothing that a little sleep won't cure . . ."

He was in the video store, playing nice uncle to his nephews, when she walked through the door. Even the air around him seemed to change, seemed to charge with something vital and alive.

She was beautiful. Her body, her face. Her long dark hair.

"Can we get this one? Can we?" His five-year-old nephew tugged at his sleeve.

"Sure." He nodded without taking his

eyes from her. "Get whatever you want."

"Can I get a big box of Raisinets?"

"Sure."

"Can I get one, too?" The older of the two boys asked.

"Sure. Whatever you want. Go ahead. I'll wait here."

He watched her move through the stacks of movies, and without thinking, followed as if drawn to her by an invisible force.

*This one. This one. This one . . .*

The closer he got, the more perfect she appeared to be.

He walked toward her, then behind her. She glanced up when he brushed against her.

"Sorry," he said. "These narrow aisles . . ."

She smiled and stepped aside to allow him to pass. He looked at the movie in her hands. *Sister Act.*

"That's a fun one," he said, smiling in his warmest, most casual manner. "My nephews liked it a lot."

"Whoopi Goldberg and some singing nuns." She smiled back. "What's not to like?"

"Hey, we're ready to go now."

One of the little bastards was at his elbow.

189

The other appeared right behind him. "Can we go home now?"

"Sure, boys." He tried to beam affectionately at them, wasn't sure he'd gotten it right, but she didn't seem to notice. She'd already moved on. "Sure . . ."

They dragged him to the candy counter, and he barely paid attention to what he was paying for. Not that he cared. He wanted to wait around to see where she'd be going from here, but he couldn't seem to drag things out long enough. The boys were already on their way out the door, and he should be right behind them. What if they were kidnapped? How would he explain that to his brother and stupid sister-in-law?

Though if the boys were his kids, he might consider kidnapping a favor. Boring little brats. Demanding. Annoying.

He followed them into the parking lot, then drove home the long way. Which eventually took him down Brighton.

He slowed when he passed the house where he knew she was staying. There was one car in the drive, the car she'd driven last night. He was wondering how she'd managed to get here so quickly, when another car drove past him. It, too, slowed as it approached the bungalow. He eased up on the gas and watched in the side mirror as she got out of the car.

"Hey, there's a car coming!" his nephew yelled from the backseat.

He swerved to avoid it.

"Didn't you see it?"

"Sure I saw it. I had plenty of time." His eyes kept darting to the mirror. She was out of the car now, striding up the sidewalk on long bare legs. He pulled to the side of the road, permitting a convenient few cars to pass him on the narrow street.

"That's what Daddy does. He pulls over and lets people pass. He says it's polite," the seven-year-old said.

"Now you're being polite, too. You weren't polite before," the five-year-old reprimanded him.

He watched through the mirror until she was inside the house.

*This one. This one. This one.*

*Yes. This one.*

It was merely a matter of how and when.

*How* would take a little figuring. She was living with a cop — he knew who *she* was, but he wasn't going to deal with her now, wasn't even going to think about her now. There was no room in his head for thoughts of her. Not when he had the one — truly the one — in sight. The other, no

191

longer important, could wait.

As for *when*, it couldn't be soon enough.
Never soon enough.

# Eleven

Mitch Peyton sat across the table from Regan Landry and tried his best not to stare. How had Cisco described her face? Interesting?

If the face across from him was *interesting,* he had to wonder what Cisco thought was *beautiful.*

Oh, the face was interesting enough, all right. Deep-set green eyes and a mass of tumbled curly blond hair that was pulled up in a tangled knot at the back of her head. A trim well-proportioned body under a pale pink cotton shirt, the sleeves rolled up, and black yoga pants. Bare feet.

He'd been startled when she'd opened the door and looked up at him when he arrived at her farm earlier in the day. He'd been expecting . . . well, he wasn't quite sure just what he'd been expecting, but it wasn't *her.*

It wasn't just her appearance that appealed. There was an energy to her, a vibrancy, that sent his senses into alert mode.

"Agent Peyton?" she'd asked, then glanced at the ID he held out to her. She studied it with serious eyes, then smiled at him. "Come in. Please. I've been waiting for you."

The smile had really gotten to him.

He'd barely heard a word she spoke, just followed her down the hall to the study, where she said she'd been working, and he'd probably want to see what she'd found straight off, so they might as well just start right in.

"I'm glad you came to look over these notes in person," she said. "John and I did discuss the possibility of me faxing them to the FBI, but then, there are all these other files, and God knows what's in them . . ."

She had waved her hand around at the stacks of boxes that covered most of the carpeted area.

". . . and I know there's more to this story than what we have here. I told you on the phone how scattered my father was in his record keeping?"

Mitch had nodded.

"Well, we're paying the price for that now." She'd stepped behind the desk and seated herself in the leather chair, which seemed to swallow her, and motioned for him to have a seat.

He'd pulled a chair up to the desk and sat.

"What makes you certain that there is more than those few files?" he'd asked.

"It's an intriguing story, and my father was a sucker for intrigue."

"If he was so taken by what he had, why didn't he pursue it at the time? And do you know for certain that he didn't, and maybe abandoned it, came up dry?"

"One possibility is that he may have been engrossed in something else, maybe he was wrapping up a book or just starting one. He'd develop a bit of tunnel vision when he was working. Which only exacerbated his careless filing habits. He might have an idea that appealed to him, but if he was already into a project, he'd have put the idea aside for the time being. Then again, I don't know that he didn't pursue it beyond what I've found thus far. I suspect that there's more, but I haven't found it yet. And of course, there is the possibility that he did write it off as not being worth pursuing. I did explain all this to John Mancini. He thought you should take a look, given what's going on in those little beach towns."

She'd opened a file and turned it to him, then eased herself half out of her seat to reach across the desk.

"These are the letters I found. See the numbers in the corners?"

He'd glanced at the letters.

*Hey, Landry, remember me?* A seven inside a circle in the upper right-hand corner.

*Hey, Landry, did you miss me?* Numbered eleven.

"When my dad started to gather his notes to start putting a project — a potential project — together, he numbered the pages in the corner, just like this, to show the order in which he was going to present them in his first draft."

"Maybe there were other things . . . photos, reports, something . . . that he would have put between these two."

She'd shaken her head. "He would have kept the letters together, chronologically, and reports separate, though also in chronological order, numbered separately as well. If he hadn't received any other letters, this one, the one with the seven in the corner, would have been numbered one. And the one numbered eleven would have a two in the corner. There were other letters. I'm certain of it. I just don't know what he did with them."

"Why wouldn't he have kept them together?"

"Why can't pigs fly?"

He'd stared at her.

"I just mean, that's a question that has no answer. My best guess is that the other letters arrived when he was engrossed in something else and he stuck them in a file so they wouldn't get lost before he could get back to them."

"Then forgot where he put the files."

She nodded. "That's my daddy."

"So how do you know where to start?"

"I'm going box by box."

"That shouldn't take too long." He'd started counting boxes.

"There are more in the basement."

"Oh."

"And in the attic."

"I see."

"He also used one of the small outbuildings for storage."

"I'm beginning to get the picture."

She'd smiled again. "Good."

She'd sorted through several other files, then handed him two sheets of paper. "These are the lists that got my attention. The first one is pretty much self-explanatory."

*"Victims attributed to the Bayside Strangler, June 1979–August 1979,"* he'd read aloud, then scanned the list of names.

"Have you confirmed that these were, in fact, the 1979 victims of the Bayside Strangler?" he'd asked, looking up.

"I've confirmed the first four. That's as far as I got."

He'd reached for his briefcase, opened it, and taken out his laptop.

"We have several computers here," she'd told him as he set his up on the corner of the desk. "You didn't need to bring your own."

"I can probably go places on this one that you can't go on any of yours." He'd smiled as he turned it on. "Let's see what we can see."

"Wireless?" she'd asked, and he'd nodded.

Then he'd lost himself in cyberspace for a little while.

He'd tuned back in about a half hour later, to look across the desk and find her chair empty.

He'd taken a small portable printer from the square case that sat at his feet and plugged it into a nearby wall outlet. As the page printed, he'd sensed her in the doorway.

"I made lunch," she'd told him. "Nothing elaborate, but it's almost two-thirty, and if you ate breakfast as early as I did today, you have to be at least as hungry as I am."

"Thanks." He'd glanced at his watch. "I had no idea how late it was."

He'd gathered the two sheets of paper he'd printed and followed her to the kitchen, which was filled with afternoon sunlight. That had been almost an hour ago, and they were still seated at the table, their now-empty plates and soup bowls pushed to the side.

And he was still having trouble keeping his eyes from her face.

"All these names were in the FBI files?" she was asking.

"In files we have access to."

"Of course." A half smile teased one side of her mouth. She lowered her voice to an ominous tone. "We have our ways . . ."

Mitch laughed.

"So we know this is for real." She placed that list aside and slid the second list to the center of the table. "What do you think about this one? What do you suppose it means?"

"Since it was with the Bayside Strangler list, I have to think the lists are related. Otherwise, as haphazard as your father was in his record keeping, wouldn't they be in separate files if there was no connection?"

He tapped on the first notation on the second sheet of paper. "Something happened in Pittsburgh in May of 1983 that caught your dad's attention. And in February of 1986, in Charlotte. So we have to figure out what caught his eye on those dates."

Regan frowned and stared at the list.

"He did keep some files — and again, I use that term very loosely — of newspaper clippings. Wide brown folders, you know what I mean?"

"The kind that have accordion sides, to expand?"

"Yes. Maybe if we look through those, one of these dates will jump out at us."

"It's worth a look, sure. Where are the files?"

"There are some in the office, in one of the filing cabinets. Let's take our coffee with us. I'm curious now to see if there's anything there."

"Lead on." He pushed the chair back from the kitchen table and stood. "Maybe we'll find the key in one of them."

They sat on the floor around a large round coffee table and went through first one file, then another. They were into their second hour of searching, when Mitch said, "Wasn't there a Corona on that list?"

"Yes," she said, and moved some papers aside to check the original list. "Here it is. August '86. Corona." She looked up at him. "I'm not sure I know where Corona is."

"This clipping is from August 15, 1986. Dateline Corona, Alabama." He skimmed the small clipping, then read aloud. *"Police have confirmed that the body of the woman found in East Park on Saturday morning was that of thirty-one-year-old Andrea Long of Corona. Identification was made by James Long, the husband of the victim, who'd reported his wife missing Thursday night . . ."*

"Does it say how she died?"

"She'd been strangled."

"Raped?"

He read a little further.

"Yes."

"There's a coincidence," she said with some sarcasm.

"I'll bet your dad thought so."

He took his cell phone from his pants pocket and dialed information for the number for the sheriff's department in Corona, Alabama, but wasn't at all surprised to find that no one on the weekend shift seemed to know anything about a 1986 murder. He left a message for someone to call him back, then snapped the phone shut.

A few taps on his keyboard, and he dialed another number.

The answering machine picked up, and he began to leave a message. "Hi, Jessica, it's Mitch Peyton, FBI. I worked with you on a case in Montgomery a few years ago, don't know if you remember me or not. I'm looking into an old case — murder victim named Andrea Long, August '86 — and was wondering if you might be able to shed a little light on — Oh, hey, Jessica. How are you?"

He chatted for a few moments, then cut to the chase.

"I was hoping you could . . . no, I don't have any other information, just the name of the victim, an approximate date of death, and the fact that she was strangled and sexually assaulted . . . Well, for starters, I was wondering if the case was ever solved. If not, if there was a list of suspects . . . Sure, that would be great."

He put his hand over the mouthpiece. "Regan, do you have a fax machine?"

She nodded and pointed to it where it sat atop a two-drawer file cabinet next to the desk.

He made a scribble sort of motion with

one hand and she wrote the number of the fax machine on a piece of paper and handed it to him.

"Listen, anything you have, fax it to me at this number. I'll give you my cell number and email address as well . . ."

He recited the information slowly, and after a few minutes of chatter, he ended the call.

"She's going to look through the files and she'll let me know if she finds anything. But it probably won't be until Monday. She's on her way out."

"Is she with the FBI?" Regan asked.

"Alabama Bureau of Investigation."

"So that's one of the ten on the unidentified list. Encouraging, wouldn't you say?"

"Well, it certainly gives direction to our search."

"Pass that news clipping over here, and we'll start a file on this one." She searched the stack for an empty file, wrote *Andrea Long, Corona, Alabama, 1986* on the side, then set it on the cushion of a nearby chair to keep it separate. "Now, let's see what else we can find in this folder . . ."

Over the course of the evening, they matched up one other clipping. Gloria Silver, Memphis, Tennessee, had been found raped and strangled on March 17, 1987.

Mitch reached for his cell phone.

"Let me guess," Regan said. "You're calling the Tennessee State Police."

He shook his head. "Tennessee Bureau of Investigation."

"Do you really think you'll get someone at eight forty-five on a Saturday night?"

"Is it that late?" He glanced at his watch.

" 'Fraid so."

"Guess it's true what they say about time flying when you're having fun. Let's wrap this up for tonight, then start fresh on Monday. By then, I should have been able to track down a few more names, and maybe we'll have a response or two."

"Fine with me." Regan rubbed her eyes. "I guess I need to put this aside for a while anyway. My eyes are all but falling out of my head."

"What time Monday is good for you?" Mitch gathered up his laptop and put it into its case, then slid it into the larger case, along with the small printer.

"Whatever time you get here. I'm an early riser." She stood and stretched. "And maybe by then I'll have found clippings that match up with the others."

"You'll be working tomorrow, then?"

"Sure. Writers don't always get weekends, you just sort of work when you have something to work on, so I'm used to it."

"Sort of like working for the Bureau," he said. "You work the case until it's done."

"Exactly."

Mitch followed her down the hall to the front door.

"You're not driving back to . . . where did you drive from today?"

"I drove up from Maryland. But I'm staying at a motel on Route One."

"Well, I'll see you on Monday."

She opened the door and he started through it.

"But you have my card, right, in case something comes up . . ." he paused to ask.

"I do. And you have my number . . ."

He nodded and walked to the car.

She stood in the doorway while he loaded the black case into the trunk, then got into the driver's side and turned on the engine. The headlights shone far into the back field, and in their light, several deer startled. The light swung out around the field and made a yellow path as he turned the car around, and he waved to her when he drove past.

Regan stepped out onto the porch and leaned over the rail to watch the taillights grow smaller as they traveled the long lane, then disappear after he made the turn onto the main road. She sat on the top step for a while and stared up at the sky, where the clouds were beginning to fade and the stars were starting to appear. Her eyes followed the lights from a plane as it moved across the night sky. She thought about the dates and the places on the lists and about the fact that it was beginning to look like each date and place represented another woman whose life had been snatched.

More than she'd bargained for when she first picked up the phone to call Chief Denver, more than she could have imagined when she called John Mancini. She was grateful that he'd sent someone to help her sort through all the information.

Grateful, too, she found herself thinking, that the someone he'd sent was Mitch Peyton. Their work styles were so similar, their focus equally complete, it seemed she'd been working with him forever.

She couldn't help but wonder about him. He'd appealed to her the minute she'd opened the door and looked up into his face. Not the most handsome man she'd ever seen, to be sure. His eyes were an odd shade of blue, so pale as to almost be gray, and his nose looked as if it had met a fist or two sometime in the past. But his voice was deep and soothing, he smiled easily and often. It had been comforting to have someone to wade through the boxes and files with, reassuring to know that someone would work with her to find answers to the many questions her father had left behind. Answers that could possibly lead to finding a killer. Mitch had certainly seemed to think so.

In the past, it had been her father who had done all of the frontline investigations into the actual crimes, she who had put it all in order. This was gruesome work. Not for the faint of heart.

Would she prove to have a faint heart, she wondered. In the end, would she be capable of alone doing what needed to be done to write the kind of books she had worked on with her dad?

For years Josh sheltered her from the ugliest realities of their work. Now there was no one to stand between her and the horror, the madness she'd be stirring up. Was she smart enough to do this on her own? Was she strong enough?

Time would tell, one way or another. She stood up and took one last look at the heavens, hoping she was up to the challenge of following in Josh's footsteps. Yes, it was difficult work. Yes, it was tiring, and at times the information she had made no sense at all. She'd never realized how like a giant, convoluted puzzle her father's work was. Sometimes it seemed like a maze with no exit. A story written in a foreign language, one you didn't know.

The work was interesting, absolutely. Intriguing, without question. And, too, just a little bit fun.

But there was always that bottom line, that behind every name there was a face and a story, a family waiting for closure.

And a killer waiting to be caught.

# Twelve

Cass leaned over to touch her toes, then straightened up and flexed her shoulders. Placing one foot on the outside wall of the garage, she pushed forward slightly, knee bent, to stretch a different set of muscles.

Amazing what a good night's sleep could do. She felt rested enough to crave a long run on the beach. It had been more than a week since she'd had a decent run, though it felt much longer.

She shook her head when she looked back on the past nine days, days that had held so much pain, so much horror for the families of those young women, in so short a time.

She took ten more minutes to properly stretch, then opened the back door and called in to Lucy.

"Luce! I'm going for a run. Are you sure you don't want to come with me?"

"I don't have running shoes," Lucy called back.

"I told you I have an extra pair if you want to borrow them. They should fit you."

209

"I'll take a rain check." Lucy appeared at the screen door. "I'm still greasy from the beach."

She held out an arm slick with suntan oil.

"You missed an excellent beach day, sleeping beauty."

"I needed the sleep more than I needed the sun."

"While you're gone, I'm going to shower all this stuff off and then I'll start dinner. I think you need a really wholesome dinner tonight."

"I thought last night's dinner of crabs and French fries was just perfect."

"Too much fat." Lucy wrinkled her nose. "But what are crabs without a little butter and a big bowl of fries with Old Bay? Now, tonight, we'll eat healthy."

"What exactly did you have in mind?" Cass eyed her suspiciously.

"Something yummy. I'll run to the fish market as soon as I get cleaned up. We'll have something broiled, maybe sea bass or tuna or whatever they have that looks good and is today-fresh. And a big salad."

"I think there are some fries left from last night."

"I tossed them. We had our bad fats for the week. Tonight it's healthy seafood and a salad."

"Sounds good. Fat or no fat." Cass leaned down to retie a shoe. "I'll be back in forty-five minutes or so."

"Do you have your key?"

"In my pocket. Why?"

"I want to lock the house while I shower and then when I go to the store."

"Good idea." Cass heard the click of the lock as she set off in the direction of the driveway.

Once on the sidewalk, she adjusted her sunglasses and began to jog slowly to the end of the street, five houses down. The house immediately to their right and the two houses nearest the corner were still vacant, the summer renters not having arrived yet. It was okay, Cass thought, she didn't mind not having neighbors. It was enough she had someone sharing her house.

Though she had to admit she didn't mind Lucy's presence. If anything, she was beginning to enjoy it. She'd forgotten what it was like to share living space with someone else, she'd been on her own so long.

On the one hand, it was nice. On the other, it reminded her of those awful days, the ones after she had lost her family and had gone to live with Lucy and Aunt

Kimmie and Uncle Pete. She and Lucy had shared a room for a few months, while Aunt Kimmie had the second floor finished off with two new bedrooms and one bath, so the girls could have their own rooms. It had been the worst time of Cass's life. And yet, in Lucy she'd found a true friend, in spite of their differences.

Cass jogged up the narrow wooden boardwalk onto the beach, reflecting on some of those differences. Lucy was now, always had been, supremely girly. Even as a child, Lucy's bathing suits had been pink, or pale blue, or white. She always wore ribbons in her hair, like her mother and her aunt, Cass's mother, did. She jumped rope occasionally, but spent most of her time at home reading or with her dolls, so it was no real surprise when she married young and began a family right away.

The only time Cass had ever seen her cousin sweat was when she played basketball. Everyone assumed Lucy wanted to play only because Cass did, but then she'd played with surprising aggression.

They'd been very close in high school, Cass reflected as she ran along the water's edge. They'd remained close until Lucy married that rat-bastard David. What had she seen in him, anyway? He wasn't a good conversationalist, he wasn't funny or particularly smart or even all that good-looking. What had Lucy seen in him?

Not that it mattered now, Cass thought as she ran a zigzag pattern around the towels of several sunbathers who lay on their blankets, wrapped in towels, the late-afternoon sun not nearly strong enough to ward off the chill.

"Hey! Cass!" someone called from behind.

She turned, to find Rick Cisco approaching.

"I thought that was you," he said as he jogged up to join her.

"You're a runner," she said, judging his practiced gait.

"When I have time. Today seemed like a good day to take a break and get in a few miles."

"It's a good day for it. Not too hot, the humidity hasn't kicked in yet."

"How far are you going?" he asked.

"As far as the next jetty. About another half mile."

"Mind if I tag along?"

"Suit yourself."

She broke into a run and he matched her pace.

They ran in silence, their running shoes

pounding softly against the sand, their breath coming in equal measure. When they reached the stone jetty, she stopped and looked out to sea.

"I usually walk out to the end," she told him.

"I'm game, as long as you don't mind the company."

She did, but she shrugged it off. *You can't always be alone,* she reminded herself. *Sometimes you have to share your space with other people. This week seems to be one of those times. Buck up and get used to it.*

She looped her thumbs in the pockets of her running shorts and walked the length of the jetty, picking her way across the rocks. At the end, she searched for the flattest rock she could find, and sat on it. She glanced up at Rick, who had followed her, and patted the rock next to her.

"It's not exactly cushy, but it's about as flat as you'll find."

He looked down at the proffered seat uncertainly, then lowered himself carefully to the rock. His long legs hung over the side and his feet rested on the rocks below.

"This is nice," he said. "Great view."

She pointed off to the left. "The charter boats are starting to come in."

"What do they fish for?"

"Tuna. Blues. Whatever is running. They have to go pretty far out for both, this time of year."

"You do a lot of fishing?"

"None, actually. Not at all."

"Oh. You sounded so knowledgeable."

"My dad had a charter. He used to go out every day. He loved it. He was such a smart man, he could have done anything he wanted. All he ever wanted was to fish." She smiled, remembering Bob Burke's love of the sea.

"Does he still fish?"

"He died."

"You lost both parents?" He turned to her. "I'm sorry."

"On the same day," she said softly.

"What?"

"They died on the same day."

"I'm sorry, Cass. Was it an accident?"

"They were murdered. My parents and my little sister."

"Jesus, that's rough. I'm so sorry . . . I had no idea . . ." He flushed as if embarrassed to have heard it. "Did they find the person?"

"Yes. A transient, guy who'd been hanging around town for a few months. My dad used to give him fish when he had a really good catch. That always killed me, you know? That my dad was so nice to this guy and he repaid his kindness by . . ." She shook her head slightly and turned her face from him. "Anyway, he was tried and convicted and sent to prison. He died about . . . I think it was maybe ten years ago or so. Cancer."

"I'm sorry," he said again. "I just don't know what else to say."

"It's okay. You had no way of knowing. Thanks." She stared out toward the horizon, not able to make eye contact with him. All of a sudden, he felt too close, though there was a space of almost three feet between them. She felt suffocated.

She stood abruptly.

"I need to get back to the house. Lucy's making dinner," she muttered, and turned toward the beach.

"Who's Lucy?" He swung his legs up over the rock and stood up. "Roommate?"

"My cousin. She's staying with me. Actually, she and I own the house together. It was our grandmother's."

*Oh, shut up,* she told herself. *You're starting to babble. Best to just go.*

She was disconcerted to find him behind her when she jumped down from the jetty onto the wet sand.

"Running or walking?" he asked.

"Running." She took off down the beach.

She figured he'd keep on going when she got to Brighton Avenue. He did not.

"This is where I came in, too," he said.

"Oh. Where are you staying?"

She slowed to a walk as she approached the wooden boards.

"At the Brighton Inn."

"Oh. Nice place." She nodded and continued walking briskly. That meant he'd probably walk up Brighton, past her house, to Atlantic.

"It is nice. The rooms are a bit old-fashioned, but it's homey and the food is terrific."

"The restaurant is pretty well known. I've eaten there many times over the years, though not recently. They were always known for their seafood, which is to be expected, considering that it's a block and a half from the ocean. Be grateful it isn't July or August."

"Why's that?"

"The humidity can get pretty fierce down here. Last I heard, the Brighton still hadn't installed central air."

"Well, let's hope we find our guy soon so that I'm long gone come the dog days."

They paused at the corner for traffic, then crossed the street. At the third house from the corner, a large brown-and-black dog barked loudly when they passed. Rick stepped between the animal and Cass but never broke stride.

"It's okay, June-bug, it's okay," Cass called to the dog, and it sauntered across the short patch of sand that served as its front yard, wagging its tail languidly. When it reached Cass, it sat in the middle of the sidewalk and she petted it affectionately.

"You're a good girl, Junie," she crooned as June-bug looked up at her with adoring eyes.

"Hey, Cassie." The screen door opened and a woman in her seventies came down the steps slowly. "Grab her collar for me, would you?"

"I've got her, Madge. She's not going anywhere."

"Not even if she wanted to. Too much arthritis and not enough energy to chase cars these days." Cass's neighbor laughed dryly. "And I'm not just talking about the dog."

The woman carried a leash and walked favoring one leg.

"This damn knee of mine . . ."

"I thought you had it replaced last year."

"That was the right knee. Guess I'm

going to have to break down and have the left one done now, too. I'd hoped I was done with all that. Anyone who tells you there's nothing to it is flat-out lying to you." Madge leaned over to grab hold of her dog. "Now, who's this nice-looking young man?"

"Rick Cisco, ma'am." He smiled and held out a hand for her. She took it and used it to hold on to while she snapped the leash onto the dog's collar.

"You're a tall one, aren't you? Not too many young men around here taller than Cassie. She's tall for a girl, isn't she. But you've noticed that, I'm —"

"Ah, Madge, Rick is with the FBI."

"Nothing wrong with that, honey."

"I mean, he's only here to work with our department."

"Oh, on that serial killer? Evil business, that is." Madge shook her head. "I lived through it the last time, back in, what was it, 1980?"

"Summer of 1979," Cass told her, but Madge didn't appear to have heard.

"Horrible that was, back then. God almighty, you were afraid to stick your head out the door, never knew where he was going to strike next." The woman shivered. "Worst summer of my life. Never seen anything like it. I was hoping I'd never see the likes of it again, and here we are, that evil business just like before."

She looked up at Rick.

"You think the FBI can catch him?"

"We're working with your police department and we'll do our best to track him down."

"Good, 'cause they didn't catch him the last time. Didn't catch him and now he's back."

"Madge, we haven't determined if this is the same killer. There's a very good chance we're dealing with a copycat."

Madge shook her white head. "It's the same. He's back. I can feel him." The older woman shivered. "Just like he was standing right next to me."

"Well, the Bayside Strangler or a copycat, we're doing our best to find him," Rick assured her.

Cass took a step or two away, and Rick followed.

"In the meantime, Madge, you keep your doors and windows locked and keep that watchdog of yours," Cass said.

"Oh, some watchdog Junie is. Say, is that Lucy Donovan? Not Donovan anymore, though. What's the married name?"

"Webb."

"Right, right. She married Lloyd Webb's grandson. Summer people, as I remember. My stars, I haven't seen her in a couple of summers. Are her boys with her? It's been awful quiet, I haven't heard kids." Madge craned her neck to get a better look at the car that had just pulled into Cass's driveway. "I heard the house next door here is rented for the summer, but no one's been around yet. Don't know if the people have kids or not."

"Lucy's boys are at camp for a few weeks. I'll tell her you said hi."

"You tell her I said for her to stop by and see me some morning. I always liked Lucy, she's a fun girl. Always makes me laugh." Madge waved in the direction of Cass's house. "Yoo-hoo, Lucy . . ."

"Hi, Madge!" Lucy called back as she opened the trunk of the car and began unloading several bags of groceries.

"I'd better go and help her. See you later, Madge," Cass said as she turned toward home.

"Nice meeting you," Rick told the woman.

"Nice meeting you, too, FBI man." Madge waved.

"What do you think of Madge's theory that this is the old Bayside Strangler back again?" he whispered as they walked away.

"She could well be right about that. Though usually her theories are a bit more suspect. Like the one about the soul of Winston Churchill having entered Ronald Reagan's body in 1967 and convinced him to run for president."

"Huh?"

"Don't ever discuss politics with her. You've been warned."

"You are just in time." Lucy directed her comment to Cass, but was looking directly at Rick.

"Lucy, this is Rick Cisco. He's the agent the FBI sent to work with us. I ran into him on the beach. Rick, this is my cousin, Lucy Webb."

"Pleasure," he said. "Can I give you a hand?"

"You're a savior." She smiled prettily. "I just did my nails."

"Hey, never let it be said that the federal government failed you in your time of need." He lifted the remaining three bags from the trunk of the car. "Lead the way."

Lucy beamed and led him up the driveway. Cass picked up the bag Lucy'd set on the ground and apparently forgot about. She followed the mini-parade into the house.

"I thought you were only going to the fish market," Cass said as she put the bag on the counter.

"Well, as long as I was out, I figured I might as well shop for the week. That way, I can take advantage of the good beach days we're supposed to have this week." She smiled at Rick. "Must work on my tan."

"I can see that you've spent some time in the sun. You've got some nice color."

"Oh, do you think so?" Lucy held her arms out in front of her.

Cass stood behind Rick and rolled her eyes. Lucy saw and laughed out loud.

"So, where are you staying?"

"The Brighton."

"It used to be real nice." Lucy started to unpack a bag.

"It still is." Rick turned to Cass. "Well, I'm going to get out of your hair. I'll see you in the morning. We'll get together with the county lab person . . ."

"Tasha Welsh." Cass nodded. "I'll give her a call this afternoon and see what her schedule is for tomorrow."

"What time do you think you'll be in your office?"

"I'll be there by seven. No later."

"I'll see you then."

"Can you stay and have dinner with us?" Lucy asked him.

"No, no, but thank you."

"Seriously. We have tons of food. I'm used to buying for an all-male house and haven't figured out how to cut down on the portions for just me and Cass. Really. It wouldn't be an imposition." Lucy smiled at Cass. "Would it, Cassie?"

"Not at all." Cass smiled, too, between clenched teeth.

"Thanks anyway, but I'll take a rain check. I have to go clean up."

"So does Cassie." Lucy grinned. "I insist."

"Cass?" he asked tentatively.

"Oh, it's fine. Really. And Lucy is a wonderful cook."

"If you're sure . . ."

"Sure. Go on back to the Inn and change, and be back here . . . when, Luce, an hour?"

Lucy nodded. "Perfect. Dinner should be on the table by then."

"Okay. Great. I'll see you both then." Rick left by the back door.

"I'm going to kill you," Cass said when Rick was safely out of earshot.

"No you're not. You're going to thank me someday. I saw the way he was looking at you."

Lucy opened the refrigerator and tucked away cartons of yogurt. "That is one hot guy, Cassie-girl. You won't find many like him wandering around Bowers Inlet in the off-season, that's for sure. I did you a favor. Anyone could see he's interested in you. He was itching to find a way to spend some quality time with you. I'm just helping him out a little."

"Oh, please." Cass shook her head and went upstairs.

"You have forty-five minutes, Cassie. And I'm doing your face . . ."

As it turned out, there'd been no time for a facial makeover, nor, for that matter, time for dinner.

Cass had barely gotten out of the shower when her cell phone rang. She wrapped a towel around her body and rummaged in her bag, which she'd left on the floor in her bedroom.

"Burke," she said right before the call went to voice mail.

She listened quietly, without reaction.

"Where?" she asked, then, "I know where to find Agent Cisco. We'll see you in ten."

She towel-dried her hair, and instead of the pretty shirt she'd been planning on wearing — pale yellow with a little ruffle at the hem, so different from the plain white or dark-colored T-shirts she favored for work — Cass slipped a navy tee over her head. She pulled a pair of jeans from the dresser and stuck her feet into her running shoes, then hoisted her bag, checked for her gun, her holster, and her camera, and took the steps two at a time.

"I thought you were going to wear that cute little —" Lucy took in Cass's demeanor and paused. "Do not tell me . . ."

"Over in Hasboro. I'll wait for Cisco at the car." She grabbed a few bottles of water from the refrigerator and some granola bars from the cupboard.

"Cass, eat something. Look, dinner is ready . . ."

"I can't, Luce. I'm sorry, but I can't eat and then go there and look at —"

"Oh, my God, of course you can't. I don't know what I was thinking. I'll make up plates for you and Rick, bring him back with you when . . . well, when you've finished up."

Cass looked out the window in time to see Rick's car pull up out front.

"I'll see you later." Cass went out the front door.

Rick had just opened the car door and

226

had one foot on the curb when Cass ran down the drive.

"I just got a call from Chief Denver," she told him as she reached him.

"Where this time?"

"Hasboro. Two towns south."

"Get in," he told her as he climbed back into the car and slammed the door.

She opened the passenger-side door just enough for her to slide in. She handed him a granola bar as he shifted into drive and hit the road.

"Lucy said she'd hold dinner. This will have to do for now."

He watched from the shadows as the car pulled away and took the corner on two wheels. If he leaned back against the corner of the house next door — gratefully, this one had yet to be rented for the summer — he could see into the kitchen but not be seen.

This was good. He wanted to watch her for a while.

She passed by the kitchen window several times and he wondered what common little task she might be engaged in.

Not that it mattered.

Soon enough, nothing else would matter.

They'd be together — finally, together —

and this time he would get it right. He had to. He'd waited so long . . .

His hand slid into his pocket and he fingered the key to the room at the pretty bed-and-breakfast in Cape May where he'd made reservations for the two of them. They'd spend a few wonderful days together there. He'd already booked them on one of those pelagic boat trips for tomorrow, so that she could watch her beloved seabirds in their natural habitat. He'd bought her new binoculars — a really special pair that had a camera built right in, so she could take all the pictures she wanted. Then after a few days, they'd head off to the Outer Banks, where he'd rented a house for the rest of the summer.

He sighed. This would be the best summer of his life. He just knew it.

Everything he'd gone through to get to this moment, it had all been worth it. He thought of all the ones who'd tried, over the years, to trick him, all the ones who'd pretended to be her. Well, he'd taught them a lesson, hadn't he?

She walked past the window again.

Oh, but this one . . . this one. This one . . .

*This is the one.*

# Thirteen

Rick followed Cass's directions to the inlet where the latest body had been found. He parked on the road and together they walked over coarse yellow stone down to the bulkhead where a crowd of law-enforcement types had gathered. As they approached the group, the body began to come into view.

Cass had just reached the fringes, close enough to see the body of the young woman, close enough to see the arms flung over the head, the dark hair spread out like a cape, when one of the members of the Hasboro police force stepped forward.

"Hey, Caplan . . ." Cass began, and he grabbed her by the arm to halt her forward motion.

"Don't bother, Burke, this isn't your crime scene," he said unpleasantly. "You're out of your jurisdiction here."

"Well, I know that," she hemmed slightly, taken aback by his reaction to her presence, "but Chief Denver called and asked me to —"

"Denver has no say here, either. As far as

I'm concerned, you're a civilian here. And that makes you a trespasser. I suggest you leave. I'd hate to have to arrest you."

"What the hell, Caplan?" She shook off his arm.

"The way we see it, you've had several shots at this guy, and you've come up with squat. Now you can step back and let the big boys show you how to catch a serial killer."

Out of the corner of her eye, she saw several of the other Hasboro cops shake their heads and look away in embarrassment, while a few of them smirked in her direction.

"Look, I've been at several of the scenes, I can —"

"You can turn ass and go back to Bowers. We don't need you."

She shrugged and turned to Rick.

"I'll call Lucy and have her come down to pick me up. You'll want to stay."

"Who are you?" The Hasboro detective pointed to Rick.

"Special Agent Rick Cisco. FBI," Rick responded stonily. "Who's in charge here?"

"Well, it ain't you." Caplan folded his arms over his chest. "I do not believe the Hasboro PD requested assistance from the FBI. You can leave with Burke."

Rick stood quietly and watched the detective posture.

"Detective Burke, I'll give you a ride back." Rick motioned to the road.

"But . . ."

He took her elbow, and she shook off his hand.

"Not now," he whispered through clenched teeth.

Cass turned and took two steps before almost colliding with Tasha Welsh.

"Where do you think you're going?" the tech asked her.

"I've been uninvited. Territorial little bastards, those Hasboro cops," Cass seethed.

Tasha shrugged. "Their loss. You home later tonight?"

Cass nodded.

Tasha leaned close to her. "I'll let you know if I find anything that might be of interest to you."

To Caplan, Tasha said, "Well, you can't kick me off your turf, so how's about you just step aside and let me do my job. I don't suppose you've gotten a decent photographer on your force?"

"Stupid fuck," Cass muttered as she opened the passenger door and got into Rick's car. "I can't believe he all but threatened to arrest us."

She called Chief Denver and was annoyed to get his voice mail. She left messages for him at his office, his home, and on his cell, then tossed the phone into her bag in disgust.

Rick started the engine at the same time he speed-dialed a number on his cell.

"John, it's Cisco. We have a situation in New Jersey we need to talk about. Call me back." He left the terse message as he made a U-turn in the middle of the road.

"I imagine my boss will have a few words for the Hasboro PD before the night is over."

"I can't believe you're taking this so calmly."

"It's not as if it's the first time I've been asked to leave a crime scene." He checked his rearview mirror before making a turn onto the highway. "Looks as if we have an escort."

Cass turned in her seat. A Hasboro cruiser followed several car lengths behind them.

"Arrogant bastards." She smacked her hand on the dashboard.

"Don't let them get to you. We'll take care of it."

"How do you propose to do that?"

"I won't. John will."

"Is John all-powerful?" she said sarcastically.

"Pretty much." His eyes never left the road. "Look, this happens sometimes — high-profile case, the local agency doesn't want to share the limelight. They need to be put in their place, so to speak. But we've been told not to make it an issue, to let the brass tell the locals how it's going to be. That way, you're on the scene, you're not pushing anyone around, you're not dictating to anyone, you're not the bad guy, you can still work with these people. That's the way my boss wants to handle things, that's how it's done in our unit."

"Your unit? Is that different from your average, everyday FBI unit?"

The slightest bit of a smile almost touched one corner of his mouth.

"The agents in our unit report directly to our boss. And he reports only to the director."

"So I guess that's a yes."

He almost smiled again.

She was still seething when he pulled up in front of her house.

"I'm going to drop you off, then I'll head back to Hasboro. I expect I'll hear from John within the next ten minutes. I want to

233

be on the scene as soon as possible."

"I can't believe they wouldn't even let us look at the body."

"You looked at it."

"Yeah, but I didn't get close enough to see . . ." She paused. "Did you see it? Her? The victim?"

"Yes."

"Did something look off to you?" She had gathered her bag onto her lap. "I showed you the photos from all of the other crime scenes. Did you notice how this woman's face was straight up, not turned to the side, like the others were?"

"I didn't have enough time to notice much of anything," he said.

"I don't know, it's a little thing. The other victims were posed so exactly, they could have been superimposed upon one another. This one . . ." She sighed. "Then again, one of Hasboro's finest could have moved her."

"We'll find out if one did."

She opened the car door and got out, slammed it closed, then leaned into the open window.

"If you don't get a golden ticket onto the crime scene, stop back. Lucy was saving dinner."

"I might do that. In any event, I'll keep

in touch. I'll let you know anything I find out. You suppose your friend, the tech, will remember to call you?"

Cass nodded confidently. "She'll call. She's solid."

"I guess I'll talk to you later."

Cass stepped back from the car and turned to the house.

"Bastard Caplan," she growled as she walked up the front steps.

She opened the screen door and walked across the porch to the front door. The outside light was off.

Odd.

It was supposed to come on automatically, at dusk. Maybe the bulb had blown out. She'd ask Lucy to pick up a new one if she had time this week.

Between visits to the beach, of course.

Cass smiled to herself. Her cousin was a piece of work. On the one hand, Lucy was kind and helpful and trying hard to deal with a bad situation; on the other, she was self-centered and frivolous and thoughtless.

And, Cass realized, she loved her in spite of it all.

She fished in her bag for her keys, then gave up and knocked on the door. She leaned against the jamb and waited.

"Lucy?" She knocked again.

There was a banging sound from inside. Cass dropped her handbag and searched through it quickly and found the key and her gun.

She jammed the key into the lock and turned it with frantic fingers, then she stepped into the semi-darkness, the skin at the back of her neck prickling. Her eyes had yet to adjust to the light, but movement to her right, in the living room, drew her attention.

"Don't move," she said firmly.

The figure on the floor rose quickly and sprang for the kitchen before she could react.

"Police," she shouted, as the figure began to disappear into the dark room.

She dodged the chair he flung in her direction, then tripped over it.

Cursing, she aimed and fired off two shots. She was almost to the back door when she heard a moan from the front of the house.

The sound stopped her cold in her tracks.

"Lucy?" She turned slowly and walked back toward the living room.

"Lucy?"

She switched on the hall light.

"Oh, holy mother of God."

Lucy lay on the living room floor, her dark hair spread out around her head like a halo.

"No, no, no, no . . ." Cass rushed to her and dropped to her knees. "Lucy, no. No."

"Cass?" Rick called from the front door. "I heard shots. What's going on?"

"Lucy, please . . ." Cass sought a pulse.

"Jesus, Cass . . ." Rick stepped into the room.

"Call for help. Call now. I don't think she's breathing." Cass began mouth-to-mouth while Rick summoned help.

"Let me try," he said, but Cass waved him away and continued to force air into her cousin's lungs.

"I think I'm losing her." Cass looked up frantically.

"My turn." Rick eased Cass out of the way and took over as the sirens began to scream in the distance.

"Don't die, Lucy," Cass pleaded wildly. "Please don't die . . ."

# Fourteen

Too anxious to sit, Cass stood against the cinder-block wall in the emergency room of Bayshore Memorial Hospital and did something she had not done since she was nine years old. She chewed her fingernails to the quick.

"Here." Rick handed her a can of soda. "I don't know what you drink, but this is the only kind they had left in the machine, so I guess it doesn't matter. It's cold — almost cold, anyway — and it's wet."

She nodded her thanks and held the can close to her body. Rick took it back, popped the tab, and returned it to her.

"You'll get more out of it if it's open."

"Thanks," she whispered, then took a few small sips. "What do you suppose they're doing to her?"

*Trying to keep her alive* occurred to him.

Instead, he replied, "I'm sure they're checking her out thoroughly."

"I should know that. I do know that." She swallowed hard. "It's different when it's you. When it's someone you're close to."

Rick gave her shoulder a squeeze intended to reassure. He doubted that it did.

"Detective Burke?" a nurse called from the desk.

"Here." Cass raised a hand and hurried over. "How is she? Will she be all right?"

The nurse looked puzzled, then looked at the clipboard in her hand.

"Are you here as part of an official investigation . . . or . . . ?"

"She's my cousin. Lucy Webb."

"Are you the next of kin?"

"Yes, yes . . ." Cass paused. "Oh. Actually, no. She's married but —"

"I'll need to speak with her husband."

"They're separated. They're getting divorced. Right now she's living with me."

"If he's still legally her husband, I'll need to speak with him. Do you know how I can contact him?"

Cass tried to stare the woman down. It didn't work.

"I have his number," Cass finally acquiesced.

"Good." The nurse handed Cass a small pad of white paper and a pen, and waited while Cass wrote the number.

"Please. Just tell me if she's going to be

all right." Cass tried to soften her stance.

"She's breathing on her own," the nurse said.

Rick stepped up, his badge extended.

"Agent Cisco, FBI. Nurse . . ." His eyes scanned her name tag. ". . . Natale. The patient is a victim of a violent crime. I will need to speak with the doctor treating Ms. Webb at the earliest possible time."

The nurse glanced first at Rick, then at his credentials, before looking back at Cass, who had not moved.

"I'll ask Dr. Peterman to speak with you as soon as he's finished."

Rick nodded. "Thank you."

"And thank you," Cass said softly.

"Don't mention it. Now come over and sit." Rick took her arm. "We don't know how long we'll have to wait."

"You don't have to wait with me. I know you want to get back to Hasboro, to the scene of the crime," she said, as if not realizing the scene of the most recent crime was her own house.

"I doubt they miss me." He smiled gently. "Besides, I'd rather keep you company. It might be a long night. Try to relax a little. I know it's hard, not knowing what's going on."

"They're going to call that boneheaded

240

husband of hers," Cass said on an exhale. "I wonder if he'll come."

"He'll come. He'd have to be made of stone not to care about what's happened to her. She's still his wife."

"Hopefully not for much longer."

"Sounds as if there's a little conflict here."

"No conflict. He's just not the man for her." She raised an eyebrow. "I'm waiting for you to tell me that that's not my call."

"I'm not going near it, Burke."

"In case you think I'm being harsh on the guy, she doesn't think he's the man for her, either."

"Her choice."

"Right." Cass nibbled on a nail. "He's been cheating on her. He's totally wiped out her self-confidence."

"She seemed pretty self-confident to me."

"Appearances can be deceiving."

"I guess." He looked down at her and saw a woman ready to pass out from fatigue. "Why don't you try to get a little rest while you can? Here, lean on me."

"You're a pretty good guy, Rick Cisco." She rested her head against his upper arm, then realized what she had done. Uncomfortable with such intimacy, she moved her head slightly so that it leaned against the wall instead of him.

"For an FBI agent." He moved her head back to where it had been, telling her, "Relax. I don't bite."

"I've got no problem with the FBI." She ignored what he'd done and closed her eyes, too tired to make an issue out of it, though still uneasy with the close proximity to this man who was still pretty much a stranger. "You've been . . . respectful. Kind."

"Let's see what the Hasboro cops are calling me in the morning," he said, and she tried to smile at his attempt at humor.

A young boy with his arm in a cast came out from one of the treatment rooms, his face wet with tears, holding his mother's hand tightly with his good hand.

A young mother walked her sobbing baby back and forth across the lobby in an effort to comfort her. The automatic doors to the emergency entrance opened silently and a woman with a bruised and swollen face came in, aided by an older woman who wore a gauzy wrap skirt over her bathing suit, and a worried expression on her face.

Cass quietly watched each drama unfold. After a long ten minutes, she asked,

"Where did you come from?"

"Maryland."

"No, no. Tonight. You dropped me off at the house and left. Why did you come back?"

"I never got off your street. I was almost to the stop sign when I saw your neighbor come out of her house . . . the older woman who lives up the street?"

"Madge."

"Right. Well, she came out her front door and was moving about as fast as she could in the direction of the corner, so I stopped to see what was going on. She said her dog —"

"June-bug."

"Right. Apparently there was a stray cat in their backyard all afternoon, giving old Junie fits. The first chance she got, she took off out the front door and chased the cat around the corner, Madge in pursuit, with her cane in one hand and the dog's leash in the other. I parked the car and chased the dog. Found her a few houses up, the cat glaring smugly from the roof of someone's car. I brought the dog back and was handing her over when I heard the gunshots."

"Did you see him?" Cass sat up. "He took off out the back."

243

"No. I didn't see anyone. Honestly, I just ran toward the house and came inside." His arm felt suddenly cooler without her head resting against it. "Tell me again what happened."

Cass repeated the story, the third time she'd done so since arriving at the hospital. The first was for Chief Denver, who'd met her at the ER and stayed long enough to make certain Lucy was still alive before leaving to personally oversee the investigation at Cass's house. The second had been to the officer assigned to take her official statement.

She'd just gotten to the part where Lucy's attacker ran out the back door, when she looked up to see Tasha Welsh coming down the hall.

"Cass, I heard what happened. I'm so sorry. Is your cousin all right?" Tasha took the chair next to Cass's and turned it so she could sit facing her.

"We haven't heard a thing. She's still with the doctors."

"What a horror." Tasha shook her head. "Are you okay?"

"I'll be fine."

"Was it our guy . . . our killer?"

"I have to think so, but at the same time . . ." Cass hesitated, as if thinking it

244

through. "He'd already struck once tonight. He's never hit two women in the same night before. It doesn't make sense to me."

"Well, here's something else that won't make sense." Tasha leaned forward. "The other victim, the one in Hasboro? She wasn't raped."

"She wasn't?" Cass frowned. "But all the others were."

"Right. And something else. Remember I told you about the fibers?"

"The fibers you found in the hair of the other victims?"

Tasha nodded.

"Pink ribbon, did I tell you the lab reports came back? Pink satin ribbon. Real silk, not synthetic. Every one of the other victims had trace of it, and get this — the fibers matched perfectly."

"Same kind of ribbon?"

"Same ribbon. We were able to trace it to the manufacturer. They stopped making that ribbon eighteen years ago." Tasha tapped a finger on Cass's knee for emphasis. "But this one tonight? Nada. No fibers."

"You're sure?"

"It was the first thing I looked for. There was something, I don't know, awkward about the way he left this one. It looked different to me somehow."

Cass nodded in agreement. "I thought the same thing. The legs weren't really right."

"Exactly. Similar, but not the same. A little haphazard. As if he was in a hurry and didn't take the time to get it exactly right. Doesn't make sense, does it?"

Cass looked at Rick.

"A copycat, maybe?" she suggested.

"Maybe he was in a hurry. We'll need the report from the investigating officers to see what else they found," he said.

"Well, don't hold your breath until they offer to hand that over," Cass reminded him.

"I can get it," Tasha told them. "Might take me a few days . . ."

"Maybe your boss can get it sooner," Cass said to Rick, who nodded.

"I'll give him another call in the morning if I haven't heard from him."

"And another thing," Tasha said. "In the past, the killer has made an effort to hide the bodies somewhat. This one over in Hasboro, he left her right out in plain view. Right there on the lower dock."

"Like I said, maybe he was in a hurry," Rick said. "Maybe he was afraid he'd be discovered if he took too long."

"Not his style," Tasha insisted. "If he was afraid of being seen, he would have left her someplace else. I think he wanted the body to be found, and fast."

"How long had the body been there, you think?" Cass asked.

"I heard one of the detectives say that the family in the first house there off the bulkhead had gone out crabbing on their boat around three," Tasha replied. "They found her when they came back, around five-thirty. So she'd been placed there somewhere within that time frame."

"He was taking a chance, wasn't he?" Cass said thoughtfully. "Broad daylight, the middle of the afternoon? It's not like him to be that careless."

"He wasn't careless," Rick said.

Cass looked up at him. "He wasn't?"

"He didn't get caught, did he? So far, no one's come forward to say they saw someone there."

"You could easily get away with it," Tasha nodded, "if there were no other boats out at that end of the dock. And obviously, none were."

"Plus, it's early in the season. Not as many people around yet," Cass said thoughtfully. "But still, why would he take such a chance?"

"I think Tasha's right. He wanted her found," Rick told them. "And he wanted her found today."

"Why do you suppose that would be important to him?" Tasha asked.

"Maybe because he had another target in mind. Maybe this victim was incidental to him," Cass thought aloud. "Or he could have wanted to draw our attention to her, and —"

"And away from someone else," Rick finished her thought.

"Lucy," Cass said flatly.

"Could be. He needed to get you out of the way, so he provided a diversion," Rick suggested. "She fits the type exactly. Right age, right build. Pretty woman with lots of long dark hair. If he's been watching her, he'd know she lives with a cop. He'd have had to lure you out of there to get to her. How best to lure a cop? With a dead body. Smart on his part."

Cass winced at the thought of another innocent woman losing her life being considered nothing more than a means to an end.

"But not smart enough to realize that he went out of my jurisdiction, or that the Hasboro boys were so territorial they'd send me packing the minute I arrived."

"You can thank those Hasboro boys and their petty mentality for saving Lucy's life," he pointed out.

Cass put her face in her hands.

"Oh, God," she said, "if I'd stayed longer we'd probably be sitting in the morgue right now."

The headlights illuminated the wooden gate and he left the car in gear when he went to push it aside. Then he drove through the opening, got back out, and closed the gate. No need for a well-meaning somebody to come along and wonder who might be wandering about this time of night.

He drove with only his fog lights on, lest some passing car see the reflection from the brighter beams and call the police. Not that he thought the police were merely sitting around this night, waiting for something to do. No, he'd seen to that, all right.

The dirt road wound about a quarter mile into the marsh before splitting off in two directions. He took the road to the left and followed it for about five hundred feet. Sensing he was near his destination, he slowed, then brought the car to a stop. He killed the lights and the engine, then opened the glove box and took out the first-aid kit he always carried with him. He got out of the car and went straight to the trunk, from which he took a suitcase. He walked along the path to the blind and carried the case with him up the steps to the shelter. It was awkward, because the case was heavy now after all these years, and one of the fingers on his left hand hurt like hell. He placed the case on the floor of the blind, then climbed in behind it.

He sat next to it and opened the first-aid kit. Taking the small flashlight from his pocket, he shined it into the case. He assembled a small bottle of peroxide and a roll of bandages in front of him; then, holding the flashlight between his teeth, he unwrapped the strip of his shirt he'd previously tied around the throbbing finger. He poured peroxide over the ragged wound to clean it, then wrapped it with the gauze.

It was a minor wound, and it wasn't the first time he'd been shot. But it was the first time he'd been shot by a woman.

And that woman. *That woman . . .*

He felt a terrible burning behind his eyes, and his hands began to shake. Hatred rolled through him, so strong and so fierce, he almost became nauseated.

If it weren't for her, he and his love would be together right now. On their way to Cape May, to start their life together.

If it weren't for her, everything would be all right right now. *Right now . . .*

But instead, he was alone, hiding like a frightened animal in a dark swamp.

And his love . . . oh, his poor love . . .

Well, that was all *her* fault, too. If it weren't for *her,* his love wouldn't be . . .

He paused, remembering the way his love had tried to fight him. Why had she done that? He hadn't planned on hurting her. Why didn't she understand that?

His fingers touched his face, outlined the scratches her fingernails had made.

Why had she been fighting him?

If she hadn't tried to fight, he wouldn't have had to hit her so many times.

If she hadn't tried to scream, he wouldn't have had to put his hands around her throat and . . .

But he hadn't wanted to hurt her, never meant to hurt her — he loved her! He would have stopped, he told himself, he wouldn't have tightened his hold on her, if the other one hadn't come in, waving that damn gun around. He'd been confused then.

For a moment, he'd forgotten where he was and whom he'd been with. A fog had seemed to roll through him, clouding his mind. He'd watched his hands at her throat as if in slow motion, and it seemed as if they belonged to someone else.

By the time his head had cleared, it was already too late. He was dodging bullets, running for the door, and he'd had to leave her there, on the floor.

He was sick with the knowledge that he had only himself to blame.

He should have killed *that* one — the other one — when he'd had the chance.

# Fifteen

Regan was on her second cup of coffee when the doorbell rang on Monday morning. She glanced at the clock: 7:45.

"I've got some good news," Mitch told her when she opened the door, "and some . . . well, some theories."

"Give me the good news first." She waved him in and he followed her down the hall into the kitchen. "Then you can give me theories."

"The good news is that I have names for two more of the victims on your father's mystery list."

Mitch set his black case on the floor next to the kitchen table and took out a folder.

"May 21, 1983. Pittsburgh, Pennsylvania. Elaine Marchand. Age twenty-nine." He glanced up at her. "Want to take a wild guess on the cause of death?"

"Strangulation. After having been sexually assaulted."

"The file didn't specify the order, but that would be my guess."

"What else do you have there?" She

253

leaned over to peek, and he folded the paper to shield his notes.

"Depends. Are you going to drink all that coffee yourself?" he asked.

"Sorry. I'll get you a cup." She went to the cupboard and took out a mug. "You were saying . . ."

"Charlotte, North Carolina. February 1, 1986. Raquel Sheriden." He watched her pour the coffee and waited until she turned back to him. "Age . . ."

"Late twenties, early thirties. Raped and strangled."

"You're good at this," he deadpanned. "Ever think about working for the government? I hear the FBI is looking for a few good agents."

She smiled and handed him the mug.

"I'm going to go out on a limb here and guess that none of these murders have been solved."

"You really are good at this." He sipped the hot coffee carefully.

"Where did you get all the info?"

"From the Bureau computer files." He poured half-and-half into the cup and stirred it with the spoon she'd used. "And that's not all I got."

"What else?"

"I have a list of over forty other uncannily similar, unsolved murders that have occurred over the past twenty-five years. Same MO. All different parts of the country. Heaviest in the south for several of those years, though. We'll have to take a look at that."

"Forty!" Regan's eyes widened. "Forty . . ."

"And those were only the ones I was able to find with ease. God knows how many there might be that were never entered into the system."

"So there could be more."

"There could be way more," he said soberly. "Now, of course, we have some work to do to determine if these others were in fact likely victims of our man. We'll have to take a look at each case individually, but the coincidences are uncanny."

"What about these other places . . ." She searched the table for the original list, found it on the bottom of the pile. "Turkey, Panama, Croatia . . ." She looked up at him. "How do we find out about those places?"

"That will be a little trickier, but I have someone at the Bureau working on that. In the meantime, look here." He took two maps from his case and spread one out on the table, moving the coffee cup out of the way. "This is a map of the United States. I've circled in red all of the cities we talked about, but it's a little hard to see, so I bought some colored pushpins. Is there a place we can hang this?"

"How about over there on the basement door?"

"Works for me." He tacked the upper corners to the door. "This will be fine, as long as no one wants to go downstairs."

"Show me." She pointed to the map.

"Let me get the pins in place. We'll start by pinpointing the places on your dad's list with red pins."

"The known victims of the Bayside Strangler."

"Right." He proceeded to place red tacks into the map. "Now, for those murders along the Jersey Shore, I'm placing one red tack to represent all, since it was basically one place. Then we had Pittsburgh . . . Charlotte . . . Corona . . . Memphis . . ."

Regan stepped closer to take a look.

"Are we going to assume that the dates and places on that list represent murders?"

He nodded. "I think it's a safe assumption. When you look at the whole picture, everything points that way."

Mitch leaned back against the counter. "I think we agree the Bayside Strangler and the man who committed these other murders are the same person."

"It certainly looks that way."

"And I think that whoever he is, and for reasons that we don't yet understand, he wrote to your father over the years." Mitch walked back to the table for his mug. " 'Hey, Landry, remember me?' "

"He sent Dad notes to keep him up-to-date on his activities. Bragging about his exploits. And my dad started to keep a record of when he received them, and where they were postmarked."

"We need to find the rest of your father's files and see what he did with all of this information."

"He would have turned them over to someone," Regan said. "Something like this, so many victims in so many areas, he'd have gone straight to the FBI. He'd have kept copies of the letters, but he wouldn't have kept this to himself."

"I think we'd have better success searching the file boxes here than we would at the Bureau. Without knowing where he sent the information or to whom, or when, there's no telling where it might be now. I'll ask John Mancini to have someone there in the office look into it, but it's such a long shot, it's almost not worth the time.

Unless an official investigation was started and documented, it will be impossible. With the passage of all these years, you have offices closing or moving, agents dying, retiring, or relocating. Your father's files may be a mess, but we're fairly certain that somewhere in the midst of it all we'll find what we're looking for. We have no such assurance relying on the Bureau records."

Regan studied the list again.

"These dates range from the early eighties right through the late nineties. My guess would be that he passed it along as soon as he realized what was happening."

"You think he understood that the killer was telling him every time he struck?"

"I think my dad would have figured that out. Remember that this was not unusual." She waved the page at him. "He'd been contacted by killers many times over the past thirty years. Some wanted to confess to him, some wrote to taunt him. Others challenged him. Catch me if you can, that sort of thing."

"Why your father?"

"It all started with a book he wrote in 1975. He'd interviewed a killer named Willie Miles, who was on death row in Florida for murdering his wives . . . that would be three former wives. My dad said he'd followed the case for the newspaper he was working for at the time, but thought it was a pretty interesting story."

"Your dad's background was in journalism?"

"Yes. Anyway, apparently Willie got chatty on his cell block and talked about how this writer from up north had come to see him, and how he was going to be famous because this writer was going to write a book about him, and one of the other inmates picked up on it. This second one wrote to Dad a few times. I guess he had told someone else there about it, and before my dad knew it, he was getting mail from other men on death row, too. Then some who were not yet on death row, and some from other states. And then some who had not as yet been caught."

"Why do you suppose they reached out to him?"

"I think they thought he'd make them famous. Write a book about them, too. The press had picked up on the story, about my dad getting all this mail, and I guess everyone wanted their fifteen minutes. It did die down after a few years, but from time to time he still heard from inmates." She smiled wryly. "Sometimes they wrote just to tell him how wrong he was about something or other he'd written. That's how he came into contact with Curtis Channing, the serial killer who, ultimately, was responsible for his death."

"The killer who put your dad's name on the hit list that he passed on to someone else."

"Archer Lowell. The man who shot my father."

"And you're certain — you are positive — that your father saved all this correspondence?"

"In one place or another. I'd bet on it."

"Right. It all comes back to finding the right box."

"I'm afraid so."

"We can scour the boxes while we wait."

"Wait for what?"

"For someone to respond to my inquiries. I sent a lot of emails and made a lot of phone calls yesterday to my office, as well as to several local police departments, state law enforcement agencies, whomever would have investigated these other homicides, asking them to fax over copies of their investigative reports."

"All forty victims plus the four from Dad's list?"

"Might as well take a look at the big picture. To that end, I have a bunch of bright yellow pins. We'll use those to mark those other forty victims I tracked down on the computer."

"Why segregate those?"

"Because we still have to put that list in order of date and integrate them into a master list. As we set up files on each of those, and confirm that they're most likely victims of the same killer, we'll exchange the yellow pin for a red one."

"And when we have all red pins, we'll have a complete list."

"Until others come out of the woodwork."

"Let's take our coffee into the office and check that fax machine. I thought I heard it ring earlier." Regan reached for the remote, and was about to turn off the television. "That's that police chief from one of those bay towns . . ."

She increased the volume.

". . . but you'll have to ask the Hasboro Police Department for that information," he was saying.

"Can you give us any information on the condition of the woman who was attacked last night? Has she been able to identify the man who attacked her?"

"I really can't give you any information,

Heather. This is an ongoing investigation . . ."

"But you can confirm that this woman did survive the attack?"

"One of the young women who was attacked over the weekend did survive. That's all I want to say at this time."

"Chief Denver, Bowers Inlet Police Department, we thank you for your time." The camera switched back to the morning host. "We'll be right back."

"There's been another one. Another murder in Bowers Inlet." Regan frowned.

"At least one, apparently. Did you hear him refer to another police department? Started with an H."

"I didn't catch the name."

"The Bureau sent an agent to Bowers to work with their department after the first four murders. Let me give him a call, see what's going on."

"While you do that, I think I'll move all this paperwork of yours into the office. There's some plywood in the barn, we can bring a piece in and pin the map on it, stand it up in front of the bookcases."

She gathered up the files on the kitchen table and took them down the hall to the office. After setting the papers on the large desk, she raised the shade on the window and let the morning in.

"I had to leave voice mail for Rick. In the meantime, how about you show me where the plywood is?"

"It's right over there, in the barn." She pointed out the window, then opened the top desk drawer and took out a key, which she handed to him. "This is for the main door."

"You're not coming?"

She hesitated. "I'll stay here and see if I can put this in order. Looks like someone was eager to share." She pointed to the fax machine, where a pile of paper overflowed the receive tray. The red light blinked furiously, indicating it was out of paper and had more pages to transmit.

"Okay. I can go right out the back door?"

She nodded and reloaded the paper tray, then hit the *Resume* button. Within seconds, the fax began to print again. Page after page after page.

Regan looked out the window and watched Mitch stride across the wide drive to the barn. He unlocked the door easily and went inside. Less than five minutes later, he was on his way back, holding a large piece of plywood over his head.

"There's a lot of good wood in there,"

Mitch was saying as he came into the room. He lowered the wood and leaned it against the bookcase. "And a lot of caution tape. I'm sorry, Regan. I knew about what happened to your dad there, and I just wasn't thinking."

She nodded. "It's okay. The tape is still in there?"

"Yes. Haven't you . . . ?"

"No. I haven't been in there since the day he was shot. I just can't bring myself to go in." She smiled sadly. "It must sound silly to you."

"Not at all. In a way, I'm surprised that you're living here."

"I hadn't intended to. I came back to clean out my dad's things, pack up my personal belongings, family things I wanted to keep, then have the property sold. I hadn't planned on staying. But I saw the story about the women being murdered at the shore, and it reminded me of those notes I found . . ."

"And you couldn't walk away from the story."

She shook her head. "I don't think I can. Not until all of this is resolved."

"Well, let's see if we can make some progress here today, so you can get on with your life. Toss me that container of tacks, would you, please? Let's get the map up."

"You have a ton of faxes here," she told him as they secured the map onto the plywood backing.

"That was fast." He leaned the map against the bookshelf and reached for the pile of paper she handed to him. He leafed through, reading aloud, "Pennsylvania State Police. Alabama . . . Texas . . . New Mexico . . . and the Georgia Bureau of Investigation sure has a lot to say."

He skimmed the fax messages that accompanied the various reports.

"Leary, Georgia. Colquitt. Ideal . . ." He shook his head. "Apparently they're still going through their records."

"And there are more faxes coming through." She pointed to the machine, where sheet after sheet slid into the tray.

"Let's put these in order by date so we have a chronological — That's my phone."

He pulled the ringing phone from his pants pocket and answered it, then wandered to the window and looked out while he listened.

"I think we need to have a sit-down-and-share, Cisco," he said after several moments. "There or here, doesn't matter . . . Okay, sure, I understand. I can be there in . . ."

Mitch looked at Regan and asked, "How far is it from here to the beach?"

"New Jersey has a whole coast made up of beaches."

"Bowers Inlet."

"Maybe an hour and a half. Depending on which way you go."

"You know a shortcut?"

"Sure. I'm a Jersey girl. We never take the main roads."

"Have lunch waiting for me," Mitch said into his phone. "I'll be there before noon."

He folded the phone and slipped it back into his pocket.

"What's going on in Bowers Inlet?" she asked.

"Seems the latest victim — the one the chief of police was talking about on TV? — is the cousin of the only detective in Bowers Inlet."

"But she's alive?"

"Alive, but still unconscious, so they haven't been able to get any information from her about her attacker."

Regan sat down on the arm of a chair and covered her face with her hands. "This is going way too fast. It's way too big. I can't keep up with it."

"I'm sure the police in Bowers Inlet feel the same way."

"Okay, we need a game plan." She stood, her hands on her hips. "We have to keep this organized or it will get out of hand. We'll lose sight of some information that might prove to be important later on. Let's start by getting the map up. Put pins in all of the locations where we think there's been a murder that could be connected."

"Maybe you can do that while I drive down to meet with Cisco." Mitch handed Regan the list and the box of pins, then began to gather all the faxes. "Maybe by the time I get back —"

"Uh-uh." She shook her head. "I'm going with you. The deal with John Mancini was that I'd open my files to the FBI, but in return, I get information up front."

"I'm not sure that *up front* means you get to tag along."

"That was the deal." More or less. "I can help you with this. For the past few weeks, I've been going through my father's files. There may be things I've read that might mean something to your investigation."

"Such as . . . ?"

"Something I hear, or see, in Bowers Inlet might ring a bell with something I read in one of his files."

Mitch searched his pockets for his keys.

"Besides, you need me." She folded her reading glasses and searched for their case amid the papers on the desk. Finding it, she tucked the glasses inside and dropped it into her handbag.

"I do?"

"Sure. I know all the shortcuts."

# Sixteen

"I'll bet this backs up but good later in the summer," Mitch observed as he drove over the two-lane bridge that led onto the small island where several of the bay towns were located. "Who still has two-lane bridges these days?"

"You'd be surprised." Regan smiled. "I remember when some of the causeways ended in drawbridges. I'll bet some still do."

"Doesn't seem very efficient."

"You don't come to the Jersey Shore looking for efficiency." The smile widened slightly. "If you want efficient, you go to Florida."

She pointed to acres of salt marsh off to her right where, twenty feet from the causeway, two herons fished amidst tall reeds.

"This still looks the way much of the shore area looks. There are miles of marshes and back bays, areas that will never be developed." Her right arm drifted out the window and rose and fell as her

269

hand rode the noontime breeze. "This is convertible weather. We should have taken my car."

"I can put the sunroof down," he offered.

"No offense, but why bother? On a day like today, you want more than the fresh air. You want to be able to lean your head back, get some sun on your face. You want the breeze along with the fresh air."

"Fine. If we ever come back, you can drive."

They passed a marina, where several boats of various sizes sat at their moorings, others sat on concrete blocks or on trailers. A sign advertised live bait, along with an all-you-can-eat clam bar. A Sunfish was heading out to the bay, and a couple of kids in a small outboard politely gave the sailboat a wide berth. They chugged past it slowly, then gunned the motor and took off, the Sunfish tossing in their wake.

Regan took a deep breath, the smile still in place. "My dad used to bring us to a place like this when I was little. I don't remember the name of the town, but I remember how it smelled. Salty and warm. It was a big deal for me. The beaches are so different from the beaches in England."

"You lived in England?"

"Until I was twelve. My mother was British, living in London when she met my father. They married there, then moved here when my father's writing career took off." Regan stared out the window. "She never really did adjust . . ."

"Where is she now?"

"She died a few years ago."

"I'm sorry."

"Thank you."

They rode in silence until they reached the main road into Bowers Inlet.

"Looks like a nice town," Mitch said as he took a left onto Mooney Drive. "Nice little houses on little sandy lots . . ."

"Like every little town on the Jersey Shore," she told him. "They all look pretty much the same — except for maybe Mantoloking. Of course, there are differences, but in most places, you pretty much always see the same kind of little beach cottage, the same narrow two-lane streets. The same little ice-cream shacks, the same little grocery stores . . ."

"What's with Manna— what was it?"

"Mantoloking."

"What, no beach cottages? No ice cream?"

"Let's just say the cottages are a lot bigger there." She mused. "But every shore town has a place to get ice cream. It's mandated by code, I think."

"Does the Bowers Inlet code require the residents to name their cottages?" He read the names as he drove by. "Sanctuary. Bill's Bungalow. Summer Breeze . . ."

She laughed. "There's the police station, on the next corner. Do you think your friend is here yet?"

"There's his car," Mitch said as he parked next to a black Camaro. "Let's go on in and see what's what."

They entered the cool lobby of the police station and waited while the receptionist called back to the chief's office. A pleasant blond woman with an easy smile and a professional manner came to escort them to the conference room.

"Lovely day out there, isn't it?" She beamed. "We've had some great beach days this past week."

She led them to the last door at the end of the hall.

"Everyone's already here, you go right on in." She held the door open for them.

"Thank you," Regan and Mitch said at the same time.

"You're welcome." She closed the door quietly behind them.

"Agent Peyton?" No doubt who was

running this show. The man at the end of the table was obviously the chief of police. He had *in charge* written all over him.

"Yes, sir." Mitch placed his black satchel on the floor next to the table and extended his hand.

"Chief Denver here," the chief introduced himself. "This is Detective Burke. And I'm assuming you and Agent Cisco know each other."

"Detective." Mitch nodded a greeting. "Cisco."

"And you are . . ." The chief pointed to Regan.

"Regan Landry, Chief," she said before Mitch could introduce her.

"Are you with the FBI, too?"

"No, actually, I'm a —"

"Ms. Landry is a consultant for the Bureau on this case," Mitch spoke over her.

"A consultant? What kind of consultant?" Denver's eyes narrowed.

"Ms. Landry has information about the Bayside Strangler that she's been sharing with us," Mitch said.

"If you have information about the Bayside Strangler," Denver stared at Regan, "why didn't you share it with us?"

"I did try, Chief Denver." She arched a brow. "Actually, I tried on three occasions.

None of my calls was returned, so I called the FBI."

"Let's see what you've got, then," he grunted, vaguely remembering those pink While You Were Out slips, but not recalling exactly what they said. "Something about a writer?" he asked.

"Yes, sir. I'm a writer. And I will most likely write a book about this case."

"And that entitles you to sit in on an official meeting how . . . ?"

"Because right now I'm bringing more to the table than I'm taking away."

Regan opened her files and handed Denver the notes her father had received. He studied them without comment at first.

"How do I know these are legit?" he asked. "How do I know that you didn't make these yourself, to get into the investigation, give yourself an edge over the competition? You don't think you're the only person who might want to write a book about all this, do you?"

"No, of course not. But since my father apparently had planned on doing that some twenty years ago, I think I have first dibs on the story."

She opened the file flat onto the table.

"My father — Joshua Landry — you may have heard of him? — received correspondence over the course of several years from someone I — and Agent Peyton — believe to have been your strangler."

"Joshua Landry. Of course, of course. Wrote some good stuff." Denver softened. He looked at Mitch. "You believe her? You think Landry was contacted by our strangler?"

"I do. The information we found in Josh Landry's files dovetails perfectly with information I've culled from the FBI computers. Look here . . ."

Mitch proceeded to show Denver the lists of victims they had compiled, the news clippings, the faxes he received that morning from several of the investigating departments.

"Huh." Chief Denver nodded slowly. "It answers the question *What's this guy been doing all these years?*"

"He never stopped, sir. He simply moved around. Looks to me as if he was pretty careful to hit small towns, where they were less likely to have the sophisticated equipment and investigative techniques being used by some of the departments in larger cities."

Denver nodded again. "Tougher to track the pattern if the agency doesn't bother to report to the national data banks. Not that we had those twenty-six years ago. It's only been the last eight, ten years that we've been keeping all our records on computer. Took us that long to get our computer system in, train somebody to use it, then have the data entered. Wouldn't be any big surprise to me if some of these small towns down south" — he tapped on the list Mitch had given him — "still haven't gotten all their open cases on record."

"That's why we requested information from the state agencies as well as the small local police and sheriff departments. We're hoping by the time we're finished, we'll have a complete list, be able to pinpoint exactly where he was every year since 1983."

"Since 1983, eh?" Denver adjusted his glasses and glanced down at the list. "In 1983 he was in Pittsburgh, according to this list. Where do you think he was between August of 1979 and May of '83?"

"That's one of the blanks we're hoping to be able to fill in."

"What do you know about your victims, Agent Peyton?" Detective Burke asked.

"Well, let's see. We know that they were about the same age, they were all killed in the same manner."

"Rape followed by strangulation isn't a

particularly novel way of killing someone. What else do you have?" She turned in her seat and focused on him.

"I have some news clippings that were in Landry's files." He gestured to Rick to send his file back to him. Rick slid it down the table. Mitch took the clippings out and laid them in the center of the table. "Take a look."

Cass stood and studied the squares of newsprint.

"Chief, maybe you should look at these women."

Denver did, then spread out photos of the women who had been murdered over the past week and a half.

All five in the room stared at the pictures.

"I can't believe how closely these women resemble one another." Regan was the first to speak.

"Neither can I," said Cass, "but the appearance is obviously important to him. It's one of the few things we know for certain about him. That he only likes dark-haired women of a certain age and body type."

"And that he poses them all in the same manner," Rick added.

"What?" Mitch turned to Rick. "What manner is that?"

"Here." Cass passed a photo from Linda Roman's crime scene across the table. "And here . . . our victim number two. Then three . . ."

Mitch studied the photos, then looked at Denver.

"Have you thought about bringing in one of the Bureau's profilers? I think we need some insight into this."

"I've put in a request. We're just waiting to hear who and when," Rick told him.

"Never worked with one myself, though of course I've read the books. John Douglas. Hazelwood. Ressler. Interesting topic," Denver said. "And all those TV cop shows seem to have one pop up at times like this."

"How much of this information are we going to release to the press?" Cass asked.

"None of it, for now." Denver looked around the room. "Unless someone has another idea?"

The two agents shook their heads. Regan didn't react, knowing she had no say in such decisions.

"I can't believe this guy has been getting away with murder for so long," Rick said. "How the hell has he stayed under the radar all this time?"

"Obviously, he's moved around a lot,

judging from the list Agent Peyton has," Cass noted.

"But to have no suspects here," Mitch said, "and so far, the reports I've received from these other agencies indicate no suspects there, either."

"Maybe we should go back to those agencies — Georgia Bureau of Investigation, for example, had several old cases on record — and see what evidence their cold files hold. There might be something that contains some DNA."

Cass nodded. "Right. At the very least, we could start comparing DNA samples. That way, we can confirm if he was in fact involved in these cases, instead of speculating. Who knows, some of the file boxes could contain old clothes worn by a victim, or something found at the scene that might contain hair or skin. You never know what might have been saved."

"Or what might have been tossed out," Denver noted.

"Nothing ventured, nothing gained," Rick countered.

"And we should ask if these bodies . . . these other women . . . were left posed in any particular manner. That seems to be his signature. As telling as the DNA," Mitch said.

"And don't forget the fibers in the hair," Cass added. "Who knows how long he's been doing that."

"What fibers?" Regan asked. "How long he's been doing what?"

"Our crime scene tech found traces of light-colored silk in the hair of our current victims. She tracked it down — it's silk satin ribbon that was last made eighteen years ago."

"You haven't released that information to the press?" Mitch asked, and Denver shook his head.

"I think we need to keep as much close to the vest as we can for now. All this fits together somehow. We don't have a clue yet. I figure the less we give him, the better."

"I agree," Mitch said.

"What's that all about?" Regan frowned. "He's tying a ribbon in their hair?"

"But he takes it with him," Cass told her. "We've never found ribbon on any of the bodies. Just the fibers."

"That's signature as well, isn't it?" Regan asked Mitch.

"It would appear to be," he responded.

"Two signatures? Do serial killers have more than one?"

"Keep in mind what a signature is."

280

Mitch leaned back in his seat, his arms folded across his chest. "It's that special something unique to the killer that gives meaning to the killing. It's what he needs to do to get fulfillment from what he does."

"So he poses these women and ties silk ribbon in their hair . . . then takes the ribbon with him? What does he get from that?" Regan seemed to be thinking out loud.

"My gut tells me he's reliving something that's important to him, but I think that's a good question for our profiler," Rick said. "She will have a better feel for this than I do."

"Okay, here's another thing. Forgive me for stating the obvious," Regan said, "but if we believe that the killer is the original Bayside Strangler — and we all seem to think he is — it follows that whoever is here now was here twenty-six years ago. But maybe not in the intervening years."

"Because there haven't been any other bodies — that we know of — until now," Rick said.

"Oh, well, that narrows the field," Denver said.

"Actually, it does," Regan insisted. "If we understand that this person has been all over the country — he's been halfway around the world — and has left a trail of bodies, though none of them here till now, then we have to think he's been gone all this time. The killings may have started here, but he definitely took his show on the road for a long, long time."

"The question is, what brings him back now? What brings this full circle?"

Denver and Cass exchanged a long, meaningful look.

"What?" Rick asked.

"The reunion," Cass told them. "This week is reunion week. People have come from all over. They're taking down the old high school and dedicating the new one. It's an all-classes thing."

"Maybe he came back for that," Regan said.

"And once he got back here, the urge to kill — to repeat the past — was too strong," Rick concluded.

"How many people do you think are in town for this reunion?" Mitch asked.

"It's not only Bowers Inlet," Cass told him. "It's Tilden, it's Dewey. Hasboro. Killion Point. All the little towns along the bay. It's Bay Regional High. We all went to the same schools."

"So we're talking about how many

people?" Rick asked.

"Couple hundred," Denver replied.

"How do we narrow that down?" Regan frowned.

"Okay, look, we have to assume there's an age range we can work with. He had to have been old enough in 1979 to have done to those women what he did, but still be young enough today to be physically strong enough to overcome healthy, strong young women."

"Let's say at the youngest, could he have been fourteen, fifteen, back then?" Cass suggested. "And the oldest he could be now? Mid-fifties, if he's in really great shape?"

"We can use those as a starting point," Denver agreed.

"And we can narrow that group even further," Regan offered, "by figuring out who on the first list has been gone from the area and is here now."

Mitch nodded. "And do an Internet search to track who's been where in the intervening years."

"We can do better than that." Denver pushed a button on the intercom. "Phyl, I need you to call over to the high school and tell them I need a copy of every yearbook from 19 . . ." He paused and looked around the group. "What we say, fourteen or fifteen years old back in 1979? He would have graduated in, say, '81 or maybe '82. If he was older than that . . . let's see, it's 2005, say he could be at the oldest maybe fifty-five? He'd have graduated . . ." The chief did some mental calculations. "Say 1968? Let's go back as far as 1960. I'd hate to have missed someone because we didn't factor in some unknown element."

He turned back to the intercom.

"Phyl, ask them for all the yearbooks between 1960 and 1985. Just to be on the safe side. Tell 'em we'll send a patrol car over to pick them up."

"Will do," Phyl replied crisply.

"We can look them over." Denver addressed Cass. "You, me, Phyl. We can at least get a head start on eliminating people we know never moved away or ever traveled around like we think this guy has done."

"If you get me the list of names," Mitch told him, "I'll start tracking them through the bureau. If we can get social security numbers for them, we can track them that much faster."

Denver shook his head. "Don't think the school will hand those out."

284

"Maybe you could ask for everyone on the list to give a DNA sample," Regan suggested. The entire group turned to stare at her as if she had suddenly sprouted an extra head.

"What?" she asked.

"We'll have the ACLU all over us if we try to pull something like that," Denver told her.

"They've done it in several places over the past few years. I read about it. The police in Massachusetts did this earlier in the year," Regan protested.

"Right, they did," Mitch agreed. "And the ACLU was all over them. These DNA 'sweeps' have been used eighteen, nineteen times. Only turned up a suspect once, and that was within a very small community of possibilities. Besides, the police department you're talking about in Massachusetts did that as a last resort. We've only begun to narrow this down. You wouldn't be able to do that without a fight. And fighting with potential suspects will only waste time. I say we follow the plan the chief outlined — narrow down the list by year of graduation, then see if we can determine who's been out of state, out of the country. Then maybe — just maybe — we'll have a list of potential suspects."

"Well, then, unless someone has something else to add?" Denver scanned the faces at the table. "No? Okay, then, Agent Cisco, you'll follow up with the profiler?"

Rick nodded. "I'll make the call today."

Cass stood and stretched, then said, "If there's nothing else, I want to get back to the hospital."

"Rick told me on the phone about your cousin being attacked," Mitch said. "How's she doing?"

"She was the same this morning," Cass told him. "The doctors said she would come out of it, but they can't predict when. She apparently was oxygen deprived for a time, we don't know how long — and then there's the trauma, the shock. She could come out of it tonight, or not for another week or two. No one wants to predict."

"I hope it's soon," Regan told her as she gathered her files. "I hope she recovers quickly from this."

"Thank you." Cass turned to Rick. "If you have another few minutes, I'll stop back in my office and see if the lab reports on the victim they found on the dock have come back from Tasha yet."

"Ahhh, Cass . . ." Denver remained seated. In his hands, he held his glasses, which he appeared to be toying with. "I'll get the lab results from Tasha and pass them on to Agent Cisco."

Cass stared at him blankly.

"I need to take you off the case, Cass."

"Off the . . ." Cass dropped her bag. "What are you talking about, off the case? It's my —"

"Cass. You're too close to one of the victims. And beyond that, I don't know that you might not be the next target."

"That's bullshit." An angry Cass grabbed a section of her own hair. "No long dark tresses here, Chief. And we all agreed he's only going after women with long dark hair."

"He also hit two women in the same day. Something he hasn't done before. I don't think we can safely predict what he's going to do."

When she started to protest again, Denver cut her off. "You messed up his game plan, Cass, when you walked in on him with Lucy. He has to be pretty pissed at you right now."

"All the more reason for me to stay involved. I can draw him out."

"I'm not using you as bait, Detective. And I'm not asking for your opinion. I want you to take a few days' leave. I want you out of sight for a while."

"So you want me to just go home and sit on my butt while the rest of you chase after this guy?" Cass was wide-eyed.

"Actually, no. You're going to have to find someplace else to stay. Your house is off-limits. Have you forgotten it's a crime scene?"

Cass grabbed her bag and walked from the room, slamming the door behind her.

"I knew she would not go gentle," Denver murmured.

To Rick, he said, "Can you keep an eye on her? She's not going to want to stay put, and we can't afford to lose her."

Rick nodded, and with Regan and Mitch left the conference room. Denver went to the window, which opened onto the back of the building and the parking lot. Cass shot through the back door and stalked down the sidewalk to her car. Denver could almost see her fingers trembling with rage.

"Sorry, Cassie," he said aloud.

He thought back to the attack she'd survived as a child, recalled the efforts he himself had made to breathe life into her small body.

He sighed, knowing that at that moment she hated him. Well, he could take that if it meant keeping her out of harm's way. And he wasn't even sure that it would.

All he knew at the moment was that evil was afoot in the bay towns, and the probability was that the face it hid behind was a face he'd looked on at some point over the years, possibly a face he knew well.

It could be someone he'd met at the Dockside Bar last night, where so many of the old gang had gathered. Or one of the guys who over the course of the evening had stood next to him at the bar and asked about his older brother, Dan, or his younger sister, Karen.

Dear God, it could be anyone.

Maybe one of his own classmates. Even one of his friends. Or one of Dan's.

He thought back to Dan's group of friends, the kids who used to hang on the Denvers' front porch every night of every summer. Of the guys who used to call the house, hoping to get a date with Karen.

Pretty Karen, who back in the day wore her long black hair parted in the middle.

A chill crawled up his spine.

He buzzed Phyl.

"Phyl, how are we doing with those yearbooks?"

# Seventeen

"Cass!" Regan hurried across the parking lot to catch up with the angry detective before she could hop into a car and speed off.

"You don't have to run, Regan," Cass told her flatly when the two women were within twenty feet of each other. "I don't have a car here. I came right from the hospital this morning with Rick."

"Look, I know you're upset . . ."

"Oh, please," Cass muttered under her breath.

"This is a bad time for you, I understand that. With all that's going on here in Bowers Inlet, your cousin being attacked, then you getting taken off your case —"

"I need to get to the hospital," Cass cut her off. "Will you drive me?"

"Where is it you want to go?" Rick asked as he approached her.

"I need to check on Lucy." Cass leaned against Rick's car.

"You have a phone on you," he pointed out. "Use it."

"I want to see her."

"If her condition hasn't changed since this morning, there's no point in spending another few hours sitting in that hospital room, glaring at Lucy's husband, and having him glare back at you." His tone softened. "You haven't eaten since . . . when? When was your last meal?"

"Sunday sometime. Lunch, maybe. I don't know."

"And you last slept when?"

"Saturday night."

"Look, you put a call in to the hospital. If Lucy is awake, I'll drive you over. If not, you'll come with us and get some lunch, and we'll figure out where you're going to stay."

They stared at each other for a long moment before Cass took her phone from her bag and dialed the number for the hospital. She meandered around the car, speaking softly. When she completed the call, she dropped the phone back into her bag.

"She's still not awake," she told the three who waited by Rick's car.

"We can grab some lunch . . . you have a favorite place?" Rick opened the passenger door for her.

She shook her head.

"Then let's go back to the inn where I'm

staying. The restaurant there is pretty good. I imagine Regan is ready for lunch, and I've yet to see Peyton here turn down good seafood. Or any food, now that I think about it."

Mitch nodded as he unlocked his car. "Lead on. We'll follow you."

"Any chance I can go home and get a change of clothes and some things I'll need?" Cass asked Rick as she got into the passenger seat.

"How about we stop after lunch and see what's going on over there? I'm sure they have someone from the department at your house until the scene has been processed. Maybe by then they'll be finished and you'll be able to slip in and grab a few things."

"All right." She leaned back against the headrest and closed her eyes.

"You okay?"

"Yes. Just . . ." She sought the word.

"Tired? Overwhelmed? Pissed off?"

"All of the above."

Rick eased onto the street and into the line of traffic.

"I know this has been hard on you. The attack on Lucy, in particular. And I know you have to be beyond pissed at your chief." He checked the rearview mirror to ensure that Mitch was following. He was.

"You have no idea."

"Of course I do. Don't think you're the only person who's ever been plucked from a plum case in the middle of it."

"This is my case." Her jaw tightened. "I don't appreciate being tossed off it. What am I supposed to do while you and everyone else is working on it?"

"Denver told you to take a few days off."

"And do what?" She was beginning to steam again.

"He asked me to keep an eye on you."

"What? That is the last straw," she growled. "I can't believe he did that. I do not need a baby-sitter. No offense, but I don't need to be —"

"Of course you don't. But if you'll calm down for a second, I think you'll see that this can work to your advantage." He put on his right turn signal to alert Mitch to the upcoming turn into the parking lot.

"How do you figure?"

"I'm supposed to stick with you, but I'm also supposed to be working the case. Well, hell, I can't be in two places at once. Our profiler will be here. She'll want all the information on all of the victims. Who better to tell her about Lucy? And who better to tell her about the other crime scenes? You were there. You'll have insights into this that no one else could have."

"I don't want to be off the case. I want to work."

"I can appreciate that. But right now, this is what we have to work with. You can play a big part in this still. Just not on the clock." He pulled into the lot and parked.

"He shouldn't have taken me off the case."

"Well, I have to disagree with you there." Rick got out of the car and waved Mitch toward an empty parking space.

"You what?" Cass swung open her door, hopped out, then slammed the door for emphasis and glared at him over the roof.

"I think Denver has a point," Rick said calmly. "I think the killer is highly pissed off right now, and the person who pissed him off is the person most likely to incur his most immediate wrath. And since that person is you, I think Denver was right to put you in the background for a while."

"I thought you just said you knew what it was like to be yanked off a good case."

"I did say that. And I do know what it feels like. It sucks. But in this case, it's not unreasonable." He rounded the car to her side. "This is one mean son of a bitch we're after here, Cass. Now, I have no doubt that you can handle yourself damn well. You did an admirable job scaring him off last night. You saved Lucy's life. And I'd be willing to bet real Yankee dollars that you gave him a damned good scare. But all of that does not change the fact that he's mightily pissed at you. I think your department needs you. I think Lucy needs you. We cannot afford to let him get to you. And he will try, the first chance he gets. If I have to wear you in my back pocket until we get our hands on him, that's where you'll stay until this is over. I'd rather have you actively involved in the investigation, and I've already told you how you can do that. The choice is yours. You can work with me behind the scenes, or you can pout and go sit in a room someplace until this is over. Your choice."

Cass stared at him, her expression unreadable.

"Like I said, Cass. Your choice," he repeated.

They both turned at the sound of Mitch's car doors slamming.

"This is lovely," Regan was saying as she got out of the sedan. "What a beautiful old inn."

"It's a great place to stay. Nice room.

Ocean view. Quiet." Rick glanced at his watch. "If we hurry, we can make the end of the lunch hours. They stop serving at two."

He turned to Cass.

"What's it going to be?"

"I guess the crab cakes," she told him, and without looking back, fell in step with Regan and Mitch.

"Which way is the dining room?" Mitch asked.

"Straight through the lobby," Rick replied. But once they stepped inside, he paused in the doorway, then directed the others to go on in and get a table. "I'll only be a minute."

It was closer to five minutes, but Rick joined the others as the waitress was passing out menus. Mitch appeared to be on the verge of comment, but said nothing.

"I'm assuming all the seafood entrées are good," Regan was saying.

"You can't miss with any of them. I had the sea bass the other day, and have had the soft-shell crabs and one of the soups," Rick told them. "All pretty terrific."

"Nothing like what you get back home in Texas, eh?" Mitch closed his menu and placed it on the table.

"Nothing at all like Texas," Rick agreed.

"That's where you're from, Texas?" Cass asked.

Rick nodded.

"You don't seem to have much of an accent," she noted.

"I'm from there, but I haven't lived there for some time."

"I see," Cass said, but Rick doubted that she did. He just wasn't up to talking about the years of New England boarding schools. He wasn't in all that good a mood to begin with.

The waitress reappeared, took their orders, and promised to be back in a flash with their iced teas.

"By the way, I spoke with Annie McCall," Rick announced. "She'll be joining us tomorrow afternoon."

"That's as soon as she can get here?" Mitch asked.

"She's wrapping up something else today. Tomorrow is the best she can do."

"Who's Annie McCall?" Regan asked.

"Anne Marie McCall. Dr. McCall. She's our favorite profiler," Mitch explained. "Not to mention the best I've ever worked with."

"What makes her the best?" Cass unfolded her napkin and rested it on her lap.

"She's a psychologist, but besides being

book smart, she's a real master at understanding behavior. Especially aberrant behavior," Rick told her. "She's really good at putting the pieces together. You'll see when you meet her."

"I'd like to meet her, too." Regan frowned. "I'm sorry I'm going to miss her."

"We can always drive back tomorrow, if you'd like. I want to be part of the sit-down with her," Mitch said. "You're welcome to come along."

"The sit-down?" Cass leaned back to permit the waitress to serve her drink.

"The preliminary meeting we have where we toss around whatever information we have. We'll give her a chance to review the records, the interviews, the lab reports, all of that, but we like to discuss the cases informally. Some of our best insights come from those moments of idle chatter."

"It hardly sounds idle," Regan noted.

"I guess *unstructured* is probably a more accurate term," Mitch said. "It's sort of a brainstorming session."

"Any chance I could be a part of that, too?" Cass asked.

Rick nodded. "Absolutely. You will be the star witness. We can't have that powwow without you."

Cass looked momentarily pleased, the guarded expression she'd been wearing lifting a little. Then she asked, "And after she leaves? Will I still be invited to the powwows?"

"You'll know everything that's going on when I do," Rick promised.

"That wasn't the question."

"No, but that's the answer." He handed his menu to the waitress. "I think we're all ready to order. Cass? Regan?"

Orders were placed and glasses replenished. The conversation drifted from the current investigation to the information Regan had found in her father's files.

"That's really interesting," Cass said. "You write books about old cases and try to solve them at the same time? How many have you solved?"

"On my own, none." Regan smiled. "But my dad had quite a record."

"I've never read any of his books, but I will definitely look for them."

"I'll try to remember to bring you a few."

"Thanks, Regan. That's nice of you. And it does appear I'll have some time on my hands, so maybe I'll even get to read a couple of them." Cass turned to Rick and asked, as if it had just occurred to her,

"When do you suppose I can move back to my house?"

"I don't know. We'll look into that later. After we eat. You're not the only one who missed out on dinner last night, you know."

"I saw you nursing that bag of chips from the vending machine this morning, so don't even pretend that you haven't eaten in days." Cass almost smiled.

"A snack-sized bag of potato chips doesn't count for anything. It doesn't even rate a true snack designation, and it sure as hell did not make up for the dinner and the breakfast I didn't have."

"Here." Mitch passed the basket of soft rolls to Rick. "I realize they're not organic stone-ground whole wheat, and God knows they probably aren't as good as the ones you make in your little kitchen, but you can buck up, just this once, and eat what the rest of us eat."

Rick grinned, and without comment buttered a roll, which he proceeded to devour.

"You make your own?" Cass pointed to the basket.

Rick nodded. "I have on occasion made my own bread. Not very often, but I have done it. Much to the amusement of some of my fellow agents, I might add."

"You never should have mentioned it," Mitch told him.

"What was I thinking?" Rick shook his head good-naturedly.

"Where did you learn to do that?" Cass asked.

"My grandmother baked every day. Cakes, cookies, breads — all from scratch. I often stayed with her when I was little. She said everyone should know how to bake their own bread and do their own taxes. So I learned both at an early age."

The waitress brought salads, and Cass picked at hers, watching Rick out of the corner of her eye, and tried to envision those large hands kneading a mound of dough.

"So, what's on the agenda this afternoon?" Mitch asked.

"Well, I'm going to get copies of everything we have and make a file up for Annie, then I'll have it sent to her overnight. That way she'll have a head start on the case before she gets here. I'll check in with the lab." Rick hesitated, then turned to Cass. "Do you think your friend Tasha would get copies of all the lab reports for us? We still don't have the ME's report from the victim on the dock."

Cass nodded. "I'm sure she'll give us whatever she has."

301

"Even if you're off the case?" he asked.

"Especially if I'm off the case."

"Can you give her a call?"

"Now?"

"Yes. But the reception is poor in here. You'll have to take the phone into the lobby."

"I'll be right back." Cass picked up her bag and left the room.

"Is the reception in here really that bad, or were you trying to get rid of her for a few?" Mitch asked.

"Both, actually. While I was in the lobby, I switched rooms from a single to a two-bedroom suite with a sitting room between."

"You move fast. I had no idea you were such a player," Mitch said wryly.

"Hey, this is strictly in the interest of justice. She needs a place to stay, and she needs to stay where I can keep an eye on her. She won't like it, but neither of us has much of a choice. I figure she's got another twenty, thirty minutes in her, tops, before she just flat-out collapses. The woman is running on empty right now. I just wanted to make sure she was taken care of when she hits the wall."

"Considerate of you." Mitch still bore the slightest trace of a grin, which Rick chose to ignore.

"She's going to want things from her house. Regan, can you go over with me later to pick out some clothes that you think she might need over the next few days? And some . . . stuff. Whatever stuff it is that women use."

"Sure. I'd be happy to. But why don't you take Cass?"

"Because I think she'll be out cold before too much longer. I'd like her to have her things here when she wakes up. And I don't think she should be in that house right now."

"She doesn't strike me as the squeamish type, Rick," Regan noted.

"I don't mean to imply that she is. But I think there's a possibility the killer might be watching her house. In that case, he could easily follow her. Let's keep her whereabouts under wraps for at least twenty-four hours, if possible. Give her a chance to rest before the real crazy stuff begins."

"What crazy stuff?"

"I expect that by this time tomorrow, the chief will have a viable list of names. That, along with Annie's imput, should put us closer to a suspect. Sooner or later, this guy will strike again. I think it's all going to begin to boil over within the next few days."

He looked up as Cass entered the room

303

and headed for the table.

"And, unless I'm mistaken, I expect we'll have him in our crosshairs by the end of the week. Until then, one of our priorities is to keep *her* out of *his*."

"You're going to keep me out of what?" Cass slid into her seat.

"We're going to keep you out of harm's way," Rick told her.

"Nice of you."

"What did Tasha have to say?"

"She'll drop a copy of everything she has to you here. I didn't know where I'd be staying." Cass smiled up at the waitress, who began to serve their entrées. "I thought if she dropped them off to you, we'd all see them."

Rick nodded. "Good thinking."

"Wow. A whole meal." Cass blinked at the plate that was set before her. "Vegetables and everything."

"Let's see how much of it you can eat before you fall asleep."

"This will only serve to revive me, Agent Cisco," Cass told him.

Rick smiled. He doubted she'd make it through dessert.

She did, but barely. Halfway through her cheesecake, Cass was struggling to keep her eyes open.

"You okay there?" Rick asked.

"I think I'd like a cup of coffee," she replied.

"How about a nap?"

"I'll be fine. A little caffeine . . ."

"Cass, I took the liberty of getting a room for you. It's actually part of my suite on the second floor. Your own bathroom. Balcony, with a view of the ocean. I'll give you the key and walk you up. You need to get some sleep."

"I need to get some things from my house, then we'll see."

"Regan will get you what you need."

"She doesn't know where anything is."

"You could tell me while we're on our way upstairs," Regan told her. "I'd be happy to get whatever you want. But Rick is right. You need to rest for a little while."

"What if Lucy wakes up? I won't know . . ."

"I'll have the hospital put a call in to me and I'll come right in and wake you the minute I hear from them," Rick said.

"Promise?"

"Absolutely." Rick took Cass's arm and helped her stand.

Regan grabbed Cass's bag and followed Rick to the stairwell. Mitch stayed behind to take care of their bill.

"You know I must be tired if I'm not arguing with you over this," Cass told Rick as they climbed the steps. "All of a sudden, I can't keep my eyes open."

"It's your body's way of insisting you let it rest for a while." Rick steered her in the direction of his rooms. He unlocked the door and led her and Regan inside.

"See, nice sitting room here. This door opens into your room."

"Where do you stay?"

"That door over there is my bedroom." He opened her door and motioned to Regan to follow Cass inside. "Cass, Regan is going to help you get settled. If you need anything, you let me know. I'll be right outside."

She nodded and disappeared into the room with Regan, who emerged less than five minutes later.

"She's out cold. Are you sure you didn't slip something into her food?" Regan asked softly.

"I didn't have to. She was wobbly in the chief's office. I'm surprised she lasted through lunch."

"So, what's next?"

"Next is you and me go to her house and pick up whatever it is she'll need for the next few days." Rick opened the door to the hall and looked in the direction of the stairs. "As soon as Mitch gets here, we can go."

"You look a little beat yourself," Regan noted. "Why not stay here and get some sleep. Mitch and I can find the house and get Cass's things."

"I want to see how the investigation is going there. And I want to look around the house, make sure nothing was missed. Then we'll come back and I'll see if I can get a few hours of sleep before something else happens."

As it turned out, Rick was able to get more than a few hours of sleep. It was almost five the following morning when the ringing of his cell phone woke him. He sat up and listened to the caller carefully, then rose and pulled on his pants and shirt. In bare feet, he padded across the carpet to Cass's door and knocked lightly.

"Cass?" He opened the door. "Cassie?"

She sat up, startled and disoriented.

"What . . . ?" She looked around, trying to place herself.

"You're at the Inn, Cass. The hospital just called. Lucy is awake, and she's asking for you." He gestured to the chair near the foot of her bed. "Regan left your clothes and things there. If you can get up and get dressed, I'll take you to the hospital."

Cass was out of bed in a flash.

"I'll be right there," she told him. "I can be ready in a minute. Just give me one minute . . ."

Rick closed the door and went back to his room to finish dressing, grateful they'd both gotten a good night's sleep. He had the feeling they'd had the last real rest either of them were likely to get until this was over.

# Eighteen

Cass pushed past David Webb as she entered the hush of the hospital room, ignoring his attempts to speak with her. She went directly to Lucy's bed. Her knees weakened at the sight of her cousin lying there with a ring of bruises around her throat and tubes in her nose.

"Lulu." Whispering the old childhood nickname, Cass leaned in close and took Lucy's hands in her own.

Lucy's voice was so muted, Cass at first wasn't certain she'd spoken at all. She murmured something, a string of words, and Cass put her ear up to Lucy's mouth.

The color drained from her face as she listened carefully to Lucy's labored words.

"Are you sure, honey? Are you absolutely sure that's what he said?" She tucked a loose lock of dark hair behind Lucy's ear.

Lucy nodded slowly, almost apologetically, then closed her eyes. Cass lingered for a moment, rubbing Lucy's hands gently before turning toward the door, where Rick awaited her.

David caught Cass by the arm as she started past him. "What did she say?"

"Nothing that concerns you." She tried to shake off his hand to walk around him.

"If she said anything about me . . ."

"Don't flatter yourself. She has more important things on her mind at the moment. Now, if you'll excuse me —"

"The doctors said she'd probably be ready to leave by the end of the week. Just so you know, I'm taking her home."

Cass turned back to him. "Why?"

"Why? Because she's my wife, that's why."

"Oh. You finally remembered." Cass walked past him and left the room.

"She needs to be home. She needs to be with her sons," David called to her from the doorway, but Cass refused to turn around.

Rick fell in step with her and they walked toward the elevator.

"Where's the fire?" he asked.

"Any place but here." Her breath was coming in little, short puffs. "Just get me out of here."

He led her to the elevator and took her arm when the doors opened. He punched the L button and leaned against the side of the car, studying her face and wondering what Lucy could have said that had un-nerved her. They reached the lobby and she stepped out of the car as soon as the elevator doors opened. She headed for the exit to the parking garage as if fleeing a burning building.

Rick kept pace with her as they neared his car. He unlocked it with the remote when they were still ten feet from it, and once inside, he turned on the ignition, but didn't put the car in gear.

"Are you going to tell me what she said that has you upset? Did she recognize the man who attacked her? Give you any clue as to who he is?"

Cass shook her head. "No, she didn't say anything like that. She's having trouble speaking, you know, because of the bruising to her throat. But she said . . . she said . . ." Cass cleared her throat and appeared to be attempting to collect herself. "She said that while he was attacking her . . . while he was attempting to rape her . . . the entire time he was strangling her, he was calling her *Jenny.*"

"Jenny?" Rick frowned. "What the hell does that mean?"

"Rick, my mother's name was Jenny," Cass said softly.

"I remember. You showed me the memorial at the bird sanctuary." He appeared puzzled. "But there are lots of women named Jenny. I can see why it might rattle you a bit, but —"

"I told you my mother was murdered. I don't think I told you she'd been strangled. June 1979. Twenty-six years ago."

"Twenty-six . . ." Rick frowned. "In 1979. The same summer the Bayside Strangler started his run here. Jesus, Cass, are you telling me she was one of his first victims? Don't you think you could have mentioned this earlier?"

"No, she wasn't. At least . . . no. Well . . . no." Cass was clearly confused. "The man who killed her . . . killed my father . . . my little sister . . . he was arrested. He was tried and convicted."

"Did he confess?"

"No." She nibbled on the nail of her right index finger. "No. He never did."

"Maybe we should go speak with him."

"Tough to do. He died about ten years ago, remember?"

"Right. Maybe Lucy's attacker had another Jenny in mind."

"The thing you need to know is, Lucy looks almost exactly like my mother." She closed her eyes and leaned back against the headrest. "Now that I think about it, all of

312

the victims look a bit like my mother. Pretty, with long dark hair . . ."

"No one ever connected your family's murder with the Bayside Strangler?"

She shook her head. "Why would they? This was an entire family that was wiped out — almost wiped out. The others — they were all attacks on women only. The MO was entirely different, too. My family . . ." She swallowed hard. "No one else was attacked in their own home that summer. Looking back, I can see why there was no connection made. And I'm still not sure there is a connection. I don't want there to be a connection."

"Where were you?" he asked. "Were you away from home on the day of the attack?"

"I was there," she said, then turned to stare out the window.

He wanted to ask how she had been spared, but the look that had come over her face warned him off.

"We need to talk to Chief Denver. You need to tell him what Lucy said."

Cass nodded but did not speak.

Rick started the car and they drove in silence to the police station. They walked straight back to the chief's office and Cass barely knocked before opening the door and walking in.

"Cass." Chief Denver looked up from his desk, started to say something, but her expression stopped him. Instead, he asked, "Cassie, what's happened?"

She told him about her conversation with Lucy.

"He called her *Jenny?*" Denver asked incredulously. "She was sure?"

"She was sure."

"But what the hell . . . ?" Denver stared at her blankly. "Why the hell would he . . . ?"

"Chief, I wonder if I could have a look at your police file on the attack on Cass's family," Rick said. "I'm assuming you still have it?"

"I guess it's still in the storage room. When we moved into the new municipal building seven years ago, all our old files were packed up and stored. I can have someone look for it. I don't recall giving an okay to get rid of any of them, so I'm assuming we still have it. What do you want with it? What are you thinking?"

"I'm thinking there's a connection to the Bayside Strangler that somehow slipped by everyone back then."

"No way did we miss a goddamn thing. No damn way. What the hell would make you even think such a thing?"

"Let's start with the attack on Lucy

Webb and the fact that her attacker called her *Jenny*."

"There are a lot of women named Jenny."

"With long dark hair, who were strangled to death by a killer who only targets women with long dark hair?"

"I'm telling you, Cisco, I was part of both investigations back then, the Burkes' and the Strangler's. I was among the first officers on the scene at the Burke home. I can tell you that not much slipped past anyone. We all knew Bob and Jenny. We went over that house with a fine-tooth comb. We found the killer hiding in the garage, covered in Bob Burke's blood. There was no doubt who was responsible for those killings." Denver's voice rose with anger and he spoke as if he'd forgotten Cass was in the room. "I carried that child down the steps, bleeding from her neck to her waist, cut up like —"

Cass bolted from the room.

"Jesus, I can't believe I just did that." Denver ran a hand over his head. "Holy mother in heaven, I can't believe I did that."

Rick started after her, then stopped at the door, and over his shoulder asked, "By 'that child,' you mean Cass's sister?"

"No, I mean Cass. Bastard stabbed her in the chest five, six times, left her for dead. It's a miracle that she lived. I still don't know how she survived."

"I'll need to see that file as soon as you can get your hands on it. Today if possible." Rick closed the door and went in search of Cass.

He found her in her office, seated at her desk, the lights off, the window shades drawn. He could think of nothing to say that could possibly comfort her or matter to her, so he said nothing. He merely pulled up the chair at the desk she'd offered to him several days ago, and waited for her to come back from wherever it was her memories had taken her. He was pretty sure it was no place good.

They sat in silence for almost twenty minutes before his cell phone rang. He answered it, listened intently, then said, "We'll be there. Thanks."

Cass raised her eyes to meet his.

"That was Mitch. Dr. McCall — the profiler we told you about — has had a change of plans and can't be here until around two o'clock tomorrow."

Cass nodded absently.

"I'm going to want to tell her everything that's come out today. Including the fact that you were on the scene when your mother was murdered."

"I wasn't there," she told him, her face still white, her eyes huge and round and haunted.

"But Denver said you'd been attacked . . ."

"I came into the house after it was over."

"But you saw him."

She shook her head. "I don't remember. It happened so fast. He was just a blur."

"All the same, Annie is going to want to talk to you about it." And probably more than that, he knew, but he'd leave all that for Annie to go into.

"In the meantime, what would you like to do?"

"Do?" She frowned, as if not understanding the word.

"How would you like to spend the rest of the day? Is there someplace you might like to go?"

She thought about it for a moment, then held out her hand. "Give me the car keys. I'll take you."

Rick had no idea where they were headed. All he knew was that right now, Cass appeared to be in a somewhat fragile state of mind, and he'd go wherever she wanted to go if that would help keep her together until Annie arrived. As a psychologist, Annie was much better able to handle this, she'd know what to say and what not to say. For the most part, Rick just wanted Cass to hang on for another day. He leaned back in the passenger seat and waited until they arrived at their destination, wherever that might be.

They were several minutes out of town, on a road that was edged on both sides by marsh. Tall cattails crept to the shoulder of the road on the right side. A mile or two down the road, the cattails began to recede and they came to a clearing. In the center of the clearing sat a house with cedar shingles weathered to a rich brown. Cass turned into the drive and turned off the ignition. She got out of the car without a word and Rick followed.

The house had obviously been abandoned long ago, as had the boat that sat dry-rotting on cinder blocks near a dilapidated garage. A rusted child's swing set stood at the far end of the yard, the swings long gone, and around the foundation of the house, stubborn flowers bloomed in spite of years of neglect.

Cass went directly to the back steps and sat down on the second step from the bottom. Rick sat next to her, and she moved slightly to the left to accommodate him. They sat in the same way, he noticed. Feet on the step below, arms resting on their thighs.

"Where are we?" he asked, knowing that whatever this place was, it was important to her.

"My house."

"Your house? This is where . . . ?"

She nodded.

"No one lives here?"

"Not since then."

"Who owns it now?"

"I do."

"You do the outside work?" The grass had obviously been cut recently.

"I have someone do that every week."

He looked over his shoulder and studied the structure.

"I guess you'd have to do a lot of work to sell it."

"I wouldn't sell it. I'd never sell it," she said quickly. "It's all I have left."

"You think you'll move in someday?"

She shook her head. "I haven't even been inside since that day. I went straight to my aunt and uncle's after I was released from the hospital."

"Has anyone been inside?"

"Maybe my grandparents, while they were still alive. The police gave my grampa the key when they finished up. I found it on a hook near the back door after he died."

"Where's the key now?"

She dug in her pocket and pulled out her key ring.

"Right here," she said. "I know what you're thinking. You think it's stupid to hold on to a property for all these years if you're never going to do anything with it. Several acres of ground, this close to the bay, it does have great value, I know that. You wouldn't believe what I've been offered for it. But I can't bring myself to live here, and I can't bring myself to part with it. I can't go inside, but I can't stay away. It's the last place we were a family. The last place I saw them."

Cass looked over her shoulder at the house. "Sometimes I think they're still here, just inside the door. Sometimes I think I see my mother at one of the windows."

She glanced at him, looking for a reaction.

"You must think I'm loony."

"I can understand why you would want to see her. I can understand why you would look for her here. Whether you sell the house or keep it, whether you go inside or not, it's no one's business but your own. If it comforts you to sit here, that's what you need to do. You suffered a terrible loss, Cass." He reached over and took her hand. "Denver told me about what happened to you. I'm sorry. I don't even know what to say, how to say how sorry I am for all you went through."

She nodded an acknowledgment and stared out at the cattails.

"When I was little, the cattails didn't come up so close to the back here. They did on the side, but out here, out back, it was open all the way to the marsh. There are tidal flats back there, and Lucy and I would use pieces of wood to make little bridges so we could walk out there. We had a plank we carried with us to put down; we'd walk across the water, pick up the plank, and take it with us to the next little stream . . ." She paused, remembering. "Sometimes the mosquitoes would be so fierce. And the flies! Oh, man, we would get those green flies out there . . . big enough to lift you up and carry you out to the bay. We'd come in some days covered in welts, and my mother would dab at the bites with calamine on cotton balls."

She swallowed a lump and tried to smile. "It's funny what you remember, isn't it? The things you remember from your childhood?"

Cass sighed, and looked up at him. "What do you remember from your childhood, what's the first thing that comes to your mind?"

"Falling out of the hayloft in my grandparents' barn when I was three," he answered without hesitation.

"Were you hurt?"

"Broke both arms." He moved aside the hair that hung slightly over his forehead to show off a jagged scar. "Landed face-first on the dirt floor."

"You're lucky you didn't crack your skull open."

"Apparently I had a hard head. I also took some hay with me when I pitched off the loft."

"Like I said, lucky."

"It was only the first in a long series of mishaps. I had a bumpy childhood. I was a bit on the reckless side, I guess."

"Did you spend a lot of time on your grandparents' farm? Is this the grandmother who taught you how to bake?"

He smiled that she remembered.

"Yes. I lived with them pretty much until I was five."

"And after that?"

"I still spent a lot of time with them. I just didn't live with them full-time."

"And your family? Brothers? Sisters?"

"Two half brothers, two half sisters. All younger. One mother, one stepfather."

"What happened to your father?"

"I never got to know my biological father very well. I was the product of a youthful indiscretion, as the saying goes. My mother married my stepfather when I was five. He's really the only father I know."

"They're still in Texas?"

"Yes. All of them."

"Do you go back often?"

"Not so much anymore," he said softly. "I did while my gram was still alive, but now there doesn't seem to be much of a point to the trip."

Cass wished she could ask about that — about why there would be no point to visiting his mother or the others — but knew better than to pry. She knew what it was like to carry around things you hated to talk about, about the feeling you got when someone started to probe amongst all those places you kept to yourself. As sure as she had her secrets, Rick Cisco had some of his own.

She found herself hoping that maybe

someday she'd find out what they were.

Rick looked at his watch.

"The afternoon is just about gone. You want to hang around here for a while longer?"

"I guess not." She glanced up. The sun was well off to the west. "We missed breakfast. And lunch. We should probably get something to eat."

"Amen to that."

She smiled. "There's a place not far down the road that makes great burgers."

"You're reading my mind." Rick stood up, suddenly aware that he was still holding on to her hand. He pulled her off the step, but did not let go. "Feel any better?"

"I do. A little. Maybe a little more at peace." She made no effort to pull her hand away as they walked toward the car. "I always feel more settled after I've been here for a while. I know that must sound crazy, after everything that happened here."

She smiled almost apologetically and added, "We were such a happy family, Rick. I know, it's easy to idealize your childhood, your family . . . but truly, we were all very happy."

She stood next to the car and looked back at the house, her eyes darting from one window to the next before focusing on a bay window on the second floor. He followed her gaze, but saw nothing there.

*Maybe she's imagining someone there,* Rick thought as he walked around the front of the car. *Could be she needs to see someone there. Well, if it gives her comfort, who's to say . . .*

He glanced up again as he opened his car door, and for a split second wasn't sure that he hadn't seen something in the bay window. A shadow maybe. He looked over the roof of the car to where she stood, then back up to the window. Whatever he'd thought he'd seen was gone.

*Power of suggestion,* he told himself as he got behind the wheel. *Nothing more than that.*

# Nineteen

Through the open conference room door, Cass could hear the approaching *click click click* of high heels on the tile floor as they moved briskly, efficiently, in her direction. She looked up at the precise moment that the wearer of those shoes stepped over the threshold.

"Ah, here's Dr. McCall," Rick announced, and rose to greet the attractive blond woman who carried herself and her handsome leather briefcase with confidence.

"Agent Cisco." She smiled. "And you must be Chief Denver."

She left her briefcase on the chair nearest her and walked to the head of the table to offer her hand, which Denver shook somewhat gently.

"Thanks for coming, Dr. McCall."

She nodded and moved on to the next chair, where Cass sat.

Rick made the introductions. "Annie — Dr. McCall — this is Cass Burke. Detective Burke."

"It's good to meet you."

"I've heard a lot about you, Dr. McCall," Cass said. "Agents Peyton and Cisco tell me you're one of the best at what you do."

"Well, I guess you'll have formed your own opinion by the time we're through here." She looked at the empty chairs that stood around the table and asked, "Where is Agent Peyton? I understood he'd be sitting in on this meeting."

"I spoke with him about an hour ago," Rick told her. "He's been tracking information about some older kills that he believes may be related to these. He said something about being in the middle of receiving some faxes and wanting to stay until everything had come through."

"Then he'll be along in his own time. Or not, knowing him. He did say he had information that would put a new light on what's going on here." She returned to her place at the table. To Rick, she said, "Let's hope he makes it in the next twenty-four hours. We both know how he is once he gets a hold on something. He has a tendency to lose track of time."

"Annie — um, Dr. McCall . . ." Rick started.

"Let's keep this somewhat informal,

Rick. I have no problem with first names, if everyone agrees?" She glanced around the table. Cass and Denver nodded.

"Go ahead, Rick, you were about to say . . ."

"I was going to ask if you'd had an opportunity to review the files we sent."

"Not as thoroughly as I'd have liked, but I did get through most of it." She opened her briefcase and took out a pad of yellow legal paper, skimmed several pages of notes, then folded the pages back until she came to a blank sheet. "It appears you have a serial killer — apparently the same one you had . . . let's see, twenty-some years ago."

Denver nodded. "That's correct."

"But no suspects, then or now."

"Right again."

"You were on the force at the time?"

"Yes."

"Then I would think you'd be the obvious one to start with, Chief. Since I didn't have time to completely read through everything, why not bring me up-to-date. From then till now."

Annie sat back in her chair while the chief recited all the known facts about their killer. As she did so, Cass studied the profiler, who wasn't at all what she'd expected. Dr. McCall — Annie — appeared to be in her mid-thirties, and was so petite, she made Cass feel uncomfortably like an Amazon in comparison.

A somewhat slovenly Amazon, at that. Cass looked down at the clothes she had pulled on in haste earlier in the day. Light gray sweatpants and a short-sleeved sweatshirt. At least they matched, she reminded herself.

In contrast, the profiler wore a linen suit that had yet to wilt, a pale pink tank under the unlined jacket. She wore large round gold earrings, and a gold bracelet next to a watch with a brown leather strap. The diamond on the ring finger of her left hand caught the afternoon sun from the adjacent window. Her makeup was perfect, not overly done, just enough to enhance, as Lucy would have said.

At the thought of Lucy, Cass rested her elbow on the table and her chin in her hand. Poor Lucy. That she had been attacked was bad enough. How would she feel if she was forced to recover back in Hopewell, with that miserable excuse for a husband . . .

"Cass?" Rick touched her arm.

"Oh. Sorry."

"Annie was asking if there was anything

else you picked up from the crime scene that you might want to add."

Cass gave it some thought before shaking her head. "Nothing that isn't in the reports. I tried to be as thorough as possible."

"And the reports from the other towns . . . ?" Annie looked back at her notes. "Dewey. Hasboro?"

"We haven't received all the written reports yet," Chief Denver told her, "but in speaking with the chiefs of police in each of those towns, I can tell you we have identical crime scenes."

"With the victims posed in the same manner?" she asked.

Denver nodded.

"I wonder, Chief, if you could call those chiefs of police and request that they fax over the crime scene photos?"

"I've already asked, Dr. McCall. We only received the ones from Dewey."

"I'll take a look at those, if I could. Meanwhile, Rick, please put a call in to home base and request that someone call the Hasboro police chief and remind him Chief Denver is still waiting for copies of their files." She smiled. "Remind him it isn't nice to not share."

Rick excused himself from the room.

"May I see the original photos from your crime scenes?" Annie asked. "Only the recent ones for now."

Denver handed her several envelopes. The profiler removed the photos, one by one, studying each, occasionally glancing back at her notes.

"So we have someone who is highly organized. He's studied his victims well enough to know where they go and when they're most vulnerable. Obviously, the fact that these women are all of the same general physical appearance is key. He's repeating something. Over the years, he's perfected his technique. Brings everything he needs with him, leaves little behind." Her voice was low, as if speaking more to herself than the others at the table. "And he's fixated on leaving them in a particular manner. The posing, the hair fanned out . . ."

She tapped her fingers on the table absently, then looked at the chief.

"Are there photos of the earlier victims? The ones from 1979?"

"Not as many, and not as good. Back then, I remember we thought it was a little ghoulish to take as many pictures of the body as we do now, from all the different angles." He passed several envelopes to the

331

opposite end of the table. "I wish we'd taken more."

Annie poured over the images of the old crime scenes.

"Are these in order?" She frowned. "I'd like to see them in order, to study the progression."

Denver started out of his seat, but Cass had already slid down a few chairs.

"They should go like this," she was saying. "Alicia Coors, she was the first one. Here in Bowers. Then Carol Jo Hughes — also in Bowers — then Cindy Shelkirk. She was the first victim in one of the other bay towns, she was killed in Tilden. Terry List, she was from Dewey. Mary Pat Engles . . . Tilden . . ."

And so on, through all thirteen victims. Annie sat quietly and watched Cass as she placed the victims in order of their deaths.

"Well, then, let's take a look and see what these ladies have to tell us." Annie's eyes went from one to the next.

"He was much younger then, I'd say. Not yet an adult. He was unskilled in this business, these first times out. And he didn't have his game on back then. He hadn't evolved."

"What do you mean?" Cass asked. "He hadn't evolved into what?"

"Into the methodical killer he is now," Annie responded without hesitation. "Here, in these early kills, these crime scenes have little in common with the recent ones. There's no thought whatsoever to placement of the body . . . see how carefully the arms and legs have been positioned in these current scenes? Back then, it was all about the killing. There seems to have been an anger, a recklessness at work there that I don't see in your latest victims. Notice the bruises on the side of this woman's face? He smacked her around a bit before he got down to business. And this one, too. His technique was raw then, the killing had an almost desperate quality." She paused to take a sip of water from a bottle she retrieved from her oversized handbag. "The current kills are almost passionless."

She screwed the white plastic cap back on the bottle as Rick came into the room and gave her a thumbs-up, meaning the requested files would be on their way. She nodded an acknowledgment and continued.

"The victims themselves, though, there's where he was making his statement back then. All around the same age, same body type, and of course, the hair. Whoever he was killing, over and over, he had been totally fixated on her hair . . ."

"Ah, Annie, I think there's something you need to know that isn't in that file we sent you," Rick said.

"Oh?"

Rick turned to Cass as if asking a silent question, to which she responded with a slow nod.

"Cass's mother was the victim of a murder here in Bowers Inlet twenty-six years ago. Her entire family was attacked. Cass was the only survivor."

Denver bristled. "That was completely different, I told you. Why are you bringing it up?"

"Chief, I can't help but see the similarities —"

"What similarities? Don't you think if there'd been similarities, we'd have noticed?"

"— and with Lucy being attacked — Lucy, who looks so much like Cass's mother . . ."

"Whoa, wait a minute. I don't have a victim named Lucy." Annie skimmed her notes. "Who's Lucy?"

"Lucy is my cousin. She's been staying with me for the past week," Cass told her. "Sunday night, she was attacked."

"By this killer?" Annie tapped on the photos.

"We believe so."

Before she could say anything else, Rick touched Cass on the arm and said, "Tell her what Lucy told you."

"He called her Jenny," Cass said. "Repeatedly. He called her Jenny the entire time."

"Wait, wait." Annie held up both hands to stop them. "Start from the beginning. Who is Jenny?"

"Jenny was my mother's name."

"Your mother . . . who was murdered that summer."

"Yes."

"Before or after the other killings?"

"Before."

"Cass . . ." Rick touched her arm. "I think you need to tell her the whole story."

"Is this necessary?" The chief stared at Rick.

"I think it is. Annie?" Rick sought her input.

"I agree. If Cass is in agreement . . . ?"

Cass nodded.

"Let's start by you telling me everything you remember about the day your family was attacked." Annie paused, then asked, "Cass, may I record this interview? I'd rather be concentrating on what you're saying instead of having to take notes."

"Absolutely, do."

Annie took a small recorder from her bag and placed it on the table between her and Cass. After the initial introduction and the asking and granting of permission to record, Annie repeated the question.

"Cass, can you tell us what you remember about the day of the attack on your family? What is the first thing you remember?"

"I woke up early — the sun wasn't up yet. I went into the bathroom and it was still dark, but I heard my father downstairs. He was taking a charter out that day, so he'd be gone long before dawn. I stood on the top step and was going to go down to the kitchen to ask him not to take the last brownies with him — we made them the day before, Mom and Trish and me. Well, Trish didn't do a lot, she was only four . . ."

"How old were you, Cass?" Annie asked.

"I was six. I'd turn seven later that summer."

"Okay, go on."

"I was going to go downstairs, but then I heard the back door close, and I knew I'd never catch up with him. My dad was very tall and he walked really fast. By the time I'd have reached the kitchen, he'd have been in the car and backed down the drive, so I just went back to bed. My sister and I had started summer camp that week, and I was excited about going, so I couldn't fall asleep. I was still awake when my mother came in to get me up."

"What were you excited about?"

"Oh, just the whole camp thing. It was different from my everyday. One of my friends was having a birthday party that afternoon. It was going to be a picnic on the beach. And I was still all revved up from the day before. The bird sanctuary had been officially opened, and we'd spent the entire day there." Cass paused momentarily, remembering. "My mother drove us in the morning — we stopped to pick up Lucy. She was my age and my best friend. When camp was over for the day, Lucy's mother — my Aunt Kimmie, my mother's sister — picked us up and drove us home."

"What time was it, do you remember?"

"After lunch. Sometime around two."

"When you arrived home, did you go directly into the house?"

"Yes. Well, that is, Trish went in first. The minute we pulled up in front of the house, she jumped out and ran for the door, crying because Aunt Kimmie was going to take Lucy and me to the party, and Trish hadn't been invited. She ran into the house before I was even out of the car."

Cass swallowed hard and Rick left the room momentarily. Through the open door, they heard the thump of a can of soda being ejected from the machine outside the conference room. He returned in an instant and handed the can of Diet Pepsi to Cass, the tab already popped.

"Thank you." She took a long drink. "Thanks."

"What happened next?" Annie asked.

"Lucy and I got out of the backseat. I went up to the house. It was so quiet . . ."

"Wait a minute. Lucy got out of the car with you?" Rick asked.

"Yes."

Rick frowned. "I don't remember seeing her name in any of the reports I read. Did she go into the house?"

"No."

"Where did she go, if she didn't go with you? Did she just stand there by the car, waiting?"

"I think . . ." Cass tried to recall. "I think she might have gone into the back-yard. I think she said she was going to wait on the swings. You saw them, they're still there, in the yard. To the far right of the house."

He nodded.

"Anyway, I went inside. I heard something on the second floor, so I started up the steps. It all happened so fast after that. I saw . . . I saw Trish. He threw her." Cass's hands began to shake. "He just picked her up and threw her, like a doll."

"This is all in the file. Does she have to go through this?" Chief Denver protested.

"I'm afraid so, Chief." Annie took over again. "Cass, you saw him?"

"No, no. I didn't see him. I wasn't looking at him, I was looking at my sister. She had flown through the air . . . and I was wondering how she was doing that. I ran up the steps and he grabbed me."

"From which direction?"

"I don't know. I only remember being surprised. I don't know where he came from. He started stabbing at me then . . . with the knife." Cass fought to control herself, and Rick moved his chair closer to hers but did not touch her.

"Then you saw his face."

"No. No, I didn't. I'm sure of that," she protested. "I think I blacked out after the first time he cut me."

"Now, all this time, your cousin, Lucy,

was outside, playing on the swings?"

"I guess she would have been, yes."

"Did anyone talk to her about what she might have seen?" Annie directed the question to the chief.

"No. No reason to. We found the killer in the garage." Denver's jaw tightened. "The girl was in the backyard when we got there."

Annie's attention returned to Cass. "What happened next?"

"I don't know. Chief, you would know more than I."

"Mrs. Donovan — Cass's aunt — started to wonder where her niece was. She got out of her car and went into the house to find out what was taking so long. She stepped inside and heard some sound — she described it as a soft moaning sound — from the kitchen. She went in, and found Wayne Fulmer — he had a room in one of those old motels out along Route Nine, hung around town most days — Wayne was crying, sitting on the floor next to Bob Burke's body. His hands and clothes were covered in blood. According to Mrs. Donovan's testimony, she started screaming, 'My God, what have you done?' And Wayne, he started screaming back at her, 'No, no, not me. Not Wayne.' Then he ran out the back door, and she went up-stairs, screaming for her sister. She found you where you'd fallen," he nodded to Cass, "on the steps."

"Who called the police?" Annie asked.

"Someone driving past saw Wayne run-ning down the road, covered with blood. By the time we got there, he had run back into the Burkes' garage to hide, that's where we found him."

"Was the knife recovered?" Rick asked.

"We found it on the floor at the bottom of the steps."

"Prints?"

"The handle and blade were so slick with blood, we couldn't get a print."

The chief slanted a glance in Cass's di-rection to see her reaction, but there was none.

"When you questioned him about why he was there, what did he tell you?" Rick asked.

"Said he'd run into Bob down at the ma-rina an hour earlier and that Bob told him he'd had a big catch, that if he stopped by the house, Bob would give him some fish."

He began to fiddle with his glasses.

"You have to try to understand how this hit the community. Everyone in town knew and liked the Burkes. Bob's family lived here before there was a town. Nothing like this had ever happened in Bowers before. As far as I knew, nothing like this had happened anywhere around here. It left everyone speechless. Everyone was up in arms when the news leaked out about us finding Wayne hiding in the garage. That we had had that murderous scum living right here in Bowers Inlet, walking our streets . . . well, people were pretty outraged. But relieved, you know, that he'd been locked up."

"Frankenstein's monster," Annie murmured.

"What?" Denver frowned.

"The scene from the old *Frankenstein* movie just popped into my head. The one where the angry mob is chasing the creature."

"We were angry, Dr. McCall. Good people — a wonderful family — had been massacred in their own home. Everyone felt that if it happened to them, it could happen to anyone."

Denver sighed heavily. "I knew Bob and Jenny, had known them all my life. My brother had gone to school with them, and back in high school, he had the biggest crush on Jenny."

The chief felt everyone's eyes on him then, and shook his head. "Don't even think it could have been him. We lost him in Vietnam. He was long gone, come the summer of '79."

He cleared his throat.

"Anyway, we were talking about the day . . . that day. We — me and Jack Cameron, he's dead now about six or seven years — we went into the house, and it was like walking into a horror movie. Cassie was there on the floor upstairs, covered with blood. We thought she was . . . well, we thought there were no survivors. Then we noticed that she seemed to move, and we called an ambulance. Gave her mouth-to-mouth to try to keep her going." He wiped a tear from his face without seeming to notice he had done so. "I'd never seen anything like it. The carnage. That little girl, her neck snapped like it was a twig. And Jenny there on the bedroom floor . . . Bob on the floor in the kitchen. And Wayne Fulmer cowering in the garage, whimpering and shaking and covered in Bob's blood." He looked at Rick. "Who would you have thought did it, Agent Cisco, if you'd walked into that scene?"

"Well, I admit it looks pretty bad for Wayne."

"We had no DNA back then, just fingerprinting. And that wasn't always accurate, depending on who was reading the prints. None of this electronic matching. No profilers to come in and tell us what kind of personality we were supposed to be looking for." He stared at Annie with dull resentment.

"Chief, I'm sorry. We're not accusing you, we're not judging you —" Annie began, but he cut her off.

"Yes you were, Dr. McCall. You were judging, and you were criticizing and you were accusing us of shoddy police work. Don't judge our actions or our decisions twenty-six years ago by the way we do things today. We didn't have the tools back then." Denver got up and left the room before anyone could stop him.

"Shit," Rick said softly.

Cass rose to go after her boss.

"Let me, Cassie. This was my fault. I'll talk to him." Rick followed Denver from the room.

"Cass, could we finish up here? I only have a few more questions for you." Annie reached over and laid a hand on Cass's arm.

"I think I should go in and see if he's okay." She gestured in the direction of the chief's office.

"Rick made the mess, Cass. He'll clean it up."

"All right. I'll give him five minutes to come back in. If he hasn't cooled off and come back by then, I'm going to go and talk to him. It usually doesn't take him much more than that to calm down, no matter what he's angry about."

Just then, Cass's cell phone rang, and she glanced at the number displayed on the small screen.

"I need to take this," she told Annie.

"Khaliyah. How are you?" She rose and walked to the window.

"I'm okay, Cassie. I was wondering how you are. I saw on the news, about your cousin. I wanted to make sure that you . . ." The girl paused, her voice shaky. "I just wanted to make sure that you were okay, that's all."

"That's really sweet of you. I appreciate the call. But I don't want you to worry about me. I'm fine."

"I went by your house and saw the cops there and stuff and the yellow tape all around the place and I got scared," Khaliyah admitted.

"No reason to be scared."

"I wanted you to know you can come and stay here, with me, if you need a place to stay."

"That is the nicest offer. Thank you,

Khaliyah. But I have a place."

"Someplace safe?"

"Absolutely safe, yes." Cass's throat caught, so touched was she by her young friend's concern.

"But if anything changes, if you need to . . ."

"You will be the first person I call. Promise."

"I guess our one-on-one is off for a while."

"Nah. I'll be there."

"You will?"

"You betcha."

"Are you sure?"

"Positive." Cass hesitated for a moment, then added, "But let's try to get there a little earlier this week. That way we can wrap up while it's still light."

"Okay. Six?"

"Six is good. Unless you hear otherwise from me."

"Great. I'll see you then."

"Khaliyah . . ."

"What?"

"Ask Jameer if he can drive you this week, okay? Until this is over? I don't think you want to be walking around town."

"Okay. I'll ask him."

"If he can't, you'll call me, right?"

"Right."

"I'll see you then. And thanks, Khali-yah." Cass closed her phone and dropped it into her pocket.

"Sorry," she said to Annie. "Where were we?"

"We were —" The door opened behind Annie and she turned in time to see Rick and the chief coming back into the room.

"Sorry for the interruption." Chief Denver nodded at both women.

He took his seat at the head of the table, and Rick sat down next to Cass again as if nothing had happened.

"What else did you want to ask me?" Cass asked Annie.

"Do you remember anything else about that day? Do you have any other images in your mind?"

"Going down the steps for breakfast, behind my mother. Thinking she looked so pretty. That I'd never be as pretty as she was."

"What was she wearing?"

"A white shirt. Pink-and-white Capri pants," she answered without hesitation. "She had her hair tied back in a ponytail, like she always did, and it was swinging . . ."

She demonstrated with one hand.

"I used to untie it whenever I could. It

was sort of a silly game between us. That morning as we were going down the steps, I reached out and grabbed hold of the ribbon and pulled it, thinking her hair would fall free, but she had used a rubber band, too, so the ponytail stayed. She laughed, like she'd outsmarted me that day, and she tied the ribbon back into her hair."

"Maybe we should give Cass a break," Rick said abruptly, looking directly at Annie. "I think we could all use a little break."

Cass frowned. "We just had a little break."

"Oh. Excellent idea." Annie had noticed his expression, which said, *Just trust me.* "You know, I sat for several hours in the car on my way over here, and I would dearly love a chance to stretch my legs."

She turned to Cass and asked, "Is there any place close by where I could get ice cream? I'm dying for an ice-cream cone."

"There's a place a few blocks from here."

"Would you mind showing me? Are you up for a little walk?"

"Sure. Why not? Let me get my purse. I put it in my office."

After Cass left the room, Annie turned

348

to Rick and asked softly, "How much time do you want?"

"As much time as you can give me."

Annie nodded, and walked into the hall, closing the door behind her.

Rick turned to the chief and said, "We really need to look at the Burke homicide file, Chief. I'm sorry. I meant what I said back in your office. I'm not trying to step on your toes and I'll apologize in advance if you think otherwise. But right now, I need to see that file if it's still around."

"Of course it's still around. There are a couple of boxes of stuff that we found at the scene. We're not total rubes, you know," Denver snapped. "What exactly are you looking for?"

"Whatever the evidence can tell us. Whatever there is that can tell us something we don't already know."

# Twenty

"You're sure this is everything?" Rick looked up at Denver. He'd just gone through the contents of the three boxes of evidence that they'd lugged in from the department's storage room at the end of the hall, where they'd been since being moved from the garage of the former chief of police when the new municipal building was dedicated. "These are the only boxes?"

"That's all we have. Three boxes. I can vouch for that myself. All we ever had."

"Any chance that another box of evidence was left in the garage when this stuff was moved here? A smaller box, maybe, that could have been overlooked?"

"No. I was one of the officers who cleaned out the chief's garage after he died and brought the files here and put them in the storage room. I can tell you, every speck of evidence that was put in there came back out. The room is always locked, and Phyllis has the only key. You want something, you have to ask her for it, like we had to do."

"The chief . . . what was his name?"

"Wainwright."

"How was it that all your evidence boxes found their way into Chief Wainwright's garage, anyway?"

"No other place to store the stuff. The old station was only three small rooms." Denver shrugged. "Didn't seem like a big deal back then. We didn't think about things like chain of control or evidence being tampered with. We didn't have anyplace else to store the old files, so when he built that big new garage, we took over part of it. Besides, it was a solved case. We had our man. He'd been tried and convicted. You can say what you want now, Agent Cisco, but that jury was convinced. There was no damned reason to think that anyone other than Wayne Fulmer was involved. I'm still not certain there is now."

"Let's both keep an open mind, Chief. I'll allow that the evidence was pretty solid against Wayne and you'll allow that maybe things weren't what they seemed at the time. Now, what did Chief Wainwright keep in the other part of the garage?"

"He had an old car he was working on. Restoring. Don't remember what it was, frankly."

"So anyone could have gone into the garage and gone through the boxes?"

Denver frowned. "Not likely. Wainwright's property was all fenced in back there. Top of that, he had the biggest, meanest dog on the Jersey Shore, had the run of that garage. The chief had one of those dog doors and the dog used to come and go. I can tell you from my own experience, that was one unfriendly dog. I can't imagine a stranger getting past him."

Rick took one more quick look through the box holding Jenny Burke's clothing.

"You want to tell me what it is you're looking for?"

"First thing, I'm looking for the ribbon Jenny had in her hair that morning. Cass said she wore a ribbon in her hair."

"Yeah, I remember seeing it at the trial. The hair ribbon, her earrings. A thin gold chain she wore around her neck, it had a little heart on it. All those little things were in separate envelopes."

Denver looked at the inventory.

"Says here there's a ribbon, look right here. *One pink ribbon.*" Denver leaned over the side of the box, pushing Rick aside. "It went in, it's still here . . ."

He rooted around in the box for a few minutes, muttering, "Could'a fallen out of the envelope, gotta be in here someplace . . ." then looked up, puzzled.

"It's not here."

"I didn't see it, either."

"Where could it be?" Denver frowned. "It would have gone in, right after the trial."

He began to remove items from the box, one by one.

"Here's the chain with the heart . . . the earrings. No ribbon. Maybe in this box . . ." Denver started searching through a second box. When he came up empty-handed, he moved on to the third.

"Why would someone take the ribbon and leave the gold jewelry?" Rick wondered aloud.

"Right. If you were going to steal from the evidence box, why wouldn't you take the items that had some value? Of what use is —" Denver stopped in mid-sentence and turned to look at Rick.

"Those pink fibers the lab found in the victims' hair," he said flatly.

"That's what I'm thinking. Question is, how did he get it?"

"How did who get what?" Cass came into the room, followed by Annie, who, realizing that Rick could have used a little more time, gave him an apologetic smile. "We got you both some ice cream."

Cass proceeded to unpack the bag. "Chocolate for the chief . . . I know that's his favorite. Annie thought you liked coffee, Rick."

Rick nodded. "I do. Thanks."

"What's in the boxes?" Cass frowned, then glanced at the label on the side of the box closest to the end of the table.

*Burke homicide.*

Cass looked from Rick to the chief and back again.

"You know, you didn't have to send me out for ice cream, as if I were a child." She addressed the men, angry with both. "I'm really insulted neither of you thought I could deal with this, that I wasn't professional enough or stable enough —"

"Don't blame them," Annie interrupted. "That was me. I could tell from Rick's expression that something was bothering him and it appeared he needed us to clear out. I wasn't sure why. Ice cream was the only thing I could think of, since I skipped lunch and ice cream is the first thing I ever think of when I'm hungry. I apologize. It wasn't intended as anything more than a means to buy Rick a little time for . . . whatever it was he wanted to do."

"Apparently what he wanted to do was go through the evidence without me present. I'm not that fragile, Rick. I know what evidence boxes contain. In case you've forgotten, I've been a detective for several years, I've seen dead bodies . . . hell, who do you think took the photos of those victims?" She pointed to the stack on the table.

"I'm sorry, Cass. It just occurred to me to look for something specific, and I didn't want you to be upset if we found it." He blew out a long breath. "I'm sorry. I was absolutely out of line. I should have thought it through. If I had, I would have realized that you didn't need to be patronized. I'm really sorry. I don't know what else to say."

"Did you?"

"Did I what?"

"Find what you were looking for?"

"No."

"And what was it, may I ask?"

"The ribbon you pulled out of your mother's hair that morning."

"It wasn't there?" She frowned.

"It's gone. The chief remembers that it had been there after the trial. But it's gone now."

"He took it. He has it." Cass stared up at Rick, her anger pushed aside for now. "The fibers Tasha found . . . she said it was from ribbon that hasn't been manufactured for years . . ."

"How's that fit in with your profile, Dr. McCall?" Denver asked.

Annie set her bag on the conference table and reopened the file. She drew out the envelope of photographs the chief had given her when she arrived and spread the pictures across the table. Without being asked, Denver took a folder from one of the boxes and removed a photo, which he handed to Annie. She studied it for several minutes, then placed it on the table, ahead of the others.

"This puts it all into perspective," she said matter-of-factly. "This has it all make sense."

Her eyes went from crime scene photo to crime scene photo.

"Explain it to me, then, because I'm not following." Denver crossed his arms over his chest. "How do you explain the fact that he killed all the Burkes? Except you, of course, Cass, though God knows he tried." He paused to ask her, "Are you sure you're up to this? You know, no one would think less of you. This is your family we're talking about here."

Cass waved away his concern and nodded. She'd never seen the photos of the crime scene from her own house, and, despite her bravado, wasn't looking forward to it now. At that moment, her pride kept her in her seat and focused on the photos on the table between her and Annie.

"See, I'm saying the Burke homicides don't fit the pattern, Dr. McCall. Jenny Burke was attacked along with her whole family. And Jenny Burke was not raped. All the other victims were attacked alone — every one of them raped and strangled — none of them in their homes."

"It all falls into place when you realize that Jenny Burke was his first victim." Annie turned to Cass. "Earlier you said your father always left the house very early in the morning. That he took charters out on a regular basis."

"That's right. He fished just about every day, took charters out at least five times a week in the warm months."

"What time did he usually arrive home?"

"It must have been around four-thirty, most days. I don't know that I could tell time when I was six, but I do remember my mother saying, 'It's time to clean up for dinner, Daddy will be home before the clock strikes five.' Knowing now what I know about charters, I'd guess that by the time he got back to the marina and tied up the boat, cleaned it up from the trip so it was ready to go again the next day, four-thirty might be closer. If they had a really good morning, though, if the fish were running really strong and everyone in the party caught what they wanted, he'd have brought the boat back in early. There would have been no reason to stay out."

"Which apparently was the case on that day."

"According to Henry Stone — he worked for Bob — they were back to the dock by twelve-thirty, and left for home shortly before one," Denver told her. "Actually, when Bob was attacked, he was standing at the kitchen sink, cleaning that morning's catch. Had his back to the door."

"And what time did the attack occur?" Annie asked.

"We got to the house around two-thirty or so, I think. So it had to be before that."

"Earlier I said I thought our man was young. Disorganized. That maybe this had been his first kill. Now I'm convinced that was the case." Annie lowered herself into her seat. "I don't think he went to the Burke house intending to kill anyone. I think he went there to see Jenny — he knew her from someplace. I think he was

358

totally fixated on her. Maybe he fancied himself in love with her. Maybe he fancied that she was in love with him."

"Obsessed," Rick offered.

"Exactly." Her gaze returned to the photos. "See how Jenny's body is positioned? She's fallen onto her side, her arms are over her head. And every one of his subsequent victims is in the same position, the more recent ones more carefully staged. I think he's carried that picture — that memory of Jenny — in his head for all these years."

"You're saying you think he's killing her over and over?" Cass asked.

"I think it's more accurate to say that each time he's hoping it ends differently," Annie murmured. "I think he attacks these women because they remind him of Jenny, but each time he's thinking, 'This time I'll get it right. She won't fight me, I won't have to hurt her.'"

"How could he possibly think a woman isn't going to fight being raped and strangled?" Cass asked.

"He doesn't think of it as rape. He thinks his victim wants to be intimate with him. He only strangles her when she doesn't cooperate," Annie explained.

"Then you think that he believed that

my mother wanted to have sex with him?" Cass asked, indignation on the rise.

"I think he did believe that, yes. Which is no reflection on your mother. Please keep in mind, we're talking about a delusional personality here." Annie opened the Styrofoam container that held her ice cream, and almost unconsciously began to swipe off small bites with the plastic spoon. "Assuming that we've discovered the why, we still need to discover the who."

She licked at the spoon, a faraway look on her face.

"Who would she have been in contact with . . . someone young, inexperienced . . ."

"The department secretary and I have been going through yearbooks, trying to compile a list of who would have been around back then, who's back in town now. Within a certain age limit, of course." Denver explained to Annie that a large multiclass reunion was occurring that week. "We're trying to pin down some likely suspects, but our list is only partially complete."

"What criteria are you using to cut the list?"

"Well, since we got word that there were other identical killings, in different states

— even different countries — over the years, we figured someone whose job required them to move around a lot. Or someone in the military, perhaps," Denver said.

"Peyton is going to put the names into the Bureau's computer, see what spills out, once the list is complete," Rick said.

Denver remained skeptical. "I'm still not sold one hundred percent on your theory that the Burkes were killed by the same man, Dr. McCall. How do you explain the fact that Jenny wasn't raped and all the others were?"

"Jenny Burke's clothes were ripped, according to the report you sent me, Chief. He didn't rape her, because he was interrupted. Which probably infuriated him. Bad enough that he hadn't expected her husband to be there, bad enough that he had to kill him. Which must have rattled him big-time. He would have panicked when he found that she wasn't alone in the house." Annie appeared to be speaking to herself. "That would have thrown him off completely."

Rick nodded. "I'm following you. He comes into the house, expecting it to be empty, except for Jenny, who he might even think is expecting him, that she wants him to come to her. He sees Bob in the kitchen, and maybe acts impulsively, sees the knife and uses it. Then he goes upstairs, probably covered in Bob's blood . . ."

Rick stole a glance at Cass. She was white, but holding her own. *Trying to be professional, even while the details of her parents' deaths are being discussed,* he thought.

Denver told them, "Jenny's clothes had blots of Bob's blood. We thought she was surprised upstairs, and tried to fight him off . . ."

"Which would have confused and incensed him," Cass added a comment for the first time.

"It's likely that you and your sister arrived home at right about that time," Annie said. "And then he really panicked. Your mother would have tried to warn you."

"So he panicked again and strangled her. When Trish came up the steps, he was probably in a rage." Cass squeezed her eyes closed. "And when I came in . . ."

"He would have been completely out of control by then. Totally out of his league. He panicked and ran out of the house . . ." Rick paused. "Why didn't anyone see him?"

"What?" Cass opened her eyes.

"Why didn't anyone see him leave the house? Your aunt was out front, right? She would have seen him if he'd gone out the front door." Rick started piecing it together. "Your aunt said that when she came into the house, she went right into the kitchen. That someone was there in the kitchen, covered in blood."

"Wayne Fulmer," Denver supplied the name.

"Did he ever say that he saw someone else in the house?" Rick asked the chief. "Did he say that someone ran past him?"

"No. He never said anything about seeing anyone else. He testified that he came up the back steps and knocked, and when no one answered, he peeked through the screen door and saw Bob on the floor, so he came in, thinking that maybe Bob had fallen, but then he saw all the blood on the floor. He said he tried to pick him up, claims that's when he got Bob's blood on his clothes, then he heard commotion, and the next thing he knew, Cass's aunt was standing there screaming her head off."

"I read the reports. His story never seems to have changed," Rick noted.

"No, it never did." Denver seemed pensive.

"So we're back to the question of how this guy got out of the house if no one saw him," Annie said. "If someone other than Fulmer committed the murders, why didn't anyone see this second guy?"

"He could have gone out through the basement door," Cass told them.

"Where is that, in relation to the rest of the house?" Rick asked.

"The door to the basement is behind the main stairwell in the house," she told him. "There's a walk-out into the backyard from the basement."

"Cass, you said you thought Lucy was in the backyard."

"I thought . . . she said she was going . . ." Cass frowned. "But that would mean that she would have seen him."

Cass looked up at the chief. "Did she say anything about seeing anyone come out of the basement?"

"We didn't ask her what she saw," he said softly. "It never occurred to us to ask."

"She's never said anything to you, all these years, about seeing someone in the yard?" Rick asked Cass.

"No. Not a word."

"She may have blocked it out. She may not want to remember who — or what — she saw," Rick told her.

Annie touched her arm. "Cass, do you think your cousin will agree to being hypnotized?"

"No. No way. You can't ask her to do that." Cass shook her head vehemently. "She is in no shape for that. She's been through a lot this week, her larynx is damaged, she can barely speak . . . no, we can't do that to her."

"Cass, she may remember something, something that might help identify the man who was there that day. There wasn't anyone else there," Annie reminded her.

Cass shook her head. "Maybe if she wants to, when she gets out of the hospital, but not now."

"Well, I guess that leaves us back to the yearbooks and at the mercy of Peyton's computer skills. Excellent though they may be," Annie said to Rick.

"Okay. Chief, could you check with Phyl and see if we can have whatever list she's compiled so far? I think we should at least start with —"

"You're wrong," Cass said to Annie. "There was someone else there."

Annie tilted her head slightly to the left.

"I was there. Maybe if Lucy's buried something . . . well, maybe I have, too. Maybe there's something I saw . . . something I don't remember." She frowned. "I don't think I saw him, but I really don't remember."

"Are you sure you're up to it?" Annie asked.

"Yes." Cass nodded. "Absolutely. Let's do it. Right here. Right now."

"Are you sure? You may remember things you wished you hadn't."

"I'm sure," Cass insisted.

"If you're sure . . . first, let's get you comfortable." Annie stood.

"I'm fine," Cass told her. "I'm okay right here."

"I'm afraid I'm going to have to ask you both to leave the room." Annie looked apologetically from the chief to Rick, adding, "The fewer distractions, the better."

"Okay. We'll be looking over the list of names that Phyllis has been preparing," Rick said as he left.

"I'll call her into my office, we'll work in there." The chief paused on his way out of the room. "You sure about this, Cassie? You don't have to . . ."

"I really do have to," she told him. "But thanks."

Denver nodded and closed the door behind him.

"Okay, what do we do first?"

"I want you to get as comfortable in that chair as you can." Annie looked at the chair Cass was sitting in. "Is it possible to be comfortable in it?"

"I'm fine. Let's just do it."

"All right, then. I want you to close your eyes, and concentrate only on the sound of my voice. Don't think about anything else. Only the sound of my voice. That's all you hear, Cassie. All you want to hear . . ."

Annie's voice dropped slightly lower, but Cass could hear her just fine.

"Let yourself relax, Cassie. Your mind is going to take you to a place where all is calm. My voice is going to take you there. And once you're there, nothing will matter, except the sound of my voice . . ."

Cass closed her eyes, and focused on Annie's words. When Annie told her to let herself drift on the sound, she drifted.

"I want you to start counting backwards from one hundred, very slowly, until you reach twenty-five."

Cass did.

"You're there now, Cass. It's peaceful and you're safe there. Nothing can hurt you in that place. You can see, but you can't be seen, do you understand?" Annie's voice dropped yet lower, her words soft, reassuring. "Cass, if you understand, tell me."

"I understand." The words seemed to float from her lips.

"Are you there, then, Cass? Are you feeling peaceful? Are you feeling safe?"

"I am. I'm safe here."

"Good. Anytime you think you feel anything other than completely safe, you're to tell me, all right?"

"All right."

"We're going to look in on your house, Cass. The house where you and your mother and father and sister lived when you were a little girl. Do you see the house, Cassie?"

She nodded. "I see it." She *did* see it.

"What color is the house?"

"It's brown."

"Are there shutters at the windows?"

"White ones. With cutouts that look like birds."

"Can you tell what kind of birds?"

"Seagulls. They're flying . . ." She held her hands up, palms together, the fingers pointing outward.

"What else do you see?"

"Flowers. Pink ones by the front door. Mommy made Daddy put something on the wall so they would climb up to the second floor." Her eyes moved rapidly behind closed lids. "They grew over the door."

"Are they roses? Pink roses over the door and up the side of the house to the second floor?"

Cass nodded.

"Do you see the roses blooming?"

"Yes."

"So it must be June, since roses bloom in June." Annie leaned closer to Cass to continue to reassure her. "I want you to think back to a particular June, Cass. I want you to think about the last time you were in that house. It was June. School had ended. You went to summer camp that year. You and Trish and Lucy, you all went together."

Cass's eyelids began to flutter.

"Remember, Cass, you can see, but no one can see you. Do you remember? I promise, no one there can see you."

Cass's hands gripped the arms of the chair.

"Do you want to hold on to my hand while you visit there?" Annie held her hands out, but Cass neither opened her eyes nor reached for them.

"You can hold on to me anytime you feel you want to, Cass, remember that. I promise that you're safe. I will keep you safe."

Cass nodded.

"On that day, that last day, tell me what you remember about the morning."

Cass related everything as she had earlier. Waking while it was still dark. Getting up for camp and being excited about the party she would be going to later that day. Everything, from following her mother down the steps to coming home after camp, and going into the house.

"What do you hear when you step inside the house?"

Cass shook her head.

"You don't hear anything?"

"I don't know what I hear."

"What does it sound like?"

"Just . . ." She waved her hands around, her forehead wrinkled in concentration.

"Commotion?"

"But . . . quiet somehow . . . I didn't know what it was, but the sound, it came from upstairs. I ran up the steps . . ."

"Were you calling anyone? Were you shouting?"

"I was calling my mommy, but she didn't answer. Then I saw Trish . . . she was flying through the air. She hit the wall near Mommy's bedroom. She wasn't making any noise. I couldn't figure out how she could fly."

Sweat broke out on Cass's upper lip.

"Then what happened?"

"I ran up the steps, I was calling to her. 'How did you fly?' " A look of confusion came over her face. "But she was there on the floor . . ."

Cass swallowed hard.

". . . and someone grabbed me around the neck, and picked me up . . ."

"Cass, when he picked you up, what could you see?"

She shook her head.

"Cassie, I'm going to ask you to pretend that you're looking down on this, looking down from someplace up above as the man is grabbing you and picking you up." She took Cass's hand to reassure her. "What can you see? Can you see what he's wearing?"

"Blue sleeves, rolled up." She touched one elbow.

"He was wearing a blue shirt, with the sleeves rolled up to the elbows?"

"Yes."

"Can you see his hands?"

Cass nodded slowly.

"Is he wearing any rings? A watch?"

"No."

"Does he have anything in either of his hands?"

"He has a knife." She began to shake.

"Don't look at the knife, Cass. He's dropped it, there's no knife. I want you to concentrate on what I'm saying, all right?"

"All right," Cass said, though her voice was shaky.

"I want you to tell me what he smells like."

"Uncle Pete."

"He smells like your Uncle Pete?" Annie started. "Is he your Uncle Pete?"

"No, he smells like him. Like the stuff he wears when he and Aunt Kimmie go out."

The same cologne or aftershave her uncle wore. Easy enough to trace.

"Does he speak to you? Does he say anything?"

"He's shouting, but I don't understand." Cass covers her ears with her hands.

"Listen to what he's saying, Cass. Remember, he can't see you. He can't hear you. And we took the knife away from him, remember? He can't hurt you."

"I can't understand him. He's . . . shouting. Cursing. He's angry at me. He's angry . . ."

"Cass, is there anything else you see? Anything else you remember about him?"

Cass touched her right index finger to the back of her left hand.

"The bird mark."

"What does it look like?" Annie asked, thinking Cass had said *birthmark.*

"Like the one on the letters Mommy sent out. The big bird with the . . ." Her hands made semi-fists, the fingers held out like claws.

"Bird mark? You're saying *bird* mark?"

"Yes."

Anne Marie felt a jolt. This was it, then, their first real lead.

"Cass, is there anything else you see," she asked again, "anything else about him that you remember?"

Cass shook her head.

"That's fine, you did just fine. Now, I'm going to bring you back, just follow my voice back, Cass. I want you to count backwards now, slowly, from twenty-five. When you get to one, you'll open your eyes . . . you'll feel rested and peaceful. Start counting now."

When she reached one, Cass opened her eyes and blinked.

"How did I do?"

"Just brilliantly. You may have given us exactly what we need, Cass. Now, how do we get Chief Denver back in here?"

# Twenty-one

"Cass, can you sketch out for me what you saw on the killer's hand?" Craig Denver asked after Annie related what Cass had told her while under hypnosis.

"I don't think so. I don't really remember what I saw." Cass shook her head. "I'm sorry. I just don't remember."

"It was something like this." Annie picked up a pen and her notebook. "She said a big bird, with claws like this . . ."

Annie bent her fingers to form claws, as Cass had done while under hypnosis.

"Like a hawk? Like some type of raptor." Denver studied it for a long minute, then muttered, "I'll be damned," before buzzing for Phyllis.

"Phyl, I need you to take a look at something in here."

He held up the sketch when the secretary appeared in the doorway. "What's that remind you of?"

Phyl didn't miss a beat. "Looks like the logo on top of the newsletter we get from the sanctuary. Just got one the other day."

"You still have it?"

"I think so. Let me take a look." She disappeared behind the closed door.

"I should have figured that out from your description." He turned to Cass. "Your mother was instrumental in having that bird sanctuary set up down there off Bay Road. That was a big project of hers."

"I do remember that." Cass nodded and turned to Rick. "I took you there. Down near where we found . . ."

"Right. There was a plaque in memory of your mother."

"They had a big dedication ceremony when the sanctuary was opened." The chief rubbed his chin thoughtfully. "Seems to me that was that same summer."

He looked up when Phyl came back into the room, holding up the newsletter. Across the top was the picture of a hawk, its talons extended as if reaching for something.

"What do you think, Cass?" Denver asked.

"I remember seeing writing paper in the house, on my mother's desk in the corner of the living room, that had that hawk on it. I think my mother used to send out letters on it."

"She probably would have," Phyl told

her. "She was one of the founding members of the sanctuary and was involved in all the fund-raising efforts. I was on her committee two years before the sanctuary opened. As I recall, we raised enough money to open three months ahead of schedule."

"None of which tells us why the killer would have had the image on his hand," Anne Marie reminded them.

"Oh." Phyl rested her arms on the back of a nearby chair and leaned over slightly. "Founders' Day. They have a big event every year to raise money to keep the sanctuary going. There's a fair with rides for the kids, food, a little petting zoo, that sort of thing. They set it all up in the parking lot. When you pay to get into the fair, you get your hand stamped. That means you don't have to pay for any of the events, and you can go to the sanctuary for free the entire weekend. As long as the stamp is still on your hand."

"Were they having this fair back in 1979?" Rick asked.

"That would have been the first one, I think. I can check on that, but I'm pretty sure the sanctuary was founded in '79," Phyl said.

"It was. I remember," Cass told them. "I

remember hearing my mom talk about it. She was really excited about it and happy that it was going to happen. The dedication was the day before the attack at our house."

"I can confirm that," Phyl was saying as she left the room. "I'll get the date of the dedication. It was a big deal back then."

"So our boy would have been at the dedication of the sanctuary," Rick said. "That's where he would have come into contact with Jenny."

"June first, 1979." Phyl's voice came through the intercom. "I called my sister. Says she remembers because it was her seventeenth birthday that weekend and all the kids who had volunteered to work at the sanctuary had come back to the house that night for cake and ice cream."

"All the kids who volunteered?" Rick asked. "Your sister was a volunteer there that day?"

"Yes."

"Phyl, get her back on the phone, then come in here. We need to talk to her," the chief instructed.

"Will do."

Phyl returned in less than a minute and hit a blinking light on the desk phone, then tapped *Speaker*. "Louise?"

"I'm here." The voice floated from the box.

"Louise, Chief Denver here with Detective Burke and Dr. McCall and Agent Cisco from the FBI. We need to ask you a few questions."

"Fire away."

"You were at the dedication of the bird sanctuary back in '79?"

"Yes. There were fifteen or twenty of us there that day."

" 'Us'?" Rick asked.

"Kids. From the high school." She laughed. "Mr. Raddick, the science teacher, gave extra credit to anyone who volunteered to work out at the sanctuary that spring."

Rick took over the questioning. "Not to work only that day?"

"No, no, in order to get the credit, you had to go at least one day each weekend that whole marking period."

"Did you go?"

"Most weekends."

"Do you remember who else went?" Would it be too easy to have names handed to them? When was the last time *that* had happened, Rick asked himself.

"I could probably remember most of the kids who went. Mostly girls, but a bunch of the guys went, too. Some of the real popular guys." She paused. "I remember thinking it was odd that those guys went."

"Odd in what way?"

"Guys like them weren't generally interested in that type of thing."

"Guys like who?" Denver leaned toward the speakerphone. "Do you remember names?"

Louise laughed again. "Sure. It was that whole bunch — you remember, Phyl. Billy Calhoun, Jonathan Wainwright, Joey Patterson, Kenny Kelly . . . that group."

Denver groaned.

"Those were the only boys?"

"Far as I can remember. Oh, there might have been a few of the nerdy guys, like Bruce Windsor, but of the cool guys, it was only those four. That's why so many of the girls signed up, because of them."

"Anything stand out in your mind from that day?" Annie asked.

"Not really. Just that it was hot and a lot of people showed up. I was in one of the concessions that served drinks — soda and lemonade. We were busy all day."

"Louise, did you know Jenny Burke?" Rick asked.

"Sure. We all knew her. She ran the volunteer program. We all worked with her."

"Do you remember if any of the guys seemed to pay particular attention to her, or seemed to be extra-friendly with her?"

"Not offhand. I think the guys all tried to show off for her, though. No one in particular, but it seemed they all thought she was something else. Mrs. Burke was real pretty and real friendly. I remember that at her funeral all the volunteers were there."

"Anyone stand out in your mind as being particularly upset? Or acting strangely? I know it was a long time ago . . ."

"Twenty-six years, but I remember. We were all upset. Mrs. Burke was the first person I actually knew who'd been murdered. It hit all of us pretty hard. Like I said, she was real friendly and we all idolized her. I don't remember anyone being more upset than anyone else."

"Was she equally friendly with everyone?" Denver asked.

"Sure."

"Was there anyone you ever saw her argue with, or anyone who sought her out more than the others?"

"Honestly, no, I don't remember anything like that. There could have been, I just don't remember anyone in particular."

"Well, if you remember anything else — or the name of anyone else who worked that day — give me a call back."

"Sure, Chief. Phyl, I'll talk to you later."

Phyllis pushed the button to end the call.

"Anything else, Chief?" she asked.

"Not right now. But thanks, Phyl. That was a big help."

"Okay if I leave for the day?" Phyllis glanced at her watch. "I told my husband I'd pick him up after work. His car's getting inspected."

"It's quitting time anyway, Phyl. You go on," he told her.

"Why did you groan when Phyllis's sister named names?" Annie asked after Phyl had left the room.

"Oh, well, let's see." The chief leaned back in his seat and looked at the ceiling. "She named the sons of the high school principal, the former chief of police, the mayor, and a county judge."

Rick brightened. "Great. So let's take a look at them."

Denver was tapping his fingers on the tabletop.

"What?" Cass asked.

"They were a cocky little foursome back then. Inseparable. Practically lived at one another's houses, went everywhere together. And always into something, the lot of them." He closed his eyes briefly. "They

381

were the biggest pains in my ass, frankly. Twenty-some years ago, and I still see red when I think about them."

"Were any of them arrested back then?" Annie asked.

"With Jon Wainwright's father the chief of police and Kenny Kelly's father the judge?" He snickered. "What do you think?"

"What types of things were they involved in?" Annie pressed.

"Minor things. Loitering. Disturbing the peace. Starting fights after the soccer games. Speeding, underage drinking. They never were written up for anything, but they were always pulling pain-in-the-ass things that took your time and pissed people off."

"Low-level sex offenses?" she continued. "Allegations of rape, Peeping Tom activity . . . ?"

The chief shook his head. "Not that I know of, but if there'd been any of that stuff, Chief Wainwright would have dealt with it himself. He wouldn't have involved us young guys in anything like that. Not if it involved his own son, or the sons of any of those other men."

"I guess there weren't records kept of that sort of thing."

"Not if it involved any one of those four. All the annoying crap they pulled back then, you'll never find a word written down."

"What are you thinking, Annie?" Rick asked.

"Just that if you scratch hard enough, you find that kids who have grown into adults like our killer exhibited aberrant behavior at an earlier age. You don't wake up one day and decide you like to hurt people. You've thought about it — fantasized about it — for a long time before you act upon it. I was just wondering what early behavior our boy may have exhibited. What fantasies he may have tried to act out. Peeping is a first step for many who graduate into more serious sex offenses. It's a logical place to start."

"I'm afraid I can't help you there." The chief shook his head. "I wouldn't have been brought into that loop."

"They were, what, high school juniors, seniors that year?" Rick asked.

Denver nodded. "Seniors."

"Any of them college-bound that fall?"

"All of them, far as I remember."

"So they would have been out of town by the end of the summer," Annie said.

"When the killings here stopped," Cass said softly.

"Do I dare ask if you know if any of these men are back in town for the reunion?"

Denver nodded. "They're all here. All four of them. Saw them at the clambake last weekend. Spoke to each of them myself."

"Lucy and I were there," Cass said.

"If our killer was there, he would have seen her. Would have noticed right away how much she looks like Jenny," the chief said.

"I guess it's too much to ask if you know where any of these guys have been for the past twenty-six years?" Rick said.

"Oh, well, I know that Ken Kelly keeps the family summer house here in Bowers. And Jon Wainwright, I think I remember him saying he's worked for a security company for the past, oh, I don't know, fifteen years or so. Joey Patterson, he'd gone into the Marines for a while, don't know what he did after that. And Billy Calhoun did tell me where he's been living, but I don't really remember. Someplace out west, I seem to think he said," Denver replied. "I can start asking around."

"We need to be subtle, Chief. At least for now. We'll have an edge, as long as he isn't aware that we're closing in on his identity,"

Cass pointed out. "And if we're wrong . . . And we could be wrong — a lot of people would have had that bird stamp on their hand after that weekend."

"Give me their names again." Rick reached across the table and grabbed the pen Annie had earlier used. "I'll call them in to Mitch, have him run the names. See if anything hits. Then, in the meantime, we can start backtracking to find out where each of these gentlemen have spent their time since they left high school."

The breeze began to blow hard across the marsh, sending the cattails chattering and the birds seeking shelter from the coming storm. He sat on the stump of a tree that had long ago been cut down, and stared across the clearing at the bird blind that stood at the end of the wooden walk.

His eyes kept returning to the plaque that marked a memorial for the woman he had once loved with all his heart.

*This is all your fault, Jenny. I'm sorry to say it, but there it is. If you hadn't led me on the way you did — what were you thinking, leading me on like that? Did you think it was funny? A game, maybe?*

His face twisted into a scowl.

*You don't play those kind of games with*

*people who love you, Jenny. I guess I showed you that, didn't I?*

She had always been so nice to him, right from the first day. She'd talked to him like he was an old friend, like he was on her level. Never talked down to him, never made him feel like the stupid gangly kid he knew himself to be.

It always killed him to think that his father had made him volunteer at the sanctuary as a punishment for having been caught looking where he shouldn't have been looking. If it hadn't been for that, he'd never have gotten to know her the way he did. He'd never have fallen in love with her, or she with him . . .

Oh, he'd known who she was, everyone in Bowers Inlet knew Mrs. Burke. She was a knockout, for sure. Only the kids who worked with her at the sanctuary got to call her by her first name. Jenny.

"Call me Jenny," she'd said that first day.

It had thrilled him every time he'd said her name aloud. He'd used it as frequently as possible.

He'd counted the days, Saturday to Saturday, lived for his hours working out there in the marsh, swatting mosquitoes and green-headed flies. He didn't care. He was with her, hour after hour, every Saturday.

And with every hour spent with her, his love grew until it was the most important thing in his life. Grew until he thought he'd die of it.

She wanted blinds built, he built blinds. Not one or two or three, but an entire series of them, strategically placed throughout the acres that made up the sanctuary. She'd hooked him up with a contractor who'd offered to help build the structures, and he gladly gave up his weekends to labor on something that pleased her so much.

"You're amazing," she'd said once, after having climbed the ladder to one of the blinds. "I can't believe you did this. How many have you built now? Four? Five? Simply amazing. I can't thank you enough."

*Sure you can,* he remembered thinking at the time. *I know how you can thank me. We both know how. And we both know you want to.*

Love and lust had mixed inside him, a heady brew. She must have felt it, too. No one could feel that way about someone who didn't feel the same about him. Of that he was certain. The feeling was way too big. It dominated everything in his life. She had to know. She had to feel exactly the same about him. It wouldn't have been fair otherwise.

And wasn't it meant to be? After all, the offense his father had wanted to punish him for, well, that hadn't been much of anything, right? No one was hurt, right? No harm, no foul.

It wasn't as if he'd actually touched that girl.

He stood beneath the blind and jumped up to grab the under-support beams, then hoisted himself up to the floored area. Leaning over the railing, he gazed out at the deepening shadows. It had been so many years since he'd stood in this spot, this very spot, where he'd listened to her talk about the bird counts they were doing down in Cape May.

"Thousands upon thousands of song-birds and seabirds, can you imagine what that looks like, thousands of birds feeding on the shore?" She'd shaken her head, and that black ponytail had swung seductively. "I'm thinking about taking a van of kids down next year. If you're home from school, maybe you'd like to go."

He'd nodded. *Sure. Sure, I'll go . . . I'll go anywhere with you.*

But of course, he hadn't. Oh, he'd come home from school in May, but there was no trip to Cape May for Jenny that year. Or any year after.

"You brought it on yourself, Jenny."

He said the words aloud, certain she heard him.

His thoughts turned to Cass. She had ruined things for him once again. First with Jenny, then with the other one.

He sighed deeply. She was going to have to be punished. Maybe if he wiped her out, it would be all right, like wiping a slate clean.

He found the image of wiping the slate clean with Jenny's daughter's blood highly appealing.

Maybe then he could find the one he'd been searching for and they could be together for always. She wouldn't try to run from him, and he wouldn't have to hurt her.

Well, he was just going to have to take care of it, once and for all.

He reached up to a low-hanging tree branch and snapped it off.

*Snap. Just like that.*

# Twenty-two

"Annie." Rick stood on the single brick step that passed for a porch at the Bowers Inlet Municipal Building. "Want to catch some dinner?"

Halfway to her car, Annie turned to him. "Thanks, but I'm on my way up to the Landry farm. Mitch wanted me to look over the reports he's been receiving over the past few days. Apparently a lot has come out of the woodwork. I want to see what he's got before I have to head back to Virginia."

"When do you get to see that fiancé of yours?" He was smiling as he walked toward her.

She smiled back. "We manage. He's a detective. We both know the routine."

"Think you can build a life around schedules like the ones you two have?"

"We're going to do our best."

"When's the wedding?"

"We haven't set a date yet. I'm thinking maybe around the holidays. Neither of us wants to put it off too much longer." She juggled her car keys, and they clanged softly against each other as she tossed the key ring from one hand to the other and back again.

"Sure hope I'm on the guest list." He grinned. "I have my heart set on catching that bouquet."

She laughed. "You catch the bouquet, you gotta back it up, Cisco. Is there something I don't know about? Last I heard, you hadn't had a real date since Livy Bach slammed the door in your face one night after . . ."

"Ouch." He winced at the reference to a relationship with a fellow agent, one that never got off the ground. "That's cold, McCall. Really cold."

"Your luck," she said as she unlocked her car door. "Livy's not your type."

He frowned. "What's that supposed to mean?"

"Livy is the quintessential party girl. You need a rock, my friend. Livy's a doll and more fun than just about anyone I know, but she has heartbreak written all over her. Not only for you, for anyone who tries to get too close. There are walls there I'm afraid no one can climb."

"Well, thanks for the analysis, Dr. Mc-Call."

391

"I call 'em as I see 'em." She slid behind the wheel of her car. "I love Livy dearly, but she has a lot of problems, Rick. A lot of baggage. She's not what you need."

"I am not going to bite, I swear I'm not." He slammed her door for her, then stood back while she rolled the window down. "I'm not going to ask what you think is my type or what you think I need. The last thing I want right now is to have you —"

"Hey, Cass." Annie waved to Cassie as she walked toward them. "Are you feeling all right?"

"A little tired, but I'm fine. Thank you." Cass stopped next to Rick and leaned in the window slightly. "I don't think I thanked you for . . . well, for working with me. It sounds silly to say thanks for hypnotizing me, but I'm so grateful to you for doing that."

"You must feel a lot of conflict, though." Annie watched Cass's face closely.

"In what way?" Cass stood up and took a step back from the car.

"All these years, you've thought you had closure, for your parents' death and that of your sister. For the attack on you. Now that door is wide open again. It has to make you uneasy, at the very least."

Cass nodded. "A little. I never thought

about that aspect of it, you know? Wayne Fulmer was in prison, he'd never get out. Justice had been served. Though, truthfully, when you're a child and you've lost everyone and everything, justice is merely a concept, one that has very little meaning."

"I understand." Annie opened her handbag and took out her wallet. She handed Cass a card. "All of my numbers are listed here. If you ever want to talk, please, call me. Any time, day or night. And if you feel you want or need someone locally to talk to, I'll be more than happy to help you find someone. As a matter of fact, an old friend from grad school has a practice near Red Bank — that's not too far from here, right? I'm sure she'd love to speak with you, if you feel you want to do that."

"Thank you. I might call you, if you're sure . . ."

"I'm positive." Annie turned the key in the ignition. "Don't forget. Any time."

She glanced up at Rick as she put the car in reverse. "I'll see you soon. We'll call you later tonight if we feel we have something that might shed some light on your case."

Rick nodded and slapped lightly at the fender as Annie pulled away.

"She's really nice," Cass said as she waved good-bye.

He nodded. "Annie is one of a kind. She's the best at what she does, and she's a terrific person, to boot. Everyone is so happy for her, the way things have worked out."

"What things?"

"You might have noticed the ring on her finger?"

"How could I not?" Cass grinned. "It's quite a rock."

"Annie's engaged to a great guy. Detective in Pennsylvania; we're all trying to get him to come to the Bureau. He's perfect for her." Rick watched Annie's car turn onto the main road and disappear at the stop sign.

"That's nice, that her friends all like him. I'm happy for her, that she found someone so nice."

"It's more than Evan being a nice guy." He started walking toward his car, and Cass fell in step with him. "Annie had been engaged a few years ago, to a guy I went through the Academy with. Dylan Shields was the best in our class. Just a super, super guy in every respect."

"What happened? Did he break off the engagement?"

"He was killed on a job a few years ago," Rick said simply.

"Oh, my God, that's terrible. Poor Annie. No wonder her friends are happy that she found someone."

"Happy for her, certainly, but truth be told, we're all — all of us guys who work with her," he smiled as he unlocked the car doors and they both got in, "we're jealous as hell of Evan. We're all just a little bit in love with Annie."

"I can see that." Cass smiled, too. "And I can see why. She's beautiful and smart and there's something about her . . . a real gentleness, I guess I'd call it."

He nodded. "You hit it right on the head. That's exactly it. I couldn't have said it better myself. She's one of the strongest women I've ever met, and yes, one of the smartest as well, but she has this gentle side to her. She's been a good friend. And I guess that's why we all love her."

*Lucky Annie,* Cass was thinking as Rick backed out of the parking space. What, she wondered, would it be like to have not one, but a whole passel of hunky FBI men in love with you?

And she was certain they were all hunky, if the others in his unit were anything like Rick. In her mind they were. A whole entire crew of great-looking men was so much more fun to imagine than solemn-looking men in dark suits wearing the requisite dark glasses — though it occurred to her that Rick did look pretty hot in his shades.

The thought of all those great-looking guys lined up made her smile.

The smile faded a bit when she realized this had been the first light thought she'd had in . . . she couldn't remember when. When had she last wanted to smile, or laugh, or make a joke? The events of the past two weeks clearly had not presented many opportunities for humor.

"Cass."

"What?"

"I said, what would you like to do now?" He glanced at the clock on the dashboard. "It's almost six. Dinnertime for most folks."

"Well, if you wouldn't mind, I'd like to stop at the hospital to see how Lucy's doing, but beyond that, we need to know if she thinks she's ready to meet with the sketch artist. Lucy is the only person who's been face-to-face with this guy and lived to tell about it. The sooner we can get a sketch, the better. Especially now that it appears this might be someone who could be easily recognized by people in town."

"Say the word, and I'll have the Bureau's best up here in a flash."

"Lucy will tell me if she's up to it. She seemed to be making progress yesterday. I can't imagine they'll make her stay too much longer."

"We may want to stretch out that hospital stay, if for no other reason than to keep her under lock and key. Denver's had the guard at her door twenty-four/seven, but once she leaves there, it's going to be harder to keep an eye on her. I don't know that the cops in the town where she lives would be willing or able to put her under constant surveillance. We could ask for someone from the Bureau, though."

"I can't believe the rat-bastard husband of hers is actually going to take her home with him. Or that she'll go."

"What makes him a rat bastard? Other than the fact that he looks a little shifty."

"You caught that? And you don't even know him." She leaned back into her seat, a satisfied smile on her lips. "Of course, if she goes home, she'll get to see her kids, and that's going to be really important to her. I'm sure he'll take her to see the boys. They're away at sports camp."

"I did sports camps when I was a kid. Of

course, we didn't have what kids today have. Not just the variety to choose from, but the opportunity to learn from professional athletes was never an option for us. Today, these kids can go to football camp or basketball camp or softball camp and actually get pointers from some of the best in the business."

"Lucy's boys are at a camp where they do two weeks each of several different sports, and they *do* have pro athletes come in to work with the kids. I know she's said they're having a ball. They don't want to come home."

"Do they know about the attack on her?"

"No. She didn't want them told. She figures she's better off telling them when she sees them. She'll still be bruised, but at least they'll be able to see that she's okay." Her voice dropped a bit. "It will be important for them to see that she's okay . . ." Her voice trailed off.

Rick reached over and took her left hand in his.

"This has been a rough day for you. You've held up remarkably well. If there's anything you want to do, or anyplace you want to go . . ."

"Just to the hospital." She made no effort to pull her hand away. That small bit of closeness seemed to offer reassurance, and made her feel, for the first time in a very long time, that she was not alone. It was part of his job to set her at ease, she knew. She'd played the same role — that of comforter — to others many times in the past. Still, his touch was soothing, and she was grateful for it.

They drove in silence for the remaining four blocks to the hospital. Rick parked in the garage and started to open his car door, when his cell phone rang.

"Mitch," he answered the call, "what do you have for us?"

"I'll only be a few minutes," Cass whispered as she got out of the car.

"Wait a minute . . . wait for me. Mitch, hold for a second . . ."

"I won't be long. I just want to see her, see how she's feeling. You don't have to come. Look, there are guards everywhere. I'll be fine." She was off before he could loosen his seat belt.

Rick watched her through the rearview mirror, as she disappeared into the stairwell.

He got out of the car and followed her while listening to Mitch's rundown of victims they'd found from across the country and across the years that matched the MO of the Bayside Strangler.

"Any DNA testing results available?" he asked as he opened the stairwell door and climbed the single flight of steps from parking level B to the lobby.

"How many matches?" He walked into the lobby and crossed to the elevator.

"Are you serious? And no one's put this together . . . oh, of course, right. You're right . . ." Rick punched the button for the sixth floor. "So we have a whole long string of offenses that match perfectly, a good number of DNA matches, but no description of this guy." He shook his head. "He must be incredibly good or incredibly lucky — maybe both — to have kept it going all these years without being seen."

Rick stepped off the elevator and walked to Lucy's door, where he nodded to the police officer who'd been assigned the afternoon shift, then leaned back against the door frame and lowered his voice to continue the conversation. From Lucy's bedside, Cass looked over her shoulder. She locked eyes with Rick for a moment before turning back to her cousin.

"Can you follow up with those?" Rick asked. "Sure. I can be there in the morning. One thing I should mention, though. I'll be bringing Cass along with me . . .

yeah, well, what did Annie tell you?" He glanced into the hospital room as he listened. His gaze fell on Lucy's husband, David, who sat on an uncomfortable-looking orange plastic chair, his arms folded over his chest. His every effort to join in the conversation between Lucy and Cass having been ignored, he now pretended to ignore them.

"Give me some quick directions . . ." Rick kept his eyes on the scene unfolding in the room. Lucy was wiping her eyes, while Cass appeared to be speaking softly, something comforting, he was sure. How could the woman do that, he wondered, after the afternoon she'd had? Surely, looking back on that horrific day, even from a deep hypnotic state, must have taken a toll on her emotions. He'd figured she was tough, but he hadn't known she was *that* tough.

"Give me that again," he was saying, when Cass turned and looked at him. She stood and rested a hand on Lucy's cheek, then walked toward Rick.

"Anytime." She mouthed the word, so as to not disturb his conversation.

"Was that a right or a left off Route One?" He indicated to Cass that he could talk and walk to the elevator at the same time. Once inside the car, however, his phone went dead.

"Damn," he muttered, "I was almost there."

"Almost where?" Cass asked.

"Almost to Plainsville."

"What's there?"

"A meeting I — we — have tomorrow morning. I'll tell you about it outside," he told her, as the elevator car filled when they reached the third floor. "In the meantime, would you like to go straight to the Inn for dinner? Or is there something else you'd rather do?"

"As much as I'd love a walk on the beach, I think I'd like to go back to the Inn." She followed him out of the elevator when it stopped at the lobby. "And you can fill me in on this meeting."

He took her arm and steered her in the direction of the parking garage. Neither of them noticed that of the seven people who stepped out of the elevator after they did, one trailed behind them, all the way to level B.

# Twenty-three

He drove leisurely, just another car that had been parked along Maple Avenue near the municipal building. He could have been coming from the public library, which was located in three rooms on the second floor. Or he could have been leaving the police station, having paid a ticket — or the borough clerk's office, having purchased new tags for his dog.

Of course, he had been doing none of those things. But, to the casual observer, the man driving the Chrysler sedan was just another citizen, going about his afternoon business.

He stayed several car lengths behind the black Camaro that carried his prey, just far enough to stay under the radar of the driver, who had to be a Fed. God knew he'd known enough of *them* in his day. He knew how to tail the best of them without being noticed.

The Camaro turned right on Brighton, and he followed casually. But when the driver turned into the parking lot of the

Brighton Inn, he went straight, at the same steady pace he'd maintained since he began his surveillance. He hesitated only briefly before reaching for his mobile phone. He dialed the number and waited, and was only mildly annoyed when voice mail picked up instead of a live voice.

"Hey, hi, it's me. Listen, I just had an idea. I know we all agreed to meet at Bowers Diner for dinner, but I've been having a craving for seafood since I got up this morning, and it won't go away. I was wondering if we could change our dinner plans to meet at the Brighton Inn instead. Back in the day, they had the best baked bluefish on the Jersey coast. And I worked there a few summers, you know, so I was thinking it might be nice to stop in, see how the old place has held up. Think it over, and if it sounds good to you, give me a call and I'll get in touch with the others. You have my number . . . I'll wait to hear from you."

He disconnected the call and made a turn into the parking area right off the beach. No point in going anywhere until he heard back from his friends. He didn't think there'd be a problem with the change in plans. The guys liked to get together and talk about the old times, it wouldn't matter where.

Glory days, indeed.

If they only knew.

Not that any of his old buddies would ever suspect. A smile tugged at the corners of his mouth, imagining their reactions should the truth ever come out. He could almost hear their shocked words.

*No, no, I don't believe it. Not a word of it . . . I won't believe it until I hear it from his own lips. I've known him all my life — went to school with him since fucking kindergarten . . . No, no, there has to be some mistake. He's like a brother to me . . .*

A firm shake of the head would follow as denial dug in its heels. *No, I'll never believe it . . .*

*Believe it, buds. Believe it . . .*

He took off his shoes and socks and slipped the phone into his pocket before locking the door and heading off over the dune. This late in the afternoon, this early in the season, there were mostly older kids on the beach, the littlest ones having gone home with their mommies to start dinner. Kids — teenagers, anyway — didn't bother him. He had no interest in them whatsoever. He skirted around their volleyball net and walked until he reached the surf. At low tide, the sand wore a thick layer of broken shells, forcing him to walk above the water-line. Still, the cuffs of his pants were water-marked, and he'd have to change before dinner. He shrugged it off. After all the years he'd been away, a quick trip back to his rented cottage to change his clothes was a small price to pay for a walk along the beach. His thinking had never been clearer, his focus never sharper, than when he was doing just that.

Like today. All had fallen into place with his first step upon the dune. Now, turning back, he knew exactly what he needed to do, and how he would accomplish his goal. Wasn't that lesson learned long ago, drummed into his head over and over by his father?

"You can't accomplish a damned thing without goals," the old man had lectured time and time again. "You want to succeed at something, you set the goal, you pursue it with everything you have."

Well, that was probably the only thing the old man had ever said that had made much sense to him, and had thus been worth remembering.

The ringing of the phone shook him back to the present and the situation at hand. He answered on the second ring. Of course they could meet at the Brighton

Inn. The others had already been contacted and they all agreed. Meet at seven,
first one there gets the table and orders
and pays for the first round. Just like old
times.

Now he had his goal, he had his plan.
Buoyed by optimism, he turned back and
walked across the beach until he reached
the dune. Without so much as a backward
glance at the ocean he'd missed so much
for so many years, he returned to his car
and dusted the sand from his feet. He had
less than thirty minutes to run home and
change before meeting the guys for dinner.

He was looking forward to more than
just a good meal.

"I'm glad you decided to join me," Rick
said after the waitress had served their
entrées. "You look a little worn-out. My
gram always used to say that the best cure
for that kind of weariness was a good meal
and a good night's sleep."

"Well, with luck, tonight I'll have both."
Cass rearranged her napkin on her lap for
what Rick thought might be the fifth or
sixth time.

"Luck shouldn't have to factor into it.
You ordered a great dinner, and as soon as
you're finished eating, you can go back up

to the second floor and crash for as long as you need to." He remembered his conversation with Mitch. "Or at least until it's time to get up tomorrow morning to make our ten o'clock meeting."

She frowned. "Are you sure you need me along?"

"Would I rather leave you here alone?"

"I've been looking out for myself for a long time, Rick."

"And God willing, the day is near at hand when you'll be looking out for yourself again." He lowered his voice. "But until we have this guy in lockup or on a table in the ME's office, my time is your time."

"It can't happen soon enough for me. I want to get back to work." She picked at her plate of scallops. "Besides, it seems as if everyone is waiting for the other shoe to drop. It's been three days since he attacked Lucy. That's the longest he's gone between attacks since this started."

"How likely is it he's left town?" He appeared about to say something else, but stopped as the waitress led a well-dressed man to a nearby table for four.

"Anyway, let's hope we can put this together soon, before he makes his next move."

"What are the chances we'll be able to do that?" She put her fork down. "Realistically."

"Mitch says he's got a number of DNA matches, coast to coast. We're waiting for the DNA results on the blood that was swabbed from your back door. I'm betting it's a match, all the way around."

"No offense, but DNA matches won't help us if we don't have a suspect."

"We have the potential for four."

"How do we quickly cull the herd?"

He smiled. "You sure you're not from Texas?"

"I had a roommate once who was." She resumed eating.

"While you were in the shower, I called the boss. He'll have the sketch artist here by midday tomorrow, so within twenty-four hours we should have a fair idea what this guy looks like. I'm willing to put money that someone will recognize him right away. Denver or Phyl, probably." He paused, then added, "Maybe even you. But in the meantime, we'll take a few hours tomorrow to go over what Mitch has compiled, see if anything stands out."

"I'm betting nothing does." She shook her head. "That's the thing about this guy. Nothing about him seems to stand out."

Two more middle-aged men walked past them and were seated at a table to their left.

"Sooner or later, he'll give something away."

"What makes you think so? He's been at this game for twenty-six years without a slip, Rick. What makes you think he'll get careless now?"

"Because it's personal to him now. I don't think he's used to failure. And the attack on Lucy ended in failure. No rape. No murder. It's got to rankle. That makes it personal. And let's talk about the fact that he's got to be pretty pissed off at you. You interfered with his plans, not once, but twice." He watched her face while his words sunk in. When she offered no response, he said, "You know that nine times out of ten a pissed-off killer is a careless killer."

"We don't know if he's failed in the past. We only know about his successes." She winced at the use of the word.

A gentleman passed and was greeted loudly by the group nearby.

"And that's what we'll focus on." Rick glanced up as laughter erupted from the table where four men now sat. "Sadly, it's his successes that will lead us to him. We'll have to try to be patient while we piece the entire picture together."

She brightened slightly. "Oh. Speaking of which, while I was upstairs changing right before we came down for dinner, Phyl called me."

"Phil?" He frowned.

"Phyl Lannick. Chief Denver's assistant. She said she remembered that a woman who lives across the street from her is on the board of the bird sanctuary. She spoke with her when she got home this evening." Cass speared a slice of carrot with her fork.

"And . . . ?"

"And the neighbor told her that, yes, they did use that hawk stamp on the backs of the hands of all paying customers and volunteers at the all-day fund-raisers or at weekend events. They still use the same motif." She put her fork down. "And it was her recollection that my mother had submitted the original design for the hawk."

"She did?"

"That's how Phyl's neighbor remembers it." Her voice dropped to a near-whisper. "Wouldn't it be odd, if that's the key to finding this guy? That after all these years, something that came to me through hypnosis, something I don't even consciously recall, would lead to the man who killed them? Not only my family, but all of these women."

"And that that something had been first sketched by your mother?" Rick nodded. "I don't know that I'd find it as odd, as much as fitting."

She put her fork down.

"Every time I think about what he almost did to Lucy . . ."

"But he didn't, Cass. He didn't because you didn't let him. You bested him."

"That time."

"What do you mean, that —"

"I think I need to turn in now, I'm very tired. Do you mind? Are you finished?" She folded her napkin and set it next to her plate.

"Yes, I'm finished, and no, I don't mind. But Cass, if you're thinking you should have been able to save your mother . . . save your family . . . save *anyone* . . . You can't possibly think you could have."

She pushed her chair back without meeting his eyes.

"I think I'll go on up to the room, if it's okay. Thank you for dinner. It was delicious." Without waiting for a protest, she stood, and after removing her handbag from the back of her chair where she'd earlier hung it, she left the room.

Rick signaled for the waitress to bring the check. He hastily wrote in a tip, signed his name and room number, and followed Cass to the lobby, hoping to catch up with her before she barricaded herself in her room, the way he suspected she was going to do.

From his seat, he had a perfect view of her, could at times read her lips. He watched her leave the table and hurry from the room.

Lovers' quarrel?

No. She and the Fed weren't lovers. Not yet, anyway. Perhaps in time — there appeared to be a genuine interest there, on both their parts, whether either realized it — but not yet. Too bad they wouldn't get to explore that.

Well, the Fed would get over her. He'd remember her as a dream tragically unfulfilled, that sort of thing. Despite his rugged appearance, there was a sensitivity about the Fed. It was there in the way he looked at Cass, in the way he watched her face when she spoke. But he'd move on. Everyone moves on.

It was clear something had upset her. Of course, the cause of her disturbance was immaterial to him, and whatever it was would pale in comparison to what he had planned for her. As it was, it was all he could do to keep his mind on the conversation around him. All he could think of was putting his hands around her neck and squeezing until her eyes went blank — and how very good, how very satisfying, it would feel.

He watched the Fed sign the check, watched the waitress turn to walk to the cashier.

"Miss?" He waved her over, beckoned her close, and whispered, forcing her to lean into him slightly. "Bring us a bottle of champagne, would you? And four glasses?"

She smiled and nodded, totally unaware that his gaze had fallen to the check she held casually in one hand.

He couldn't read the signature, but the name of the Fed was totally unimportant. He'd gotten what he wanted.

Room 212.

The second floor used to be all two- or three-room suites. He wondered if it still was. That would make sense. It was clear to him that she and the Fed weren't sleeping together, but the Fed was sticking as close as he could. A two-bedroom suite would certainly fit the bill.

A satisfied smile crossed his lips. He

wasn't quite sure what he'd do with the information now that he had it, but he was certain it would come in handy. Perhaps a quick trip to the second floor — merely to get the lay of the land — was in order.

"Excuse me," he said to his companions. "I'm going to hit the men's room. Order the bluefish for me if the waitress comes back, would you?"

He strolled through the room, which had filled up considerably since he'd first arrived. He waved at an old acquaintance or two on his way to the lobby. Once there, he entered the empty stairwell and climbed undisturbed to the second floor.

Room 212 was at the very end of the hall. Convenient. But which side of the building was he on? He couldn't remember. It had been too many years.

He walked to the opposite end of the hall and looked out the window to orient himself. The room overlooked the street.

Not good.

Not insurmountable, but not good.

A glance at the room locks proved encouraging, however. He'd gotten through more challenging locks with his eyes closed.

He whistled all the way to the stairs, and all the way back down to the lobby. He might need to change his plans a little, but so what? Plans should be flexible, right?

One of his companions looked up as he approached the table. "You're in fine form tonight. You look like the old cat that ate the canary."

"I always hated that cliché," one of the others said.

"Well, this cat isn't all that old." He slid back into his seat. "What say we order another bottle of champagne?"

"You buying?" the friend on his left asked.

"Sure. Why not?"

He was still grinning, couldn't help himself. He had the rest of the evening all worked out in his head — Plan B, he was beginning to think of it — and he was feeling fine.

He lingered in the lobby after the others left, on the pretext of making reservations for Saturday night.

"My brother's wedding anniversary," he explained when he left them at the door. "I'm sure he and his wife would love to celebrate here."

He did stop at the desk to ask some inane question of the young and inattentive woman on duty. There were so many people milling about the lobby and the front porch, he thought it best to make a quick surveillance of the exterior of the Inn. The windows for room 212 would be easy enough to find.

He walked around to the back of the building, and as he'd anticipated, he had no trouble locating the room, which, to his surprise, had a small balcony. Now, that had possibilities that needed to be considered. He took a few steps closer, thinking this was perhaps the way to go. But there was nothing below the balcony to climb from. He frowned, displeased. He would've liked to have gone that way.

He stood half-hidden in shadow, recalling a time when he might have been able to make the leap from the ground to the balcony, but those days were, sadly, behind him now.

Ah, youth . . .

"Hey, buddy, you staying here?" The voice cracked through his consciousness like splintered glass.

Startled, he turned to find a classmate standing on the walk not ten feet away.

"Ah, no. No. I was just . . ." Just what? Shit. Just what was he doing here?

"You here for the party up in the second-floor ballroom? Todd Lennin's?"

"Ah, yes. As a matter of fact, I am." He

417

twisted his mouth into a smile and stepped onto the walk. His brain was almost boiling over. *Great. Let's have a party on the second floor and invite tons of people who have known me all my life.* And Todd Lennin, of all people. Like he'd be caught dead at any party Todd Lennin would have.

He took a quick look around to see if the man — Carl something or other? — was alone. He appeared to be.

"You took the same shortcut we took." Carl — Cal? — gestured toward the end of the lot.

"We?"

"My wife and the Davises. You remember George Davis?" Carl/Cal was weaving slightly. From all appearances, he'd started the party a bit early.

Carl Sellers. That was it.

"Sure, I remember George." George Asshole Davis. Who didn't remember him? Only guy in the class more of a nerd than George was Carl. "Is he coming along, then?"

"They already went in. I stopped for a pack of cigarettes — can't believe I'm still smoking. It's not like I don't know any better." Carl shook his balding head and patted his jacket pocket. "I just can't seem to stop myself."

"I know what you mean."

"You smoke?"

"I'm embarrassed to admit it, but yes, I do. As a matter of fact, when you came along, I was actually looking for my lighter. I think I dropped it along the path here." He jammed his hands into his jacket pockets and tried to look forlorn. "I wouldn't care, except it belonged to my dad."

"Oh, hey, that's rough. And good lighters are hard to find, aren't they?" Carl reached into his pocket. "Me, I use these Bics. But if I had one of those old lighters, I'd use it. I love those things. My dad had one, too."

He swayed slightly again. "Hey, I'll be glad to help you look for it. Where do you think you dropped it, somewhere around the walk?"

"That's the only place I can think of. You know what it's like, you want to smoke around a place like this, you feel like you have to go someplace where you won't be seen."

"That's the gospel truth, man." His voice took on a touch of indignation. "Like we're pariahs or something."

"Exactly."

"I'll help you look for it and then we

can go up together."

"Hey, thanks. That would be great. We can catch up on old times." Like they had any old times to catch up on. Carl was never part of his crowd.

Carl followed him around the corner of the building, his head down.

"Kinda dark back here, don't know how you're going to find anything. Maybe we should wait until the m—"

One blow to the back of the head and Carl was down. One quick and expert twist of the neck made sure Carl was down permanently.

Looking around to assure himself no one had stepped onto the path, he lifted Carl's body and carried it to the Dumpster at the back of the building. With a grunt, he tossed it unceremoniously over the side. He then bent over at the waist, his hands on his knees as he struggled to catch his breath.

Damn. In his prime, he could toss a body over his head without breaking stride.

Yeah, well, those were the days. He'd turned forty-five in February. Not exactly prime time, not for this sort of thing.

He brushed his hands off as he walked back to the parking lot, asking himself if that had really been necessary.

*Yes, damn it. It had.*

There was so much burning anger inside of him right then, the blood in his veins felt molten. The pressure was becoming unbearable.

Carl had ruined his night, coming along when he did, and seeing him where he'd been standing. If at some point in the future a woman was found dead in room 212 — *that damn room right up there* — surely Carl would recall whom he'd seen in the parking lot that night and he'd remember where he'd been looking.

Especially if the woman was Cass Burke.

Besides, he was feeling pissy. More than pissy. The night had started out so promising, but with a party three doors down from her room, he'd have to wait. He couldn't take the chance he'd be seen. He cursed under his breath.

The blood was pounding in his head so loudly, it sounded like the ocean. And his hands were starting to shake — never a good sign. His skin was beginning to itch.

There was only one way to scratch that itch.

Looks like he'll have to go to Plan C.

Somewhere, there'd be someone. Someone with long dark hair and promise in her eyes.

Before the sun rose tomorrow, he would find her.

# Twenty-four

"Tell me again why we're going to Plainsville?" Cass sat back in the bucket seat of Rick's Camaro and strapped the seat belt.

"We're going to exchange information."

"I think we've given Mitch pretty much everything we have. What's left to exchange?"

"He's apparently hit the mother lode with his request for information from the law enforcement agencies he contacted. He says he's got a pretty impressive time line of our man's activities over the past twenty-some years. I'd say that alone is worth the trip."

"Why doesn't he fax it to us?"

"Apparently it's still coming in. Remember, it's been less than a week since he sent out his requests. Some agencies are still getting their data together." Rick stopped at the corner and turned to her. "Is there a problem here that I don't know about? Is there a reason you don't want to go? Because if there is, let's talk about it now, before we get onto the highway."

"It isn't that I don't want to go." She shifted in her seat to face him. "It's just that I feel I should be here with Lucy this afternoon. When she meets with the sketch artist."

"You can't be in the room with Lucy when she and Kendra get together. Kendra wouldn't permit it."

"Why not?"

"She wants as few distractions as possible. If she's dealing with a child, maybe she'd let a parent in. But other than that, she prefers to be one-on-one with her subject."

"Oh. Well, then . . ."

"I expect we'll be back here by the time Kendra is finishing up, so you can see Lucy when it's over. But I doubt Kendra would let you sit in."

Cass nodded. "All right, then. Let's go."

Rick took a left and headed toward the bridge between Bowers Inlet and the mainland.

"Pretty, isn't it?" He nodded toward the bay as he crossed over the narrow bridge.

"Beautiful. I love it. Love seeing the sun set over it every night."

"Have you ever lived anywhere else?" he asked.

"Only when I was in college. Other than

that, my whole life's been on the Jersey Shore."

"Where'd you go to college?"

"Cabrini. Outside Philly."

"I know it. I went to Penn."

"Is that where you dropped the Texas accent from your speech?"

"Actually, I lost that a few years earlier." He slowed for the entrance to the Parkway. "I went to boarding school in Connecticut."

"How'd you end up there?"

"Not my choice." He turned on the radio and began to search for a station that was more music than static. "My mother's idea."

"Oh." She wanted to ask what had prompted his mother to send him away at a young age, but hesitated.

"She felt it best at the time." He knew she was too polite to ask, and knew, too, that they had at least an hour together in the car. They had to talk about something.

"You mentioned once that she had re-married."

"Married. She and my father had never been married." He settled for classic rock out of New York.

"Right. Sorry."

"It wasn't your fault." He smiled. He

knew it was an awkward subject. "When she married my stepfather, and began having a family with him, I guess she felt the contrast between us was too great. Caused people to ask too many questions that were embarrassing to not only my mother, but her husband."

"What contrast?"

"All of her children with Edward — her husband — are blond and blue-eyed. I, being one-fourth Mexican, stood out like a sore thumb in the family portraits."

"You're part Mexican?"

"I sometimes think that's my best part." He tried to smile again, was less successful this time. "My grandfather — my mother's father — was Mexican. My grandmother was Swedish. Some combo, eh?"

"What about your father's parents?"

"Irish and Italian."

"Quite a combo, indeed."

"And you're, what, Irish and . . . ?"

On the radio, Sting was singing about fields of gold.

"The Irish is that apparent?"

"Oh, yeah." This time when he smiled, it was genuine.

"Irish and German and French."

"Gotta love America." He shook his head. "Gotta love that melting pot."

She looked out the window at the seemingly endless vista of scrub pine. Less than a mile away, new shopping centers and strip malls abounded. The changing face of the area wasn't totally to her liking.

"Did you hate boarding school?" she asked softly.

"At first, yes. Yes, I did. After a while, though, I adapted. I learned to make the best of it."

"How?"

"Well, for one thing, since I was bigger than everyone else, I wasn't bullied much. For another, I was a strong athlete. And I was smart."

"What sports did you play?"

"Football and baseball."

"Were you very good?"

"Actually, I was," he admitted. "All in all, once I got used to the fact that I wasn't going home until the end of the term, I was okay. I adjusted."

"You were a smart little boy, then. Lots of kids rebel when they're sent someplace they don't want to be."

"Is that the voice of experience speaking?"

She nodded. "After I lost my family, I went to live with my aunt and uncle — Lucy's family."

"And things weren't good there?"

"It wasn't bad," she said. "I know they did all they could for me. And being with Lucy was a comfort, in a way. She and I had always been very close. But . . ."

"But it wasn't your home, and it wasn't your family."

"I felt as if I'd walked into someone else's life. I wanted my own life back. I wanted to go home," she said simply. "I wanted my mother and my father and my sister and my house. As much as Aunt Kimmie loved me, she was Lucy's mother, not mine. And Lucy, as close as we were, was not my sister. I wanted things to be the way they'd been. I never really was able to accept what had happened."

He'd turned the radio down when she'd started to speak, he wanted to catch every word. He knew instinctively this was not something she spoke of often. He wanted her to know that he understood this, and therefore offered her his full attention.

"So you rebelled how?" he asked.

"Name something." She laughed dryly. "I drank. I smoked. I stayed out at night. Much to my aunt and uncle's dismay. They just didn't know what to do with me. Looking back, I feel bad that I put them through so much. They tried really hard."

She bit her lip and stared out the window.

"I'm sure the situation was difficult for your aunt, too."

"I had no concept of that as a child. I wasn't aware of anyone's pain except my own. If she grieved, I didn't sense it. I only knew that my entire world had collapsed under my feet. I had no sense of anyone else's suffering back then."

"Well, you were pretty young."

"Seven that summer." She bit her lip and stared out the window. "When I became old enough to understand things a little better — which wasn't until I was in college — I was surprised that I had survived it all. You simply don't realize how much pain the human spirit can endure."

"You seem to have turned out all right." He reached over and took her hand. "Better than all right. You might be the strongest woman I've ever met. And I've known some truly tough women."

"I didn't have a choice."

"Everyone has a choice. You get into situations you hate, places you don't want to be, you have a choice. You go with it and make it your own, or you fight against it relentlessly. Smart is knowing when to stop fighting. Strong is knowing when to move past it and take what you have and turn it into something you can live with."

"Easier for some than for others."

"Don't kid yourself, Cass. It isn't easy for anyone."

Having no response, she turned her face to the window once again, and watched the trees whiz past as the car sped along. She'd already revealed more of herself to him than she had to anyone in a long time, and she wasn't sure why.

She leaned forward and turned up the volume on the radio. Right then, she had nothing more to say.


"So, what have we got here?" Mitch asked as he followed Regan into her office. "Anything new come in since I left last night?"

"The fax machine hasn't stopped," she told him. "It's eating me out of house and home. Well, out of paper, anyway."

She pointed at the stacks neatly arranged atop the desk. "These came in late last night, this other stack was in the tray this morning. The ones that are still in the tray have arrived since the time I got up at six, emptied the tray, and made my breakfast." She paused. "Speaking of which, have you eaten?"

"I have, thanks for asking. The restaurant next to the motel does a decent omelet. But if there's coffee . . ."

"There's always coffee. I think you know where to find it by now." She pointed him in the direction of the kitchen.

"Need a refill?" he asked from the doorway.

"I do. Thanks." She handed him her cup.

The fax machine beeped, signaling more incoming.

"Released a flood here, I do believe," she muttered to herself as she stapled the pages of the last fax together.

Mitch returned with two cups in hand. "What was that?"

"I said, we've opened the floodgates. I can't believe how many unsolved murders are out there." She shook her head. "And these are only the ones that fit our profile."

"Well, let's take a look and see how many actually do."

She handed him a stack of papers.

"These are already separated. They're from all over the country."

He sat in one of the leather chairs near the corner of the desk and leafed through the faxes.

"This looks like the real deal here, this

one from Texas. This could be our guy." He continued reading, his face a study in concentration. "This one, the one from Idaho, not so sure. Let's see if there's any DNA we can compare to the DNA profile we already have."

He bent over the pages, turning them thoughtfully.

"I like this one from Kentucky," he murmured. "Let's see what else they have on him . . ."

"Before you get too engrossed, there's another fax you need to look at before Rick arrives." She handed him a folder. "This came in from your office early this morning. I kept it separate from the other faxes."

He opened it and paged through it. "The scoop on the four names Rick gave me. Christ, any one of these could be our guy . . . did you look at these?"

She nodded.

"That was my first thought, too. All of them are in a position to get around."

The sound of a car door drew her to the window.

"Rick and Cass are here." She disappeared from the room, the sound of her footsteps leading to the front door. She was back in a moment, Rick and Cass in tow.

"This is an incredible home," Cass was saying. "The grounds are beautiful."

"Thank you. My father's doing — I'm afraid I contributed nothing to the décor, nor to the landscaping." Regan smiled and pulled a chair closer to the large desk. "Cass, have a seat. Rick, if you'll pull that chair up, we can get right to it."

Regan took the chair behind the desk, and sat back, motioning for Mitch to begin.

"First of all, we've had phenomenal response to our requests for information from agencies around the country. I'm still going through them, but thus far I've got a pile of an astonishing sixty-seven unsolved murders that fit our killer to a tee."

"Sixty-seven?" Cass gasped.

"Sixty-seven that merit a closer look, yes. No guarantee it's him, but they're looking damned good. There are another several dozen that are long shots, but all in all, I think this guy has been busier than any of us could have imagined."

"Well, if we take those sixty-seven and put them in order of date, we should have a pretty fair idea of where he was in what year," Cass said thoughtfully. "If we match that up with where the four prime suspects were during those times, we should be able to determine which one is our man. Or if none of them are."

Mitch nodded. "We're already on that. John is having someone back at the office feeding the data into the computer as we speak. He should have something for us soon."

"Chief Denver needs to know all this," Cass told him. "He should have all the information you have."

"He already does," Mitch assured her. "I spoke with him yesterday afternoon, faxed over the nuts and bolts. Didn't get to send him everything because his fax machine jammed."

"Damn thing." Cass shook her head. "We've been having problems with it for months. We just haven't gotten around to replacing it. Give me copies of whatever didn't go through, and I'll deliver them this afternoon."

"I'm one step ahead of you." Regan smiled and handed her a brown envelope. "All copied and ready to go."

"Thanks." Cass slid the envelope onto the floor between her and Rick's chairs.

"Well, let's look at what you do have on these four," Rick said. "Let's see what they've been up to since leaving old Bowers High."

"Bayshore Regional," Cass corrected.

"Whatever. Let's take a look."

"Regan, can you toss these through the copier behind you? Let's give everyone their own set." Mitch handed her the stack of papers he'd withdrawn from the folder, and she stacked them on the copy machine to her right and pushed *Start.* The machine printed and collated four sets in slightly more than a minute. Regan collected and stapled them and passed out the packs.

"Okay, let's take a look at William Calhoun. Age forty-five, currently separated from his wife. Resides in a small town outside of Albuquerque, New Mexico. William is a pilot who's logged in many a mile with Universal Airways."

"He looks good," Rick said.

"He looks even better when you learn that there's a large number of unsolved murders along the border, not too far from where he lives," Regan told them.

"Before you get too happy over Calhoun, take a look at Jonathan Wainwright. Son of the chief of police who investigated the murders back in '79," Mitch reminded them. "Widower whose wife died under questionable circumstances. Like Calhoun, he currently lives in the southwest. Left college after two years to join the army.

Special Forces for nine years, then left the army to work for a private security firm."

Rick's head shot up. "Mercenary?"

"Possibly, with that background," Mitch agreed. "We're looking into that, too.

"Then we have Kenneth Kelly. Son of Judge Kelly. Divorced three times. Two children, one by each of the first two wives. Latest ex-wife lives in London. Four years of college followed by a master's in international studies. Has worked for the U.S. Commerce Department since grad school. London, Brussels, Sofia . . . this guy's been around."

"They've all been around," Rick muttered.

"And the last one? That was only three," Cass pointed out.

"Joseph Patterson. Same age as the others. Single. Never married. Son of a man who was mayor in Bowers for fifteen years. Did a stint in the Marines, then went to work for JTS for the past eighteen years. Sales — he managed most of the south and the southwest."

"JTS. The software company?" Cass asked.

Mitch nodded. "Right."

"He would have done a lot of traveling . . ."

"It could be any one of these guys." Rick shook his head. "They all had jobs that permitted them to travel. Domestically and internationally."

"So how do we narrow it down?" Regan asked.

"With luck, Lucy will do that for us," Regan said. "She's meeting with the FBI's sketch artist in about two hours. Hopefully, we'll have a face by the end of the day."

"And with the information we get from the Bureau's computer, by then we'll have zeroed in on every place this guy has been for the past twenty-six years."

"Do you think Denver should bring all four in for questioning?" Mitch asked.

"I don't know. By the time he gets them rounded up and into the station, we could have Kendra's sketch. A positive ID would be better than pulling all four in and hoping that the face she draws belongs to one of them."

Mitch nodded. "You have a point, Rick."

"This could all be over within the next twenty-four hours," Cass said as if she couldn't quite believe it.

"If the cards all fall our way." Rick nodded, then added, "Not that they usually do."

"Can I fax these to the chief?" Cass asked. "I think he needs to see them right away. Let him decide if he wants to start pulling one or all of them in for some preliminary questioning. The danger there, of course, is that without probable cause to hold them, we can't act on even our strongest suspicions. We'd have to let them walk when they want to, and then the Strangler could just flat-out disappear."

"Let's do it." Mitch pointed to the fax machine. "But do it now, before we get another incoming. That machine hasn't been silent for more than fifteen minutes since Tuesday."

Cass slid the four pages into the fax machine and entered the number for the police department. The pages went through, but when she looked at the confirmation page, she frowned.

"System failure," she read.

"Try it again. Maybe the machine is overheated," Regan suggested.

Cass entered the number again and hit *Send.*

The results were the same.

"I think I'll give Denver a call and let him know we have this. We can drop it off when we get back to Bowers."

She speed-dialed the number for the station, but got a busy signal. She disconnected, then dialed the chief's cell phone.

He answered almost immediately. "Denver."

"Chief, it's Cass. I'm here in Plainsville with Rick at Regan Landry's home. She and Mitch have put together some information on the four possible suspects that you'll want to see. I tried to fax it to the station but it didn't go through."

"Good luck getting anything through that machine today," he said curtly.

"It's acting up again?"

"It's jammed, been running nonstop." He paused for a moment, then said, "I take it you haven't seen the news today?"

"No. We left Bowers early and . . . don't tell me there's been another . . ."

"Around nine this morning, they found the body of a man who's in town for the reunion, broken neck." He declined to tell her that the body was found in a Dumpster outside the very inn in which she was staying, all but under her bedroom window. He still hadn't decided what to make of that. His gut told him there were no coincidences; on the other hand, as far as they knew, the Strangler had never targeted that particular type of victim, or killed in that manner.

"Who was it?"

"A guy named Carl Sellers. Someone snapped his neck. I doubt you'd have known him. He's in his mid-forties . . . left Bowers for college and I don't think he's been back but maybe two or three times since." Even as he spoke the words, it occurred to the chief the victim had most likely been a classmate of the four they already had in their sights. Coincidence? His gut gave another twitch.

"And Cass — we just received a report of a woman going missing last night, early this morning, from downtown Tilden. She fits the description. They haven't found her body yet."

She hung up the phone without waiting for the chief's good-bye. Turning to Rick, she said, "We need to go. Now. Back to Bowers."

"There's been another murder?"

"A man in town for the reunion." Cass turned to Rick. "Chief says he's in his mid-forties."

"Same as these guys." Rick tapped on the folder. "Classmates, maybe?"

"How the hell does that fit in?" Cass was already at the door. "And a woman went missing in Tilden last night. Chief says she fits the description of the others. They're still looking for her."

"Anything else you think we need to take back to Bowers?" Rick asked as he gathered the papers.

"We have a bunch of DNA matches — matches to one another, obviously nothing to match to your vics, but still . . . if we can pinpoint any one of these guys — or any other suspect — as having been in these cities on these dates, we'll have the start of some serious evidence."

"We'll take whatever you have ready. The rest —"

"I'll wait outside, Rick." Cass waved to Mitch and Regan. "Thank you both. I'm sorry. I really am. But I have to go."

"Go." Regan nodded, and Cassie did.

Regan picked up the envelope Cass had left on the floor and handed it to Rick. "This has most everything we have so far. We'll make copies of anything we get in today and we'll bring it to Bowers Inlet if we can't get the faxes through. Right now, Cass is jumping out of her skin. Take her back, Rick. She's dying to get her hands into this."

"She's still on leave, as far as I know. She's not going to get her hands into anything. Denver isn't going to let her near it."

Regan pointed out the office window.

Cass paced impatiently alongside Rick's car.

"I don't think I'd want to be the one to tell her that."

# Twenty-five

Craig Denver looked out onto the parking lot of the Bowers Inlet Police Department and wondered what the hell was going on in his town.

Women turning up dead, a man found in a Dumpster with his neck broken, a young girl missing and most likely dead as well. What the hell had happened to the sleepy little bay towns he'd loved all his life?

"Chief?" Phyl opened the door between her office and his and poked her head in. "I made some iced tea. I thought you might need something cold about now."

"Thanks."

She came into the office with a tall glass in her hand. Chief Denver slid an envelope over and gestured for her to place the glass on it.

"Do you have a minute?" he asked.

"Sure." She stood uncertainly at the end of his desk.

"Sit." He waved in the direction of the chairs and took a sip of the iced tea. "No one makes iced tea like you do, Phyl. I swear I'd keep you on even if you were a total incompetent, just to have a supply of your iced tea in the summer."

She sat, crossed her legs, and waited.

He rubbed his temples as if in pain. "Honest to God, Phyl, I can't keep up with all this. For the first time in my life, I'm second-guessing every move I make, every decision. I should have brought all four of those guys in for questioning yesterday. I didn't, and now a man is dead and a woman is missing. What the hell was I thinking?"

"You were thinking if you try to push the killer too fast, you'll lose him, send him back into whatever hole he's been hiding in for the past twenty-six years. Which hasty action may well have done. Without probable cause, you have no arrest. Without evidence, you don't have probable cause. You can't hold four men because you think one of them might be a killer."

"You sound like a cop, Phyl."

"I sound like you sounded yesterday. Those were your arguments when you went back and forth with the DA's office."

"Still, maybe —"

"Forget maybe. You don't even know that Sellers was killed by the same guy. As much as you say you don't believe in coincidences, I gotta tell you, they happen."

"What the hell do you make of all this, Phyl?" He stood and began to pace. "All these women, now Sellers . . ."

"I don't know, Chief." She shook her head, understanding that he didn't expect her to have answers, he needed to bounce something off her. She was well practiced at letting him take his time getting to it.

"Did you know him, Carl Sellers?"

"I did. He was in my sister's class," she nodded, "though not a very popular guy, and he certainly wasn't in with the group of guys you're looking at. He was one of those who was just there. No real friends, no real enemies, not that I recall, anyway. One of those who left the Jersey Shore, ended up in some big city someplace — I think I heard he's been living in Chicago — where he became very successful. Didn't come back home much. Just sort of a schmo who got lucky when he grew up."

"That was my impression, too, the little I remember about him." He sat on the edge of the desk, sipped his tea, then put the glass back onto the envelope. "Feels like it's all connected somehow, doesn't it? I can't figure out how, damn it. I'm having a hard time seeing the Strangler all of a sudden going from strangling women to breaking a man's neck."

"Maybe it was just a robbery after all. His wallet was missing, his watch."

"Maybe so." Denver's fingers tapped out an agitated rhythm on the desktop.

"You know, there have been a lot of social activities this week, Chief. Those four . . ." she pointed at the file she'd earlier placed on his desk with the faxes from FBI Agent Peyton, "they've been at pretty much all of them. I've seen them myself."

"And what did you think, Phyl? You get strange vibes from any of them?"

"They're all strange, if you ask me. But if you're asking me if any one of them looked more likely than the others, well, no." She rested an elbow on the edge of the desk. "Billy Calhoun, he's still a loudmouth. Used to drive everyone crazy in school because he could get away with anything, his father being principal. And Jon Wainwright? He was always in the background, you know? Sneaking around. Kenny Kelly, well, as the son of a judge, he could have gotten away with murder back then. And Joey Patterson is still the goof he always was." She paused, then added, "It's funny, remembering how they were when we were in school. Everyone thought they were so cool. Now they're all just middle-aged men with balding heads and expanding waist-bands."

The chief pretended to flinch. "Lot of that going around these days, Phyl."

"You wear your bald head well, Chief." She smiled. "But if you're asking me if there was anything about any one of them that gave me the willies, or made me think, 'Yeah, this one's the serial killer,' I'm going to have to disappoint you. They all look normal. Just like everyone else." She shook her head. "But that's what makes it so scary, you know. Whoever he is, he looks as normal as anyone."

"The beast is rarely marked on the out-side," he muttered.

"What?" she asked.

"Something Chief Wainwright used to say. The beast is rarely marked on the out-side. Inside, he's ugly and evil as sin. Out-side, he looks like anyone."

"Maybe that's what makes him a beast."

"I have a call in to the FBI; I'm asking for a few more agents. I need someone watching each of the four around the clock, see who goes where. I've tried sur-veillance with the few men I have, and I don't have enough bodies to keep tabs on four people, twenty-four/seven. It's impos-sible. Best I could do was to cover two of

447

them. Not good enough." He shook his head. "Obviously, not good enough. And I still have someone posted at Lucy Webb's door around the clock. I can't take the chance of leaving her unguarded."

"Maybe if we work with the other PDs . . ." she began but he waved her off.

"I'm having a real problem with a couple of these departments. Except for Tilden, everyone seems to think they can handle this alone. Look to make a name for themselves, I guess. Dreaming about a book deal and an appearance on *Good Morning America*, maybe Letterman, for whoever brings this guy in." His disgust at the prospect was evident. "And in the meantime, people just keep dying and disappearing."

He shook his head.

"You know, if we'd known about some of these modern investigative techniques twenty-six years ago, we might have had him then. If we'd known how to lift fingerprints from skin, lift trace evidence, or even the profiling they do today, we might have gotten him." Denver shook his head almost apologetically. "As it is now, we did everything right, as right as we could. Got the lab working, though why it takes so long to get results on some of these things is beyond me. Got the FBI in here right away. Got the profiler down here . . . we've got a sketch artist in to talk to Lucy Webb, see if we can get a picture of this guy. And another woman has still gone missing. Whatever we do from here on out, we're still a day late, in my book."

"That will be huge, the picture. We'll have him, once we have his face. Especially if it's someone local." She glanced at her watch. "It's two now. The artist is still with Lucy. Maybe in another hour or so we'll have him ID'd. That should make you feel optimistic."

"I'll be optimistic when I have someone sitting in that back room."

"What did the profiler say?"

"She believes he started this as a young man, that the Burkes were his first kills. That he was after Jenny, just unfortunate for Bob that he came home early that day, and that he didn't expect the kids to come home when they did." He tapped his fingers on the side of the glass. "Said that he hadn't gone there with the intention of killing Jenny, that he thought she'd be waiting for him. That he was obsessed with her, and thought she felt the same way about him, but when she started fighting him, he went into a rage and killed her. That he keeps killing all these other women who look like her because each time he thinks maybe it will turn out right for him, but when it doesn't, he ends up killing again."

"Never saw that coming, back then. The killings all seemed so different."

"That's what we thought at the time."

"Did she say anything else about him, anything that could give us an idea of what kind of person he might have been back then?"

"She asked if he had a record as a juvie. I told her that if any of these four" — he slid the list from the file and placed it in the center of his desk — "had gotten into any serious trouble, I'd have been the last to know. No rookie was going to be made privy to that sort of thing. But she — Dr. McCall — thought that was significant, any early criminal activities."

"What kind of activities?"

"Stuff other than speeding and starting fights on the school grounds. She asked specifically about sex offenses. Flashing. Peeping Tom–type stuff. She said sometimes guys who engage in that sort of thing when they're young graduate to more serious sex offenses later on." He shrugged. "I couldn't help her with that. I don't know who'd'a known about it, if any of those boys had been up to stuff like that."

"I did," Phyl said softly.

It took him a moment to respond.

"What? You did what?"

"I knew."

His eyes narrowed. "Phyl, what are you trying to say?"

"I know who the peeper was." She picked up a pen that sat at mid-desk, reached for the list, and circled a name. She then turned the sheet of paper around for him to see the name she'd marked.

"You sure?"

"Positive."

He frowned. "How do you know?"

"I was the peepee."

Denver's jaw dropped.

"Right." She nodded firmly. "I'm the one he peeped."

"First I ever heard of this."

"I imagine it is. But as you said, as a rookie, you wouldn't have been brought into it."

"Son of a bitch." Denver slapped his hand on the top of his desk.

"That's pretty much what my father said at the time."

"Is this the face, Lucy? Is this the man who attacked you?" Kendra Smith held up the sketch she'd made from the description Lucy had given her. It had taken well over two hours, and though she knew her subject was rapidly tiring, she needed to have every detail right before she left the hospital room. The devil's in the details, as her mother used to say. When it came to creating a composite, the details were crucial. An accurate sketch could make the difference between catching a killer and accusing an innocent man. Kendra took her responsibility very seriously. Once she signed her name to the picture she'd drawn, there would be no mistakes.

"That's him, yes. That's him." Lucy's voice was almost nonexistent after a couple hours of speaking. Her throat was still bruised, but she'd insisted on completing the sketch as soon as possible.

Cass knocked on the partially closed door. "May we come in?"

"You're just in time." Kendra looked beyond Cass to speak directly to Rick. "We just finished."

"Cass, this is Kendra Smith," Rick introduced the artist. "Kendra, Cass is the detective here in Bowers Inlet . . ."

He paused as Cass embraced Lucy.

"And she's also Lucy's cousin," he added.

"Well, Lucy's a trooper. She did an incredible job. In spite of the fact that she tells me there was low light in the room where she was attacked, she kept her eyes open." Kendra held up the sketch she'd completed. "Agent Cisco, I believe this is your man."

Dark hair going light at the temples and receding slightly. Thick neck. Eyes deep and wide apart. Chiseled jawline, ears close to the head. Lines around the mouth and eyes.

"Lucy, had you seen this man before? Before the night he attacked you?" Cass was asking as she reached for the sketch.

"I think I did. I think he was in the video store last weekend when I went in for a movie. Was that Saturday night?" Lucy squeezed her eyes tightly closed. "God, it seems like so long ago."

Cass patted Lucy's arm. "You did a terrific job, Luce. I'm so proud of you."

She took the sketch from Rick's hands, and paused. Turning back to him, she lowered her voice and said, "He was in the restaurant last night. He was with three . . ."

She took a deep breath, then nodded slowly. "He was with three other men. What are the chances the four we've been

453

looking for were right under our noses?"

Rick took a second look at the sketch.

"Shit, you're right. He was there." He rubbed his chin. "No coincidence that he was at the Inn. He must have been watching you, Cass."

"Let's get this over to the chief. I'll bet my life he'll recognize this face." She leaned over and kissed Lucy soundly on the cheek. "You did it, Lulu. We're going to get him, and you were the one who led the way."

"If you do get him, it will have been worth it," Lucy whispered.

"No ifs. He's ours now." Cass turned to Kendra. "Thanks so much. This is excellent work."

"Lucy did the hard part," Kendra said modestly. "I'm only the translator."

"Whatever you call it, you have a gift. Thank you." Cass headed toward the door.

"Thanks, Kendra. I'll let you know when we get him." Rick followed Cass into the hall and stepped around the officer who was standing guard.

"I'll race you to the elevator," Cass said, but as they approached the small lobby between elevator cars, they noticed both cars had arrows pointing up.

"Forget it. Let's take the steps." Rick

grabbed her by the arm and steered her toward the stairwell.

They ran down several flights then through the double doors that led to the lobby, and out the side door that opened to the parking garage. Up one more flight to Rick's car, then out onto Claymore Boulevard, which led directly into Bowers Inlet. Five minutes more and they were at the police station.

Cass barely knocked on Denver's door.

"We have a face," she said breathlessly as she held up the sketch.

"And I have the name," Denver told them.

"Do we know where he is?" Rick asked.

"We know where he's been. He leased a house over on Darien Road. I already called for a warrant. Judge Newburg is signing it as we speak. It should arrive about the same time we do. We'll start there."

"Chief, I want back on the job." Cass's hands settled on her hips, her arguments already on the tip of her tongue. It was clear she was ready to fight if she had to.

"With restrictions. One, you don't go inside until we know for certain if he's there . . ."

"How many officers do we have?" Rick

asked before Cass could respond. "Besides the three of us."

"I have three more meeting us at the scene and I've already requested backup from Tilden."

"But we're lead, right?" Cass paused in the doorway.

"I said you could come along with restrictions," Denver reminded her. "I know the temptation to nail this guy is going to be overwhelming for you. But let someone else bring him down, you hear me? It's in everyone's best interest if you do not put your hands on him. If you can't go along with that, you stay outside until it's over. Are we understood?"

"Sure. I understand." She nodded, her mouth a straight, grim line. "You want this clean."

"It's going to be clean. What I want is to avoid any complications in the future. I want this done professionally — not that you're not professional, Cass — but for you, this is highly personal. You were one of his first victims. I don't want your fingerprints on him when we take him down. And I want him alive to answer for every last victim."

She nodded. She didn't like it, but she understood. Someone else would have to bring him in. Which was okay, though not the way she wanted it to end.

What she wanted was to bring him down, alone. What she wanted was to look into the eyes of the man who had murdered her family, hold a pistol to his heart, and fire.

# Twenty-six

The bayside cottage that Jonathan Wainwright rented for the season — intending to buy, according to his brother's wife — was unlocked, as if the occupant had just stepped out to the small patio off the dining area. The rooms were immaculate. Nothing cluttered the counters in the kitchen. No dishes had been left in the sink. The living room furniture was as smooth as if never sat upon. The bathrooms appeared to have been scrubbed down with Clorox.

The beds in both upstairs rooms were expertly made. The clothes in the closet were in perfect alignment, as were the socks and underwear in the dresser.

In the refrigerator, they found an orange, a bottle of seltzer, an unopened pound of butter. A dozen eggs sat in their box. A tub of cream cheese and a jar of salsa stood side by side with a six-pack of Coke on the top shelf.

There was nothing to suggest the identity of the person who lived there.

"You didn't really expect him to be here,

did you?" Cass asked softly.

"No. Would've been nice to waltz right in and snatch him up. But that rarely happens. Even on TV." Chief Denver moved through the living room, back into the kitchen, his hands in his pockets. "I suspect he's off disposing of his latest conquest. I only wish I knew where."

A uniformed officer stuck his head through the doorway. "Chief, the crime scene tech is here."

"Send her on back."

"Before I get started, tell me just how far I can go," Tasha Welsh asked as she came into the room, lugging the heavy black bag that accompanied her everywhere. "How broad was your warrant?"

"Broad enough." Denver nodded solemnly. "What did you have in mind?"

"I'm thinking the traps from the bathroom sink, for one, since the place is so clean. We'll roll for fibers, and we'll bag the bed pillow, hoping for some hair samples, but if we have to go to skin cells for the DNA, the bathroom sink is always a good place to start." Her gloved hand held up a disposable razor. "Chances are, he shed a few shaving."

She popped the razor into the bag.

"Do whatever you have to do to get as

much as you can," Denver told her.

"Already bagged his shoes. Maybe we'll get a trace of soil from the bottoms, and maybe we can link that to one of the places where the bodies were found." She started back out of the room, then turned and said, "You never did find the actual crime scenes, did you? We don't know where he's been taking these women to kill them?"

Denver shook his head. "No. We don't have a clue."

"It's someplace that means something to him," Cass said aloud. "Someplace where he feels safe . . ."

"Well, he grew up around here. Maybe we should start with the house he grew up in," Rick suggested. "Or that garage where the evidence was stored."

"Not a bad idea," the chief said. "Let me get someone over there to talk to the present owners."

"Disappointed?" Rick asked Cass after Denver had left the room.

"I didn't expect him to be here. He still has a victim, someplace. At least I'm assuming he does. The body hasn't been found, and God knows, everyone's been looking for her." She paused. "Her name is Lilly Carson, had you heard? She lives with her widowed mother, she's twenty-eight years old, the single mother of a six-year-old son, and she just got her master's degree in education last month. She supported herself and her son and put herself through grad school by working as a bartender at Jelly's down in Tilden. That's where she was last seen. Leaving Jelly's after her shift was over, two-forty in the morning."

Cass went to the window and gazed out.

"Where did he take her?" she murmured. "Where does he feel safe?"

"Denver says he has a brother and sister-in-law in town. They gave us a description of the car he's been driving, maybe they can give us an idea of where he might go. Someplace that's important to him. Or one of his buddies might know where he'd go."

"Let's get started, then. You want to take the brother, I'll start with the friends?" Cass asked.

"No. Just because we think he's occupied with someone else isn't a good enough reason to leave you exposed. We'll go together. And we'll stick together until we find him."

She nodded halfheartedly and went off to tell the chief where they were going.

Jonathan Wainwright sat in the bird

461

blind, his back against the wall, literally and figuratively. On the floor near his feet, Lilly Carson lay, bound and gagged and still unconscious. His mind went back and forth between killing her right then and there or holding on to her. His brother had called his cell phone, wanting to know what the fuck was going on, the police had been there, asking a lot of questions.

"You haven't done anything stupid, have you, Jonny?" his older brother, Steve, had asked, a touch of derision in his voice. "You're not still doing . . . you know, the stuff you used to get in trouble for, are you?"

"If you're asking me if I've looked into anyone's bedroom window lately, the answer is no," Jon had replied calmly, then disconnected the call.

But he was far from calm. Somehow, they had put something together. The one who didn't die, that's who it must have been. She must have told them.

Jenny.

Or another Jenny wannabe?

He rubbed his eyes. He just didn't know anymore. Sometimes he thought he knew. Sometimes he felt so sure . . .

The woman on the floor of the blind moaned softly.

*What to do with you? What to do . . . ?*

Killing her would be as mundane as tying his shoes at this point. The thrill was definitely gone. She held no appeal for him now. The moment had passed.

But alive . . . maybe she could serve a purpose.

He stood up and looked down on her. Lilly's long dark hair spread around her and fell across her forehead in a silken wave.

*What a shame,* he told himself. *What a waste.*

He leaned over the side of the blind and looked around. The sanctuary was exactly that today. His sanctuary. A slight breeze blew through the trees and the marsh grasses, and a few birds called every once in a while. Other than that, it was quiet. Peaceful.

He rested his arms along the top rail and began to think. *Plan it out, son,* his father would have said, *for Christ's sake.*

He nodded a silent response. *Okay, Pop, I've got a plan for you. I only wish to God you were still around to see it all play out. You think I embarrassed you when I was a kid? You ain't seen nothing, old man.*

Resolved, he lifted the woman and opened the door to the blind. Carefully picking his way down the steps, he started across the marsh to the small rowboat he'd tied up at the edge of the bay. He dumped Lilly unceremoniously into the bottom of the boat, and she groaned when her head hit the seat. Ignoring her pain, he pushed out through the shallows. When the water was above his knees, he slid over the side of the boat and picked up the oars.

He looked straight ahead as he rowed, glancing down one time to see Lilly watching him through terrified eyes.

"Oh, don't look at me like that. I'm not going to dump you over the side. Uh-uh. You're much too valuable alive. Much more."

He rowed quietly and kept as close to the shoreline as he could. When he reached his destination, he hopped out of the boat and dragged it up through the reeds. He lifted a frightened Lilly and hoisted her over his shoulder, pushing his way through the thick growth of cattails to the house that stood at the edge of the marsh — the house where it had all started, twenty-six long years ago.

# Twenty-seven

"Can you give me five minutes?" Cass asked Rick as he slowed down in front of her house.

"I can give you all the time you need," he told her, "but I'm coming in with you."

He turned off the engine and they got out of his car. She waved to a neighbor across the street, and stepped aside as a happy toddler drove his miniature car toward her on the sidewalk. The boy's mother smiled apologetically as she kept pace with her son.

Cass pushed aside the crime scene tape that still draped her front porch, and unlocked the door with her key. She stepped inside tentatively.

"It seems like forever since I've been here," she told Rick as he followed her into the front hall.

"Well, it's been a pretty intense week."

"It hasn't even been a whole week," she reminded him. "Hard to believe, isn't it?"

"It seems like I've been here longer than

that. I feel as if I've known you for more than a week."

She paused at the stairwell, one foot on the bottom step, and studied his face. He was watching her watch him.

"I know what you mean. I feel the same way," Cass told him.

"Good. That's good." He smiled.

"I'll be right back." She broke eye contact and ran up the steps to her room.

She grabbed her last clean pair of jeans and a T-shirt from her dresser — she really did need to get some laundry done — and stuffed them into a small tote, along with her running shoes, before going into her closet. From the top shelf, she took a small handgun already in an ankle holster and strapped it on. Around her waist she wore a belt with a clip that held her revolver. She reached up to the shelf again and felt around for the twenty-two she had, on occasion, concealed in the small of her back. Finding it, she slid it into place and tugged her shirt over her belt.

"You look as if you mean business," Rick said from the doorway. "You really think you're going to need all that?"

"One way or another, we're getting him today." She met his eyes in the mirror that hung on the closet door. "I'm not sure how, but this is ending today."

"I'm all for that."

"What do you say we pop in on Mr. Calhoun and see what he has to say. Maybe he'll have some thoughts on where his good friend, Mr. Wainwright, might be spending a quiet day."

"Well, neither of his other friends had much to say," Rick reminded her. "I doubt he'll be of much help, but let's give him a try."

"You think Wainwright knows that we know it's him?" she asked as she turned to him. "Do you think he's caught on?"

"If he's tried to go home, he's caught on. And there's a damned good chance his brother has tipped him off. He sure seemed to have an attitude when it came to his little brother."

"I felt that, too. As if he wasn't at all surprised that the police wanted to talk to him. Almost as if he was expecting it."

"You think his brother knows what he's been doing?"

"No. If he had, he would have turned him in long ago. Steve seems like the type who'd carry his sibling rivalry into his middle age. I think if he had something on Jonathan, he'd have been more than happy to blow the whistle on him." She reflected for a moment. "I feel pretty certain that Steve doesn't have a clue as to what his brother has been up to all these years."

"Still, I think we should stop back at Steve's and see if he's thought of anything else since we spoke with him. Let's see, that was four hours ago, and —"

"Oh, shit." Cass took a quick glance at her watch. "It's almost seven. I told Khaliyah I'd meet her at six. Come on, Rick. I'm really late."

Cass pushed past Rick and ran down the steps. She searched her bag for her cell phone and hit the *Speed Dial* key.

"Damn. She's not picking up. We're going to have to stop at the playground."

"The playground?" He followed her outside. "Now?"

"Long story. I'll tell you in the car."

Khaliyah was practicing foul shots when Rick pulled into the parking lot next to the basketball court.

"I'll be right back."

Cass jogged to the court and reached for the ball Khaliyah lobbed in her direction. She caught it handily, but did not take a shot. Instead, she passed the ball back to Khaliyah.

"I'm so sorry, but we're going to have to postpone our game tonight. I know I said

I'd never bail on you, but —"

"You're not bailing." Khaliyah bounced the ball a few times before picking it up and holding it against her chest. "You're here, aren't you?"

"Yes, but I can't stay."

"It's okay. I understand. You're a cop, Cassie." She began to bounce the ball again.

"Where's Jameer? I thought he was going to drive you."

"He's here. He just walked over to the stand to buy us some water. He'll be right back."

"Stick with him, would you? Make sure he takes you home."

"Sure." Khaliyah turned and dribbled in the direction of the basket. She took a shot, missed, got the rebound.

Cass watched, hands on her hips. "You're good, girl. But you need to practice if you think you'll beat me next week."

Khaliyah laughed. "Any week. I can — and have — beaten you. I'll beat you again."

Cass went to the girl and gave her a sisterly hug. "Be careful. I don't like thinking about you being out while this man is still on the loose. He's very dangerous. Very bad."

"Don't worry about me. I'll be fine. You're the one who needs to be careful." A flash of concern crossed the girl's face. "Please don't let him hurt you."

"I'm going to do my best to avoid that."

"Well, you go on back to work now and catch this guy so you have plenty of time to rest up for next week."

Cass grinned and waved to Jameer, who appeared at the opposite end of the court.

"You call me if you need me. I'll have my phone with me. You have the number, right?" Cass called to Khaliyah as she headed toward the parking lot.

"You programmed it into my phone," she called back to Cass and pointed to the gym bag that sat on the ground near the end of the bench, the cell phone Cass had given her resting on top.

"Don't hesitate to use it."

"I won't." Khaliyah waved good-bye to Cass, then challenged Jameer to a game of one-on-one by pitching the ball in his direction.

"That's your buddy?" Rick was waiting at the end of the path.

"Yeah. She's a terrific kid."

"She's a beauty. Looks like a good ball-player, too."

"Both true. We've got high hopes for her.

We're looking for a scholarship to a Division One school. She's going to go places." Cass paused to look back once, then patted Rick on the arm. "Now, let's go see if Steve Wainwright has come up with anything new since we last spoke with him. Then we'll move on to Billy Calhoun."

Jonathan watched from the bleachers as Cass and Rick made their way back to the parking lot. He was sick to his stomach, just looking at her. At that moment, he ached to feel the skin of her neck under his hands. Ached to watch her die for all the pain, all the frustration she had caused him.

Ached to finish the job he'd left unfinished years ago.

He was sweating, his nervous system on overload.

He turned his attention to the young girl on the basketball court. Obviously, she was someone important to Cass.

His eyes followed her as she spun around the boy who attempted to block her shots. Beautiful, strong, and young. Too young, he reminded himself. Not much more than a child, really. He wouldn't think of doing to her what he wanted to do to Cass. The very idea disgusted him.

After all, he did have his standards.

The action moved to the basket at the far end of the court, where several other young people had gathered, boys and girls. The game interrupted, the players stopped to chat with the newcomers. He eyed the gym bag on the ground near the bench, not twenty-five feet from him now.

*"You programmed it into my phone,"* the girl had said when Cass had asked if she had her cell number.

Nonchalantly, he hopped off the bleachers and strolled by, his hands in his pockets. When he reached the bench, he bent down, as if tying a shoe, and reached over to grab the phone, which he tucked into his pocket. A glance at the group assured him that no one had paid any attention to him. He straightened up, and continued on his way.

Pulling his baseball cap down over his forehead, he pushed his dark glasses back, and with his hands in his pockets, he walked leisurely through the playground and into the park that led toward the bay. From there, he'd walk over the dunes and find a nice quiet place in which to sit and think about how best to fit this little unexpected bonus into his plan.

# Twenty-eight

"What are we looking for?" Cass asked the chief, who'd called her back to Wainwright's rented house.

"We're looking for anyplace he might have stashed his souvenirs."

"Do we know for certain he kept them?"

"We know none of our victims' wallets have ever been found. I spoke with the profiler, Dr. McCall, late this afternoon. She feels very strongly that he would keep them all in one place, and he'd keep them close to him. We found the car he's been driving, and we have some techs going over it, but nothing so far. The house is our second choice."

"If it's here, we'll find it."

"Give me a call when you do. I'm heading over to Lilly Carson's. I need to assure her mother we're doing all we can to find her daughter. Then we're gearing up for a press conference just in time for the eleven o'clock news. I'm releasing the name, the sketch, everything we have on him. I want him to know for certain that we're breathing down his neck. I want this bastard."

She frowned. "What do you think the chances are he's left town?"

"It's possible, but somehow, I'm thinking he hasn't. We found his car twenty minutes ago, there's no train service through town, and the bus only runs three times each day."

"He easily could have stolen a car, or even a boat."

"Yes, he could have. No reports of that yet, but then again, he could take a car from any street. Most of the summer people park their cars when they get here, then walk to the beach or to town. It might take a while to notice if your car isn't where you left it. As for boats, we always have one or two of those missing. We have two now, as a matter of fact. I have an officer looking into that."

"Chief," one of the uniforms called from the doorway. "I think we have something."

Cass followed Chief Denver into the house and up the steps to the second floor. A portion of the wall behind the bed had been pried free, and a large trunk had been dragged into the middle of the floor.

"Open it," Denver instructed.

"Want me to shoot it open?" an officer from Tilden asked.

"No, I don't want you to shoot it, you might destroy evidence. Try something else."

"I got a tire iron in the trunk of my car," someone offered. "Maybe we can pry it open."

"Give it a try, and if it doesn't open, take it back to the department and see what tools we have that might get that lock off." Chief Denver looked at his watch. "I have to get over to the Carsons'. I'm already late."

Cass stepped out of the room and pressed against the wall as the chief passed by on his way to the steps.

"If nothing else, maybe we'll be able to give someone closure," she said to Rick, who stood across from her on the narrow second-floor landing. "Think of what might be in there. For parents, or husbands, or siblings of women who disappeared over the years; maybe we'll finally be able to at least let them know they can stop wondering."

"Let's not get our hopes up. For all we know, the trunk holds his old baseball cards and a few *Mad* magazines."

Her cell phone rang and she looked at the incoming number.

"Khaliyah, hi," she said. "What? I can't

hear you. The reception is poor here. Hold on . . . let me try downstairs . . ."

She ran down the steps.

"Is that better?" She paused, but still could not understand what was being said. "Let me go outside . . ."

She went through the front door and onto the lawn, where thin patches of grass stubbornly grew in the sand.

"Much better," the voice on the phone told her. It was not Khaliyah's. "Now, step out a little more. There, that's good. I want to see you."

"Who is this?"

"Oh, Detective Burke, I think you can figure it out."

"Where are you?"

"Closer than you think. Now, listen carefully. I have Lilly Carson. She's alive, but whether she stays that way, well, now, that's going to depend on you."

"What do you want me to do?"

"I want you to turn and walk to the end of the driveway . . . right now. Don't look at anyone, don't give a sign to anyone. I can see you. One wrong move, and I'm out of here. And Lilly Carson will die."

She did as she was told.

"There, that's a good girl. Now walk down the street to your right, all the way down to the very end. Good, good. See the red sedan on the opposite side? Wave to the driver, Cass."

She did. He waved back.

"Now, I want you to cross the street. Stay in the shadows there, we don't want anyone to see you. Now walk straight to the passenger's side."

He leaned over and opened the door.

"First thing, take the gun from your waistband and drop it right there on the ground," he demanded. "Then you can toss out that little number you have strapped to your ankle."

"How do you know I have —" she started, and he laughed.

"Because all you chick cops think it's cool to strap a little handgun to your leg."

He chuckled as she pulled her jeans up to her knee and exposed the gun.

"You're all so predictable." He shook his head. "Take it off and drop it."

"Someone will find it."

"Well, hopefully it won't be some little kid, right?" He gestured for her to get into the car. "Of course, if that little kid should turn out to be one of my nephews, maybe that wouldn't be so bad."

She got onto the passenger seat.

"Close the door."

She did.

"Now, I'm going to remind you that a young woman's life is at stake here, so don't try to grab the wheel or yell out the window or do anything stupid . . . which reminds me, put the cell phone right there in one of the cup holders, where I can see it."

She popped the phone into the nearest cup holder and he immediately picked it up and tossed it out the window.

"Any other weapons I need to know about?"

"No. Just the two."

"That's what I figured. I've never known a woman who packed more than two." He smiled with self-satisfaction.

The twenty-two felt as if it had begun to glow in the small of her back. She was so conscious of it, for a moment she thought surely he could see it.

"Where's Lilly?" she asked, her heart pounding with anticipation. She was on an adrenaline high, to be this close to him, to the man who had destroyed her life.

"Lilly's waiting for us."

"Where are we going?"

"I want it to be a surprise."

He drove along the bay for several min-

478

utes before pulling over to the side of the road.

"Get out," he told her, and she did.

"Now we're going to take a little walk, Detective Burke." He took her arm and steered her into the marsh. "Again, I remind you that a young woman's life is at stake, so don't think to try to overpower me with some cheesy martial arts move. You do know martial arts, don't you, Cass?"

She nodded.

"I figured you would. Trust me when I tell you, you could never best me."

Something hard and round butted her in the middle of her back.

"Just a little insurance," he said, "in case you decide your life is more important than poor Lilly's. Though I doubt you would. You're the type who would want to be a hero, aren't you, Cassandra? Idealistic to a fault, right?"

The ground was becoming softer, wetter, as they continued into the marsh. Soon Cass could feel the ooze beneath the marsh grass sucking at her shoes with each step she took. They were almost to the bay now — she could smell it, salty and pungent. Where the hell was he taking her?

He pushed her forward lightly and her

feet slid into water. They walked along the edge of the inlet for another minute before she saw the outline of a small boat tied up to the bulkhead of a long-forgotten dock.

"On board." He shoved her from behind. "Here. Sit right here . . . no, turn around. I want you facing the other way."

Again, she did as she was told, praying his hands wouldn't graze her lower back. Sitting as she was, he was within a foot of the handgun hidden there. With her back to him, she felt certain he could see the small bulge of the gun.

*Thank God it's so dark,* she thought. *Maybe he'll miss it completely.*

"Don't think I don't know what you're thinking," he said in her ear.

"What am I thinking?" she asked calmly.

"You're thinking maybe you can jump over the side and swim for help."

"Actually, I was wondering what corner of hell the devil is saving for you."

He chuckled. "All of them, my dear. All of them."

He rowed on, her anxiety increasing as the minutes passed. Had anyone realized she was missing yet? Surely Rick had. Surely he was looking for her right now.

The oars splashed lightly as the boat made its way along the edge of the marsh.

There was a time when she had known every nook and cranny of the marsh, every little tidal pool and inlet. But it had been years since she'd taken time to explore the back bay, and she was now totally disoriented. When he headed toward shore and jumped out to pull the boat to land, she had no idea where they were.

"Out," he told her.

She stepped out of the boat and made her way through the soft sand to the firmer shore, where the grasses grew eight feet tall and thick as a hedge. He guided her to a place where the cattails had been tamped down slightly into a path.

"Walk." He nudged her forward, the gun in his hand once again.

"Where are we?" she asked. "Where are you taking me?"

"Why, Cassandra Burke, I'm surprised you haven't figured it out," he replied, a touch of glee in his voice. "I'm taking you home."

# Twenty-nine

"How could she have just disappeared like that?" Rick ran a worried hand through his hair. "She's vanished."

"That's ridiculous. Are you certain she isn't in the house?" Chief Denver pressed. "Did you think to look in the backyard?"

"We've been through every room of the house, Chief. I'm telling you, she isn't here, and no one saw her leave. She got a phone call from Khaliyah . . ."

"Khaliyah Graves?"

"I don't know the girl's last name, the girl she plays basketball with."

"What did she want?"

"I don't know. Cass said the reception was bad, and she was going to take the call outside. That's the last I saw of her."

"Khaliyah lives over on Westbrook, but I don't know the house number. Hold on, Rick, let me see if I can contact the department, see if we can get the girl's number."

Rick paced the sidewalk outside Jon Wainwright's house, his phone close to his ear. How could it be that Cass had disappeared seemingly into thin air?

Beads of sweat broke out on his forehead. He knew that she hadn't just vanished. He knew, too, that she wouldn't just walk off the scene, without at the very least telling him what she was doing. He shook his head. She'd do more than tell him. She'd take him with her.

She'd have to. She didn't have a car.

"We got through to the girl. She says she didn't call Cass. Says she can't find her phone, she thinks someone took it from her gym bag while she was playing basketball."

"I guess we know who that someone was, don't we." There could be only one explanation, and the very thought of it turned Rick cold inside.

Wainwright had her.

Rick didn't know how he'd done it, but he was one hundred percent certain he had.

"Get the men who are still there to start canvassing the neighborhood. See if anyone saw her. I'll see how quickly I can get out of the Carsons'. With Lilly still missing, I can't do a quick hello good-bye. In the meantime, you keep in touch, you hear?"

"Will do."

Rick closed the phone with a snap, then went into the house to call together the officers on the scene. He told them what had happened, what he and Chief Denver suspected, and what the chief had directed them to do. There was a mass exit out the front door, as the officers took to the streets in search of a sign of Cass or someone who might have seen her.

Within minutes, someone called from across the street.

"Here. I've found something."

"What have you got?" Rick rushed to him, and looked down. Two handguns lay on the ground in the haze of an officer's flashlight.

They stood silently, staring at the ground. Finally, the officer said, "How'd he get her to do that? Cass would never give up her guns, leave 'em lying on the ground like that."

Rick knelt down to inspect the guns. He picked up the ankle holster he knew she had strapped on only hours before.

But there'd been three guns, he knew. If two were left here, she still had a weapon. Assuming, of course, that Wainwright hadn't found it and turned it on her. He hoped that wasn't the case.

Rick punched in a number on his cell,

and waited while it rang.

"Annie, it's Rick Cisco. We have a problem here in Bowers Inlet . . ."

He filled her in, listened, then thanked her. He disconnected, and immediately dialed the chief's number.

"We found two of her guns, but not her," Rick told him as he strode to his car. "Annie thinks he took her to where it all began. I'm thinking the bird sanctuary. I'm headed there now."

"I'll send a few cars out to meet you," Denver said before Rick hung up.

The street was too narrow to make a U-turn, so Rick threw the car in reverse and drove backward to Bay Avenue, where he took a left. Wishing he had lights and sirens so everyone would get out of his way, Rick followed the route he remembered to the sanctuary.

What was Wainwright's plan? Were his hands, even now, around her neck, strangling the life from her? Rick's heart skipped a beat, imagining Cass fighting for her life.

"Fight the bastard," he said aloud. "Fight him with everything you've got. Just hold on . . ."

Rick stopped the car at the entrance to the sanctuary, got out, and moved the gate aside. He drove straight through, his tires kicking up sand and small stones as he sped down the road to the Jenny Burke Memorial. After the second turn, he slowed, his high beams glancing off the rails on the side of the road at the left. Finally, he saw it, and pulled over. His Glock in one hand, a flashlight in the other, he closed the car door softly.

Rick stood by the side of the road and strained his ears to listen. He heard . . . nothing.

Finally, there was a rustle overhead, followed by the *whooooooooo whooooooooo* of an owl. The winged predator took off from its perch and disappeared into the night, leaving Rick with his mounting fears.

He found the path that led to the blind and followed it. When he arrived at the structure, he stood in the shadows and watched, and listened. Nothing. No movement, no sound.

He climbed the ladder silently, the Glock still in his right hand, but when he reached the top and looked over, he realized he'd been wrong. The blind was empty. He shined the light around the interior, but there was nothing.

"Where the hell are you?" Frustrated, he

banged a hand on the floor of the blind before heading back down.

Cass stiffened when Jonathan pushed her through the cattails and the weathered brown house appeared in the moonlight.

"See?" Wainwright whispered in her ear. "Just like I told you. I brought you home."

"Is she here?" Cass asked, her mouth dry.

"You'll be able to answer that yourself in a moment." He forced her to the top of the concrete basement steps, and she hesitated.

"Don't be a child," he told her, shoving her down the steps and through the basement to the stairs that led to the first floor. "Nothing to fear down here."

"Where's Lilly?" Cass asked as she was pushed through the door and into the living room of her childhood. Miraculously, everything was just as it had been twenty-six years earlier. The dark green sofa had, long ago, faded pale from the sun that beat in through the front windows. A magazine from 1979 lay on the floor next to a chair. After the murders, Cass's grandparents had come into the house one time, and then only to get the things that Cass needed. Clothes, favorite toys, important papers. They had then simply locked the house when the police were through. Incredibly, to the best of Cass's knowledge, no one had been inside since. Except for the thick layer of dust that covered everything, and the cobwebs that hung from the ceilings, all was as it had been.

"Lilly is upstairs."

"I want to see her."

"Patience, Cass."

"Uh-uh. I want to see her now."

"As you wish, then." He gestured with the gun. "Up you go. And don't forget who has the gun."

"Oh, I haven't forgotten."

She climbed the steps slowly, the child within her screaming silently with every step. Her hands shook and her knees threatened to simply give out. It took all of her willpower to force herself to continue forward. She could not be a coward. She could not fail Lilly.

There'd been no chance to save her mother. She hadn't gotten to her sister in time.

This time, she was not a child. This time, she was not helpless.

This time he would not win.

She stood on the top step and took a deep breath.

"Where?"

"Why, in Mommy and Daddy's room, of course. Honestly, Cass, you should know the game by now."

"Is that what this is to you? A game?" She started to turn to face him but he jabbed her in the back.

"Figure of speech," he hissed in her ear. "Now, go on, go on into Mommy's room and see what we have waiting for us."

She stepped in through the darkened doorway. In the light from the moon overhead, she could see a figure lying on the floor. Wainwright jabbed it with the toe of his foot, and the figure moaned.

"You said you'd let her go," Cass reminded him. "Do it now."

"No, that's not exactly what I said. I said I wouldn't kill her. And I won't. I'm a man of my word."

She turned slowly and saw the smirk on his face.

"But you're not going to let her go, are you?"

"No. No, I'm not going to let her go. Sooner or later, someone will find her. Maybe she'll still be alive." He shrugged. "Maybe not."

"Why?"

"Oh, please. I've seen all the same TV shows. Keep the bad guy talking until the guys in the white hats arrive. You think your Fed boyfriend is going to figure out where you are?" He snorted. "The guy doesn't look that smart. And we both know *Denver's* not that smart. Obviously. Did he tell you we sat at the bar in Gabby's Place two weeks ago and bought each other drinks?"

He laughed. "I proved twenty-six years ago that I'm smarter than old Craig. I'm still smarter. Smarter than him, smarter than my old man. I do have to brag, though — it was a kick, watching the old man scramble around back then, acting like he was on to a lead here, a lead there. He didn't have a clue. Not a fucking clue." He laughed again. "You should have seen him when he got those letters I sent. All agitated. He knew the killer was smarter than he'd ever be. Well, I proved that, didn't I? The man went to his grave years ago, still didn't have a clue."

"Why my mother?"

"Why not your mother?" He spun her against the wall in a rush, the gun now in her face. "Don't you know what she was?"

"No, Jon. Why don't you tell me?" she whispered.

"She was Jezebel, right out of the Bible." His voice dropped. "She was the most beautiful woman in the world. She was . . . everything."

"She was a married woman with children."

"She would have walked away from all of you, to be with me."

"Did she tell you that, Jon?"

"Every time she looked at me, I knew."

"So you killed her? You killed the woman who loved you? That makes no sense."

"I didn't plan on . . . that wasn't supposed to . . ." He appeared suddenly confused. She used the moment to swing the door into his body, hoping to slam his gun hand into the jamb.

She missed.

"Bitch!" he screamed at her, and twisted her arm behind her back.

Her hand struggled to get the small handgun from the small of her back. It caught in the waistband of her jeans and she cursed loudly as he tried to pin her against the wall. His gun was in her face, his finger on the trigger.

From somewhere outside, a car door slammed.

His eyes darted to the front of the house; the brief hesitation was all she needed. She wrenched her hand free and jammed the gun into his chest. And fired. Once, and the gun dropped from his hand. Twice, and he slumped against her. Three times, and his body began to fall.

The door crashed open on the floor below, and she pushed Jonathan Wainwright to the floor.

"Cassie?"

"Rick? I'm here. I'm here . . ." Her voice caught in her throat. "I'm here . . ."

He took the steps two at a time, slowing only when he reached the top.

"Wainwright . . . ?"

She pointed to the floor.

"Are you all right?" He went to her, put his arms around her.

"I am now." She wanted him to hold on, hold on and on and make this nightmare go away. But . . . "Lilly Carson is over there. She's alive, but I don't know for how much longer. I don't know what he's done to her."

They moved farther into the bedroom and he snapped on the light. Lilly lay on her side, her dark hair spilled across the carpet. Cass's knees went weak.

"Lilly." Rick knelt down next to her. "Lilly, can you hear me?"

Slowly the woman opened her eyes and blinked against the light.

"We're going to get help," he promised. He reached for his phone just as cars pulled up outside. He looked at Cass. "Go tell them she's here. Tell them to get an ambulance ASAP."

Cass nodded, and willed her legs to move to the stairs.

"Up here," she called down with a shaky voice. "She's up here . . ."

Cass sat on the bottom step and watched the activity around her. Once again, the home she had shared with her family had turned into a crime scene.

Tasha Welsh arrived, as did the medical examiner. Both stopped to squeeze her shoulder and offer congratulations on their way up the steps. Cass couldn't bring herself to go up with them, not right then. She still didn't trust her legs to take her anywhere.

"How did you know?" Cass asked Rick when he sat down next to her and took her hand. "How did you know where to find me?"

"Annie said he'd take you back to where it all began. At first, I thought that meant the sanctuary, where he met your mother. When I got there and realized he hadn't been there tonight, there was only one other place he could have taken you. This is where the killing began. I'm only sorry I didn't catch on sooner."

She sat as if still in shock.

"Not that you needed my help," he told her. "You did just fine without me."

"I've never killed anyone before," she said simply. "I'm glad it was him."

"I didn't hear you say that." Chief Denver approached the steps. "I need you to hand over your gun, Cass."

She handed it to him without comment.

"You know the county will investigate, as they do every time an officer is involved in a shooting."

She nodded.

"The shooting was totally justified," Rick interjected. "He had a gun on her. He was going to kill her."

"No doubt in my mind about that. No one's questioning the justification, Agent Cisco. It's just a formality."

Denver knelt before Cass and studied her face. "Cassie, are you sure you're all right?"

"I can't believe it's over. It's over. He's really dead?"

"He's really dead," he assured her.

"All of my life, I was haunted by what happened here." She looked around the

494

living room at furnishings that were at once both strange and familiar. "I thought about coming home that day, about him being here. I thought about stopping him in time."

"Well, this time you did that." Denver patted her knee and stood up. He went past them to the steps to the second floor.

She and Rick sat in silence for a long time. He looked to the top of the stairs, where the lights had all been turned on and brown stains marred the pale carpet.

Old blood, not new.

Her blood, not Wainwright's.

"When you said you dreamed of stopping him, you meant that first time. Not this time, now. But then."

She nodded.

"I wanted to save my parents. My sister." Her eyes filled with tears, and Rick knew the dam was close to bursting.

"You were six years old."

"I know that. I do. And I don't blame myself for not saving them, Rick, I swear I don't." She swallowed hard, her bottom lip trembled. "I just wish *I could have* . . ."

"Come on, Cass, let's go." He stood and tugged at her hand. He wanted to put his arms around her and comfort her, make all the pain go away.

"Go where?"

"Anyplace but here."

He parked on the street that she'd directed him to and turned off the ignition. He took off his shoes and socks while she did the same, then together they set off on foot, taking care to keep to the narrow boardwalk that led over the unlit dunes.

In silence they followed the sound of the ocean across the dark beach to the waterline, then walked a half mile up the beach, the tide swirling at their feet. Cass paused at the foot of the jetty.

"This might be a little tough to maneuver in the dark."

"I have a flashlight in the car."

"That's the easy way."

It was too dark to see her face, but he could almost feel her smile.

"Go on, then." He took her hand.

They picked their way slowly through the smooth rocks until they reached the end. Cass lowered herself carefully to perch on the end of the jetty, and Rick did the same. He put both arms around her and pulled her close.

"I want you to know I would have ripped him apart with my bare hands if he'd hurt you," he told her.

"I'm glad it didn't come to that."

He wanted to say that he thought it was best that she had been the one to kill Wainwright, but it was stating the obvious. Instead, he tightened his hold on her and just held on. When she turned to him, he leaned down and kissed her mouth. She tasted of tears, and she kissed him back, so he kissed her again. And again.

"I meant it when I said I felt as if I've known you for a long time," he whispered.

"I thought that was just a line."

"A line?" He frowned. "You thought that was a line? I don't do lines."

She laughed softly, and he tried to remember when he'd last heard her laugh.

"I swear —"

"Shhh. I was just teasing you. You looked so serious, so earnest for a moment."

The clouds that had covered the face of the moon drifted aside, and light spread in rivers across the water. The tide lapped against the rocks, and she stuck out her foot to catch it.

"It's really over, isn't it, Rick?"

"It's really over."

She leaned against him and sighed.

"Do you want to go back to the Inn?" he asked.

"In a little while."

"How do you feel, Cass?"

"I feel at peace, Rick. For the first time I can remember, I feel at peace."

He couldn't have asked for more than that.

Cass came out of the kitchen carrying a large spray bottle of water and a scraper, when she heard a car pull into the drive. She went to the dining room window and watched the driver of the Camaro get out. She tapped on the glass and pointed to the front door.

"Hey," she said as she opened it.

"Hey, yourself." He kissed her, then stepped inside and looked around. "What are you up to?"

"A lot can happen in three weeks."

"I'm sorry. I was out of the country. I couldn't get in touch. I figured rather than call and try to make excuses on the phone, I'd drive up here and make excuses in person."

"Apology accepted." She closed the door behind him. "You know, I never thought I'd step back inside this house, let alone ever consider living here. But it was the strangest thing, after that night . . . I don't know, I just wanted to be here. I thought if I got rid of the . . ."

She motioned in the general direction of the second floor and the kitchen.

"You know, the telltale signs. If the walls and the floors were cleaned up, maybe it could be all right. I had someone come and clean out the bad stuff — take out the old carpets and clean the walls and the kitchen, and it's as if all the bad karma is gone now."

"I have to admit I was surprised when I stopped at the police station and Denver told me you were thinking about living here again."

"Lucy wants to live in Gramma's house, which she is totally entitled to do. She wants to move down here with her boys for the rest of the summer, once they finish up at camp. She isn't going back to David. I could certainly stay there with them, but it's going to be a bit crowded. I got to thinking that I have another place to live. I wasn't sure I could do it, but once I came back, it seemed the ghosts were gone. The bad ones, anyway. I can live with the others. I'm not one hundred percent certain, but I want to try. I thought giving the rooms a new coat of paint would be a good place to start."

"Well," he said, looking around, "you

have your work cut out for you. Fortunately for you, I'm an expert at home repairs — and a whiz at painting. Did I ever tell you that I paid for a summer in Vienna by painting houses? No? Well, remind me to tell you about that sometime. For now, I'm all yours. You just tell me where to start."

"Don't start something you don't intend to finish, Agent Cisco." She poked at him with the wallpaper scraper, then started up the steps to the second floor.

"Don't you worry, Detective Burke." He grinned and followed her up the stairs. "I've got two weeks' vacation saved up. More than enough time to finish whatever it is you've got in mind."

# Epilogue

Regan lifted the last box and hoisted it against her chest before starting down the basement steps. She figured her father's old papers had rested quite comfortably in the basement for all these years, they could remain there for a few more. She'd hoped to get more sorted out, but she was running out of time. She had promised her editor a first draft of the book about the Bayside Strangler in ten weeks. She'd have to go through the remaining boxes another time — right now, they were proving to be a distraction.

She slid the box onto the storage shelf and turned to go back up the steps, when her foot caught on the edge of a smaller box that must have fallen from a nearby shelf. She tripped over it and landed on her hands and knees.

"Damn."

She picked herself up and leaned over to lift the box. The bottom, having apparently spent too much time on the damp basement floor, fell out, spilling its contents.

"Shit," she muttered, and knelt down to gather the papers that littered the floor.

She scooped them together, stuffing them back into the file they'd slid from, then she realized what she was looking at.

She took the file to the light, and read the name. Puzzled, she gathered the rest of the papers and carried them upstairs, where she deposited them on the top of her desk.

Old elementary school report cards, all bearing the name of Edward Kroll.

Odd . . .

The doorbell rang and she left the file on the desk while she went to the front hall. She opened the door, to find Mitch Peyton on the other side.

"You're late," she said. "I thought you'd be here a couple of hours ago."

"Oh, sorry. I got caught in traffic on I-95. Is now a bad time?"

"No, it's not a bad time. Come in." She stepped aside to permit him to enter. "I have the items you were looking for, they're all ready for you."

"I can't believe I left all those reports here. I don't know what I was thinking."

They went into the office and she handed him a fat brown envelope. "Everything's in here."

"Thanks, Regan. I appreciate it."

His gaze fell onto the papers that were stacked upon the desk. "You started the book already?"

She nodded. "I did, but that file isn't part of it. I don't know what that is."

"What do you mean?"

"I found a box downstairs that held some old report cards. Look, they're all for someone named Edward Kroll, who, back in the forties, attended St. John the Baptist Elementary School in Sayreville, Illinois."

"Who's Edward Kroll?"

"I have no idea. I've never heard the name before." With a finger, she drew out first one, then another of the report cards. "I can't imagine why my father would have had them."

"Maybe Kroll was someone your dad was investigating."

"Maybe." She picked up one of the report cards and read a written comment aloud. " 'Eddie is an asset to the class. He has an aptitude for math, is inquisitive, and is an excellent reader.' Signed by Sister Mary Matthew." She flipped the card over. "Second grade."

"Well, his name is sure to turn up again, if your father was interested in him enough to keep his report cards from grade school."

"That's what I thought, too. I'm sure there must be other files. But . . ." She dropped the report card on the desk.

"Right. With your dad's filing system, who knows where they might be."

"Same old story." She laughed. "It certainly makes going through his papers an adventure. I never know what I'm going to find. Sometimes I wonder if he didn't plan it that way, just to keep me intrigued."

"I guess I'll get this to my car." Mitch patted the envelope and headed for the door. "Thanks again, Regan. I appreciate it. I don't think my boss would be too happy if he knew I'd left some of my investigative reports here."

She walked him to the door, and watched him open the trunk of his car. He dropped the envelope in, then walked to the driver's side.

Closing the front door, Regan wished she could think of something to say that would bring him back inside, if only for a while. She'd been thinking a lot lately that the house seemed so quiet, so empty, since the Strangler case had been wrapped up and Mitch had returned to Maryland, and she was once again alone.

The doorbell rang.

Wondering what Mitch could have forgotten, Regan opened the door.

He stood there, a dark blue blazer slung over his shoulder.

"I was just wondering — now that we have work completely out of the way — if you'd like to go out to dinner with me. If you don't have other plans for tonight, that is."

"You mean, like a date?"

"Yes." He grinned. "Like a date."

"Oh." She smiled, waved him inside, and closed the door behind him. "Give me a minute to change."

"You don't have to change. You look perfect."

"Well, I'll need my keys . . ." She disappeared into her office and returned with her handbag.

"So," she said as they walked to the door, "what did you have in mind?"

"I was thinking about this Mexican place outside of Princeton. I had dinner there one night and thought maybe you'd like it. They have one of those sort of traveling trios that roam around the restaurant, singing to the customers."

"I know the place. It's one of my favorites, actually." She locked the door after they both stepped outside.

"Mitch." She grabbed his arm when they

were halfway to the car. "Did you really forget to take those files?"

"Of course not." He grinned. "I made copies of a few reports and left them on the desk. You don't really think I'd leave my files someplace, do you?"

"I thought it would be out of character."

"I just wanted an excuse to come see you."

"I'm glad you did. I've been dying to tell you about this old case I found in the bottom desk drawer last week . . ."

# About the Author

**Mariah Stewart** is the bestselling author of numerous novels and several novellas. A RITA finalist for romantic suspense, she is the recipient of the Award of Excellence for contemporary romance, a RIO (Reviewers International Organization) Award honoring excellence in women's fiction, and a Reviewers' Choice Award from *Romantic Times* magazine. A three-time recipient of the Golden Leaf Award and a Lifetime Achievement Award winner from the New Jersey Romance Writers, she has been inducted into their Hall of Fame.

A native of Hightstown, New Jersey, she lives with her husband, two daughters, and two rambunctious golden retrievers amid the rolling hills of Chester County, Pennsylvania. She is a member of the Valley Forge Romance Writers, the New Jersey Romance Writers, and the Romance Writers of America.